THE PRINCESS AND THE BULLY

TIFFANY RANSIER

INDIGO HEARTS PRESS LLC

Copyright © 2021 by Tiffany Ransier

All rights reserved.

No part of this book may be reproduced in any form or by any electronic or mechanical means, including information storage and retrieval systems, without written permission from the author, except for the use of brief quotations in a book review. This is a work of fiction. Names, characters, places, and incidents either are the products of the author's imagination or are used fictitiously. Any resemblance to actual persons, living or dead, businesses, companies, events, or locales is entirely coincidental.

Ebook ISBN: 978-1-949079-15-9

Paperback ISBN: 978-1-949079-16-6

Hardback ISBN: 978-1-949079-17-3

Published by: Indigo Hearts Press LLC

Editing: Pretty Little Book Editing

Cover design: Indigo Hearts Designs

 Created with Vellum

For anyone who wants to change for the better.

BLURB AND WARNING

Please be advised that this story is dark. There may be scenes that will trigger you. This includes scenes having to do with mental health. If you believe this book isn't for you, please don't read it.

I'm a princess. I was fine with the way my life was – partying all day and night. But my parents weren't.

Now I'm a student at Southern Goldsworthy University. The best for the rich and elite.
Heath Goldsworthy, campus heartthrob and oldest son of the Dean, came into my life as the first true friend I've ever had.
He gave me a new start. Something that I was very grateful for.
Now he's missing...
And I'm the top suspect responsible for his disappearance.
His sister hates me, but his brother hates me more.
He wants to make my life a living hell until I confess what happened that night.

But I can't confess what I don't remember.
And why does he keep messing with my emotions? I hate playing his games.
The Dean's son doesn't just go missing.
Someone is responsible and they don't want me to remember.
I have to find out who before it's too late.

TABLE OF CONTENTS

Prologue	1
Chapter 1	5
Chapter 2	27
Chapter 3	37
Chapter 4	59
Chapter 5	71
Chapter 6	89
Chapter 7	105
Chapter 8	125
Chapter 9	137
Chapter 10	153
Chapter 11	165
Chapter 12	181
Chapter 13	195
Chapter 14	209
Chapter 15	219
Chapter 16	237
Chapter 17	251
Chapter 18	271
Chapter 19	281
Chapter 20	295
Chapter 21	309
Chapter 22	323
Chapter 23	331
Chapter 24	353
Chapter 25	367
Epilogue	379
Author's Note	385
Also by Tiffany Ransier	387
About Tiffany	389

PROLOGUE

Mera

Thirteen years ago

The rain is coming down hard. Mother says I shouldn't run in the rain, so we have to hurry and make it to the treehouse.

"Come on," I yell to my new friend. What's his name again?

I can't remember.

It's a long way to the big tree where the treehouse is.

"Oh, I see it," he says. I grab his hand in mine. "Come on, if we hold hands we won't slip."

He smiles and nods. He has a nicer smile than the boys I usually play with.

It's really cold when we reach the tree and both of our clothes are soaked. Mother won't be happy about that. The treehouse helps block some of the water from reaching us. Mother says it's bigger than what most kids get. That's all because I'm a princess.

I walk up to the ladder. "Hey, since this is your first time, you go first."

"Thanks," he says, grabbing the first wooden slat and pulling himself up. Once he's through the hole, I start climbing up.

Mother says that way someone won't accidentally fall on me.

He laughs. "It's high up here. This is great. I need to get my dad to make one for me."

He looks so happy. At that moment, I realize that he's kind of cute. I usually think boys are icky. He seems different though. We stand at the railing and watch as the rain comes down. Suddenly I hear a thud. "What's that?" I ask looking around.

He points down. "Looks like clumps are coming down."

I bend over the railing and spot big white clumps all over the grass now.

"It's helling!" I shout excitedly.

"I think it's hailing."

"Same thing." I say, crossing my arms together. "The birds are going to get hurt if we don't get the nest off the roof."

I point above our heads. "It's up there."

"How are we going to get it?" he asks.

If only my sister was here, she'd be able to reach it easily. Without her, one of us would have to step on our tiptoes on the railing and grab it.

"I'll just stand on the rail and reach for it."

The smile leaves his face and he grabs my arm. "No, let me do it. You might start to feel scared and look backwards."

"It's okay," I tell him. "I can do it." Someone needs to inform him that girls are just as strong as boys are.

"Please, Pinkie. Let me do it," he says, tugging on my pink hair strands.

He looks so sad asking. I can't say no. "Okay."

He smiles. "Just give me a kiss before I do." He puckers his lips.

"A kiss?" I giggle. "That's for adults though, at least that's what Mother says."

He makes a shhh motion. "Don't tell anybody. I can keep a secret. Can't you?"

Nodding, I step closer. Closing my eyes, I hear nothing but the rain coming down as I lean forward. Eventually, I feel something warm and slightly wet on my lips. I stay there for a second and then move back.

"There!"

His face is red. "I'll go get that nest now." He moves to the railing and hoists himself up, one leg at a time. He doesn't need to stand on his tiptoes like I would.

"I got it!" he yells and a few seconds later, I watch him crouch down, safely handing me the nest. The baby birds inside it start chirping. I'll have to put this back when the weather clears or else their mother won't be able to find them.

After he hands it to me, I put it down and reach my hand forward to help him off the railing. As he reaches toward me, his foot slips, and I scream as he topples back, falling over the side. "Rain Boy!" I yell.

I peer over the railing and find him sprawled brokenly on the ground, against a rock with red coming off of his head.

Oh no. This is all my fault. I scurry down the steps quickly and run for the castle. But after that I never see him again. My Rain Boy.

CHAPTER ONE

Mera

Bang bang bang.

The hell is going on? Why is someone banging on my door? They should know not to disturb me.

And ouch, why does my head hurt so...

Oh wait, I got drunk again.

Peeking an eye open, I'm immediately met with the wooden part of the bar counter, not the tall white doors of my room with the gold around the trim and the matching gold handle.

I didn't even make it home last night. Fuck, Mother is going to kill me.

With a groan, I place my hands on the floor and maneuver myself to my knees. Almost there.

Bang, bang, bang.

Fuck, that hurts. Who's banging on the door when the bar doesn't even open until eleven.

Is it past eleven?

It can't be. George would have shoved me right out the door at ten so he could get ready to open.

Wincing, I reach up to the counter, sit back on my ankles and pull myself up. I can't believe I fell asleep behind the bar. Usually I sleep it off in the back room or make it home. Why didn't I this time?

Oh, now I remember. It must be because of my dear friends V, T, and W. Still sitting on the counter is a giant half drank bottle of vodka, a drained bottle of tequila and at the very end, one of whiskey.

And this was the second bar. Why did I go so hard?

Oh that's right. Mom is still insisting I go on the annual trip around our country with her and Father. I might've been okay with it if Cate was coming, but she's in her last year of Uni and doesn't want to take time off. Therefore, I refuse to go.

Stepping around the counter, I spot my three "friends." Josh, Evelyn, and Amanda. All sprawled out on the floor by the bar and around the stools. They can't drink as much as I can, but it seems like they drank enough to pass out before going home.

Their parents will probably be pissed.

Ha. Too fucking bad for them. And they didn't get to steal money from me this time because I brought none with me. George put it on my tab.

They've been my "friends" all through middle and high school, yet I'm nothing but an ATM in stilettos for them. Stories that draw on my sympathy, birthday presents for birthdays that are nowhere near close, stealing my card info, and more. Naively, I hoped once I was done with my early years in school that I'd make a lot of great friends and memories I'd never be able to forget. Memories that I'd treasure for years to come.

Well, it never happened. The only thing I've come to realize is that I don't need them, or anyone.

With a chuckle, I grab my tiny purse from the edge of the counter and sling it over my shoulder. Bending down, I pick up the clear heels I must have shucked off before passing out.

If I had to pick a best friend, the only choice would be–

Bang, bang, bang.

God that hurts.

"You're still fucking banging, huh?" I stomp over to the wooden door, and unlock it with my free hand.

It's a miracle that the three of them haven't woken up from the commotion.

Pulling the door open, I find a very pissed off expression that looks out of place on the face of an angel. Her platinum blonde hair like my own, with green eyes instead of my blue ones, and nude lip gloss with smoky eyeshadow. How does she manage to look so perfect so early in the morning? I don't think I'll ever look so pristine.

"Sis, I think you've really done it this time," she says gravely, crossing her arms. "Let's go."

A heavy sigh leaves my mouth. Shit. If Cate is this pissed, I've really fucked up this time. I should've gone home.

Without missing a beat, she turns her back to me and starts walking without even checking to see if I'm behind her. Her back is straight in perfect posture and her hair, unlike mine, is in a high thick bun.

Closing the door behind me, I hurry to follow.

How could two sisters be so different? She's everything my parents want. Prim, proper, and perfect. And here I am, a riotous mess in her shadow. I'll never step out from it. It's something that I came to terms with a long time ago. I don't despise her for it, though. It's who she is.

As we walk along toward the parking area, I can hear the rustling of the bushes across the street. Of course, the paps are out and salivating over whatever details they can twist to suit the news cycle.

I didn't even get a chance to look in a mirror. I can see the headlines now, *Drunk Princess gets picked up by Lovely Princess. Youngest Princess Goes Wild Again. King and Queen Can't Control their Little Princess.*

Whatever, fuck them.

The clicking of her heels echo on the pavement until we reach a lone black sedan parked on the side of the road. There's barely anyone around, so I'm right in my assumption that it's still early.

Our chauffeur, Peter, pops out of the driver's side as Cate steps around the car to get in the back. By the time he comes around to my side, I've already wrenched my own door open, threw my heels in, and plopped onto the seat with a huff.

Closing my own door with a click, I settle back in the seat and cover my forehead with my right hand.

"Home, Peter," Cate orders.

I feel her gaze on me, burning with disappointment as I turn to stare out the window.

"What were you thinking, Mera?"

"I was just trying to have a little fun."

"And what about your duties? Did you honestly not remember that we had to be there for the opening of the new royal museum?"

Oh shit, that was today?

"Why didn't you remind me?" I groan.

"Should I have to remind you of everything?" With a sigh

she grabs my hand and places it between hers. Glancing at her out of the corner of my eye, I watch the anger in her eyes fade. "Take this seriously, Mera. You are a princess. Prove to everyone that you're more than a party girl."

"What if I don't want to? I like the way I am. I like the way things are. And what does it matter anyway? You're the crown princess, not me."

A fact that I'm so very grateful for. Running a country sounds boring and tedious.

"That doesn't mean you should act out and bring shame to the royal family. Mother and Father have both had enough, and I'm afraid, my dear baby sister, that this is the straw that's broken the proverbial camel's back."

"What are they going to do? I'm already finished with high school. They wouldn't trust me to send me off to the northern and southern castles by myself. What can they do, Cate, really?"

Scoffing, I cross my arms and watch as we finally start to climb up the hill leading to the palace.

"I heard the word college mentioned, Mera."

"College? They think that's a punishment. I'll have Peter drive me, party when class is done, and then repeat every day. They made sure I passed high school, I'm sure they'll make sure I pass college. What's the big deal?"

She lets out a real laugh, not just one of those small tinkling ones she does to seem classy, like a lady. And that scares me more than anything.

"America? As in the United States of America?"

"That's correct," Mother says, glancing at herself in the mirror.

I flop down on her bed in the middle of the expansive room and cover my mouth with my hand.

No, no, no.

"Father, please tell me I don't have to go."

He fixes me with a regretful look as he removes his bowtie in the opposite mirror across from Mother.

"Darling, we love you, and because we love you, we let you do what you want. You are our precious Mera. But we can't let this go on any longer. This constant partying. The constant money draining from those friends of yours. We've both had enough."

"You need to get out there and find your life, like Mary Catherine."

Clenching my teeth at the comparison, I dig my nails into my palms for a minute and then let go. "So three years then?"

"Four," she chimes in. "Four wonderful years at Southern Goldsworthy University."

Four?! College here is only three years. And even more, that's her alma mater. I feel like I might've said something about that college to the press once. What did I say? Oh well, it doesn't matter now it appears.

"That's not fair!" I retort.

"It's plenty fair. You will go there for four years and hopefully grow to be more than this party girl persona. You will figure out what you want to do and when you get back you'll be a whole new you. If we see good behavior, maybe we'll let you come home during the holidays. Keep in mind, that's my alma mater and the Dean is under strict instructions to report back to us on your behavior."

Good behavior must be code for no outrageous partying and especially no drinking. What the fuck am I going to do then, in America no less? But unless the Dean has eyes all over campus, he won't know what I'm doing all hours of the day.

Ugh, this is such a fucking drag already.

"You will leave tomorrow."

What? "That's too soon!" I yell.

"That's too bad. The semester starts on Monday and you don't want to miss a moment of class."

"But Mother-"

"Wilhelmera, this is final. Say goodbye to your friends and settle your affairs today and be ready to go bright and early tomorrow morning."

Anger pools in my gut as tears of frustration fill my eyes.

"Don't look too disappointed. The Dean's son will be there and you guys can go-"

I cut her off, instead stomping out of their room to be immediately met with Cate. She gives me a small smile and pats my shoulder in what's supposed to be a comforting gesture, but all it does is make me more furious. I don't need her comfort. I needed her to be on my side and help stop this. They always consider what Cate says. The door closes with a click.

Whirling around, I walk down the long hallway, under the high gold ceilings, passing the guest rooms and the few maids dusting and cleaning. Rounding the corner, I finally reach the tall white doors with golden handles and trim. Wrenching it open, I stalk inside and flop on the pristine bed, still made up from yesterday.

Scooting my body up to the headboard, I grab one of the big fluffy pillows and scream into it.

This can't be happening.

Knock knock knock.

"What is it?" I groan.

The door creaks open. "Princess, your friends are waiting downstairs in the foyer," Angelina says.

She's been my personal maid for two years. I overheard her defend me from the other maids, and she's been my favorite ever since.

"Just send them up," I reply with a sigh, staring up at the ceiling.

"Of course."

I've been laying here for hours and this still doesn't seem real. How can they just ship me off like this?

A chorus of hey's cut through the air, all annoyingly fake. I peek to watch all three of them entering the open door with forced smiles on their faces.

Typical.

They all flop down on the black couch against the opposite wall.

"Last night was fun, wasn't it?" Evelyn asks.

"It was great! We should go out earlier today. Maybe go shopping and have a meal at The Crown?" Amanda suggests.

Right. The Crown. The most expensive restaurant in downtown Kardenster.

"What do you think, Mera?" Josh's charismatic voice makes me sit up to look at them. Josh has forever been trying to use that charisma to become my boyfriend. Never in a million years, asshole. I know where that's been.

I guess the only good thing about all of this is that I get to say this. "Sorry, no can do guys. Tonight's my last night and I'm going to spend it packing."

Glancing at each of them, I watch their fake smiles fall from their faces. Josh manages to keep his face neutral, but the girls frown.

Amanda straightens against the back of the couch. "What do you mean, Mera?"

"Yeah, where are you going?" Josh asks, brows furrowing.

"The U.S. Specifically, Southern Goldsworthy University. And I won't be back for a long time, apparently."

Annoyance forms in their eyes as they all turn to look at each other.

Evelyn giggles a bit. "On graduation night, didn't you shit talk that place during that impromptu interview with the press? I wouldn't want to be you when you get there. Please tell me they won't make you actually go and embarrass yourself, Mer."

Oh yeah. I was super drunk and I just wanted to be left alone, so I said whatever came to mind. Mother was upset for months.

"Come on, there must be something you can do," Amanda says, poking her lip out.

Anyone who wasn't paying attention might think this was real, that they really had three good friends who were just looking out for them. But I know they're just acting this way because they're going to miss the money and the free stuff.

"Well, I guess we'll go then," Josh says with a sigh. "Group hug?"

Inwardly, I roll my eyes, but stand up all the same and let them hug me without hugging back.

Amanda and Evelyn leave first, knowing that sticking around won't do anything for their wallets.

"Bring us back some cool souvenirs. We'll see you when you get back," Josh says and then he finally leaves too.

I walk to my door and go to close it when I hear the echoes of their voices as they walk down the grand staircase.

"No more free booze. My dead grandma's birthday was coming up in a few days too."

"I was so sure we were going to fuck before this weekend was over."

Clenching my teeth together, I close the door and run back to my bed and flop down on it.

Fucking leeches.

The next morning, I'm standing in front of the plane steps in a pink tank top with my pink hoodie and dark blue jeans with my pink bag on my shoulder with "Princess" bedazzled on the side.

"You're going to be fine, sis," Cate remarks, touching my shoulder. "Sorry Mother and Father couldn't be here. Running a country and all."

"Yeah I know and I will."

"That's a big change from yesterday."

I chuckle a bit and turn to look at her. "I thought about it all night long and as much as I hate that this is happening, I can't stay angry about it. I'll just have to make this place my bitch, princess style."

She grins and pulls me into a hug. "That's the baby sister I know. Now listen, if you get into the same sorority Mother did, she might have more mercy on you. As soon as you get there, get an application for Zeta Delta Beta."

Sure, I can do that. What sorority wouldn't want a princess as a member?

"Now go, and try not to enjoy the parties too much, hm? And if you need me, I'll always answer the phone," she says, letting me go.

I walk up the stairs and take one last look behind me at beautiful Kardenia. The rolling green hills, the cool blue lake, and the clear sky are only a piece of what I love about my home.

"See you, Cate," I say, turning around and finally going inside.

"I love you!" She yells as the steps are drawn in and the door closes.

With a small smile, I mumble, "I love you too," and settle into one of the many empty seats.

"Buckle up, princess," one of the pilots hollers from the cockpit. "It's going to be a long twelve hours."

A great benefit from not sleeping all night. I get to sleep now. I pull out a pair of pink fluffy earmuffs and an eye mask.

It only takes a few seconds for me to completely drift off.

A hand touches my shoulder and I jump. Wrenching the earmuffs and eye mask off, I lock eyes with the pilot. "Sorry I scared you, but we're here. Time to go."

The scare wears off and I glance toward the window. The afternoon sun is streaming in. "Already?"

I didn't think I'd sleep the whole flight, but I guess that's what happens when you party all night and only get a few hours of sleep a day.

By the time I get out of my seat, the door is open, the stairs are down. Hitching my bag over my shoulder, I walk out to find it blazing hot. But I don't want to take my hoodie off just yet. Of course in Kardenia it gets hot sometimes, but I don't think I've ever felt heat like this before.

I amble down the stairs and hop into the waiting car that takes off the moment the door closes. "Good afternoon, Princess, and welcome to sunny Southern California. It's currently 105 Fahrenheit, which is pretty common for this time of year I hear, so make sure you drink plenty of water."

As if I didn't know from the way my skin burned the

moment I stepped out of the nice air-conditioned plane. "Thanks."

"Oh and the King and Queen asked me to let you know that while they are keeping your cards active, you won't be allowed to spend more than necessary. No big clothing purchases. No electronics. Only food and school related items will be allowed. The minute they see a huge purchase they will cancel your cards and you'll be left with nothing."

"Wonderful," I mutter and glance out the window as we make our way onto the highway. "Why is there so much traffic on this highway?"

"Freeway," he quips. "This is normal for a weekend afternoon."

At least the air is on. I grab my earbuds from my bag and pop them in, shuffling my music library and getting lost in the beat.

After what seems like forever, the door opens and my eyes widen as I realize I didn't even notice us pull up. That means...I'm here.

My stomach flutters a bit as I pull my hair into a high ponytail.

This is it. I grab my bag and slide out and into the heat. The sight of the tall trees catch my eyes first, followed by the tall glass building only 500 feet away with the words Administration emblazoned on the top.

Is that where I have to go? It would've been helpful if they had some sort of map mounted and someone to take my bags. I really have to lug them around until I find where I'm supposed to go? Glancing down, I eye the first two and the third is in the driver's hand and promptly plopped down next to the other two.

"Have a good time," he says with a bow and hops into the car that zooms off.

Yeah, thanks for just taking off and leaving me. A few laughs sound off in the distance. As they grow closer, I can tell they're the mocking kind. The kind I wouldn't have to deal with at home. Everyone there respected me.

This is my new reality.

Clutching my bag closer, I mutter, "They better not be coming toward me." It's too fucking hot to deal with catty people. I wipe the beads of sweat off my forehead as I feel their eyes on me. Thankfully, they're walking past, but when they finally get into my view, I see them turn and hide giggles behind their hands.

"Bitches." I say it loud enough for them to hear me and they frown, but keep on walking.

"You know, it was probably that princess bag of yours and that hoodie that tipped them off to who you are."

I look over my shoulder to find a tall guy with a charming smile that seems so model-like. Who is this guy and what is he doing at this college? He runs a hand through his hair which grants me a view of his toned biceps in a short-sleeved shirt. "Sorry, you're a little late. I was waiting out here for a while, but it's a hot day today. I'm your campus guide."

His eyes, as green as the trees around us, meet mine.

I half-expect to see hatred or annoyance. I mean he has to know about what I said about this place. But for the first time ever, my expectations are out the window. I can't detect anything. This hasn't happened before. "Traffic sucks here."

He chuckles. "Yeah I know. I'm Heath, by the way."

"Mera."

"Yeah I know. Princess Mera." He does a little bow, making a show of it and earning a laugh from me before grabbing two of my bags.

"So Heath, does everyone know I'm coming today?"

"Ah, you haven't been on the internet, have you? It leaked

online twenty hours ago that you were going to be a student here. My dad told me last night that I'd have to show you around."

Typical. At least this place is gated and the paps can't come on campus. I wouldn't doubt it was my "friends" who leaked the info for money. It wouldn't be the first time.

"Well, don't worry. I won't force you to do anything except help me carry these to my dorm room." I'm sure this is the last thing a guy like him wants to do.

"Hey. Let me do my job. My dad will kill me if he doesn't think you're fully satisfied. Follow me."

We start down the concrete path between the lines of trees. "And your dad is…"

"The Dean."

I glance to my left to find a tight smile on his face for a brief second before flitting back to his charming one. "Heath Goldsworthy at your service."

"So you practically own this school, I take it?"

"That's right. We do things our own way here, sometimes way off of the norm of other college campuses."

As we make our way to an open concrete area with a bunch of tables, chairs, and benches, I hear a chorus of yells.

"Heath!"

"Bro come hang out when you're done."

"Get some lunch with us."

Heath nods in their direction. "Sorry guys, not today."

A few girls glare in my direction, and a few of them wave erratically at Heath until he smiles in their direction. That one smile causes a few kisses to be blown his way and I look away once I see how uncomfortable Heath looks.

"Got your own fan club, huh?" How could he not with a perfectly chiseled jaw like his?

"However did you notice?" He snorts and turns a corner. A tall six-story building looms several feet away.

A few minutes later, we come to a stop in front of it. I use my arm to wipe the sweat off, which doesn't do much for me, so I'm ready to go inside. Heath grabs the top of his shirt and wipes the sweat beading on his forehead, giving me an amazing view of the bottom of his six-pack.

A lump pools in my throat and I cough loudly.

"Your throat is probably dry. Let's head in so you can get some water."

The moment we walk in, all heads turn in our direction. God, I hate when people do this. Every girl's eyes light up when they see Heath.

"Oh Heath!"

"Heeeeeath!"

"You look so tired, let me get you a water."

One of them practically hurts herself, jumping off one of the couches and racing to the refrigerator at the far end of the room. She quickly puts the bottle in his hand, brushing along his finger as she lets go.

God, how does Heath stand this? Is he the only hot guy on campus?

"Thank you...what was your name again?"

"Jenny."

"Thanks, Jenny. I appreciate the gesture, but my friend here is thirsty too. Mind getting one for her?"

Friend? He probably doesn't mean that.

Jenny seems to notice me for the first time as her eyes slide over to me. Turning her nose up, she turns around, moving her hips in an exaggerated motion as she retrieves another bottle.

"Here you go!" she says in a fake ass peppy voice.

"Thanks."

After taking a few big gulps, Heath's water is gone, and he tosses the bottle in the recycling bin near the door. I'm still sipping mine when he starts toward the middle of the room where the two elevators are.

I wonder what floor I'm on. Not that it matters, since I won't be in this dorm for very long.

It opens and we step in. He presses the number five.

"Room 515. Almost the top floor. Sadly, there's no view for the freshman dorm. It's actually in the worst spot. Now the senior dorm, that's where you'll get a view of the quad and the trees. The science building."

"It doesn't really matter. I'll be in a sorority soon."

The doors open and I step out first with him right behind me. "Oh? And what sorority would that be?"

"Zeta Delta Beta."

He bursts out laughing and I turn around to look at him. "What's so funny?"

We stop in front of a door with the number 515 on it. He sets my bags down and digs a keycard out of his pocket, sliding it quickly. Once we've set everything down, and I've sat at the edge of one of the beds with nothing on it, I look in his direction.

"Well? What's so funny?"

He covers his mouth to hold another laugh and then crosses his arms. "I just don't think you're going to get in."

"What? Why not? Anyone would love to have an actual, real life princess join their sorority. That was the sorority my mother was a part of. How could I not be let in?"

He sighs. "The simple, honest truth is…my little sister can be a bitch. She's president as of tomorrow, and I just know she'll find a reason to not accept you, even with you being a legacy."

"She can't do that. I *need* to get into that sorority."

He glances toward the lone window in the room like he's thinking hard, and there's a long moment of silence. "I don't really know you that well and considering you called all the guys who go here, fuckboys…"

I wince and bite my lip and try to remember exactly what I said in that interview.

"…which does include me, I *should* be the asshole that you expect me to be and say you're on your own. But, I won't. I'll ask my sister for an application and when I do, I'll put a few good words in her ear about you."

Oh my God, I could hug this guy. "Thank you so much, Heath!"

A slow smile spreads across his face, and this one actually reaches his eyes. He digs in his pocket, bringing out a slip of paper. "Here's your schedule."

History. English. Algebra. Bio. Art.

Fun stuff. Said no one ever.

"Oh shit, I have class tomorrow and no school supplies."

"Well I guess with your parents being the King and Queen they wouldn't have time to take you out to buy them. Lucky for you, your guide knows where the student store is. Let's go."

After the run to the student store, Heath takes me around the whole college. I've never seen so many open glares in my life. I've also never seen so many thirsty girls in my life. Heath is basically a prince in his own right.

From the student store, to the class buildings, to the cafeteria for lunch. Luckily it wasn't a huge thing since Heath went in the side entrance to get sandwiches from the sandwich place. We ate and continued to the woods around the lake and then all the way back around to the administration building and the small financial aid one behind it. This whole time, he's carried my bag full of supplies.

We sit on the bench outside the financial aid building and drink the last bit of our water from the cafeteria.

"Was your sister sad to see you leave?" he asks, propping his hands behind his head and leaning back.

"A little, I think. We've never been apart for long."

"It must be nice to be so close. I don't know if my little brother and I will ever be that close. We could go months without talking to each other and be happy about it. It wasn't always as bad as it is now, but…anyway, let's get you back to the dorm so you can unpack."

Suddenly, I remember how I thought this was going to be a terrible day. It was completely the opposite, and it's all thanks to Heath. "Thank you," I mumble.

"For what? Being a decent person? It must be hard being somewhere brand new and alone at that. This is your brand-new start. So, since you're not half bad, let's be friends." We lock eyes as he puts his hand out, and I slowly shake it.

"Well, well, look who I've finally found."

Heath's head whips around, and I turn to look too as a guy pops around and stands in front of the bench. I see the grimace on his face first, a stark contrast to the smile I saw on Heath's face. I hate that it's even possible, but he looks even more devastatingly handsome than Heath does. His ocean blue eyes are piercing and cold, but underneath that, very subtly, I can see a hint of anger.

This has to be his brother.

"Why were you looking for me, Callan?" Heath asks, crossing his arms. The smile he had on his face is long gone.

"You skipped lunch for this? So you could show *her*

around," Callan's eyes move toward me and the anger in them grows.

"Dad told me—"

"Fuck Dad. And fuck her, she didn't need a guide. She has eyes and a mouth to ask people for directions. Don't you remember what she said about us? Fuckboys and spoiled bitches. Yet here she is, joining the lot of us."

I can't stop the eye roll that happens. "So he didn't eat lunch with you. What's the big deal? And I'm pretty sure you've said rude things while you've been drunk too."

"Just mind your own fucking business," he retorts.

"You know, it's crazy. You look an awful lot like Heath but all of the asshole gene was put into your DNA."

His blue eyes grow dark at that, and I almost regret saying it.

"That so?" He glances behind me, sarcastically looking around. "Where's Mary Catherine? Oh wait, she didn't embarrass her country every day and get shipped off to the United States. That's a real princess if I ever knew one."

Anger explodes from my chest. "Fuck you!" I shout and get off the bench.

"Fuck you, too, princess" he responds. Towering over me, he glares down like I'm the gum on his shoe, so I scowl back. Up close, I can see even better just how gorgeous he is, with his perfectly proportioned face and thick eyelashes.

And then the strangest thing happens, I see a cloud of rain above his head, messing up his perfect hair and making it drip to his face. It startles me, I back up slightly, blink, and it's gone.

"Callan." Heath sighs and stands up. "I'll let you know if I need to miss lunch again. See you later."

He grabs my arm and leads me away with my bag on his shoulder.

I follow without resistance and eventually, he lets go. He doesn't say a word the rest of the way to my door.

"If he ever bothers you, just let me know, okay?" he says quietly.

It's a nice gesture, but I won't walk the other way if I see him coming. From what I've seen so far, he'd probably be overjoyed if I ran off like a scared puppy. "Sure. Thanks for everything, Heath. I really need a fresh start and I feel like that's what I'm getting."

Heath stares at me for a minute and opens his mouth like he wants to say something, but he doesn't. With a slight nod in my direction, he sets my huge bag of supplies at my feet and heads back for the elevator.

In one go, I swipe the card and grab the bag with my other arm, hauling it in.

A gasp makes me turn my head to the bed on the left, and a girl with auburn hair claps excitedly. "Finally, I get to meet my first roommate! I'm Scarlett."

I sit the bag on the floor next to my bed and meet her halfway in between our beds. "Nice to meet you, Scarlett. I'm Mera."

She chuckles and her warm hazel eyes light up. "Can I hug you? I thought I should ask first since you're, you know, a princess."

"Sure!" Bewildered, I open my arms, and sure enough, she grabs me in a quick hug.

"Need help unpacking? I already did mine yesterday."

Is she kidding? Why would she take on extra work? Oh well, I can't say no to help. "Yeah, I mean. Sure."

She smiles and goes over to the other side of the bed and starts with my biggest suitcase. An hour and a half later, we've made quick work and I'm all settled with my bag packed for class tomorrow.

"You have a *ton*, girl. I'm so jelly of those designer clothes."

"Lots of designers give them to me for free. Free advertising. Though I guess for my remaining time here, I'll be stuck with out-of-fashion clothes."

She winks. "It's not so bad, trust me. I'm here on scholarship so I have to save every penny."

The door suddenly clicks and we both turn and watch it open. I expect to see another pretty girl like Scarlett. Instead, my mouth drops open as a person as tall as Heath in a black hoodie dragging two roller suitcases behind them. They lift their head up and my eyes widen as I see it's a gorgeous *guy*. Almost as gorgeous as Heath. Is this a California thing?

He rubs a hand down the back of his head and his cheeks turn a bright pink. "Um, hey, I'm Peyton. A mistake was made with housing."

"I'll say," Scarlett says with a grin. "I'm Scarlett and this is Mera."

"Nice to meet you guys. I know the last thing you want to do is share your space with me. I barely got in on a scholarship and I can't afford to live off campus either, can we just keep this between the three of us?"

Scarlett laughs. "Sure, our RA won't notice the tall guy coming out of the elevator every morning."

"She said she's cool as long as there's no funny business. And there won't be."

Scarlett and I turn to look at each other. I shrug and she nods, turning back to him. "We're good with that."

A grateful smile spreads across his face. "Thanks."

"Why don't we get dinner together once Peyton's done unpacking? I may be poor as shit but I have a raggedy Honda Civic in the parking lot. Let's go get dinner somewhere off campus."

"Sounds good," Peyton replies.

They both turn in my direction and I slowly note how their eyes and expressions tell me the both of them really do want me to come. Like how real friends would act. Is this how it feels to have people who actually want your company and not your money? They didn't ask me to pay for it or even pay for the ride there.

"Yeah!" I say excitedly with a small smile.

"Awesome."

"Nice, this won't take long."

Maybe, this year won't be so bad after all.

CHAPTER TWO

Callan

Four seats. There are only four seats at our table for lunch today. I pull out the only empty one, next to my sister and eye my parents.

"Where's Heath?" I ask.

"He's busy, as he should be," Dad replies as he straightens his tie. His dark brown hair is swept to the side with gel. His blue eyes, exactly the color of my own, avoid mine, instead choosing to land upon Mom sitting beside him.

I never feel like I have his full attention. He'd always rather be looking fucking elsewhere.

"Busy doing what?" I ask, leaning back in the chair and crossing my fingers together.

A flash of annoyance appears on his face and stares me down with a look that says how dare I even ask another question about it. "He's showing our newest *special* student around."

Of all days for him to assign that job to Heath, it had to be today. Every Sunday we have lunch as a family and it's always like this. Dad reminds us exactly what our purposes are, and when it comes to my siblings and I, I'm on the lowest rung. Not to mention that he has to interact with someone as spoiled and entitled as she is. Everyone has seen her interview from a few months ago about this college. No one wants to have her here. "Fucking really? All she has to do is go to the Admin office and one of them could show her around. That's part of the job that we pay them to do."

"That *I* pay them," he says, tipping his thumb in his direction. "Heath is going to make sure that we get more international students enrolled at this college. We've never had many and this is our opportunity. If Clarise's daughter has a great time, she's bound to recommend this place to everyone she knows. You know they pay triple the regular tuition. Heath has never–"

"Failed before," I interject. "I know." Like I haven't heard that millions of times.

He smirks, waving a passing waitress over and I grit my teeth. The waitress takes our orders for our drinks and meals. The minute she's gone, he starts in again.

"Son, this is your freshman year. This sets the tone for the next three years. Look at Heath. Honors classes, football, fraternity president, the president of three clubs, and he does volunteer work at the library and student union."

Yes, because Heath can never stop being perfect for one second in his life. And I hate him for it.

"Mom, you've heard Callan is going to join Alpha Alpha Alpha, right?" Collette pops in. She flashes a smile in my direction, communicating with her eyes that I shouldn't say anything more and to let her handle this. She's aware that she's Mom's favorite as Heath is Dad's favorite.

Mom nods. "Yes." She massages Dad's shoulder. "Isn't that amazing, dear?"

"That's *fine*, but why can't he become the president of another fraternity. Why settle for simply being a member? You are a Goldsworthy and you are destined to be more than that."

My blood starts to boil with every word and I clench my fists on the armrests. He never stops.

"I mean look at your sister, she's going to be president of Zeta Delta Beta. You're really just going to let the two of them leave you in the dust?" He scoffs and shakes his head.

"Now dear, Callan will do his best to make us proud I'm sure." She throws a careful smile in my direction. And she sickens me for how compliant she is, bending to his every whim. If he divorced her, she would be lost without him.

"He needs to do better though, especially with that Silverstone boy going there. God knows we need to keep our family above them."

Of course, he'd bring up the Silverstones. Our families are forever locked in some sort of unspoken competition. Their son, who I fucking hate, applied and Dad was forced to accept. They're responsible for the software system our school uses for tracking attendance, grades, and online classes. How could he tell them that their son couldn't go to SGU?

I can't fucking deal with this anymore. I need to get as far away from the both of them as soon as possible. He's a lot more harsh without Heath. Seeing his shiny trophy in the flesh puts him in a better mood. Collette places her hand on Dad's. "We won't disappoint you."

He nods at Coll, while Mom beams at her. She's forever

wrapped around her finger. Fucking sickening how neither of them have ever shown me a modicum of support they give them. I can't help but despise Collette for it too. The moment I'm ready to jump up and leave, our food comes. I shovel it down and race out of there without a goodbye to any of them.

It takes hours for me to track Heath down. Literally trekking all over campus in the fucking heat. The only place I haven't checked is the admin building area. All this time and he's still hanging out with her. How fun could it really be showing someone around who thinks you're nothing more than an elitist fuckboy?

I stop in front and see only a few people inside, none of them being Heath, so I round the corner, walking all the way to the end of the path to the financial aid building. Immediately I spot his familiar head of brown hair on the lone bench, and next to him a platinum blonde one.

Whether they're done talking or not, I need to talk to him. *Now.*

"Well, well, look who I've finally found."

Heath's head turns in my direction and so does hers. My brother squints his eyes against the afternoon sun so I move in front of them. The bench is pretty small so they're not sitting that far apart.

"Why were you looking for me, Callan?" Heath asks, with a twitch of annoyance on his lips.

This is rich. Am I cockblocking him? Is that the reason why he's still showing *her* around? And the fact that he doesn't know why I'm looking for him pisses me the fuck off. He knows how Dad is.

"You skipped lunch for this? So you could show *her* around." I study her face. Her pink lips purse and her crystal blue eyes fill with judgement as she looks me up and down. Suddenly, I see a weird flash of pink in my head. I shake it away.

"Dad told me–" Heath starts.

"Fuck Dad. And fuck *her,* she didn't need a guide. She has eyes and a mouth to ask people for directions. Don't you remember what she said about us? Fuckboys and spoiled bitches. Yet here she is, joining the lot of us." Heath's expression remains unmoved by my outburst.

She rolls her eyes at me. "So he didn't eat lunch with you. What's the big deal? And I'm pretty sure you've said rude things while you've been drunk too."

Holy fuck, can she just shut up for a minute? "Just mind your own fucking business."

But of course she doesn't. "You know, it's crazy. You look an awful lot like Heath but all of the asshole gene was put into you."

Ha. So she's no different than everyone else. This might be the fastest I've hated anyone. She's been here less than a day and thinks she knows everything. I'm *so* fucking glad it's Heath and not me, because I couldn't deal with her and right now, I just want to leave. I don't even fucking care about talking to Heath and he can go back to trying to get his dick wet, but not before I can hit her right where it hurts.

"That so?" I look around the whole area. "Where's Mary Cathcrine? Oh wait, she didn't embarrass her country every day and get shipped off to the United States. That's a real princess if I ever knew one."

That pretty face of hers changes in an instant. "Fuck you!" she yells getting off the bench.

"Fuck you, too, princess." She glowers at me like an angry

little chipmunk. I know by her unwillingness to back down that I hit the right button. Every guy in America wants to meet Mary Catherine. Not just because of her beauty but because of how she carries herself. It's hot honestly. But Wilhelmera? No. She's spoiled, entitled, and I can easily tell she's going to be a problem.

She gets a startled look on her face for a second and backs up. Now she wants to fucking back down a little?

"Callan." Heath sighs and his mouth forms a thin line. "I'll let you know if I need to miss lunch again. See you later."

I watch him grab her arm, leading her away from me.

Whatever.

As I take the first step on the Alpha Alpha Alpha stairs, someone steps in my way. I'm ready to push them back to the side where they came from, until I see Noel's wide eyes and hands in the air.

"Hey, I come in peace. You look like you're going to kill someone."

Behind him, two others step out. Tyrell and Vincent.

Vincent claps me on the shoulder. "Lunch was a bitch wasn't it. Just ignore it, man."

"We're going to have the time of our lives. Let's enjoy it," Noel urges, his brown eyes heating up with excitement.

Tyrell stays quiet, but he nods in agreement.

Noel and Vincent have been my friends since childhood. Tyrell only since freshman year of high school. He never says much, and sometimes I wonder about what lurks behind his blue eyes, but I know these guys are the only people who will ever fully understand me.

"And hey, you got to move in early. You didn't even have to bother with the guys' freshman dorm," Vincent says.

I can't deny I have it easier than the three of them. Nodding, I walk between them and step inside. Turning around, I eye the three of them. "You guys get dinner without me. I'll see you guys tomorrow morning. Professor Harper's an ass and I have to be ready for him to call me out."

"History blows," Noel adds and then they're gone.

I raid the refrigerator to the upset of some of the AAA guys, but what can they say when I practically own this house. They stay out of my way as I go upstairs to my room on the second floor right near the stairs. Coincidentally, the furthest room from Heath's at the end of the third floor.

Heath's see you later echoes in my head as I flop down on the bed and pull out my drawing pad and pencil from the nightstand. I end up drawing a shoddy version of the bench they were sitting on. Why this of all things?

If I could just relax a little bit...but I can't. I can't afford to relax anymore.

With five hard tears, the drawing is in pieces and I throw them to the floor along with the drawing pad and pencil.

Thank God there's no one else sharing this room with me because I think about now I'd tell them to get the fuck out and find another room to stay in.

Bright and early, I make it to the dining hall to grab some French toast and coffee. Everyone else seems to have had the same idea because it's packed and every line is long.

"We'll go and get breakfast. You find us a table."

"Thanks," I reply and start to search for an empty table. Near the end of the dining hall, I spot four empty spots at the end of the table and lucky me, it happens to be right next to Collette and her three friends. It's not really a surprise at all. Lots of girls run the other way when they see Collette.

She might seem nice at first, but underneath there's a monster. She can be as ruthless as I can. We're twins after all. Anyone who crosses her is shit out of luck.

I'm not sure how Vincent is going to take this since he doesn't want to be anywhere near Ashlynn. Oh well, I don't fucking feel like going up to the second floor.

I pull the one out next to her and sit. "These seats better be free."

Coll jumps a little and turns with a scowl on her face that softens when she sees it's me. "Oh. Callan. You can sit." She turns her head to the right, presumably to look at Ashlynn and whispers something I can't make out.

"So that's her, huh?" The girl sitting across from Coll asks.

What was her name? Geri? Galleria?

Collette giggles behind her mouth and nods. "Gemma dear, we must not give her the attention that she's so desperately seeking. Here, she's a nobody."

I straighten in the chair and instantly notice the shiny head of platinum blonde hair. A girl with curly blonde locks flanks one side of her and on the other is what I believe to be a guy in a hoodie. Ugh, I need to get away from here. The second floor it is.

I slide my chair back and Collette gives me a questioning look. "See you later," I mutter.

I'm several feet away when all of a sudden I hear a chorus of gasps. *The fuck?*

Turning back, my mouth drops open at the sight and a laugh bubbles in my throat, but I quickly swallow it.

Maybe, karma does exist. Because of her, I sat through

my father's bullshit without Heath and then had Heath brush me off.

I think seeing this makes it worth it all, though.

In the span it took me to walk over here, the princess and her friends also got up and so did Collette. Maybe Collette was going to follow me?

But in any case, the glass that's being held in the princess's hand is now empty because the contents are on Coll's new shirt and sweater. By the orange tinge to the shirt I'd say it was orange juice.

And I'd also say, Wilhelmera of Kardenia has fucked up and nothing can save her now.

Collette's mouth hangs open in shock and she shrieks and clutches her fists at her side.

This, I'm going to fucking enjoy.

CHAPTER THREE

Mera

"Since we're all done eating, we might as well head to class early," Scarlett says with a sigh. "First class on a Monday morning and it has to be history. Why?"

"It's not so bad as long as the teacher isn't a jackass," Peyton mutters, rubbing a hand across his eyes.

"Let's just get there and get seats next to each other." I stand up quickly, swiveling around and stop in my tracks when I notice the guy getting up from the table a few feet behind us. His trademark scowl is parked on his face and he's turning around to leave.

Did he see me? I guess he's going to a class too. Well, at least I don't have to talk to him today. I grab my bag in one hand, hoisting it on my shoulder, and my almost full styrofoam cup of orange juice in the other.

I wonder if he's going to meet up with Heath.

Someone walks by in my peripheral vision and I stumble over to get out of the way, and lose my footing for a split second. Shit. My hand tips over as I correct myself, and I gasp when I notice it suddenly feels empty.

"Oh shit," I hear Scarlett and Peyton say at the same time. My eyes leave Callan's back and move to my left.

Well, I now know where my orange juice went.

Gasps echo throughout the whole hall and I just know they're all looking over here now. This seems like a drama craving college.

A girl with dark brown hair in a bun, and bright blue eyes shrieks as she looks down at her shirt and cardigan.

"Oh my God, Collette!"

"Collette, are you okay?"

"We need to get you out of that like now, girl."

Three girls come out of nowhere and surround her, so I step back a little and say, "I'm so sorry."

I've never intentionally dumped anything on anyone. I can't say this is the first time this has happened. Usually it's no big deal, however this is Goldsworthy University and I probably just embarrassed a rich girl.

The girl I spilled the orange juice on shoves her way through her trio of friends and steps toward me. "What was that?"

"I..um...I said I'm sorry." I look at her with a questioning expression. Her previously scrunched up face falls and I start to breathe a sigh of relief. That is, until I notice the same coldness in her eyes that Callan has.

"Collette Goldsworthy does not accept your apology."

Ah. That would explain the eyes. And the bitchy attitude. Oh God, wait a minute. This is the girl that's president of Zeta Delta Beta? I'm so fucking screwed. "It's not like it was on purpose."

"Sure it wasn't. Listen, I'll call it even just give me five for my dry cleaning."

She eyes the bag at my side so I clutch it tight. "I don't have cash on me, but of course I'll give you money after lunch. $500 is no problem." If it'll make her go away and stop this show. I just want to get to my class.

Turning to her friends, she gives them a look and hoots with laughter. Her friends giggle a little, as they all stare me down.

"I meant 5 thousand, dear."

What the fuck? "Who needs five thousand for dry cleaning?" I exclaim.

She smiles smoothly. "Collette Goldsworthy does."

What bullshit. "I can't give you that, so you're going to have to figure something else out."

The smile slips off her face. "You clumsy bitch. I know you have money, you're a princess for God's sake and yet you won't give me even a morsel of it."

I grit my teeth. If I hadn't been told to keep my money spending low, I would gladly give it to her. As it stands, I can't.

"Oh I get it. You've been disowned, haven't you? They sent you here with barely a drop of money. That's why you can't afford to pay for my dry cleaning. I guess you're basically a peasant now." She chuckles and shakes her head in fake sorrow.

What. A. Fucking. Bitch.

I clench my fists at my side. If I was in my own country I would've slapped that smirk right off her fucking face.

Suddenly the crowd starts to murmur and gasp. What now?

From my right side, I abruptly feel a light touch to my shoulder with my bag strap on it.

"What's the problem, sis?" A few squeals sound off throughout the hall at his deep voice. I don't have to look to know it's Heath. The tension between his sister and I eases a little as she regards Heath with a welcoming smile.

Murmurs echo throughout the hall.

"He never comes to breakfast."

"Wasn't he showing her around campus yesterday?"

"Are they friends?"

"This *klutz* stained my new shirt and cardigan and she needs to pay for my dry cleaning."

The hand on my shoulder tightens and I look at Heath out of the corner of my eye and then back to her.

"You know we have plenty of money to pay for it, Coll."

Her brows draw together. "And?"

"And here." He digs in his back pocket, pulling out his wallet and then a card. Reaching for her hand, he opens it and places the card in and pulls her fingers over it. "There. Now can you relax?"

Her mouth drops open. "Why? Heath, stop being a knight in shining armor and let her pay."

I scoff. "Yeah, I offered $500 and that's it. You're choosing to be a bitch about it so how about I give you nothing instead?"

She gasps and I shut my lips together as my hand flies to my mouth. I probably shouldn't have called his sister a bitch in front of him. Heath definitely won't like that. I'm also a billion percent positive my chances of getting in Zeta Delta Beta are now in the toilet.

Contrary to my belief, he doesn't say a word.

"Did you hear that, Heath? Are you going to let her get away with calling me that?" She cries indignantly.

Heath puts a hand under my chin, turning my attention to him. His green eyes study mine for a second, and I can tell he's trying to communicate something with them. My eyes widen as his leans in and his face gets closer.

What's he doing?

His lips come down on mine in a closed mouth kiss. Only a touch and yet, the entire hall goes wild.

And just like that, my first kiss is gone. I never wanted to give an asshole at home the ammunition to go around and say they kissed a princess like they're something special, so I've dodged every single attempt. Especially Josh's attempts.

Blinking quickly and uncontrollably, my mind tries to process what just happened. "Get to class. You're going to be late. I'll talk to my sister."

From somewhere behind me, Scarlett grabs my arm, yanking me away. I don't miss the shrieks from his sister, the angry chatter between all the girls, or the stunned expression on Callan's face that turns into full blown anger.

The minute we get out, Scarlett pulls me out of the path of the doors. "Girl. You have some major explaining to do."

"You said all he did was show you around yesterday, but did he *show you around*, or did he show you his dick?" Peyton asks, raising an eyebrow.

I cover my face. "No! He didn't. I don't think he even wanted to do that, so then why?"

Peyton shrugs and Scarlett shakes her head.

"One thing is for sure, you've made an enemy out of Collette Goldsworthy. The Goldsworthys don't pull any punches either," Scarlett says in a low tone.

Peyton starts forward. "Let's go before we really are late."

We end up with good seats at the back of the class. It's two to a table, so Peyton and Scarlett are seated at the very back in the right corner and I'm alone at the table in front of them. I'm not naive to think that no one will end up sitting next to me, I just hope it's someone at least a little less arrogant after dealing with Collette.

An older lady with white hair stalks back and forth at the front of the class. "Two minutes."

Like a tidal wave, students flood in and grab seats in a rush. Some grumbling at being forced to sit toward the front.

My phone vibrates and I quickly check it. Heath?

Heath: Let's talk later. Meet me at the Alpha Alpha Alpha basement tonight at 8. Key will be on top of the door frame.
Me: Kay, see ya.

I guess that means I'll get an answer. I shift in the chair to put my phone back in my pocket when I hear the sound of someone pulling the chair out and settling in next to me.

Holding my breath a little, I ready a nice introduction to my seat mate so it doesn't feel awkward, only to find no ordinary seat mate, but Callan Goldsworthy.

"The fuck," escapes my mouth before I could stop the words from falling out.

He glares and edges his head close to mine, staring right into my eyes with a devious glint in his eye. "We're going to play a little game," he whispers.

Before I can muster a response, Professor Harper claps. "Class will now begin."

He flashes a twisted smile and turns his attention to the front. A weird shiver goes down my spine. Any game he wants to play, I'm not interested.

She starts off with the syllabus and as she turns over the

page to read the backside, the door clicks open and everyone turns to look, including me at the person coming in.

"I'm so sorry I'm late, professor. Something came up." Collette flashes a huge smile that would probably work on anyone else as she takes the last seat in the room toward the front.

Even though she's not my favorite person, I can't help but wince for being part of the reason for her being late.

Professor Harper clears her throat. "This is the first day so I'll accept that excuse. Let this be a lesson to everyone. If you want to pass my class, come to class on time. Be ready to learn. Slacking off is unacceptable. I don't care if you're a Goldsworthy or a Silverstone, or even a princess. Everyone is held to the same standard in this class. Is that understood?"

"Yes, Professor," we all answer back.

She moves her attention back to the paper in her hand and resumes where she stopped, making sure to emphasize the big project due right before Thanksgiving. A 10-page report on an important person in U.S. History. Wow, this class is nothing but fun stuff.

Beside me, I watch Callan's fists clench and unclench so I try to pretend he doesn't even exist.

I spend the next three hours praying that somehow the professor will be generous enough to let us go early.

No such luck for me because she takes up every second of it and the moment she lets us go, Callan is the first to jump up and leave. He doesn't even push in his chair or put his stuff in his bag.

"He must have been really uncomfortable," Scarlett muses.

Collette is right on his heels, muttering, "Klutz" venomously as she walks past me.

Together the three of us leave the building and head back toward the cafeteria building.

"Who is that guy and what did he say to you?" Peyton asks, eyeing Callan in the distance.

"Long story short, he's Collette's twin brother and he just might hate me a smidge more than she does. It's a tough call though. And he wants to play a game."

"Girl, with the darkness radiating from him I'd stay far away." She laughs a little. "We've only just become friends, but I can already tell you'll make sure this year isn't boring." Scarlett wraps an arm around my shoulder and gives it a squeeze. "Right, Peyton?"

He chuckles. "Yeah. This is the most excitement I've ever had in 24 hours."

Warmth fills my chest as I realize how different it is having friends laugh with you instead of at you.

I flop down on my bed and sigh happily, enjoying the stream of air conditioning coming in. Scarlett and Peyton were only able to eat with me for a little bit before heading off to their next classes. My next one isn't until the evening though and by the time I leave to go, they'll be getting dinner.

Art class. I completely suck at it so I know it's going to be a nightmare. God, I hope I'm not stuck with a snobby teacher like high school who will fail me for my lack of creativity.

Hours later, I leave the dorm and head for the fine arts building. As I approach the building, I spot Scarlett on the phone with her back to me. She shifts the weight between her feet and moves her empty hand to her head in a clear agitated way. "I just got here, let's not do this now."

I move in front of her and her eyes widen and flash to the phone. "Gotta go, talk to you later."

"Family drama?" I ask.

She nods and moves a piece of hair behind her ear. "Yeah. I was just about to head to the dorm. You have Art 101 right?"

"Yeah, I'll see you later. Don't wait up, I have to go and talk to Heath after I get out of class too."

"Don't have too much fun." She smiles a little, but not her usual eye reaching one. It's dull in a way.

That phone conversation must have been an intense one.

I wave and head for the doors of the building, going up the first flight of stairs and then down the hall. At the far end, I spot a large sign next to the door that says Art 101.

Please don't let this class suck.

When I walk in, I take a stool at the table in the far back. No professor in sight, but they must not be far since the board already has the instructions for our first project.

And lucky me, there's no stool next to mine so I'll have this entire table to myself. I scroll through my phone and wait for class to start, vaguely hearing more students coming in and the stools scraping against the stone floor as they're pulled out.

"Looks like everyone is almost here," I glance up to find a friendly looking guy who doesn't look much older than us at the front. Honestly the complete opposite of Professor Harper. How did he get this job?

I hear a loud grunt from the left and to my absolute horror, I see Callan pull a stool from the empty table to my left and drag it over to the empty space beside me.

"Are you ready to play yet?"

There's enough room between tables due to the larger

room that talking in a normal voice wouldn't be heard at the table in front or to the left of us.

"Just leave me the fuck alone, Callan."

"No."

"Okaaaay class. Let's start making magic." He walks by, setting down a piece of paper, the syllabus, and a huge white paper where I assume I'll be drawing a ball like the one on the board. "Read the syllabus at your own convenience and the first project is due next Monday. Instructions are on the board along with samples. If you need me, I'll be at my desk."

Stopping at the front, he pulls out his chair, and really does just sit.

How can two classes be so different?

Immediately, the silence evaporates. Everyone is talking to a friend and yet here I am, stuck with him.

I expect to hear Callan talk about the game he keeps bringing up, but to my utter surprise, he seems to ignore me completely and start on his drawing.

Lifting the page of the syllabus up, I flip it over to find it's only one side. The only thing it says is that there's thirteen projects and one final. We can do as much extra credit as we want and attendance on Wednesdays isn't mandatory. I didn't even choose this class and I already love it.

Ha. If I fail a project I'll just do some extra credit.

This is perfect.

I squint at the board to read the instructions and start to draw the ball.

A snort reaches my ears.

"What's so funny?"

"You're fucking terrible at this, that's what funny."

"Haven't you ever heard keep your eyes on your own paper?"

But his words get to me so I stop what I'm doing, look

between the instructions, the sample drawn on the board, and my paper.

Maybe I'll just ask the professor what he thinks. Hesitantly, I get up from the stool and walk around Callan to get to the aisle leading up to the front. As I walk, I can feel eyes on my back as the chatter quiets a bit.

"Professor Schmidt, when we start with the ball, we do a light outline right?"

He looks up from his phone and looks from me to the board. "Well, yes. Um, who are you sitting next to?"

He peeks around and points to the corner. "Mr. Goldsworthy right? He's perfectly able to show you the correct approach for this piece."

With a dismissive nod, he goes back to his phone and I have no choice but to go back to my seat. Fucking hell.

As I sit back down, I look at my mess of a ball and sigh. Angrily, I erase the whole thing.

He snickers. "Beg me Princess and I'll help you."

"Not gonna happen," I reply resolutely.

A twisted smirk forms on his face and he continues his sketch of the ball. I watch his hands flex as he moves the pencil with short strokes, starting on the shadow of the ball on the counter. He seems like he knows exactly what he's doing. Does he actually like art?

"You know, I'm better with my hands than my brother is."

I don't respond, instead choosing to spend the rest of the two and a half hours staring at the blank piece of paper in front of me while occasionally playing a game on my phone.

"Class is over, you may go," Professor Schmidt says from his seat.

It's 7:30. Almost time to meet Heath. I stuff the papers in my bag, moving past Callan then out the door. I haven't been to fraternity row yet so I need time to find AAA.

My stomach grumbles as I reach the bottom step. But I'm so fucking hungry. I need something until I can get something for dinner.

I eye the vending machine in the corner and race over. My credit card is accepted and I choose a bag of kettle corn. I'll have to eat this on the way.

It's a long trek to Fraternity Row. When I get there, I ignore the hoots and hollers from both sides, only paying attention to the greek signs on each house.

Finally, I come across AAA. I stop in my tracks. What am I supposed to say? Heath asked me to come. Yes. That will work.

I twist the knob and open the door to hear a bunch of yelling and cheering. This is the first floor so the door for the basement has to be around here somewhere. Walking away from the increasing noise from the group of guys, I start down the only hallway. I peek through every open door.

A laundry room that made me want to cover my nose.

An equipment room.

A bathroom.

Another bathroom.

I turn the corner and come across a closed door with a window that looks out to the outside.

Finally, at the end of the hall, I come to a locked door. If this isn't it, I don't know what is. I'm proven correct though when I reach above the door to find a lone key. After opening it, I put the key back in place and take a step inside. No lights on so Heath must not be in here.

I think there's still a few minutes until it's 8.

I check the phone to find it's 7:55. Oh crap, my phone's at

1%. I should've charged it before Art class. Now I can't even use it to find the light switch.

After putting my phone back in my pocket, I move my hands over the walls for a switch. Maybe it's down a little more? Stepping down, I keep moving my hand against the walls, searching for the switch, but find none. And when there's no stairs left, I stop in place and look around. Complete darkness. Not even a sliver of light from a window.

God I hope there aren't any bugs in here. It doesn't smell particularly dusty at least. Stepping around in the dark, I put my hands on the walls, until I bump into something. What is this? The soft and firmness of it tells me it's either a leather couch or loveseat.

I don't feel like stumbling around in the dark anymore. I'll just wait here for him. Sitting at the edge, I keep my bag on my lap, and hopefully avoid any spiders waiting for their next victim.

The dark is so incredibly quiet it's a tiny bit unnerving. I can only hear the sound of my own breathing.

Wait. I hold my breath for a second and listen carefully.

It's faint, and so quiet it's easy to miss under the sound of my own breathing. But now, it's easy to hear. There's someone else down here. And even creepier, I can hear their even breathing which means they're close by. They're either at the other end of the couch or maybe across from me.

Maybe everyone in AAA knows there's an extra key above the door and they come down here to...oh shit, I don't know. Why would someone just sit in the dark without saying anything?

After a deep breath, I mutter, "I know someone's there."

Silence.

"What about turning on the lights? Did you enjoy hearing me fumbling around for the switch?"

More silence.

"Heath is going to be here soon. Are you waiting for him?" Highly unlikely since Heath himself told me to be here for what I'm pretty sure is a personal conversation

My heart starts to pound a little faster at the continued silence. It's starting to unnerve me.

Suddenly, I hear it. The sliding of something. Something sliding on the leather?

And then, I feel it. A large rough hand grips my left leg. I jump instantly off the couch.

"Stop. What the fuck are you doing?"

That hand is joined by another one as they grab me by the hips and yank me back down. Instead of the soft coolness of the leather, I land on something warm.

Is this the creep's lap?

One hand quickly grabs my wrist in a tight, threatening grip.

I gasp and the blood starts rushing quickly to my head. This guy is determined to keep me here. For what reason? I need to get out of here. Think, Mera.

"Let me go," I say in a low tone as my mind races.

I use my nice pair of flats to step on his foot. He grunts when my foot connects, but his grip doesn't loosen.

His breathing is no longer even, in fact, it's coming out so quickly. Is he…angry? With my eyes starting to adjust, I can finally make out a pair of wide shoulders and a fit arm.

This guy could easily do something to me if he wants to and I'm not strong enough to stop him.

Heath should be here soon. The panic slowly rises in me as the minutes seem to tick by, when suddenly, that one hand of his leaves my wrist, moving past my back to around my waist. Before I can open my mouth to tell him to stop, his other hand is underneath my legs pulling them so my feet land on the other cushion.

"Stop touching me. Let me go."

He only lets my legs go. His right hand is securely gripping the right side of my waist still, with no give in it.

I stare into the face of the man harassing me, thankful to finally make out the details.

His breathing evens out again and that's when I see it. That damn cold glint in his eye. The smirk on his face.

"Callan," I breathe.

"I told you we'd play a game, princess."

"Why?" I exclaim,

"I don't owe you an explanation."

I push at his chest and squirm around trying to get out of his lap. "I wouldn't keep doing that if I were you, princess."

I freeze and lock eyes with him. He leans forward slightly, bringing his face so close to mine I can feel his hot breath on my cheek.

"What are you doing?"

Flinching, I feel his lips ghost over mine. "I wonder who's a better kisser. Heath or me? Let's find out."

I couldn't move if I tried so I close my eyes quickly and wait for it to be over. He'll probably just do what Heath did this morning. A small peck and he'll get whatever satisfaction he wanted and be done with this stupid game. I just need to–

His lips come down hard on mine, moving so fast I gasp, accidentally giving him access to my mouth. He thrusts his tongue inside, immediately moving against my tongue.

Oh God. A small sound escapes my throat and I bite down, nicking his tongue as my mouth closes.

He chuckles and grabs my throat, dragging my face to eye level. "Do you like the taste of blood, princess?"

The hand around my throat pulls me in and his lips meet mine once more. His hand tightens so hard I have no choice but to gasp for air. He uses that opportunity to thrust his tongue past my lips. The coppery taste is strong as his blood is spread across my tongue. As my eyes start to water, I hear a resounding click.

My eyes pop open and I take in the brightness of the light in the room. In a hurry, I push against Callan's chest who immediately lets me go. Scrambling off his lap, I quickly fall to the floor. My cheeks heat up as I avoid his eyes, wiping the tears away from the corners. I can still feel the ghost of his lips on mine and his warm tongue in my mouth.

I use the table to pull myself up just in time as Heath steps off the last stair. He gives me a small smile. "Hey, sorry I'm a little late. I had to…Callan? What are you doing here?"

Crossing my arms, I eye him. He meets my eyes and moves his finger over his lips. "I was just playing a game." My stomach rolls a little as I remember how I was completely under his control. He could've done whatever he wanted to me.

Heath's smile falls. "Get out, Callan."

"Actually, now that I'm here, I think I'd like to know what's so important you had to bring her down here to talk to you? I've never even been down here before."

Heath's mouth twitches a bit at the ends. "It's solely meant for the president and his company only. And right now, she's my company. Leave."

Callan's signature frown is back as he stares Heath down, until his gaze slides toward me. "So, Wil, what's the verdict?"

"Don't call me that," I retort. Anything but that. It makes me sound like a man. Whatever, I'll answer so he'll leave. It's getting late and I'm still starving. I stare directly into his eyes as I remember how insistent his tongue was. How warm his lips were. How come I can't remember how warm Heath's were? "Heath."

His eyes brighten at that and he chuckles a bit. "I know you're lying, but it's okay. We'll play this game again."

He moves past Heath to the stairs. "Later, bro."

Heath eyes him until the door clicks behind him.

He strides toward me and looks me up and down. "What was that? Why did you say my name?"

Clearing my throat, I move my hair behind my ear. "Um. He wanted me to tell him who I liked more, you or him."

His worried eyes close with relief and he sighs. "Good. That means he's not playing one of those games. I know he likes to play with people. I've seen him go after guys for going against our family. He plays mind games until they're at their breaking point and by then they'll do whatever he asks."

Is that what this is? He's trying to break me down.

"If I had to guess, Collette must have egged him on after what I did at breakfast. When I left them, the two of them were still talking."

I bite my lip and finally ask the question I've been wondering. "Why did you do that, by the way?"

He sighs and rubs a hand over the back of his head. "I clearly remember what you told me yesterday. You said you wanted a fresh start. And if you do want that start, you can't afford to piss off my sister. The moment you spilled that orange juice, you were fucked. Zero chance of getting into Zeta Delta Beta."

"So you kissed me?"

He sheepishly grins. "Sorry, I'm a terrible kisser, right?"

I've only ever had two kisses in my life, so I can't really say. Well if I compared it to Callan's–

"It wasn't bad," I blurt. It really wasn't. It was quick and gentle, and sweet. The complete opposite of Callan's. It was nice. Like Heath.

"Good, because we'll have to do a whole lot more to be convincing as boyfriend and girlfriend. And don't worry, this isn't all for you. You'll help me keep the girls from clinging to me."

I snort and laugh. Some girls will be discouraged, but not all. "Fair enough. But how did you manage this?"

"The three of us have this rule where we can ask each other a favor for our significant others. A once in a lifetime thing. This is my favor."

He digs in the back pocket of his jeans, pulling out a folded paper. Before he even unfolds it, I know what it is.

My jaw drops as my eyes widen and focus on the paper in his hand. "Heath, you shouldn't have done this. You're too nice to me. What did I do to deserve this? We barely know each other."

He nods. "That's true, but I also know what it's like to want a fresh start and be denied it." His green eyes darken and he glances away. "Just take it."

I reach for his outstretched hand and grasp the paper. I open it up to find an invitation to Zeta Delta Beta. Wait, this isn't an application?

"You don't need to fill one out. All you have to do is complete the hazing rounds and you'll be in. If you fail them, I can't help you, I'm sorry."

My pulse quickens as I stare at the paper with my name on it. "No, Heath. This is plenty of help. I really appreciate this. Whatever it takes to get in, I'll do."

He smiles widely. "Good. Show everyone who you really are. And, I guess this means you accept."

"You spent your one and only favor. Of course, I accept. This isn't like it's forever."

"Not at all. In a few months we can break up. I'll even let you dump me."

I giggle. "Me? Dump the incomparable Heath Goldsworthy? I could never. No, I think you should dump me."

Out of nowhere, my stomach makes its emptiness known with a grumble.

"God, I'm hungry. Is there anything else you wanted to say before I go, Heath?"

His green eyes stare into mine and he shakes his head. "Yes. Do me a favor and don't tell anyone this is fake. Not even your friends."

I move toward him and give him a quick hug that he returns. "Got it." It's a simple thing to ask of me for something big like this. "Thank you, again. And I'm sorry if this inconveniences you. I promise this won't all be for nothing."

He nods and I take the stairs up to the door and walk out.

I can't let Heath down.

By the time I get to the dining hall, most places are closed. Only a few are still open, but there are still a lot of people sitting around, eating and talking. I get in line at the pizza place with only four people in front of me.

"Piggy getting back in line for more?"

Piggy?

I gaze around and lock eyes on the closest table to the pizza counter. A trio of guys, all snickering. Following their eyes, I spot a girl with her arms crossed with large glasses and short bangs headed toward me. She kind of looks familiar.

"Oink oink." The guys make piggy noises at her, snorting obnoxiously and laughing.

Fucking assholes.

So what if she's heavier? And so what if she wants more? Hell, I go and get seconds of food all the time.

I step up to the counter when it's my turn and get two large slices of pepperoni and ham.

When I'm done, I linger at the side of the counter where the napkins and condiments are. Glancing out of the side of my eye, I watch as she comes away from the counter with only a cup and approaches the area I'm in.

"It was a really hot day, wasn't it?" I ask, striking up a conversation.

She pauses for a moment, moving her cup in her hand. "Yes." She fills it up with ice first and then the pink lemonade.

Whirling around, she leaves quickly without another word.

The loud jarring from the guys continues. "Piggy got thirsty. Look at her gulping it down."

Just ignore it. She's ignoring it.

I grab my plate of pizza in my hand and leave to search for a table. There's plenty of open ones so I decide to take an empty one with two chairs.

My eyes move off my plate to watch as the guys change tables to her empty one. One of them leans down to her ear, whispering something and wraps a gangly arm around her shoulder. "Well, how about it?" he yells loud enough to capture the attention of everyone in the near vicinity.

"How about you go shove that tiny dick of yours in a light socket? How about that?"

"You bitch," he yells and moves to slap her.

Somehow I find myself right in front of their table and slap my hands down before he can reach her cheek. "Slap her, and I'll slap you."

"And who the fuck are you?" he asks narrowing his eyes at me.

Another one of them mutters, "Dude, is this that princess chick?"

"Shit…isn't this Heath Goldsworthy's girl?"

A sly smile creeps on my face. "That's right. Now I suggest you leave my friend and I alone."

"If she's your friend, how come you weren't sitting with her?" The guy who went to slap her asks.

I glance at her completely neutral face and shrug. "Friends argue."

He grimaces and nods to the other two guys. "Let's go."

As soon as they're gone, I go back to grab my pizza and then sit in the chair directly across from her. After making sure there's no one in earshot, I lean forward. "Hey, just in case they come back, what's your name?"

She blinks at me. "Gemma."

"Well, Gemma. I'm Mera."

"I know. So, how did you do it?"

"How did I do what?"

She sighs and pushes her glasses up her nose. "How did you pull Heath Goldsworthy in less than 24 hours?"

"I…uh…well. It was love at first sight really. For the both of us."

She glances down at her hands and then back at me. "Well, then I feel it's my responsibility to tell you that you should do whatever it takes to get Collette on your good side. A bad relationship with your future sister-in-law would be disastrous, right?"

Just nod and agree. "Yeah, you're right. I'll start by getting into Zeta Delta Beta and go from there. Maybe she'll let me be one of her officers." Now that's a stretch. I'll just be lucky to fucking get in.

"Well, there's only one spot. The chances of you getting that spot after what happened today and considering the amount of women applying for that position, I'd say your chances are slim to none. But hey, good luck. I'll put in a good word for you."

She stands up from her chair and I stand up with her. "Wait, how can you put in a good word?"

She smiles. "I'm their treasurer of course. Math and science are what I'm good at. I enjoy it, and that's why Collette is letting me join whether I complete the hazing or not." She laughs a little. "Anyway, I have to get back. Thanks for your generosity, Mera. In situations like these, I never really know what to do. See you again soon."

She grabs her bag off the floor and leaves with a wave. She's kind of strange, different?

I shove a pizza slice in my mouth and chew it slowly.

Oh shit, I should have asked her about the hazing. Oh well. It's been a long fucking day and I can think about it tomorrow. There's four days until then. I have to get through the rest of this week first.

CHAPTER FOUR

Callan

Every day it's the same damn thing. They come to the dining hall in the morning holding hands, almost unable to keep their eyes off of each other. He doesn't even sit with the group of guys he usually sits with. No, now he's sitting with her, Red, and Tall Boy.

A few of the girls have even come around saying how perfect he looks with her. Like he's her Prince Charming or some shit. No one can touch her on campus with him on her arm. Just how did she sink her claws into him so quickly? Whatever she's planning for my brother, he's completely clueless. If this were last year I know he wouldn't let someone like her around him. He'd intentionally hang around the brainless ones. She's nowhere near brainless.

He also never likes to indulge Collette when she's being a brat, but he's never shown it publicly. We've always stood together in support of each other against others. Whatever she's done, I'm going to undo it by forcing her out of here.

I'm going to break her until she has no choice but to run home. I just need to get her alone first.

Sadly, it's going to have to wait until after hazing is over. Ha. These poor bastards.

Our fraternity has three rounds and this is only the first.

I lean back on the couch and watch as fifty hopefuls standing around the dining table try to drain a huge bottle of vodka in fifteen minutes. It's tradition to have everyone who's pledged to down one big bottle of the president's choice of booze, and Heath has always been into vodka.

Half of them easily got through more than half of the bottle, but now they're struggling to get it down with only five minutes left.

Maybe I should've done this part to show them how it's done. Though, I prefer tequila myself.

A bottle clinks as it hits the wood table. Of course. The first to finish is Vincent. Absolut is one of his favorites. He smirks at me.

"Oh fuck," Noel mutters. He moves his head back, downing the last fourth of the bottle in one go. "There, done."

He coughs and elbows Tyrell. "Come on, hurry." Tyrell glances at him with a blank expression and continues sipping at the bottle.

Half of the other guys manage to finish their bottles, struggling hard with bright red faces. Tyrell is the last to finish as time runs out and Heath's timer beeps.

Heath comes through the doorway in the corner out of the kitchen. "Time's up. Anyone who didn't finish leave the bottle on the table. Better luck next year."

A few guys groan and stumble past me to the foyer.

"Heath come on, you know me. You know I won't be here next year," one guy says, pleading with Heath with one hand on Heath's shoulder.

Heath's business smile pops on. "Rules are rules, dude. It's nothing against you personally. Thanks for your interest."

"Fuck!" the guy yells, whirling around and kicking a chair on his way out.

And this is the easiest round. Fucking hilarious. I let out a loud laugh and Vincent comes over. "Since you're in such a good mood, come out and join us for rounds two and three."

Now *that's* hilarious.

"Fuck no. But hey, you guys enjoy it. This is your chance to find a new girl. Take it."

The smile leaves Vincent's face and he turns away.

Well fuck, he can't be stuck on her forever.

Noel pops up behind Vincent, wrapping his arm around his shoulder. "I'll take all the hot girls then if you won't, buddy."

Vincent nudges his arm off roughly and goes back to Tyrell near the table.

"It's going to take a lot more than that to get him to stop thinking about Ash."

Shaking my head, I sigh. "Yeah. I don't fucking get it. How could he let himself get that wrapped up in her?"

"I don't either. I'd rather have fun with as many girls as possible. Like I'm going to try and do tonight. Sure you don't want to come and watch the show?"

"Hope you guys are excited, because the second round starts now. Strip it all off and show what you got," Heath booms.

Fuck no. I don't need to attract the female eye any more than I already do as a Goldsworthy. They're probably lined up outside hoping to see my dick. Walking to the other side of campus buck naked? No. I'm good. "I'm sure."

About thirty guys leave the house naked with my friends bringing up the rear. None of the guys are shy about covering their dicks and that goes for my friends too. I know Noel will make certain to show his off. Heath's Vice President, Rick, will be at the other end of campus waiting for the guys to see how many guys make it. Only a select few in history have ever disappeared during the second round. It's the third and last round that can really fuck a guy over.

"You've been quiet this week."

I glance back to find Heath facing the door too.

"Yep. And you've been even busier with your new girlfriend. You've been bending over backwards to make her happy, I'm surprised you aren't with her right now."

His mouth forms a thin line. "She's busy. Don't bother her with your little games."

I'd love to see him try and stop me. "Busy with what?" I get up off the couch, moving around it and come face to face with Heath. "Don't you have enough on your plate to be worrying about what I'm doing? Why don't you focus on your fucking self?"

Ring ring. The phone in his pocket goes off and Heath turns around quickly as if he's trying to hide something. "What is it?"

I lean my head in slightly to listen in. The volume is just barely loud enough to make out a few words. The person on the other end mentions a number. Must be Rick telling him how many girls made it through. That's when I hear it. That one word that changes everything.

Mera.

Leaning away quickly, I put my hand over my mouth as

my mind races. This is it. She's using Heath to get into Zeta Delta Beta. And she's out there…right now.

That's what she's busy with.

This is almost too perfect. My little game can continue.

Heath continues talking on the phone in a low tone. "Fucking hell. She wasn't supposed to be there. Watch the both of them and call me if something happens."

By the time he turns around, I'm already completely naked and heading out of the living room.

"What the fuck Callan?" he yells.

As I wrench open the door I feel a hand grab me by the shoulder. Ha. Heath can say whatever he wants, but I'm going whether he likes it or not. "I told you that you didn't have to do the hazing."

I turn my head to look back and smirk. "Well, now I've decided to do it. On my own accord. Just give me a pass for round one."

I shove his hand away and walk out the door, entering the cool summer night air. I'm already behind, by the time I get there, someone might already have a hold of her. I need to hurry.

Breaking into a run, I start down Fraternity Row. Faintly, I hear Heath shout, "Just leave her alone, Callan. Grab anyone but her."

No. If I'm going out and showing my dick off to the world, it will only be so I can play this game with her.

Panting a little, I slow to a stop as I make it a few feet away from the group. I wipe the beads of sweat off my brow, courtesy of the long run I did. And as I suspected, half the female population was out and ogling my bobbing dick.

The moment I make it to the edge of the group, all chattering between the guys and girls near me stop. Jaws drop as I push through until they part the way for me. Toward the center I spot Noel surrounded by a few girls. At the other end toward the edge, Tyrell and Vincent's eyes are both locked to the right side of the group.

What the fuck are they staring at so hard? Is there a really nice pair of tits?

Before I can turn to look, from that same direction, I hear, "Oh God, is that my brother?"

Coll?

I cover my eyes quickly to avoid seeing something I really don't want to. "What the fuck, Coll?" I yell out, covering my eyes. "You're the president. You shouldn't be here."

Everyone quiets down.

"It's all her fucking fault. And you shouldn't be here either!" she screams back.

"Who?" I ask.

"The klutz! She dared me to."

I uncover my eyes to find Wil at the far end to the left with her head peeking around a well built guy. A cheeky smile forms as she locks eyes with me and I see a flash of pink right then. Why does that keep fucking happening? She then looks around me, presumably at Coll. "You could've said no," she says in a sing-song voice and then goes back to talking to the guy in front of her.

I wonder if she knew that Collette doesn't back down from dares. God this is annoying. I didn't come here to play protective brother but I guess I have to. Straightening, I look around, avoiding Collette's area. "All of you guys wanting to get into AAA, listen carefully, you touch Collette, you're out. No exceptions."

A throat clears from somewhere behind me. I turn to find

the only fully clothed person in the group with a hoodie and a clipboard. Rick.

"Actually, I'm pretty sure only Heath can bar someone from getting in. Not you."

My blood starts to boil at that and I narrow my eyes. "Want to try that one more time?"

His eyes widen and he holds up his empty hand. "Um no! Sorry, dude. You're right, carry on." He backs away, disappearing into the heavily wooded area.

That's what I thought.

"I bet you, you're wrong." I turn to my left as the guy in front of Wil faces me. Why the hell is *he* here?

He takes a few steps in my direction, stopping only a few feet away.

Why the fuck didn't Heath tell me that Kane Silverstone was joining AAA? He smirks at my expression. "I see Heath didn't tell you that I'd be the newest special member."

I stare into his arrogant gray eyes. "No, I just thought you were too much of a pussy to do this with the rest of us. After all, you didn't even come over to down your bottle of vodka."

He shrugs and sighs in an exaggerated way. "When I grab a woman like your sister, I want to be sober so I can fully appreciate the way her body feels in my hands. I want to be able to understand when she begs me to touch her more. I want to remember the soft sounds that emanate from her mouth."

Gritting my teeth, I curl my hands into fists at my side. One more word and I'll punch that smirk of his right off his fucking face and it won't be the first time.

"Let's make a wager. I bet you that I can get away with carrying your sister back to her dorm and still get initiated into AAA." I don't spot even a hint of fear in his eyes. There's only confidence. Does Heath have some kind of understanding with him?

After a few beats without a response, he smiles widely. "Fine, I'll save your pride. No bet, but I'm going to do it anyway."

It takes everything in me not to grab his arm as he strides past me to Collette and her group of friends.

"Don't fucking touch me, Silverstone," Collette shrieks. "Aren't you three going to help me?"

"Sorry, Coll."

"Yeah, you're on your own this time."

"Don't you remember? I told you before we left that the chances of a guy carrying you back were high."

"Shut up Gemma and –" Collette screeches.

Moments later, he files past me with Collette over his shoulders in a fireman's carry. "Light as a feather, aren't you, ballerina girl?"

She ignores him, turning her head in my direction. "I can't fucking believe you Callan!"

Ugh, I didn't fucking come here for this. She's going to be pissy with both Heath and I now.

"Sorry Princess, we'll talk soon though," he yells out as he disappears past the crowd of people.

That's right. He was talking to Wil. Did she know who he was when she started talking to him? Oh well, it doesn't even fucking matter. I can finally do what I came here to do.

Talking between everyone resumes, but quieter than it was when I first arrived.

Straightening, I walk to my left, straight for her. Her arms crossed over her breasts tighten and her eyes widen as I get closer. "Stay away from me."

I lean my head down to her ear. "Your one shot at getting into Zeta Delta Beta is almost gone. Your ticket just left carrying my sister out. I bet you're wishing you didn't dare her to come now."

She glares up at me, unmoving. As the minutes tick by, the people around us start leaving. Some of the guys are doubled up with girls because of the smaller amount of girls who made it.

"Clock is ticking, princess. Better ask me nicely."

She huffs. "I wouldn't ask you to carry me if you were the last guy here." She takes a step to the left to move around me, and I match it. She steps right and I match it again.

I wait for her angry eyes to meet mine, but instead she peeks around my arm. "Hey, you two. One of you carry me and I'll give you my number. Fair trade, right?"

I turn around to find the two guys she's talking to to be Vincent and Tyrell. Tyrell seems to ignore her, still only fixated on the three of Collette's friends, and Vincent shakes his head. "Sorry," he calls. "Callan, I'm heading back now. Good luck."

"I don't need it," I reply, watching as he steps off from beside Tyrell to Collette's group of friends.

He bends down to the tiny brunette, Ashlynn, and whispers something in her ear. Her face turns a bright shade of pink as she elbows him and he grabs her around the waist and throws her over his shoulder. "Vincent! Fucker, let me go!"

For their sake, I hope Ashlynn's father and Vincent's mother don't hear about this.

I can't say I didn't see that coming. He probably would've torn off the arm of any guy who went to touch her.

A deep laugh sounds and I watch as Tyrell moves toward the remaining two of her friends. Gemma, the smart new girl in her group and Luella. Luella's always been shy around me. She's been Collette's friend since her freshman year of high school and she's always been nice to me, even when I'm a dick. Tyrell wants to carry one of them?

Without even a word, he picks Luella up in one arm and carries her out under his arm. I almost want to give him a high five. I didn't think he had it in him.

As they pass me by, I hear Luella mutter angrily, "I fucking told you not to come near me."

Oh, I guess Luella isn't so quiet after all. I don't think I've ever heard her cuss before. Tyrell has never mentioned knowing Luella to me.

His deep voice responds in a slow, gruff tone, "Ella, if s-someone is going to carry you while you're naked, it's going to be me."

She makes a sound of deep frustration as he carries her away under his arm.

What the hell do they have going on?

"Well, that doesn't matter. There's still three other guys left and only two girls," Wil says with a nod, as if she's so positive that one of them is going to carry her. One of them being Noel.

"Noel," I boom. "Carry Gemma back."

"Are you serious?" he yells, starting to come over. "I was just about to carry Lisa."

"Don't take another step this way, and just do it."

He sighs. "Right. You owe me then."

I watch out of the corner of my eye as he goes over to Gemma, off on her own with her hands at her sides. She looks up to Noel. "You collected a bunch of numbers right, so you don't need mine?"

"Well, yes."

"Good. And you're strong enough to carry an ugly fat girl like me?" she bluntly asks.

There's a long awkward silence. One that actually makes

me uncomfortable. There's a blankness on her face. She believes every word she said.

Sure she's a little heavier, who cares, but she isn't ugly one bit. Her full lips and chubby cheeks accompanied with her rounded glasses make her very attractive.

Noel doesn't respond. Instead, he hooks one arm around her legs and the other around her back and hoists her to his chest without a hint of struggle.

"Gemma!" Wil calls from next to me. "You're beautiful and don't let anyone tell you that you aren't."

Two hands pop on to Noel's wide shoulders and her head peeks over just enough to see her eyes. "Thanks, Mera. Good luck."

Good. Now there's only the two guys left and Lisa, and by the sounds of it, they're both going to carry her like some of the other guys that had to double up. One will take her arms and the other her legs. Rick is long gone now too.

I stare down into Wil's annoyed eyes. "I'm not waiting any longer, princess." She clenches her arms together even tighter. It's funny that she thinks she can stop me from moving them away. I can move them any time I want to.

Something about the image of her being bare to my gaze makes a wave of excitement flood through me.

"Let's continue our game, Wil."

CHAPTER FIVE

Mera

I wish he'd stop with this stupid fucking game.

"Girls are probably lined up and waiting for you. Why don't you go and find one of them for your twisted games?"

He steps closer and grabs my chin, forcing me to look into his eyes.

"Because I don't want to play the game with anyone but you."

"And what will people say when they see you carrying your older brother's girlfriend naked?"

He snickers. "You think I care what those people think? No. We're going to play until you can't play anymore."

"What's that supposed to mean?"

His eyes darken a little. "Stay the fuck away from my

family. Better yet, go back home. Sweet talk your parents into letting you go home."

So he thinks he can do all of this and force me to leave? I didn't even ask Heath to help me out, he did that on his own.

And now? Well I don't want to be here, but I'm going to stay no matter what happens.

"I'm not going anywhere," I snap.

He smirks like he expected that response and lets go of my chin. "We'll see about that won't we?"

Way too quickly for my liking, he closes the tiny gap in-between us and suddenly I'm oh so aware of how warm and fit his body is as his six pack presses against my torso. His eyes, cold as ice, stay locked on mine as his toned arms reach around my shoulders.

My face heats up as I figure out exactly where his hands are headed right as they land.

His rough hands cup my ass hard, and I gasp as he picks me up easily, pulling me against him.

Of all the fucking ways he could've carried me, he's carrying me like this?

Holy shit, are his hands kneading my ass? He starts to turn around with me solely being held by the ass by him.

"Wait, I'm going to fall!" I squeak, as I teeter back.

"Then you'd better use those legs of yours and wrap them around my waist."

"Absolutely not!" I yell. If I do that my hooha will be wide open.

"Suit yourself." He takes another step forward, and I'm forced to grab his shoulders just to stay upright.

He chuckles. "Knew you'd have to grab me somewhere. Now wrap those legs around me."

"No," I say firmly.

Glancing around, I notice how almost everyone is gone. We haven't run into one person yet, thank God.

"Wrap them around me or I'll fuck you right here, right now for everyone to see."

My heart drops and my stomach churns. I look up from his neck to his eyes, hoping to see something different.

But nothing's changed. They're still hard and cold.

All of a sudden, I feel something hardening underneath me. "And if you don't believe me..." He lets me down a little bit and lifts me back up, rubbing me against his hard cock.

Bile rises in my throat and I look away from his cruel, piercing eyes, unable to stand to even look at him anymore.

He's fine with embarrassing Heath and even more, me. I'd look like the school whore, fucking my boyfriend's brother right out in the open. And I'm sure they wouldn't stop at that. They'll post us on the internet and my parents will find out. I'll really be in trouble then.

"Five seconds, princess, before my dick slides inside you. You can't see, but there are some girls coming up on the left."

No matter what I do, I'll be uncomfortable. I've already lost by even being in his arms. I don't want to lose my virginity to a monster like him.

Using his shoulders as leverage, I grip them tightly, and lift my legs up and cross them behind him. Immediately, a rush of cold air hits my nether regions. What I don't expect is his hands that travel from my ass to my legs, keeping them anchored to his sides.

As we walk by, a few girls gasp when they see us and I bury my head in his shoulder and close my eyes, not for comfort but out of complete embarrassment because there's nowhere else to turn.

"You should end this game and go home."

"I'm not going home," I say into his shoulder.

A few guys hoot and holler as we walk by.

My face burns and I can't help the tears that start to fill my eyes. I can't let them out. He can't know how much this hurts.

I take a deep breath and look out to see how close we are to sorority row. Thankfully, it isn't too much further. I move my head around as far as I can to see if there's anyone else, but there doesn't seem to be.

"What if I lied, princess?"

"What do you mean?" I ask slowly. If he'd walk just a little faster–

He drops me down lower again. "What if I fuck you anyway?"

My blood turns cold. "Let go of me," I say quietly.

"No." He rubs his cock against my folds.

"Let go of me, Callan!" I yell.

A twisted smile forms. "Sure, let me just spread you open a little and then I'll drop you down onto my dick."

His hands wander back, away from my legs and back to my ass.

"Don't," I say, pounding my hands against his shoulders.

"Beg me."

"What?" I ask, heart pounding in my chest.

"Beg me not to."

Swallowing hard, I clench my lips together and then let it go. "Please don't do it."

"Please don't do it? I don't know what you mean," he murmurs in an offhanded way.

"Please don't fuck me."

"I do have a name you know," he says, tipping his head down to look at me.

A name that I despise more than anything else in this world.

I stare deeply into his eyes. Fucking hell. I never thought I'd have to beg for anything in my life. "Please don't fuck me, Callan."

And then, something strange happens. The moment his name leaves my lips, his eyes heat up for one second, and then it's gone again. And he's looking away.

His hands go back to my legs and he walks briskly. Faster than he has this whole time. I recognize the surroundings so the moment he stops, I let go and he does the same, making me fall onto the ground right on my ass.

He turns around, leaving quickly. I can breathe a little easier. "We'll play this game again, Wil."

No, we fucking won't.

The moment I open the door, I'm met with a crowd of naked girls, and right in the center is Collette and she looks livid.

Straightening my back, I cross my arms and don't back down. "So that's it right?"

She takes three quick steps forward and slaps me across the face.

I gasp and hold my cheek, feeling the burn of the slap and the impending humiliation.

"You know, I thought you were a bitch, but I never thought you'd be a whore too. Really? It's one thing to have my brother carry you, but it's another thing to spread your legs for him like that."

The other girls behind her giggle, happy to watch her tear me down. They can laugh as much as they fucking want, I just want to know if my humiliation was worth it.

"Just answer the damn question. Am. I. In?"

"You are. Now I guess you can run along and go and give my brother, oh wait let me clarify, my *older* brother his *reward* for getting you in." She laughs snidely and turns away.

I push my fingernails into my palms, doing my very best to keep my mouth shut. Does she even know what Callan's really like?

"Oh and one more thing." She turns her head slightly. "Don't make a mess of that room, klutz. We like to keep a clean atmosphere. Can't have food spilled everywhere." She giggles and leaves with the short brunette that I now know is Ashlynn, her VP, and Luella, her secretary.

The other girls scatter, getting their clothes back on so they can go back to their dorms. Gemma smiles in my direction and grabs one girl as she goes to leave. "Brandie, this is Mera. Mera, Brandie. You guys are going to be roommates."

Brandie's eyes widen and she curtsies. "Your Highness."

"That isn't necessary. It was a sweet gesture though, thank you."

She grins and grabs me in a tight hug. "I'm looking forward to being your friend, Mera. Let's get here early tomorrow so we have a chance to chat before the party. I'll have to introduce you to my best friend Jamie too."

That was quick. I'm going to miss Peyton and Scarlett, but rooming with Brandie doesn't seem like it'll be so bad. Maybe. She can easily be a snake in disguise like my friends back home. I should be able to get a better read on her tomorrow.

"Yeah, sounds good."

After getting my clothes back on, I head back to the dorm.

God, I need to tell someone about Callan. I grab my phone out of my pocket and find her name in my phone.

It rings for a while and I say a quiet prayer. *Please please answer.*

"Mera?" she asks.

I take the turn out of sorority row and head toward the dorms.

"Cate, I did it. I'm in ZDB."

She laughs. "Oh my God. Congrats. I knew you had it in you. But hey, you're okay right? I know that hazing is rough."

I don't exactly know how to start, so I stay quiet.

"Mera?"

"I'm a princess, yet I'm completely helpless to him."

"To who?" she asks. "What asshole are you letting get under your skin?"

"Callan Goldsworthy."

"Aren't you with his older brother Heath right now?" she asks in a confused tone. "I've been seeing it everywhere online."

"Yes, but that's not real. It's fake."

"Mera? What the hell is going on?" she asks incredulously.

I come to a stop outside the dorm. "It's a long story, but it's late here and I'm tired. I'll have to tell you another night. Just know that Callan Goldsworthy is making my life hell. I just needed to tell someone."

She's quiet for a moment. So quiet, I have to look at my phone to check and make sure she didn't hang up. "Just keep hanging on, okay?"

"I will. I just wish you were here. I've never had to deal with a monster like him before."

"It's that bad?"

"Yes."

She sighs. "Just keep me updated. Talk to you soon, sis."

The phone clicks on the other end.

Suddenly, I hear rustling in the tree area to the right of the dorm.

"Who's there?" I call out. Maybe it's just an animal. There's a lot of stray cats around campus.

"It's just me." Heath comes into view and stops in front of me. "I just came to make sure things went okay."

"As okay as they could be. Callan carried me."

His mouth tightens into a thin line, but he doesn't look surprised.

"You could've given me a heads up that he was going to be there."

"That's just it, he wasn't supposed to. He was already in. But he must have heard me talk to Rick and figured out that you were there. I'm sorry for whatever he said and did. I'll talk to him after the party."

I can't help but feel relieved to hear that. "Good. But I think we're going to have to end this fake dating thing a lot sooner than we initially planned. I know you want to keep the girls away, but it might be best to find someone else who doesn't piss off your brother this much."

He nods. "Except you're one of a kind, Mera. I don't feel the pressure to put on a facade with you. I can be myself. And I haven't felt like myself in a long time."

"Are you serious, Heath? Me? But you hang out with so many people."

He rubs a hand down the back of his head and sighs. "People who expect me to act a certain way. A person I'm not comfortable being."

I wrap my arms around his chest and give him a hug.

He flinches in my arms. "Is everything okay, Heath?"

"Ah, yeah." Even after only knowing him for a week, it's easy to tell he's lying.

I lower my hands to the hem of his shirt and lift it before he can stop me.

Gasping, I touch the three large bruises covering his abdomen. "Oh God, Heath. What the hell happened?"

He yanks his shirt down and takes a step back. "Don't worry about it. I'm okay. I ran into a door. After I kick the party off at AAA, I'll be at ZDB. See you then."

He leaves before I can stop him. I don't believe him for one second. Should I really pry into his life? Real friends do that right? I'll just have to ask again tomorrow.

My first college party. Finally.

I've survived my first week of college. I've gotten into the sorority I wanted. I have every right to celebrate tomorrow.

The sound of twigs breaking to my left makes me turn my head. "Heath? Is that you?"

There's no sign of anyone stepping out. Must have been an animal. I hurry inside without looking back.

Bang bang bang.

Ugh, who the fuck is banging?

God, my head hurts. Wincing, I feel my pounding head.

Oh this. This is familiar.

Oh yeah, George's bar. This must be Cate banging on the door looking for me again.

I pop open my eyes to find a totally different atmosphere.

An empty bed across from mine. Posters of hot guys.

I glance down at my clothes to find I'm in a white tube top and dark pants. My party outfit.

Right. This is my new room and that's Brandie's bed. But it's empty? Oh shit. I didn't unlock the door so she couldn't get in the room.

Already I'm a shit roommate and she's so nice too. Wait, this means the party happened.

I don't–

"Open the door or we'll break it down!"

Like a glass of cold water is dumped on me, the fuzziness of just waking up is cleared away. What the fuck? Break the door down, why?

Hobbling over to the door, I wrench it open to find two police officers, a man and a woman, waiting with Collette at their side. Her normally perfectly made up face has long black mascara lines down her face. Her hair is a mess and her eyes are red. "You treasonous bitch. Klutz. How could you?"

"What?" I mean not that I'm surprised because she hates my guts, but what the hell?

"We need to take you down to the station to ask you some questions about what happened last night."

"I mean sure, I'd like to know what happened last night too. Some people party too hard or what? Why are you questioning me and no one else?" My first college party and I can't even remember what happened. I must have indulged a little too much last night. But this has never happened before.

The two officers turn to look at each other and then at Collette who gasps and sputters, "She's lying. She has to be lying. I know she did it."

"Did what?"

The male officer sighs. "Heath Goldsworthy. He never made it back to his fraternity last night."

I glance at the three of them. "Okay. He's a college guy. Doesn't he have a place off campus he stays at?"

"It wouldn't be a big deal, but at some point between last night and this morning, someone did this." The female officer holds up a picture. A picture of a piece of a road, but that's the most insignificant part of it. "This is on the patch of road in front of Zeta Delta Beta."

"Oh my God." I slap my hand over my mouth and tear up. That can't be real. The blood rushes to my ears as I glance at Collette's face.

She screams in my face, "It had to be you. I know you did it."

In bright red letters that are clearly spray painted on, that strip of road reads "Heath Goldsworthy is dead."

"I'll go down to the station," I murmur, frozen in shock.

"For the last time, I don't remember. It's the honest truth. If I did, I'd tell you."

"What's the last thing you remember?" the male officer asks.

"Going to sleep last night."

"And when was the last time you remember seeing Heath?" the female officer asks, writing on her notepad.

"Last night. He showed up at my dorm and he said he'd see me at the party. I'm assuming he did."

She nods. "Collette and a few of her friends said he came to the party and you made a show of drinking a lot so Heath would sleep with you."

I still in my chair. Heath did mention something. Something he did to make sure that only a few girls would be able to be alone with him. They had to down a bottle of Absolut in five minutes.

Is that...what I did?

I clench my eyes closed and try to remember, but it's all blank. Like it never even happened.

"She says you were super drunk and you made a show of grabbing Heath and dragging him to your new room. After that, no one ever saw Heath again. We've asked multiple people and not one person saw him. You were the last to see him."

"That can't be. He had so many friends. So many people know him. He couldn't have just slipped away. Heath can't be dead."

The male officer stands up. "We'll do the best we can to find him. In the meantime, please let us know if you do remember anything that might help us locate Mr. Goldsworthy."

He opens the door, leading me out and down a hallway until I'm outside the station.

The moment I step out I look around at all the cars in the parking lot. Shit I don't have a way back to campus. I pull my phone out of my pocket and find Scarlett's number.

The phone rings and rings until it goes to voicemail. Maybe Peyton's with her? It's after ten now so she should be awake.

As I'm about to click on his name in my contacts list, my phone rings and Mom's name pops up on screen.

This isn't going to be good. I heave a heavy sigh and click accept.

"Mera? Why did I get a call from the American police that you're a person of interest in the disappearance of my friend's son?"

"Because I was the last person who saw him…"

She makes a frustrated noise. "I didn't send you there to get yourself into even more trouble. We sent you to learn, not to fraternize. Certainly not to get blackout drunk, like I specifically forbade you from doing, and doing heaven knows what with a boy. You're a princess, Mera! Whether you're in this country or not."

"I know that Mom."

"Then stop embarrassing this family. How many more

times do I have to ask you that? Cate would never do something like this," she yells.

"Yeah, you're right Mom. I'm just the screw up. Cate is the trophy daughter, I get it. How dare I make a friend? How dare I find someone who likes me for who I am and not the crown that weighs upon my head?"

She sighs. "Mera–"

"No. I've heard enough." My eyes start to burn as tears well up in my eyes. Before she even get a hint of hearing me cry, I hang up the phone.

The moment I do, it's snatched out of my palm from behind me. "What?" I whirl around and find my phone gripped tightly in *his* hand.

"Where is he? Where's my brother?" Callan shouts, eyes blazing and wild.

I've never seen him show this much emotion before and it's frightening.

"He didn't make it back to AAA. I waited the whole fucking night for him. He had something to give me and he was supposed to talk to me about something. What the fuck happened?"

"I don't know." And I don't.

His eyes narrow. He doesn't believe me.

"You're lying. You guys have been hanging out all week. You expect me to believe he left your side without telling you where he was going."

I turn around to face him. "I don't remember, okay! I wish I could. I don't want this to be true." Tears fill my eyes at the thought of Heath's lifeless body being found somewhere.

He grabs me by the throat and bends down to my eye level. "You're hiding something, I know you are. And whatever it is, I'm going to drag it out of you. We're going to continue our game, but this time you aren't going anywhere."

The hand around my throat tightens and I gasp for air, breathing rapidly. "I'm going to break you down until you confess. Everything was fine until you showed up. One week of you in our lives and suddenly my brother's dead."

"I'd never hurt Heath," I spit out.

He lets my throat go, and I jerk back gasping for air. His eyes darken as they stare into mine. "I'll be the judge of that. Starting today, you're my toy. Mine to play with, mine to break." As he walks past me to the parking lot, he pushes my phone into my chest. I rush to grab it before it can fall.

When I'm positive he's finally gone, I let out a yell of frustration. Fuck. What can I even do about him now? Talk to my parents and make more trouble for them? They're already upset with me. Talk to the Dean? Yeah, like that will work. He probably thinks I murdered his son, so why would he help protect me from his other one?

No, the truth is I'm all alone in this. Whatever happens, I'm powerless.

Heath's perfect face smiling ear to ear with his signature dimples pops in my head and I sigh deeply. Going back to my phone, I finally click Peyton's name. On the second ring, he picks up. With a groggy note in his voice he answers. "Mera?"

"Peyton, is Scarlett with you?"

"Mm, no. Her bed looks slept in but she isn't here. What's up?"

"I need a ride, but if she isn't there I guess I'll have to start walking."

"Wait, hold on. There you are! Is everything okay, Scar?" There's a murmur in the background.

Peyton clears his throat and a little bit of the sleepiness leaves his voice, "Okay, we'll come get you. Where are you?"

And then clear as day, I hear Scar's voice. "She's at the police station. Heath Goldsworthy is missing and if last night makes anything clear, Mera is the number one suspect for his disappearance."

"I don't even remember what happened," I groan, massaging my forehead. This hangover is killing me.

"What'd she say?" I hear on the other end. "Hand me the phone."

Scarlett sighs. "Girl, we got there right as you were taking him up the stairs, and we didn't see you again the rest of the night. Hold on, we'll come get you. Peyton, get your clothes on so we can go get her."

They hang up and I'm left reeling. Just what the fuck was I thinking? What actually happened? I wish I could remember.

While I wait for them, I go to dial my sister. Even though she's probably disappointed in me too, I just need to rant about how fucking unfair all of this is.

My call doesn't ring once, going directly to voicemail.

That's...never happened before. I guess I'll have to call her later.

When I get back to my room, after being dropped off by Scar and Peyton, I feel completely drained. There were so many angry, sad, hateful faces, judging me when they don't know anything.

The writing on the road is still there. It all seems so surreal, like something out of a nightmare.

I've never forgotten a night at home even when I've had a lot to drink.

If I go back to sleep, will I dream about last night? I flop down on my bed and push my face into the pillow. To get more comfy, I place my hands underneath it when I feel something strange. A rough texture hits my hand.

What is this?

I yank it out from under my pillow to find a crumpled piece of paper. This wasn't here when I woke up was it?

What I find when I open it makes my jaw drop and my heart leap into my throat.

It's your fault he's dead.

No. No. *No.*

I cover my mouth and glance around. Goosebumps form on my neck and shoulders. Is this a cruel joke? How is it my fault? What did I do? This can't be true.

I cover my face with my hands and breathe rapidly. I can't. I could never hurt him or anybody. Someone out there knows. They have to know what happened if they wrote this. I need to find them.

God, I can't breathe. I clutch my chest as my world seems to spin around me.

"Oh my God, Mera!" A hand moves over my shoulder to my back. "Breathe. Come on, look at me." Another hand takes my shaking one and I finally glance over to see Brandie with her tight curls and sympathetic eyes.

"Please try to calm down, I'm sure Heath is out there somewhere. You fell for him hard didn't you?"

She rubs my back in calming circular motions and I take a deep breath slowly.

"I wish I could've been around last night to act as your alibi, but I couldn't even get in the room. I had to stay with Jamie and Kori last night."

"I'm so sorry," I say, wincing. "I don't know why the door was locked. But I could never harm him or anyone else."

"I know you didn't. You're too sweet for that. You and Heath were like two peas in a pod."

Smiling wanly, I crumple the note in my hand.

If only everyone else believed me as easily as she, Scarlett, and Peyton did.

CHAPTER SIX

Callan

When I get back to the fraternity, there's a whole crowd milling around who grow quiet as I approach them going to the door. I throw scowls in their direction in case any of them are even thinking about talking to me right now.

Not unless they have any information about Heath. That isn't likely though. They're nosy asses trying to get all the latest. I throw the door open, stomping inside.

Someone had to have seem him.

I head straight to the foyer and find a bunch of guys milling around. "Where the hell is Rick?"

They point up the stairs and I go back to the stairway, heading straight for his room. Loud music is blaring on the other side of the door. The hell?

He's just playing some tunes like everything is fine.

Opening the door quickly, I find Rick sitting on one of the beds and some other guy on the other, snoring away despite the noise.

Rick looks up at me with bloodshot eyes. "Callan, how could someone do this to Heath?"

"Listen, there's no time to wallow around. Turn off the sad depressing shit and get busy. I need you to ask every single guy who lives in this fraternity about the last time they saw Heath. Once you have everyone's answer, come find me."

He nods and I leave him to it, striding back down the hall and going up another floor.

I stop outside the third door and open it to find Noel, Tyrell, and Vincent talking quietly together.

They straighten when they see me at the door.

Noel speaks first, "We're really sorry, man." He twiddles his thumbs together.

Tyrell's mouth twitches as he nods slightly.

Vincent rubs his forehead. "Is there anything we can do?"

I look between the three of them. "You can start by telling me the last time you saw him."

"The party at ZDB," the three of them say simultaneously.

Sighing, I run my hand through my hair. I figured that's what they would say. If they knew something they would've been the first to tell me. "Right. That's what everyone's been saying. Just, let me know if you hear anything. I'm counting on you."

I exit Noel and Tyrell's room and go to the end of the hall.

To be courteous, I knock once and then open the door. There should only be one occupant in there right now. Silverstone looks up from his phone, leaning against the wall near the window. "If you're looking for Vincent–"

"I'm not. I'm looking for you." I walk straight for him and come face to face. "When was the last time you saw Heath?"

He studies my eyes for a few seconds. "Here, at AAA. I was at the Zeta Delta Beta party too, but I didn't show up until later. I was hammered."

"Fine," I respond. Not that I expected him to know anything either.

My feet are almost out the door when he says in a low tone, "But Heath Goldsworthy knew how to keep a secret. Maybe it was one of those secrets that got him killed."

In a flash I'm back in front of him, this time in his face. "If you know something, you need to fucking say it. What kind of secrets?"

A slow smile spreads across his face. "Oh, I don't know. Someone's bound to know though. Maybe the answers you're looking for are closer than you think. One thing is certain though, I'm positive you're barking up the wrong tree."

"She knows *something*. She has to."

He shakes his head. "Believe me or don't, but the truth always comes out one way or another. Now, get the fuck out of my room."

Gritting my teeth, I stomp out and slam the door.

Fucking Silverstone.

The whole second week of school is lost to me. I skip every single class, anxious to hear something, anything, from the police or my parents. But there's nothing but radio silence.

It's been a week and no one has come forward. The most popular guy in college has just disappeared without a trace.

His phone was last pinged at the cell tower within the

school's vicinity. His phone is off, going straight to voicemail. The find my phone app says the last time his phone was on, it was at school.

The weirdest part of it all is his car. The black Camaro he loved so much is gone. It gives Collette and I hope that he's just out there, driving and escaping all of this.

With his car missing, all airports, train stations, and bus stations in California have been checked. No sign of it. The housekeepers at my family's other two homes in the states haven't seen him.

He's just gone.

Even worse, I feel something I haven't felt in a while. Guilty. While I'm angry and upset, a tiny piece of me is glad. Happy even. That's the fucked up thing about it.

It's fucked up of me to be happy that now I'm the only son, and my father can only rely solely on me to take over his businesses when the time comes.

But I can't let myself go that far. I can't think like that because more than anything, I want Heath to be alive. Every time Dad doubted me, Heath was there to lift me up. He was there for every accomplishment.

That's what I need to focus on.

The first football game of the season was last night. Usually, my brother's time to shine as their star quarterback. It doesn't feel right to go and see the whole team come out without Heath leading them. I can't bring myself to do that yet.

My phone suddenly sounds off and I grab it from next to me on the couch.

Dad.

"Hello?"

"Callan, can you come over for dinner tonight? Pick

Collette up too." His voice is terse. I know I shouldn't push it, but I do anyway.

"What's going on?"

"Just be here in two hours."

The line clicks.

Shit. Did they find Heath's body?

Could there be any news? Is this why he cancelled lunch today? Not that I'm complaining.

I message Collette to ask if she knows what this dinner is about, but she's as in the dark as I am.

At six, I pull into the Goldsworthy estate driveway and park my Lambo behind Mom's pearly blue Land Rover.

"I hope this is good news and not bad news," Coll muses, as we get out. "with any luck, they'll be able to throw that klutz in prison."

For a moment, Wil's wide eyes and quivering mouth pop in my head from the police station and I shake it away.

The butler opens the door before we can knock. Passing the grand foyer and the double staircase, we turn right past the formal sitting area and head straight for the formal dining room. The table that can seat twenty is only set for four.

One chair per side of the table.

An uncomfortable feeling weighs in my gut as I notice the missing placement that's always to the right of mine.

After pulling Collette's chair out for her, I get seated in my own. A maid I've never seen before scrambles out, bringing tray after tray of dinner entrees. He went to all this trouble, but I could care less about this meal. I just need to hear whatever he has to say.

The moment she's done, Dad starts to make his plate, cutting a piece off the baked chicken.

"Are you going to tell us or what?" I ask, staring at him so eagerly stuffing his face.

He stares down to the foot of the table and then looks at me. "Eat your food, son."

"No. I'm not doing anything until you tell me what's going on."

He glances at Collette. "Coll, do you think you could pass those mashed potatoes?"

She smiles slightly at him, and obliges. Under the table, I grip my hands together tightly. Just barely keeping my cool.

Collette clears her throat. "Dad, is there any news?"

He sets his fork done and sighs. "Unfortunately. This isn't about your brother."

I lean forward, setting my elbows on the table. "Then what's the fucking point of being here?"

He turns toward me. "Your cousins. Two of them went missing last night. There was a house fire they believe Ava was in last night, but no remains have been found. And there's been no sign of Lacey."

"What?" What kind of fucked up shit is this?

Collette gasps. "No, please don't let it be Ava."

Mom gets out of chair and reaches Collette, wrapping her arms around her. "It is, and Lacey too."

Over two hundred and four hundred miles away. And on the same night, she couldn't possibly be responsible for them either.

"The police don't think their incidents are related to Heath's. Until they find a connection, his case is completely unrelated. There were no messages left for them, unlike the one written on the road for Heath."

Collette sobs. "Ava and I were going to go on spring break vacation together this year. How could someone do that to her?"

I can't help but laugh at that statement. Loudly at that. Everyone in the Goldsworthy family knows how spoiled and toxic Ava can be. She gives Collette a run for her money in the spoiled department. The wealthy in San Francisco are a different breed entirely. Ava must have run her mouth too much to the wrong person.

"No, the real question is Lacey. The nicest fucking one of us all. Genuinely nice. No one has a reason to target her."

Collette's mouth thins. "Why would anyone go after Heath too then?"

"Hell if I know, and that's what I'm going to figure out as soon as I break that princess down."

Dad slams his fist on the table, causing every dish to shake. He squares his shoulders and stares me down."Absolutely not. You are going to stay far away from her. I wish they would've asked the other one, whatever her name is, to transfer instead?"

"Cate."

Strangely, I feel a mild annoyance at him automatically assuming the same thing wouldn't have happened with her older sister.

No. There's no room for me to sympathize with her.

"Whatever. If she's responsible for Heath's disappearance, she'll slip up and we'll find out."

"His murder, you mean."

Dad glares at me and Mom gasps and holds her hand to her chest.

Collette snaps, "He's alive. He has to be."

But they're all ignoring the statistics. Missing people are rarely found after 72 hours of being missing. He's already been gone a week. His credit cards and his debit cards haven't been touched. His house hasn't been touched.

No one has seen or heard from him.

There's no way he's alive.

"I've had enough," I mutter, moving my chair away from the table and standing up. "Enjoy your dinner."

The messed up cocktail that's the four of us together without Heath is too much to handle. Everyone else has no idea what happened to him, but one person does. She knows. I still don't know if she's lying about remembering or not, but one way or another, she'll either tell me the truth or I'll force her to remember by any means necessary.

The next day, bright and fucking early, I'm waiting in front of our history teacher's class. Multiple students walk through the open door, but not me. No. I'm waiting with a full, big, plastic water bottle for her. I got the call from Collette that she's wearing a white shirt today.

She almost didn't tell me after being pissed about our argument last night.

"Callan," a voice calls in a sultry voice.

God, I can't believe she followed me here.

All throughout high school, Ginger, aptly named for her orange hair, has wanted my dick. I never paid attention to her enough to know she's rich. There's no way she was smart enough to snag one of the few scholarships my father offers.

When I don't turn around, she moves in front of me. "I'm so sorry about your brother, baby."

I grunt in response and look over her head, waiting for those annoyingly shiny locks of pale gold hair.

Ginger, never one to be discouraged, prattles on about nothing.

Five minutes later, I see those locks bouncing with her

every step closer to the classroom with Red and Tall Boy. Her eyes find mine as her friend murmurs and glances at me.

Wil freezes for a moment, with a hint of fear flaring in her eyes. Tall Boy moves around her, taking the lead. With a renewed sense of confidence, she steps forward as Red brings up the rear.

I glance down at Ginger and tilt my thumb to the side. "Think you could move over?"

She looks absolutely delighted to finally have my attention, but she doesn't move fast enough, so I move her out of the way myself. She squeals at my hand touching her body momentarily.

"Hey, princess," I say as Wil finally reaches me, in Ginger's empty spot.

Vaguely, I hear Ginger makes a frustrated sound, but I could care less about her. I won't be distracted from this.

Wil stops mid step and Red from behind her pushes her back. "Don't fucking stop, Mera. Keep going."

But it's too late. My water bottle top is already unscrewed and I dump it right over her head.

Ginger's annoyingly loud laughter erupts, almost making this moment less enjoyable.

It turns out the shocked expression on Wil's face is more than enough to keep me entertained. Red yells, "What the fuck!." Red moves in front of her, using her body to shield and push her into the classroom with Peyton.

She regards me with eyes full of rage. "Stay away from Mera."

I tip my head down, finding myself amused by her boldness. "No."

A crowd gathers around us as we block the way, and after a few annoyed whispers, Red reluctantly goes inside.

Ginger giggles and grabs my arm. "That was so great,

Callan. Maybe later I can go to AAA and we can hang out." I wrench my arm out of her grasp and walk through the doorway.

Immediately, I notice Wil's usual seat is empty. Did she change seats?

And then I follow her friends' upset gazes from the table behind us to the front.

Wil's arms are around her shoulders as she nods at whatever Professor Harper is saying.

Long after I've settled into my usual seat and the rest of the class has piled in, the professor lets her go. Her eyes immediately find mine and she scowls. Her arms leave her chest as she starts her walk down the aisle to the empty seat next to me.

I'd previously only been able to see the straps of that lacy pink bra of hers with the way Red shoved her out of the way. But now I can plainly see, like every other person in this class, how well it's holding up those tits of hers.

The very ones that were pressed tightly against my chest a little over a week ago. And though she tried to hide them, I saw those dusky pink nipples when I set her down outside ZDB.

Abruptly, I become all too aware of a problem in my pants. Fuck. I adjust myself covertly and lean back in my seat.

That shouldn't be happening.

"Oh yeah, take it off, won't you princess."

"Is that a designer bra?" a girl asks with a giggle.

I glance up to Wil's face. Her face is only slightly flushed. She's hiding her embarrassment well. Next time, I'll have to step it up.

As she takes her seat, the professor clears her throat. "The

THE PRINCESS AND THE BULLY

next time anyone comes to class ill-prepared, you will be asked to leave and it will be counted as an absence. We're here to learn, not to find a potential mate. Does everyone understand?"

Beside me, I hear Wil murmur her agreement.

Leaning over slightly, I whisper, "Our game continues now."

Her mouth drops open to respond, when the teacher starts class, forcing her to close her mouth.

Wil and her friends left as soon as the professor dismissed us. So anxious to get away, that this time I'll let her.

When I step outside the classroom, Noel, Vincent, and Tyrell are waiting for me.

Noel puts his arm around my shoulder. "Isn't there something you forgot to tell us, buddy?"

"What are you talking about?" I ask.

Vincent laughs. "You know, you had me fooled there. I thought you wanted Mera to stick around so you could play with her some more."

"I do. She's not allowed to leave," I blurt, looking at him in confusion.

"Except, why would you make a petition to get her kicked out of school if that's what your intentions are?" Tyrell asks gruffly.

"A petition for *what?*" I ask incredulously.

Tyrell holds his phone up in my phone, and right in front of my eyes on Booksmarter, the Silverstone school program, is a petition with my name at the top. In big letters, it says "Expel Wilhelmera Karden of Kardenia."

I didn't start a petition, and even more ridiculous, to get

her expelled from school? No, I want justice from my brother.

I point to the screen. "That wasn't me. I didn't do that."

"It's linked to your Booksmarter account, dude. It's definitely you," Tyrell says.

I click on my name and it goes straight to my profile.

What the fuck?

I pull my phone out of my pocket to check my account and find it pinned to the top of my profile. Created an hour ago.

"I was in class an hour ago!" I yell. "Someone fucking hacked my shit."

"Well, it's too late now," Noel says. "Once you start a petition, it's locked and can't be deleted. It has six months to get the necessary signatures. Ten thousand people go to our school so it needs five thousand. It's at three hundred already. With all the people who liked Heath, I'd say there won't be any problems reaching five thousand."

"Fuck!" I yell.

I start down the hallway and a few people give me a thumbs up. A few yell "Justice for Heath." Goddamn it.

No. I can't worry about this now. Only a few petitions have ever gotten to five thousand and even then, only two have ever gone through. There's no way this will. If it somehow reaches five thousand, I'll cross that bridge when I get to it.

The next three weeks, Wil ignores me no matter what I do. She had to have heard about that petition, but she hasn't said a word about it.

I've pulled her chair out from under her, and watched

that plump ass of hers hit the floor. I've stolen her backpack, emptied it and it's contents. Even tossed it around with my friends who were less than willing volunteers.

She even skips art classes on Wednesday just to avoid me and she's never worn a white shirt again.

Today I haven't done anything, yet, but I'm thinking I'll follow her into the bathroom after art class. I've learned that she does it to avoid me after class is over. Art class is one of the later ending ones so there won't be a ton of people around. No one will hear her when she screams.

The teacher dismisses us from his chair and I grab my bag and follow her quickly. She avoids the line for the elevator, instead heading for the stairs at the end of the hallway. This is new.

A group of girls stop chattering at the corner of the stairs as they notice her approach. The blonde closest to the railing gets a wicked smile on her face, and in slow motion, I watch as she sticks her foot out in a right angle. Wil doesn't notice, too focused on me at her heels and trips over, losing her footing and tumbling right down.

A sickening thud is heard as she hits the midway point.

And then something weird happens. It crawls up my neck slowly. Then behind my eyes. I feel it. A fuse being lit. I reach the edge of the stairs and look down to find her body crumpled and her clutching her ankle.

"Bitches," she mutters angrily, wincing in pain.

I turn my head to look at the four of them and the one who tripped her smiles and flutters her eyelashes. "Great petition by the way, Callan."

One girl backs away with the intensity of my expression. "Do that to her again, and I'll push you down these same fucking stairs."

She gasps.

I take the stairs slowly and Wil looks up at me with cautious eyes. I bend down and grab her arm, easily hoisting her up. "Wh-what are you doing?"

"I'm helping you." I glance down at her blue t-shirt and jeans and find them smudged with the dirt from the floor.

"Just let me go," she yells, pushing me so quickly I almost let her go.

I tighten the hand around her arm. "You hurt your leg, princess."

"My ankle, actually," she says wincing.

"Either you put your arm around me, or I carry you. You have five seconds to choose."

"I'll just call Brandie and Jamie."

"Wrong answer," I respond, and throw her over my shoulder with one arm and grab her bag with my other.

Behind us, I hear the girls shrieking, way too high at that for me to even begin to understand what they're saying.

As I carry her out she makes a frustrated noise. "Why are you doing this?"

I pause for a second before answering, "Because my game was ruined."

"I knew you were going to do something tonight," she screams.

She'd be no good with me backing her into a dark restroom stall. The ankle pain would be too much and she wouldn't be focused.

I drop her on the step of her sorority and immediately leave. I'm already past the next sorority when I faintly hear her call out, "Don't ever do anything like this for me again."

And I won't.

I can promise her that.

I skip Wednesday's history class and of course she skips art, so the next time I see her is Monday morning's history class.

As she sits down, I slide a note over to her. She looks a little warily at it for some reason, but then she opens it.

The game continues.

She crumples it and pushes it back to me, turning her attention to the front of the class.

When it's over, she rushes to get out of her chair without pushing it back in. I slide my chair back cleanly to block her way.

"You've got to be fucking kidding me," Red remarks behind us.

Tall Boy comes around his table and stops to my left. "Need something?"

He frowns. "Let Mera go."

I look as if I'm pondering it for a moment and then shake my head. "Nah, I don't think I will."

Wil sighs. "You two go ahead, you have class and I don't."

Tall Boy stands firm. "I'm not going anywhere without you, Mera."

"Sweet, you have a new knight in shining armor now that Heath's gone," I say, looking between the two of them.

She curls her lip angrily. "Scar, get him out of here."

"Let's just let them talk," Red murmurs to Tall Boy, pulling him by the arm.

He backs up reluctantly, looking at Wil, a distressed look on his puppy dog face. "Call me if you change your mind."

As if she'll get the chance to.

The professor looks up at us after a while with a questioning look, so I finally get up, grabbing her by the arm as I do so she doesn't try to escape. With my free one, I grab my backpack and hoist it over my shoulder. I drag her out the door and down the hall, as other people watch and stare.

"Where are we going?" she asks with a bored tone in her voice.

"You'll see."

We turn another corner and we finally reach a short stairwell. I walk up no more than ten steps and turn the handle, finding it to be unlocked.

A wave of satisfaction flows through me and I grin, turning back to look at her. "Guess it isn't your lucky day."

Opening the door quickly, I drag her behind me and out to the roof.

Above us, the skies are cloudy. Now that it's October, it's officially fall and starting to cool down. The sun isn't so relentless up here.

"Put your bag on the ground," I order.

She makes no move to do so, so I yank it off and throw it to the side. I toss mine on the opposite side.

I move her directly in front of me, holding her arm tightly and backing her up until we're close to the edge of the roof. "What have you remembered?"

She scoffs. "Nothing. You think if I'd remembered something I wouldn't go to the police?"

"Why would someone who's guilty go to the police?"

Something different passes through her eyes. "I'm. Not. Guilty." She glances away quickly, looking behind her to see how close she is to the edge.

And she's close, only a few steps more and she'll be falling over the ledge.

"So there's nothing you need to tell me? Nothing at all?"

Her eyes widen and she shakes her head. "No."

I can hear the firmness in her voice. It's almost believable, but something tells me she's lying.

What the fuck isn't she saying?

CHAPTER SEVEN

Mera

He frowns and a sadistic smile forms on his face. One that makes me want to run far away and as fast as I possibly can.

If he sees those notes, he'll think I really am guilty. I can't tell him.

"I don't have anything to tell you." And even though I know his answer will be no, I ask anyway, "Can I go now?"

"No. We're still playing our game."

No. I refuse this time. We lock eyes for a moment and in one swift move, I wrench my arm out of his grasp, which hurts like a bitch, and kick my leg out aiming straight for his balls.

He catches my leg just as it almost reaches his crotch.

Shit.

I only have a few seconds.

His right arm is dominant so I go around the left, dodging his arm that extends to grab me. I did it. I got away.

On the way to the door, I pick my bag up by the strap. I don't need to look back to know he's on my heels. I just have to push forward harder. The stairs past this door will be a struggle. As I reach the door, I pull it open and take my first step when I feel the pull of something holding me back.

Shit. I clench my fists with frustration as I feel his muscular arms go around my waist and pull me back in.

The door closes with a click.

"Thought you could get away, princess? You're not as fast as I am." He pulls my bag off and tosses it to the side.

Clenching my jaw, I try my hardest to push those large hands of his off of my waist. My efforts are for nothing as they stay unmovable. Locked on tight.

He lifts me up, carrying me back to where we were near the edge of the roof. This time he forces me on the ground on my back.

I avoid his eyes, looking at anything and everything, but the fact that he isn't saying anything is eerie.

I force myself to look up at him and watch in horror as he bends down and brushes his fingers against my gray t-shirt. "I've already seen what you look like without this. A lot of others have too. But you didn't walk around during the day shirtless."

"Stop," I mutter, slapping his hand away.

His eyes harden as he reaches down to the edge of my shirt and tugs it off. Immediately, the cooler fall air hits me. He tosses my shirt over his shoulder without a second thought.

"Now for the bra," he says, reaching his hands forward again.

"No. You can't. I'll be suspended."

THE PRINCESS AND THE BULLY

He smirks. "Beg me then, princess. Beg me not to take this black lacy bra off." His hands skate around the edges, moving up the strap.

Gritting my teeth, I look down at the ground. "Please don't take my bra off."

"Please...?"

"Please...Callan, don't take my bra off."

"Obedience. If only you were that obedient about telling me what you know, then I wouldn't have to do this." His hand travels down to my light blue jeans. Fuck, what am I going to do?

With a pull and a zip, they're unbuttoned and the zipper is tugged down. Automatically, I scoot away from him, but he gets down on his knees, his hands going behind me.

They grasp the back of my jeans and pull them off, tossing them back where my shirt is. He grabs my chin roughly. "And these matching black panties of yours. How badly do you want to keep them?"

He raises an eyebrow as I don't respond. "Well? Tell me how badly Wil."

I already had to beg him once, I'm not doing it again. What's going to happen if I keep giving him what he wants? I can't just keep giving in to him.

The hand on my chin tightens as I keep my silence.

He chuckles. "Obviously not that much then. Okay, that's fine." My heart jumps in my chest as his hand leaves my chin and goes with his other one to rest at my hips where my underwear straps lie. He slowly starts to tug my underwear down and I put my hand on his. "Wait."

"No, you had your chance. Now these underwear of yours are coming off."

What?

"No!" I scream. His hand immediately covers my mouth.

"Just so you know, our game won't end even if you scream, princess. So tell me, do I need to keep my hand here?"

I shake my head quickly before he decides to not give me that choice.

"Fine, I'll let go, but you scream again and I shove my dick right in, and whoever comes running up here will get an eyeful." His eyes get a sadistic gleam in them. "They'll see me fucking you."

I nod quickly, gulping nervously as he lets go.

I take a deep shaking breath and stare at him. "Please, Callan. Don't do this. I need my underwear."

His cold eyes stay locked on mine for a long time and he doesn't move. Suddenly, his eyes flash and he pulls me forward so I'm laying flush to the ground. He climbs on top of me and I hear the sickening sound of him messing with his jeans.

"No," I whimper. "Stop."

He eyes me for a second with an unreadable expression and then that sadistic smile of his is back. "Fine. I'm not hard any–"

My eyes widen as I feel something stiff against me that wasn't there before.

"Shit," he mutters and stands up quickly, turning around. I move to stand up and reach for my clothes when he snatches them away as I'm about to reach them.

There's an unevenness in his expression as he walks past me to the edge and tosses them over before I can even say anything to stop him.

"What the fuck!" I yell.

"Guess you better go and find those." He turns away, grabs his bag and leaves. I cross my arms over my chest as some hoots and hollers echo throughout the air.

With a sigh, I go for my bag and dig my phone out. Glad I didn't keep it in my jeans.

I can't call Peyton or Scarlett, they'll both be in class by now. What do I do? Just walk out there like this?

I close my eyes and think but nothing comes to me. I throw my dignity away as I lug my bag on my naked shoulder and exit the roof. I take those stairs slowly and peek around. Wonderful. There's tons of people around.

My cheeks heat up as I start my walk of shame down the hall. I hold my head up as people sneer and laugh as I walk past. The orange-haired bitch who's always following Callan around just happens to be in the hallway with her friends.

"Who are you taking your clothes off for now?" she jeers as I approach.

I stop and stare her down. "Why don't you go find Callan's dick and ride it to get him off my back? Oh wait, you can't because he doesn't want you anywhere near his dick."

"What was that bitch?" she snaps incredulously.

Her words fall on deaf ears as I continue walking.

"Someone take pictures and sell it to the paparazzi!" a guy yells.

The one thing I've always done is kept my clothes on, even when I'm hammered to prevent embarrassing my parents completely. Guess that's out the window now.

A story like this is bound to go viral.

As I turn the corner of the hall, I bump into someone going my direction.

"Sorry," I say quickly.

The person looks up from their phone and I find a familiar face. Gemma!

"Oh, hey Mera. Whoa." She looks me up and down. "Is there a fashion show I'm not aware of?"

I shake my head. "No. This is the work of Callan Goldsworthy."

The words leave my mouth before I can stop them. Shit. She might go run and tell Collette about this and I'll get slapped again.

I can't let her get the wrong idea. "It's not what you think, though. I didn't let him do this."

She raises an eyebrow. "Oh. So like what happened with the third round of the hazing?"

A few guys walk past me, obviously staring at my assets.

I nod quickly and she nods. "Okay, then let's go to the bathroom." She pulls me by the arm and down the hall. Laughter follows us until we're in the mostly quiet bathroom.

The few girls inside, gossiping in the corner give us the evil eye and Gemma sticks her tongue out the corner of her mouth and pushes her nose up to make a piggy nose. She makes oinking noises and the girls, startled by the weirdness, hurry out.

With an accomplished smile, she pulls her bag away from her back and digs inside, pulling out a shirt.

"This will be way too big for you, but I always keep an extra shirt with me. In case of, you know, food spillage. It's easier than walking all the way back to the sorority house."

"You're a lifesaver!"

She places the shirt in my hands and I set my bag down to put it on.

"Don't thank me yet, you can't leave this building without something on your legs." She pulls her phone out of her pocket and makes a call.

Oh God, if it's Collette she definitely wouldn't do anything to try and help me.

"Lu, you haven't left the ZDB have you?" She pauses.

"Great, bring a pair of pants to the Lit building first floor bathroom near the side entrance. Mm, they're for a friend. Just bring them and quick."

She hangs up the phone and smiles. "Problem solved. And don't worry, Luella won't mind. She has an afternoon class in the Science building so she was on her way out anyway."

"I owe you big time."

She shakes her head. "Don't worry about it. You helped me during the party so I kind of owed you."

My stomach churns at that. "Wait, I helped you?"

"Oh." She winces. "Coll did say you forgot the party. One of Callan's friends, you know the one who carried me during the final round, well he asked me out."

Oh right, the flirty guy who goes after any woman he sees.

"I told him no in front of everyone and let's just say he didn't take it well. He wanted to drag me off and talk to me privately. I wasn't sure what to say so you stepped in and told him to fuck off."

I cover my mouth and giggle a little. "Oh shit." That sounds like me.

"He looked so embarrassed. I don't think any girl has ever told him no. That was the last time I saw Heath too."

My jaw drops. "What?"

"Yeah, Heath came out of nowhere and I got this urge to make it clear I wasn't interested so I told Heath in front of him that I'd rather go out with Heath. You should've seen the look on his face. And then Heath of course brushed me off because he had you." Gemma gets quiet and bites her lip. "Sorry. Thinking about Heath must hurt."

I touch her shoulder. "No, I'm glad you told me. Thank you."

She smiles. We stand there in a comfortable silence for a

little while when the door opens. Luella walks in with a cautious smile. In a soft voice she says, "Here I come, to the rescue." She holds up a pair of beige pants. "But you might not even need these pants."

Someone out moves from behind her.

"Ashlynn, you came too?" Gemma pipes up.

She glances at her and nods slightly and then looks at me. "Are these yours?" She throws my jeans and gray t-shirt at me.

"They are. How'd you find them?"

Upon closer inspection, they're a little dingy now. I can't complain though because I never expected to get these back.

She points her thumb behind her. "Some guys out there were showing them around to everyone who'd look. Apparently someone told them they were yours and they wanted to make a pretty buck off of them. Buuuut...I snatched them away. You're welcome."

"Thanks."

Out of the three of them, I've had the least interaction with Ashlynn. Luella and I have bumped into each other a few times around the house so we've exchanged some awkward hellos.

Luella holds the pants out. "I think you should still wear these. Your clothes should be washed again before you wear them."

I glance down at them in my arms. Do I really want to wear clothes that some random guys have been drooling over?

Nope.

"Yeah you're right. Thanks. I'll be sure to give them back once I get back to my room." I turn toward Gemma. "And you too."

"No rush," Gemma says. "Hey, want to get lunch with us?"

There's a small noise from Luella and I watch her and Ashlynn share a look. Eventually Ashlynn nods. "Yeah, come have lunch with us in the dining hall."

"Sounds good," I agree with a nod.

After pulling on the pants and picking up my bag, we leave the bathroom, with Gemma and I following Luella and Ashlynn out.

Since we went out the side entrance, we have to walk to the front to start down the path that leads to the dining hall.

Luella and Ashlynn slow down so they're walking side by side with Gemma and I.

"You know, you guys didn't have to help me, so how about we make it my treat?" I offer.

It's the least I can do.

"Great. Barbecue sounds good. What do you guys think?"

"Girls?" a voice rings out from behind us.

God, it's her.

I follow their leads and turn around to see Collette with her hair pulled back in a bun and a bluish purple tutu on. "What are you three doing?"

"Going to get lunch," Gemma pipes up.

"With *her*?"

Luella clears her throat, twiddling her thumbs together. "Well, she did offer to buy."

"It's just this once, Coll," Ashlynn says.

Collette rolls her eyes and sighs. "If you guys wanted me to pay, all you had to do is ask. Come on."

She moves past us and continues down the path we were going. It's clear her invitation isn't extended to me.

Ashlynn squares her shoulders and keeps walking. Luella throws me a sympathetic look and rushes to catch up.

Gemma looks between us, with indecision on her face. I

don't want her to lose her space that she worked hard to get so I clasp her on the shoulder. "It's okay. Go ahead."

She grabs me in a hug. "I'm really sorry. This is the correct choice for now." She races off and in the distance, I see her fall into step with them.

Is that what true friendship is? Whoever you hate, your friends hate no questions asked.

I guess I can understand that.

All of a sudden, I'm missing Peyton and Scarlett. I almost wish I could go back to the freshman dorm for the night. No one took my bed so we can have a sleepover.

Yeah, that sounds great.

I send off a quick message to Scar to let her know I'll be over. I'm about to lock my phone when I see my sister's name in my contact list.

It's been a month and I still haven't heard from her. Mom and Dad said they'd get her to call me. I wonder if she's just busy with her last year at Uni. No. She still would've called me about something like this.

I click her name and just as it did a month ago, it goes straight to voicemail. Her phone is still off?

I check social media to find that she hasn't made a post for a little over a month. That's really not like her. Did something happen? Something my parents haven't told me?

I click to call Mom, who answers the phone after a few rings with a yawn. "Mera? We were just about to go to sleep. Is there an update in the case?"

"No, I'm not calling about that. I was actually wondering why I haven't gotten a call back from Cate."

Mom stays quiet and in the background, I hear Dad ask what's wrong.

"Mom?"

She sighs. "I'm sorry, dear. Cate is busy with her studies

right now. You know she's putting everything into school and the clubs and everything, along with keeping up with her princess duties. She'll call you when she can."

"Okay, but you can't put her on the phone right now? Even just to say hi?" I plead. I need to confide in someone about these notes.

"No, I'm afraid not," Mom replies firmly. "Good night."

She hangs up and I pull my face away from my phone to look at it.

Whatever. I can do this. I'll get through all of this. The notes, Callan, Heath's disappearance.

Those notes might be even worse than dealing with Callan. They've only sent three notes. Either it's my fault he's dead, that I'm a whore for letting his brother carry me, and that they're watching me.

It's had me losing more sleep than I'd like.

I get back to my room in the sorority and find it empty. Brandie must still be at her midmorning class. On routine, I reach under my pillows, checking for a note and find another one. Wait. No there's *two*?

I smooth the first one out and it chillingly reads

Are you ready to die too?

My heart drops and I sink to the floor at the thought of this person just casually being in my room. Who could be writing these? I already asked for permission to put up a camera outside the door but I was denied when I couldn't tell Collette the reason why.

I stuff the first note in the drawer with all the other ones and open the second one, dropping the note the minute I read it and jumping off the floor to my dresser. No way. How could I have missed that?

I go through every drawer. Throwing out all of its contents, but I still can't find it.

My pink hoodie. It's even bedazzled Princess M on the back.

Fuck!

I stride back to that spot on the floor and pick up the note.

Where's that pink hoodie of yours?

How long has it been gone? I only wore it a few times here. Who'd want to wear a hoodie when it's in the 90s during the day? The perfect weather to wear it is only just coming up now. Shit. I collapse face down across the width of my bed and sigh.

Fuck my life.

"I don't want to go."

"Come on, we've already had several football games and you haven't even been to one. You need to experience it at least once, right Peyton?" Scarlett asks, elbowing Peyton to her right.

Peyton grunts. I don't think he exactly wanted to come either.

"You guys, this is an exciting one. We get to play MGU!" Scarlett yells with a tiny jump.

"MGU?" I ask.

"Yeah, well this is only one of Goldsworthy University's campuses. The other one is Mid Goldsworthy University."

"It's always a close call even with Heath, right? I doubt we're going to win," Peyton says as we round the corner from the ticket booth to the stands.

"Hey Mera, you actually came!" a familiar voice from above yells.

The stands are filling up fast so I look around to find the source when I see someone stand up and wave enthusiastically. Brandie. And it looks like Jamie is with her. She points to the empty space on her left. Just enough to hold the three of us.

"You guys okay with sitting with them?"

We've only eaten breakfast with them a few times with their boyfriends. Scarlett always gets weirdly quiet around them. I don't blame her for it though. Brandie can be a lot sometimes. Her enthusiasm can come off as being annoying. Jamie balances her out as she's more reserved and happier with her head in a book.

Peyton nods and Scar flashes me a small smile. "At least it's not the top."

We get to their seats in the middle and Brandie locks me in a tight hug. "I'm so glad you came, Mera. Now you can see our boys in action. Right Jamie?"

Jamie nods and blushes. "Emerson is amazing on the field."

"Not as good as my Brett," Brandie squeals with a happy sigh, letting me go.

She cranes her neck around. "And it's good to see you guys again too, Scar and PeyPey."

I snort and Peyton clears his throat. "Well that's a new one."

The three of us sit down and chatter with them as we wait for the game to start.

As it's about to begin, I spot a familiar head that turns to scan the crowd. Oh God, it's Callan. Behind him are his three buddies that he's always with.

I've seen them around, but not Callan. He hasn't come to class at all the past two weeks. He missed turning in the outline for the history paper.

Though, if my sister was missing I'd have a hard time focusing on school too.

God, what do I care? He can miss as many classes as he wants. His father owns the school for God's sake.

Somehow, I've managed not to run into him on campus. Very, very lucky of me.

They take a seat on the last part of an open bench near the bottom.

I should wait a while before leaving in case he has any ideas of containing that fucked up game of his after this.

The game seems to fly by, and before I know it, we've won, and just barely. Most of the visiting team shakes hands with our team.

Jamie and Brandie stand up quickly and Brandie touches my shoulder and looks at the three of us. "Thanks for watching the game with us. We need to do this again. It's much more fun with five people. We're going to go wait outside the locker room for them. Later!"

Maybe I will come to another game. It wasn't so bad. I do feel glum seeing Heath's replacement on the field, but he pulled it together for them. Heath must have been great.

"Dane played great today," Scar murmurs, making it super clear how interested she is in his backside.

"I didn't think you knew any of the visiting team by name."

She shrugs. "How could anyone not know Dane Goldsworthy?"

I turn my head back to the field just in time to see the edge of his face as he follows the team off the field. "Heath's cousin."

"Yep. His father is the Dean of MGU. They're trying to keep it hush hush, but I've seen a few posts online talking about how Dane's older sister is missing. And I think they mentioned some kind of fire at Northern Goldsworthy University."

"*What?*" That's the first time I'm hearing about this.

Could Dane's sister's disappearance be linked to Heath's somehow? Maybe this can help exonerate me fully.

And then maybe they can find Heath and…put him to rest.

"Hey, don't look so down. Why don't we go out and get dinner off campus?" Scar runs a comforting hand down my back.

"Sooner or later, the person behind this will be revealed. Just watch and see, Mera," Peyton says reassuringly.

I nod and glance around, specifically at the bottom benches in the stands. No sign of Callan anywhere. "Let's go, then. I have to use the bathroom first though, so you guys just go wait in the car and I'll meet you there."

"Are you sure?" Peyton asks. "We don't mind waiting for you."

I don't want to force them to wait for me. "Nah, it's okay. There will probably be a long line of people."

They leave after a little more reassuring.

Now I just need to find where the bathroom is. Shit, maybe I should have asked them if they knew.

I walk around the area between the ticket booth and the stands, until at the very end of the field, I spot the bathroom signs.

Bingo.

There's a surprising amount of stalls inside, making a wait time nonexistent. I do my business and quickly wash my hands.

When I walk out, the moon has fully come out and I can make out a few stars. The cool night breeze almost reminds me of the night of the hazing.

"Can't believe we fucking lost. That bastard isn't even here and they still managed to beat us."

I eye a trio of football players, holding jerseys in their hands with MGU's colors of blue, white, and gold. I slow down so I don't accidentally cross into their path as I'm about to walk by.

But my slowing down seems to have its own consequence when they spot me.

For once, I'm hoping people don't know my face. I am not Wilhelmera. I'm just a normal college girl.

"Hey, dude, isn't that the princess?"

Fucking hell.

I straighten my back and go to walk past when I feel a hot sweaty hand touch my arm.

"Hey, aren't you Heath Goldsworthy's girl?"

I lock eyes with the man holding my arm and find arrogance reflecting back at me. "That's right."

He sneers. "Well I guess you're free now aren't you?"

Another guy jeers behind him, "Yeah, why don't you hang with us?"

The last voice shouts, "Come on, don't you feel bad for us? Show us some pity, pretty princess?"

I wrench my arm away with a frown. I don't like where this is going. I need to get back to the car, right now.

"Thanks, but no thanks." After flashing them a smile full of fake sincerity, I start walking toward the entrance where the ticket booth is.

The guy who grabbed my arm suddenly steps into my path, forcing me to try and go around him. "Can't say we didn't try and be nice. I'm not a guy who takes no for an answer though."

Ugh, what a fucking asshole. Just like Callan.

Suddenly, his friends grab each of my arms in a tight grip and carry me back with the original arm grab guy getting a twisted smile on his face. "Yeah!" he yells excitedly and rubs his hands together.

At that moment one person, a girl, walks by. Her eyes widen when she sees me, as if she knows exactly what kind of situation I'm in. But instead of coming to my aid, she runs away, heading straight for the ticket booth area. I watch as her bouncing blonde curls disappear as I'm dragged around the side of the bathroom wall.

Okay. I'll kick each guy next to me in the balls and do whatever I can to the other guy.

Right as I'm about to kick my legs out, I hear the sound of footsteps and a voice calling out one of their names.

Fuck.

I need to hurry then. With all the strength in my legs, I kick them both in the crotch, and they fall to the ground cupping their groins. The last guy looks at them and scowls, leaning toward me when I put my fingers out and poke him straight in the eyeballs. "Holy shit!" he yells. I go around the three of them and dash for the exit when two long arms grasp me around my middle and yank me off my feet.

No.

I dig my fingernails into their arms and the person snaps. "No matter what you do, I'm not letting go."

He pulls me back to the other guys. The guy who I poked in the eyeballs is rubbing his eye angrily until he sees me. That's our cornerback for you. Nice and speedy. Great job Kendricks."

Kendricks throws me against the wall face first, making my face connect with it. God, that fucking hurt.

"What do you guys say we steal Heath's girl from him? Even if he comes back, which spoiler alert, he won't. That loser is fucking dead."

The others burst out laughing.

"You guys laugh, but no girl can ever resist my dick once she's gotten a taste. This princess will probably cry to her parents and beg them to transfer her right away."

A cold chill goes down my back and I shiver. What can I do? My face touching the rough wall isn't helping my thoughts stay clear. The rough bits are hard and scraping at my skin.

"How come you get to have her first?" one of the guys ask.

"I caught her didn't I? Without me she would've gotten away." He keeps one firm hand on my back, holding it in place while his other travels down to my shorts. One of his hands sneaks around and unbuttons and pulls the zipper down.

My cheeks heat up as they fall to the ground. No. This can't be happening.

I should've called Scar and Peyton.

To my horror, I feel a hardness move between my underwear-covered butt. "If you do this, I will kill you when you're done," I say.

"Oh, so you actually do want to go to jail, don't you? It

wasn't enough for you to kill your boyfriend, but now you want to kill some harmless guys taking you for a spin too?"

Harmless?

His sweaty hand pulls my underwear down, exposing my bare butt. The hand on my back hasn't moved an inch, and as hard as I try, I can't move it off. Even if I did, the other three guys are waiting just behind this guy.

Why is this happening?

"Hey, what's going on here?" I hear a gruff voice ask in a friendly tone.

Callan? What is he doing here?

I hear one of the arm guys respond, "We're just having a little fun. Don't worry, we'll be leaving soon."

Shit. Callan's so twisted he might just join in with them and finally do what he's been threatening to and fuck me.

There's a long pause. "You really want to have fun with her? You know I got girls lined up who would love to have a go with you guys. You lost and they're wanting to comfort you. Come on, let's go find a few."

Kendricks immediately responds, "No, we're good. I've found one I really want and I'm going to have her. I'll try her pussy first and then her ass. By the time we're done with her, she'll be crying and begging for more." Callan's jaw clenches and his mouth twitches. "And let's be honest, your brother isn't coming back. It's been over a month, he's probably dead in a ditch somewhere, overdosed on drugs."

"Repeat all of that for me, one more time" Callan says, in a deadly tone I can barely recognize. The amount of venom behind it almost has me shaking in fear.

"You fucking deaf? I said–"

Boom! Flesh connects with flesh. The hand on my back is gone and I yank my panties up and my shorts, whirling around just in time to see Callan wailing on who I assume is

Kendricks on the ground. The other three guys are trying to pull him off and when that doesn't work, they start kicking him until he's off.

He coughs and a stream of blood hits the ground. Kendricks is holding his stomach and gasping for air. His face is already starting to swell up and turn purple with a black eye.

Callan's eyes are wild as he takes on the other three guys alone. Their punches are brutal, but he takes it in stride each time, giving them back exactly what they dish out.

His eyes lock on mine for a split second and he receives a punch to the stomach for it.

Fuck. Fuck. Fuck.

I reach in my pocket for my phone when I hear a voice shout, "What the fuck!"

They all freeze, including Callan.

I glance toward the source of the voice and find a tall guy with tousled dark brown hair and hazel eyes approaching us swiftly. That jawline is oh so familiar. I didn't get a full view of his face before and now that I have, I can't help the blush that rises to my face. Those gorgeous genes of theirs are strong.

"What the fuck happened here?" Dane Goldsworthy booms.

CHAPTER EIGHT

Callan

Fuck, my lip is busted open. I wipe my finger over my bottom lip to stop the blood from running down my chin.

Trust Daney boy to come to their rescue.

He stops in between us and Wil.

"Well?" he asks his teammates.

I spit the blood welling up in my mouth on the ground near one of their feet.

"Cap, we–" one of them starts.

One lie out of their mouths and I'll keep punching the living daylights out of them.

"They assaulted me," Wil blurts.

Dane's head turns to her and then back to them. "That's my cousin's girl. All four of you, get the fuck up and head to the bus. Coach will hear about it as soon as I'm there."

The three of them scramble forward to help the beaten guy on the ground and they help him limp away. Fucking sack of shits.

They thought they could run my game and mess with my toy. I'll be the only one to break her.

Dane helps me up off the ground and pats me on the back. "Dude, I thought you were going to wait for me outside the locker room."

"The locker room? I thought you said the bathrooms. Well whatever. I've had a lot going on with taking over from Heath and all."

He nods. "Is it fucked up to say congrats? I know these aren't good circumstances, but being the president of a fraternity is a huge deal."

"Well I guess I should congratulate you too. You're president of your AAA chapter."

"Not because I want to be," he mutters, running a hand over the back of his head. "Listen, I don't have a lot of time, so should we go somewhere and talk?"

I eye Wil, a few feet behind him. Her posture tells me she wants to make a run for it and leave, but in order to do that, she'd have to get past me. If I leave to talk to him, she'll bolt. This is the perfect opportunity to continue our game. She seems to still be a little shaken up so it's perfect.

"No, let's just talk here. Wil won't tell anyone what we discuss. Right?" I ask, staring at her.

She doesn't respond as she stares back, nonverbally fighting me with that stubborn streak of hers. I need to break that. "Big mouths get stuffed, princess. Remember that."

Her lips thin and she nods slightly.

Good.

I turn back to Dane. "So, how'd you know Lacey was missing?"

He sighs. "She called me in the morning and told me she'd be at the game. After the game, I tried to find her. She was nowhere to be found. Tried to call her, no response. I'm investigating a few leads now since the police in our area are lazy as fuck."

"And she didn't seem different at all during that last phone call?"

He shakes his head. "She was her same overly optimistic self. Nothing seemed off. We can't find her car either. It's already been so long, I don't think...fuck, I don't think she's alive anymore."

And pretty soon, no matter how much money his parents or mine shove at the police, they'll stop looking for our siblings. We'll never know what happened to them.

"Do whatever you need to do to get answers," I tell him, eyeing Wil. "I'll do the same. Keep me updated."

"Will do. But hey, where's Coll? I thought I'd be able to see her too while I'm here."

"She took the plane up north. She's meeting with Sophie tonight. I'll text you an update as soon as I hear from her."

"Great." Dane holds his hand out and I take it as he pulls me in and claps me on the shoulder. "Stay safe. Don't take any chances. I can't have you disappearing on me too."

I'd like to see a fucker try and kill me. "You too." He smiles at Wil and lopes off.

"So it's true," she murmurs.

"If you're talking about my cousins going missing, yes."

She blinks. "Well, I couldn't possibly have been responsible for them. Let's end this here and now."

I stalk toward her with careful steps. She doesn't move as I reach her, leaning down until our faces are only inches apart. "Our game continues tonight, princess. The police believe those cases are separate from Heath's. I still need to get the truth out of you. So let's go."

I grab her arm and she instantly goes dead weight, keeping her feet down hard. "Hell no. I'm not doing this again."

"You're going to keep doing this until you tell me the fucking truth Wil. Now, tell me, do I have to carry you over my shoulder again?"

She makes a frustrated sound in her throat, but she walks behind me with no issues.

We go out the side entrance close to the locker rooms. A lot of people are still lingering around, fired up about the win that we scored.

"Callan, hey!" someone shouts.

I nod in their direction.

Now that I'm AAA president, everyone wants to get on my good side. I refuse to be Heath's close though, and bend to everyone else's will.

They want something, they need to work for it.

A flash of orange steps in my path. "Callan," Ginger purrs.

"Busy," I snap, going around her.

"I'll be in my dorm, room 110!" she yells as I stride past her.

Like I'll ever remember that.

Wil's been extremely quiet. I glance back to find her texting on her phone quickly. I stop in my tracks and snatch it from her grasp. "Hey!" she yells.

I slip it in my pocket and keep walking, ignoring her.

"Asshole," she mutters.

I squeeze her arm a little tighter and she takes a sharp intake of breath. The door to the fraternity is wide open when we get there.

My new Vice President, secretary, and advisor are in the

THE PRINCESS AND THE BULLY

foyer, talking loudly about the plays in the game. They love to play football, I wonder why they didn't tryout.

"Hey, dude. How'd it go?" Noel asks.

The three of them go quiet when they notice Wil behind me.

"I'll talk to you later. I have something to do now. Don't come find me."

Noel, Tyrell, and Vincent absorb my words and go back to talking to each other as I start down the hall.

"Oh come on. Neither of you three will help me?" Wil screams to them.

No, because they know that neither of them can stop me from getting what I want.

Callan Goldsworthy always wins.

With a smirk, I open the basement door with the key. Not that extra key that Heath would sometimes leave on top of the doorway, but *his* key.

Luckily, it was in his room.

I don't turn the light on as I drag her behind me. After all, monsters lurk in the darkness. It's where I live and thrive.

I throw her onto the couch and she gasps. "Do you remember what we did the last time we were here?"

Of course she remembers. How could she forget where this game started.

I don't hear a response so I blindly move my hands around her body, brushing the softness of her stomach, and then the roundness of her tits, until finally, I find that small throat of hers.

As I'm about to grab it in my palm, she shocks me by asking. "Why did you help me? Why did you beat those guys up?"

The answer is simple enough to me. "Because you're mine

to break. My toy to play with. If you saw someone else with their hands on your toy, wouldn't you be angry?"

Her breathing accelerates and she spits out, "Just get this over with." Her voice has that same stubbornness to it.

Time to break her wide open. I feel around the table for what I put down here earlier. My fingertips graze it and I stretch forward, taking the soft cloth.

As my eyes adjust to the darkness, I make the cloth taut and put it around her eyes and tie it behind her head. "I can't. I can't see, Callan."

"Exactly, princess." I move my hands to the hem of her shirt and take it off, followed by another lacy bra. She gasps and covers herself. I don't know why she bothers because I can still remember seeing her bouncy tits from the third round of hazing.

"I've already seen everything you have to offer, princess, except what's between your legs. But I plan to see everything tonight."

Her hands jolt out to stop me, but it's too late. My fingers have already undone the button of her shorts and I yank them down without even touching the zipper.

Her small hands go to the straps of her panties as she desperately tries to keep those on.

I smirk and jerk those panties right down. She takes a sharp intake of breath. "That's what happens when you think you can stop me."

Now she's completely bare to me. I trail my hand over her soft skin and she shivers. "You're no better than them."

"I never claimed to be, princess."

She makes a low sound that I can only match with fear in her throat. Good. She needs to be more scared.

"Of course, if you tell me what I want to know, I won't have to do this."

She screams, "I don't know! I don't fucking remember anything."

I grasp those thighs of hers roughly, wrenching them apart. She cries out in shock.

"Fine. Keep telling yourself that." Her body shakes under my hands as I skim down her inner thighs.

"I wonder, how many times did my brother fuck you before he disappeared? How tight is this pussy of yours Wil?"

She doesn't respond. "Guess I'll find out for myself." I grip her right leg tightly in my left hand and move my fingers over her folds.

"Stop!" she shrieks, tilting her head to the side.

That one lone word makes me dick jump to life. And she doesn't stop saying it, she starts chanting it as I tease my fingers over the small hairs down there. I still my fingers and she stops chanting.

But doesn't she know, I'm not going to stop?

I thrust my index finger past her folds and into her pussy. She screams and attempts to scoot back, but she can't escape my large hand on her leg.

God, she's fucking tight. I pull my finger out to the tip and then thrust it back in forcefully. Her body shakes and she emits low sounds in her throat. I add my middle finger in and she shrieks and sobs. "No, *please*, Callan." Tears stream down her face, leaking out from below the blindfold.

My dick jumps in my pants. "Begging won't help this time, princess."

I thrust both fingers inside of her when I start to feel a wetness coating them. She's getting wet from this. "Your body is betraying you, princess. Do you feel how wet you are? How my fingers are sliding in so easily now?"

She runs her fingernails over my arms, cutting into them

with a biting strength. A few places twinge start to burn slightly so I know they're bleeding or almost bleeding.

"Scratch me as much as you'd like." Can't say I haven't been scratched by a woman before. Never in anger, but always in pleasure.

I add a third finger, and she arches off the couch, eyes closed and mouth open as all three slide in and out. A low moan escapes her mouth, echoing through the basement.

Abruptly, I freeze, fingers still half in and half outside as I feel my dick in my pants aching and begging for release. Fuck. I knew I'd probably get hard, but now it just hurts.

Get your dick under control, Callan. I grit my teeth and thrust inside her again and hear another moan, low in her throat as if she's trying to suppress it. It still manages to make my dick hurt like hell.

Fuck.

A loud knock sounds on the basement door. Who the fuck is that? I told them not to bother me.

After taking my fingers out of her tight, wet pussy, I adjust myself in my jeans. I only meant to try and hide this boner, but my hands slow to a stop as I feel her wetness on the tip of my dick.

I slide my eyes back to her and see the blindfold is still in place. Good. She can't see me do this. My fingers, still slick from her wetness, slide down my dick, coating it completely.

Fuck, I hate how good that feels. I pull my hand out quickly and step back. "Next time, my dick goes in your pussy."

I walk away from her and take the steps going up the stairs. This better be fucking important.

Opening the door, I find it's neither of my friends. "Silverstone. The fuck do you want?"

He smiles widely and peers over my shoulder. "Sorry to interrupt your fun. Who's that down there?"

"None of your fucking business. What do you need?" I snap.

"Don't get testy. I need to make you aware of something now that you've gotten settled into your position." He nods his head toward the hallway. "Come."

What the fuck could this be about?

I angle my head down the stairs and yell, "Leave once you're dressed."

There's no response, not that I figured I'd get one, and I let the door close behind me as I follow Silverstone to his room.

Only a few guys are around, surrounding the TV, none of them being my friends. They better hope to God they aren't the ones that told Silverstone where I was.

Silverstone closes the door behind me and pulls his phone out.

"Oh wow, your daddy bought you the newest phone. You're so cool and rich." I roll my eyes. "Can I fucking go now?"

"Shut the fuck up and look," he says, shoving the phone in my face.

A conversation between two people. Him and...I glance at the top of the conversation to find the name. Heath Goldsworthy.

I flit my eyes back down and read the messages.

Kane: You don't have a treasurer anymore do you? I can help with that. What do you say, friend?

Heath: The position is yours. The day after the party I'll announce it.

Kane: You're making the right choice, Heath.

"The fuck did you have on him?" I yell, shoving his phone into his chest.

He chuckles. "It doesn't really matter anymore does it? Anyway, I want my position."

"Absolutely fucking not. I don't need to be in the company of a Silverstone."

"Goldsworthy, I'm not asking, I'm telling. Unless you want everyone in this school to know your brother's secrets."

"Keep that fucking mouth of your shut." I prod him straight in his chest to his black fucking heart. "Keep Heath's name out of your mouth. I'll give you the fucking position. You screw up, you're out. Oh and one other thing." I deliver a right hook straight to his jaw. "Touch my sister again, and I'll kill you."

He rubs his jaw and nods slightly. "Fine, I'll leave her alone for now." A devious smile forms on his face. One that makes me want to punch him again. "I'm much more interested in a certain princess right now."

That same red I saw when I saw those guys hands on her flashes in my head once again. "If you touch her–"

"You'll...what?" he snorts. "Kill me in your brother's honor. Let's be a little more honest with ourselves, Callan. For some fucked up reason, you're interested in your brother's girlfriend. And yet you think I'm the messed up one?"

I clench my jaw. I don't need to explain anything to him. "Get out of my way." I don't want to hear another fucking word.

He holds his hands up. "Yes, el presidente."

After throwing the door open, I stomp out and rush

down the hallway and go down to the basement. I know she's gone.

The door is still unlocked and I take the stairs two at a time. When I reach the couch, I lean down and sniff it. Her scent is still there.

In my head, I see a flash of her open mouth as a moan escapes it. My cock comes alive once more inside my pants, and instead of suppressing it, I tug it out. I pull my hand off my dick and sniff it to find my hand still smells like her unique scent. I shouldn't like how she smells, but I do. It's intoxicating.

Fuck. I fist my cock, tugging it hard over and over as I imagine it sliding inside her. I remember feeling how tight she was around my fingers. Just imagining the tightness of her pussy around my dick makes my blood run wild.

Spurt after spurt of cum erupts out. Gritting my teeth, I glare down at the mess I've made. I can't do *this* again. I need to follow through with my last threat. I need to be done with her. I'll just have to lock her down here, chain her up, and fuck her until she stops lying.

CHAPTER NINE

Mera

Since my very first total fail at the first party day of the year, I've avoided every other party. And we've had a bunch. I've ignored the siren call of the loud music blaring outside the walls of my room. The laughter and excited voices that carry down the halls. The smell of the booze.

I refuse to ignore it tonight. It's Halloween. One of my favorite nights of the year. Every single year in high school I had a party at the palace. It would've been epic this year if I was still at home. My parents wouldn't have been able to stop me from opening the bar since I'm finally eighteen.

Oh well. I can still have fun tonight, I just can't get blackout drunk again to the point where I completely forget everything.

"Almost ready, Mera?" Brandie pipes up from behind me.

"Yeah, I just need to get this wig on."

"Here, let me do it for you," she says, coming up from behind me.

She picks the wig up from the vanity and slowly positions it accordingly in the mirror. "Wigs are fun aren't they? You're a gorgeous Snow White. You're so much better at makeup than me. Thanks for doing my face too!"

It's what I'm good at. After watching Cate be woken up early for events to have her face done, I decided to learn myself so I wouldn't have to be bothered.

The short raven waves and the red lipstick make my blue eyes stand out more than usual. Maybe I should dye my hair.

I move off the vanity chair and straighten my dress, making sure there isn't a wrinkle in sight.

Brandie is adjusting the angle of her witch hat on her head.

"Can you believe we actually have to go through an inspection? Her Highness is so ridiculous." She covers her mouth. "Oh sorry, I don't mean to make you feel inferior."

I shake my head. "No, the truth is, my being a princess doesn't matter one bit here. In this situation she's the queen and we're all her lackeys."

And to make sure she doesn't get embarrassed by any of us, we have to line up for inspection. She's already cleared all of the juniors and seniors costumes.

"Let's get this over with then," I say, marching out of the room with Brandie at my heels. We get down to the foyer and join the crowd of girls waiting. At the other edge of the crowd near the kitchen area, I spot a bloody Jamie in a Carrie dress. She nods to her roommate, Kori, dressed in a cat costume, who narrows her eyes at me as her mouth turns to a frown. What's her fucking deal?

Jamie skirts around the crowd until she reaches our side.

"You guys look great. I'm guessing Mera did your makeup, Brandie?"

"Of course. You know I'm not that skilled."

Jamie smiles. "I would've had to steal her away if my costume involved makeup. I'm so glad all I needed is the fake blood."

The crowd around us suddenly quiets down. Behind us, the stairs creak as feet step quickly down them. The last footsteps are light as a feather.

As if we're synchronized, we all step back, as close to the stairs as possible and form a tight line.

The four of them step in front of us, with Collette being in the forefront. She looks particularly excited tonight, but the weirdest thing is, she isn't wearing a costume. Her outfit is a more beautiful version of the tutus she wears along with a pair of glittery tights and ballet shoes. Brandie's known her for years and when she told me I honestly didn't believe her. She doesn't like to dress up in anything but, and she'll always make fun of anyone wearing a ballerina costume too.

I guess she wasn't lying when she said a soul wouldn't dare come down dressed in a ballerina costume and incur her wrath.

She starts at the end of the line closest to the hallway instead of the front door. As Collette makes her judgements, I look away and focus on her three officers in front of me.

She still hasn't chosen her fourth and last one.

Gemma spots me looking and discreetly waves with her arm glued to her side. She's wearing a hot pirate girl costume with heavy eyeliner and dark red lipstick. To her left, is Luella who notices Gemma's gaze and smiles at me. Her face is the most made up as she has white face paint and a black painted nose for her deer costume.

Ashlynn only glances my way for a moment before

flitting back to her nails. She's a traditional fairy with glittery wings and a short goofy dress with glittery eyeshadow and a blue flower wreath around the front of her hair.

Collette's Judy voice edges ever closer.

"You need more eyeliner," she murmurs to one girl.

"Different color lipstick."

"Your lips are too glossy."

"Your whole face needs to be fixed."

"Too much eyeshadow."

A few of the girls make small noises of frustration that Collette seems to ignore. Finally, she stops in front of me. Her eyes move over my face several times and. Her gaze drops to my costume and back up.

What can she say? I know I did my makeup perfectly and this costume wasn't cheap either.

A crooked smile forms on her face. "More blush on those cheeks, Mera."

What a bitch. I know my cheeks are red enough. Her mocking eyes leave mine, going to Jamie next to me. "Wasn't Carrie soaked in blood? You only have a few splatters on you." She takes another step. "Awesome makeup, Brandie, but where's your broomstick?"

I snort and she glances in my direction. "Something funny?"

Shaking my head quickly, I struggle to hold in the laughter. I guess she can say what she really thinks to anyone but me. I'll humor her by going back up to put more blush on, but I'm not actually going to. My makeup is perfect. She even said so herself, just not to my face.

Once she's judged the last person, she walks back to the front in front of her three friends. "Let the party begin. Don't have too much fun." She walks away to the kitchen and all of the girls in line go separate ways. Gemma opens the door wide open and group after group of guys come in.

Two of those guys being Emerson and Brett who hug Jamie and Brandie, respectively. Brett is dressed as a police officer and Emerson as a cowboy. Emerson reaches behind Jamie to grab her ass and Brett pushes Brandie against the stair railing, kissing her hard.

All of a sudden, I feel like a fifth wheel. I bet they wouldn't even know if I left.

Peyton and Scarlett are getting food in the dining hall before coming here to meet me in an hour.

I'll just get a few drinks and then leave for a little while.

When I get to the kitchen it's mostly empty as a lot of people are outside in the back. I grab a bottle of whiskey and pour myself a few shots.

Ah, I missed that burn.

I pour myself a few shots of vodka and then some tequila.

Yes. This is what I missed. My face is feeling warm and everything seems so much better now. I'll just have a few more shots of tequila and be on my way.

Once I'm done, I slam my shot glass down and glance around at all of the people yelling and laughing as the music roars from outside.

I stumble out the hallway and back to the foyer to find my friends haven't moved.

"I'm going to walk around campus. See you guys later," I say in a loud voice.

Jamie's the only one who acknowledges me, giving me a little wave and goes back to cuddling in the arms of her boyfriend.

I wonder if I'll ever have someone like that. Someone who's so wrapped up in me that they completely block out everyone else.

Someday.

I mean, I'm a fucking princess. My Prince Charming has to come at some point.

Gemma's alone on the porch when I walk through the doorway and she looks bored out of her mind, looking down the road. "Hey, I'm going to wander around for a bit. Want to come with?"

"I would, but Collette doesn't want me to leave." She moves her hands over her outfit. "I think I actually sort of look nice. I don't want to stay cooped up, but I don't really have a choice. See you whenever you get back."

There's a sour note in her voice that makes me wonder how long it's going to take before she can't stand Collette's bossiness anymore.

I start down the road, eventually reaching the end of Sorority Row. Tons of people are running around in their costumes with bottles of alcohol in hand.

A few large groups start whispering as they see me walking past. As I turn the corner, I spot a group of guys in devil masks and all black. So far everyone else has worn their own unique costume.

Out of the corner of my eye, I watch as they actively walk around everyone in their path and follow me. Their steps aren't too fast as if they want to get around me or too slow as if they're walking casually. No, they're keeping up with me. I walk past the library and start toward the administration building. Unlike everywhere else, there's no one around. Shit, maybe it was a mistake coming this way.

I walk a little faster, stumbling over a few cracks in the concrete and almost falling on my face a few times. Shit. Eventually I'm passing the administration building to the spot I met Heath at two months ago. And then I hear it. My heart jumps in my throat as I hear the sound of feet hitting the pavement fast.

I glance behind me to find them hastening to catch up. Wait. Something glinted in one of their hands. Was that a knife? My heart thunders in my chest as I break into a run. Into the tree covered area with benches on each side. Ugh, these flats aren't helping me at all.

Why are they chasing me? This can't be a misunderstanding, can it?

Off in the distance, I hear the sounds of laughter and yelling, but around here there's no one.

This is my very own horror movie. Just what I fucking needed.

Except, I have a phone. I yank it out of my pocket and start to dial 911 when a rough hand grabs my shoulder and yanks me backwards, causing me to drop my phone to the ground.

The brightness of my phone illuminates the darkness of the area.

"What do you want?" I ask, eyes widening and heart in my throat.

The other three surround me from the back. The person's grip tightens as they pull me closer, and something hard and sharp hits my chin. I flit my eyes down, staying still to find it's a chef's knife. So I was right.

"If you're going to use it, use it. And then my parents will hunt you down and kill you."

The person throws the knife to the ground, making a clinking sound that sends chills down my spine.

"That's better. Now go and fuck off."

They shake their head and thrust their hand forward, putting their gloved fingers around my neck. Those long fingers tighten to the point that I'm gasping for air. I move my arms up, trying to peel their hand away, but it does nothing. I shouldn't have drank so much.

Coughing hard, I start seeing stars behind my eyes. Desperately, I move my hands up, reaching for that ugly devil's mask. My fingers glide over the edge, but they angle their head back so it's still out of reach.

Is this what they meant by that note? These are the same people that killed Heath? How can I even hope to save myself if Heath couldn't?

I can't do anything anymore. My body goes limp as I sink to my knees and hit the ground. Suddenly, that pressure around my throat is gone. Blinking my eyes quickly, I intake a gulp of air sharply and touch my aching throat. God, that hurts.

The person straightens and folds their arms. "What happened to Heath Goldsworthy?" Those first words clue me in exactly to who it is.

"Callan?" I rasp, touching my throat.

The mask is slowly pulled down to reveal those cold eyes of his. His face is neutral, as if he didn't almost make me pass out.

The other guys move from next to and behind me to Callan's side. They pull off their masks to reveal that they're his three friends. I should've fucking known. No one else but them would be so arrogant as to do something like this out in the open.

"You guys are fucked up!" I yell, eyeing each of them individually. They avoid my gaze, looking anywhere else but me. Callan is the only one looking me dead in the eye.

"Just tell me what happened to my brother."

"For the last time, I don't know. It's been almost two months and I still can't remember."

Callan scowls, and hurls the mask to the ground. "Let's go."

The other guys pile their masks on top of his and follow him without so much as a word to me.

They're either as twisted as he is or extremely loyal. The same loyalty that Collette inspires in her friends.

Whatever. I'm done thinking about him and allowing him to ruin my night. I pick up my phone and check to make sure the screen isn't cracked. Thank God it isn't.

Instead of going straight to the area where we did our third round of hazing, I turn left and follow a path through the trees. I just need to take a breather. The lake is somewhere around here, I think. I've never been to it but everyone says it's peaceful.

After walking for a while, I discover it's nowhere near as close as I thought it would be. Finally, I feel the coolness in the air and I spot the shimmering water with the moon reflected on it. It's a lot bigger than I thought it'd be.

At the shore of the lake, I stop and sit down, probably completely ruining my costume. Oh well. It's quiet enough where I can only hear the crickets, the birds, and my own breathing.

Wait. Is my mind playing tricks on me? I hold my breath and listen only to hear the slow intake of breath and then its release. That's not me. Before I can even reach into my pocket to pull out my phone, my phone is wrenched out by a gloved hand and tossed away all over again.

Fucking hell it better not be cracked.

I don't even have time to worry about it as someone grabs me around the waist, carrying me into the water.

Turning my head slightly, I see that same damn devil mask. "Why won't you leave me alone? I already told you thirty minutes ago, I don't know anything."

At this point, the water's up to my chin but he's still well above it. "Let me go."

He shakes his head and my head immediately meets the water.

It was so abrupt I didn't even get a chance to hold my breath. The hand on my head is hard and unyielding, but he won't hold me here for long. I just need to be strong. I'll survive this. I always make it through Callan's games. He won't kill me. My lungs start to burn, crying out for air. It hurts.

Why is he torturing me again? I don't know what happened to Heath. I don't know! I want to scream it in his fucking face until he finally understands.

With a gasp, I open my mouth and water pours in. I tap the hand on my head to show I give. That this is enough. But it does nothing.

No. Callan. I scratch hard at the gloved hand and try with all of my strength to move it off my head. But it's no use. This hand isn't moving. It never had any intention of moving.

But I haven't gotten my memories from that night back. I still have to try and remember.

"Callan!" I scream under the water. There's no use in trying to keep my mouth closed now.

Everything hurts. It's too much. And I can't fight anymore. I close my eyes and everything leading up to this point flashes in my head. Being told I'm coming here, meeting Heath, meeting Scarlett and Peyton, and Callan. The anger inside of him. His hate for me, it's all come down to this.

He's ending the game.

His cold blue eyes are the last thing I see in my mind as everything drifts away.

Wet. Something on my lips is wet, and kind of warm too?

A harsh cough forces itself out of me, causing my eyes to open as the water occupying my stomach forcefully ejects itself out. God. I suck in a deep breath. Ouch, fuck. I clutch my chest and look around, trying to figure out where I am when it all floods back to me.

The lake is only a few feet away. Callan must have dragged me out and…did CPR?

"Are you okay?" a gruff voice asks. Jumping out of my skin, I tilt my head back to find not Callan, but Kane Silverstone. He raises an eyebrow. "Well? You good? Or do I need to drive you to the emergency room? You know crazy people are there during Halloween."

I stare down at my wrinkly hands. "Are you the one that tried to drown me?"

He snorts. "Why would I try to drown you and then offer to take you to the hospital? No."

"It's just, you're dressed like the guy."

"Yeah, I know. I was watching the whole thing. I'm a pretty observant guy. I've seen *a lot of things* I probably shouldn't have seen." He leans down, offering his hand for me to grab, so I do. "I spotted someone following you and decided to follow him. I'm always keeping an eye on Goldsworthy, you know. I really thought it was him. Don't think he knew I was there. I thought maybe he was playing a fucked up game with you."

"So you know about his games?"

"Everyone knows. But then I realized, he couldn't possibly do this. He wants answers and as far as he knows, you're the only one with them."

Something about his statement strikes a chord in me.

"Wait. So do you know something?" I ask, staring into his eyes.

A slow smile spreads across his face. "Maybe. Maybe not."

"Well if you do, you need to tell the police," I say excitedly, "and you know, get Callan off my fucking back."

He takes a few steps closer in a flash and puts a finger to my lips and taps his ear. "There could be ears listening. Anyway, the guy heard me coming and swam to the right and disappeared. I almost followed him, but I figured saving your life was more important."

"Well, thank you for *eventually* stepping in," I say wryly.

Ring ring.

Oh shit, that's my phone. I run up the shore and grab it. My screen protector is putting in work tonight. It's Scarlett. I click answer and she starts speaking fast, "Mera? What's going on? I've been calling and you didn't answer. Peyton and I are at ZDB and you're twenty minutes late. I thought something happened to you so I tracked down that asshole Goldsworthy."

"You did *what*?"

"Yeah, he's standing right in front of me right now." Her voice lowers. "And he's with some orange haired bitch who keeps sneering at me."

In the background, I hear, "Ginger. My name is Ginger, you red-haired bitch."

Scarlett chuckles. "Okay. *Okay*. Mera, babe, I'm going to hang up now so I can stomp a bitch into the ground. Call me a bitch, one more time!"

The line goes dead.

"Guess I better get you back," Kane muses.

"You heard that?"

"How could I not? Your friend is fiery. She reminds me a lot of someone else," he says, turning around and walking up the shore.

"Who?" I ask, utterly confused.

He shrugs and mysteriously responds, "Can't quite put my finger on it."

I follow behind him, staring at his back. Every encounter with this guy is strange, but I guess the first thing he said to me wasn't a lie.

That night at the third round of hazing.

He parted the crowd like he was a God. His subjects looked at him in fear. Not even the girls wanted to look at him. But I did.

And I think that's what made him come toward me. He said *"Don't be like everyone else. You'll always want me on your side."*

And I guess he wasn't wrong.

But he's surprisingly not as horrible as everyone makes him seem. We like a lot of the same bands and he even binges teen dramas like I do.

I'm laughing so hard at his jokes and quips that I barely notice the stares and whispers we get. I know I look like a hot mess. My perfect makeup has to be ruined and I'm still soaking wet with this stupid wig hanging like a damp cloth. Kane, on the other hand, quite possibly looks hotter than he usually does with his black shirt clinging to the six pack I saw in all its glory. His dark hair, normally styled well, is hanging at his temples.

He slows to a stop as we reach Sorority Row, so I stop too. "What's going on?"

He smirks. "Before we get there, can you hold out your hand for me?"

I give him a questioning look. "Uh, sure." I'm not sure what he needs it for.

He reaches behind himself and pulls out a black Sharpie. With his lips, he pulls the cap off and starts to write on my arm.

Kane Silverstone.

The fuck? His hand grips my wrist. "Stay still." Underneath his name, he writes down a phone number.

"You know, I could've just put your phone number in my phone right?"

He grins and his eyes shoot up to mine. "That would've been smart, huh?" After capping it, he shoves it back in his pocket and continues onward.

When we get there, my jaw drops as I note all of the people hanging around the steps and the sidewalk next to it.

Almost every single goddamn person I know. Jamie, Jamie's roommate, Brandie, Callan and his friends, Collette and her friends, and Scarlett and Peyton. Not a Ginger in sight.

"Silverstone?"

"Mera's with *him?*"

"Why do they both look like they've just come out of a swimming pool?"

Scarlett and Peyton are the first to walk through the crowd of people. Scar's hair for her maid outfit is a little crazy. I'm guessing that was Ginger's work.

"I was worried about you. What the hell happened, girl?"

"Me too. Did you guys take…a shower together with your clothes on? Or go swimming with them on?" Peyton asks, looking between us.

Heat rises to my cheeks and I glance over to Kane, who doesn't respond. His smile grows wider and I blurt, "No. There was an accident and–"

"What kind of accident?" Gemma pipes up. She moves her glasses closer to her face and studies me up and down intently.

"It doesn't matter, because I saved her," Kane responds with a sly smile.

A tall body steps between Scar and Peyton and I grimace when I see it's *him*. But he isn't even looking my way.

"Saved her how?" Callan asks, scowling at Kane.

He smirks. "I gave her CPR. Those lips of hers were really soft and wet."

Callan's eyes darken for a moment. So quickly, I could've easily missed it. A slow smile spreads across his face as he nods and rubs a hand over his chin. "I'm sure they were, after coming out of the lake I'm assuming? But you know, you'll never feel how wet her other lips get."

My jaw drops open and I feel the flush climbing up my neck. Oh my God, he didn't just say that in front of everyone. He moves between us with a satisfied expression, slamming his shoulder into Kane's and making no apologies as he leaves down the sidewalk.

"Did he just say what I thought he said?" Collette murmurs.

Noel hoots. "That's my boy."

If I had even a sliver of dignity left, it just went out the window.

Suddenly, everything seems so overwhelming.

Callan and his friends scaring me, almost drowning, the embarrassment, Kane. Everything starts to spin around me as I make a path through everyone, stumbling up the steps.

"Mera?" Scarlett asks, following close behind me.

"See you around, Mera," Kane calls as I walk in the door.

My chest aches as I breathe erratically all the way up the stairs to my room. A few seconds later, Scarlett and Peyton both come in.

"Did you and Goldsworthy fuck?" Scarlett asks as I yank the wig off.

"No," I manage to say as I flop down on my bed.

Peyton clears his throat. "Well, what exactly is going on between you guys?"

I steady my breathing and glance at the mirror against the wall.

I wish I knew.

I haven't been able to stop thinking about how Callan's fingers were inside me. God, my face is heating up all over again. I've been trying not to think about it. It helps that he's been skipping class again. But every time I do think about it, I keep remembering the moans that escaped my mouth. It hurt at first, but that feeling went away quickly. The only thing left was pleasure. No matter how much my brain said no, my body was practically begging him for more.

My panties were soaked on the way back to the dorm.

I tighten my thighs together as that tingling feeling starts again.

"Nothing."

Peyton raises an eyebrow, but he doesn't question me further.

Scarlett rubs my back. "Just don't let him get under your skin. The Goldsworthys are trash and the Silverstones are no better."

It's too late, I want to say. He's already gotten under my skin.

One thing's for sure, I still utterly despise him. That petition that he started needs 894 more signatures and then it'll go to the board.

Why is everything so completely out of control?

CHAPTER TEN

Callan

All night long, I stayed awake. I kept seeing her and wondering what led up to her needing CPR. Ironic that Silverstone of all people was the one to save her.

We were just with her.

He got to touch that silky smooth skin of hers.

Why does that bother me so much? It shouldn't. All night long those same thoughts circled around in my brain, like a record. I sketched in my sketchpad, but every single damn time, I always ended up drawing *her*.

Her smiling when she's walking with her friends. Her angry glares when she notices me. The fear that lurks inside in the deepest part of her fierce eyes when I play my game with her.

By the time it's almost dawn, I'm so worked up I skip

breakfast. I know her class routine by heart so I know she walks in the science building every Thursday exactly at 7:15 for her Bio class at 8. She sits in the lounge area before her class starts on her laptop, watching some drama show.

If she ever looked over her shoulder, she'd see me, but she never does.

Today, she will.

I walk in the side entrance of the building with my backpack on one shoulder and stride down the hall. In the distance, I can see her sitting with her legs crossed in the lounge chair and her Mac on her lap. There are only two other people in the lounge. One girl is passed out on the couch and the girl next to her is writing something in a journal.

Today, unlike other days, I don't make my steps quiet. And when I slow to a stop next to her, she glances up with her earbuds in, obviously expecting to see someone else as her smile turns to a frown.

She reaches up with her left hand, tugging on the cord slightly, pulling her earbuds out. "What do you want?"

I open my mouth to respond, when something catches my eye. Something is slightly faded on the top of her left hand. What the fuck is that?

I reach down and grab her hand and hold it up under the fluorescent lights.

Son of a bitch. Kane Silverstone is scrawled in that bastard's handwriting with his number underneath. Did he do that after I left or did I just not notice it?

Gritting my teeth, I move my fingers over the mark roughly.

"Hey, what the hell are you doing?" she snaps.

He must have used a fucking Sharpie. I don't respond, feeling the anger surge and roll over me as I yank her up out of her seat. She tries to go dead weight, but when she sees I have no interest in letting her go, she grudgingly goes along as I drag her down the hall by her wrist.

"Where are you taking me?"

I stop in front of the bathroom and push my hand against the door, bringing her to the sinks.

"Are you fucking serious? He just wanted to give me his number."

Ignoring her, I focus on soaping her hand and scrubbing it until that damn mark is gone. A few guys come in. Even though I can hear them pissing I know they're taking longer than necessary just to be nosy as fuck.

It takes a few scrubs, and her hand is unblemished once more. I run her hand under the water to rinse the soap off completely.

It's done, but I don't feel satisfied yet. Not one bit.

Fuck. I stare down at her hand and think about Silverstone's smug face as he wrote his number down. He did this so I'd see it. I know it. Fucker.

"Can I go now?" she asks with an annoyed tone in her voice.

"No," I state, looking up into her eyes.

Her eyebrows furrow and she digs her phone out of her pocket with her other hand. Her glossed lips pout slightly. "I have class in thirty-five minutes." She tilts her head back and stares at me. Whatever she sees makes her eyes widen slightly and that flash of fear goes through them.

I was going to fuck her, but I think I have a better idea. Something I've been saving.

"There's plenty of time," I mutter, tugging her with me as we leave the bathroom and go back to the lounge. I stop in front of her chair and let go of her wrist. "Pick your stuff up."

She scowls, rubbing her wrist. "No. I'm not interested in playing your games today."

I back her into the wall next to her chair. She lets out a gasp as I push my leg between hers and grab her neck, leaning down to her ear. "Pick it up and come with me before I do what I'm going to do in this lounge for everyone to see."

She gulps and nods slightly.

Good.

I back off enough for her to put her laptop away and put her bag over her shoulder.

"Lead the way," she says with a sigh.

"Fine." I glance over at her as she walks slightly behind me.

As I'm about to turn the corner, I watch her dart off to the last door on the left, her teacher's room and turn the handle.

But she isn't fast enough, because my hand is already on her arm, and I'm not letting it go.

"That hurts," she complains with a wince.

"And now, you really do need to be punished." I grab her bag off her shoulder and put it over mine. "Now you have no choice but to follow me."

I turn the corner and walk to the end of the hall to the first door on the right. I've been scoping rooms out for this exact purpose. There's no window on the door and no one ever uses this one because the electricity outlets don't work. You'd think a super rich school like this would fix them, but no. My dad is a fucking cheapskate when it comes to this school.

When she enters, I lock the door behind her and throw our bags to the floor.

She crosses her arms and glares. "And you know what, I

think you're the one who needs a punishment. How fucking dare you tell everyone what you did to me? You made it seem like I wanted that. I didn't enjoy it one bit."

Snickering, I approach her slowly and edge her back into a table. "You might not have wanted it, but you sure as fuck enjoyed it, princess. Don't lie to me."

Her mouth thins as she looks away. I tilt her chin up so she meets my eyes. "Should we test it out? It's been a few weeks since then."

She shakes her head quickly. "No. I don't want to."

"But bad girls deserve to be punished. You tried to run away when you could've come quietly."

"I will never come quietly to you, Callan." She wrenches her chin out of my grasp.

My last ounce of control snaps with those words. I slip my thumbs into her yoga pants and hook them around the straps of her underwear. Together, her panties and pants come down. She gasps and pushes her hand against my chest. "Stop it!"

In one smooth motion, I pick her up by her thighs and throw her onto the table behind her. She tightens her thighs together, but I pry them open with brute force.

"I'm not blindfolding you this time, princess. You're going to see exactly what I do and how I do it."

I place my index finger at her folds and tease them slowly. "Just stop this. I don't know what happened to Heath."

This isn't about Heath.

But I don't say it.

I thrust my finger into her and she gasps and jumps slightly at the intrusion. "You're fucking tight."

She bites her lip and looks away.

That won't do.

I pull my finger out and thrust it back in, several times, earning a muffled moan each time.

My cock jumps in my pants and I add another finger. Her back arches as tiny pants leave her mouth. "Please…"

"Please what?"

"Stop."

"Really? Okay." I yank my fingers out, completely covered in her, and study them. Took her less time to get wet.

"Oh thank God," she breathes.

I eye her wetness on my fingers and bring them to my mouth. "W-what are you doing?"

Our eyes stay locked as my mouth opens, letting her wetness touch my tongue for the first time. Her taste is everything I thought it would be, musky and so damn sweet. But it's so muted. I need more, directly from the source. As I pull my fingers out, she makes a small noise in the back of her throat.

I grab her thighs and yank her forward to the edge of the table.

I bend my head down to the juncture of her thighs and thrust my face in, breathing her in. Fuck. Her scent is intoxicating. Like a fucking drug to my brain.

And I need more.

She gasps as my tongue parts her folds. Her legs twitch in the grip of my arms and she lets out a sharp moan. Completely unmuffled.

"You're so vocal, and here I thought you'd be quiet knowing people are walking through the door only a few feet away and going to their classes."

Her hand flies to her mouth as I move my tongue insistently over her clit. Her soft whimpers make my cock so hard, I'm sure it's purple now.

I remove one hand from under her thigh and thrust my

fingers back into her pussy. Two at first, and then three, all the while sucking on her clit.

"It's so much," she gasps. "It feels…" She stares down at me with heated eyes.

With a smirk, I move back slightly, easing my fingers out of her.

"W-wait, what are you doing?"

"I'm stopping, princess. Unless…"

"Unless what?" she asks, biting her lip.

"Unless you tell me, it feels good."

She opens her mouth, and closes it, glancing away.

"Five seconds, princess." I squeeze two fingers around her clit and she jumps.

Her head tilts back. "It feels…good."

"I'm sorry, I didn't get that. Can you repeat that, one more time?"

Her heated eyes find mine. "Please…keep going." Her pink face turns away once more.

Fucking hell. My cock wants to be inside her now, but I oblige, thrusting three fingers back inside her. Her hips start grinding with every thrust and I switch between licking and sucking her clit, until I feel her body shudder. Her body jolts and her pussy tightens around me so hard, I think my fingers are going to fall off.

Panting, she goes still on the table, still looking anywhere but at me.

"You act like this was your first time finishing, princess. My brother couldn't make you come?"

She doesn't respond, her hand swiping the sweat off her forehead. I lick my fingers clean, but I'm far from satisfied.

Last time, I was deprived of this. This time I won't be.

I stand up, moving her thighs together and place her feet on my left shoulder.

She blinks up at me with exhausted eyes, hair splayed all over the place on the table. "What are you doing?"

"Getting off, princess."

Her eyes widen. "No!"

So selfish. But it's too damn bad she doesn't have a choice.

I yank my pants and underwear down and groan at the feeling of my cock being free.

Her eyes widen with fear as I stare down at her. "Don't."

Grasping her ankles tightly in the crook of my left arm, I nudge my cock forward, rubbing right over her entrance. She gasps and tries to move her legs, the outcome being her opening teasing the head of my cock. "Wil. Stop fucking moving."

She stills as her eyes grow watery. "If you fuck me, Callan, I'll never forgive you."

"I'll accept all your hatred, princess." I tilt my hips up and drive forward, earning a shocked gasp as I push my cock between her thighs. "Just not today."

Her eyes flood with relief, but not for long as I pull back and thrust forward. She bites her lip and closes her eyes. With every slide of my cock between her legs, my cock is teasing her clit.

Fuck. The wetness between her thighs and the tightness of her thighs are the perfect combination to make it almost feel like I'm inside her.

One moan after another escape her mouth as she muffles them with her hand.

Grunting, I pick up the pace, sweat beading on my forehead as I grit my teeth. At that moment, she does something so unexpected, my breath ceases in my throat. Her eyes open, locking with mine. Something moves through them, something I haven't seen before. I can't figure it out before they flit down. Her free hand reaches down and the tips of her fingers touch the head of my cock.

Shit. I almost came.

"Don't touch," I growl. But as I pull back and thrust forward, her fingers are still there, waiting for my cock. The touch of those small fingers are my undoing as spurt after spurt of cum hit her stomach. She yanks her hand away and I pause. "I told you not to touch."

"I was cu–. Look. Are we done now? Can you get a paper towel from that sink over there?" she asks, pointing across the room.

I move my cock out from her tight embrace and let them go. "I think you should clean up the mess you made. Why waste a paper towel?"

She raises an eyebrow as I move my fingers through the pool of cum. As I move my fingers up, she shakes her head, but I dip my fingers past her lips and smear my cum there.

"You aren't leaving this room until you get all of it in that mouth of yours." I glance to my left at the clock. "Looks like you have seven minutes until class starts. You better hurry."

"You're an asshole," she grumbles as she moves her fingers into the cum and drags them up to her mouth. This time, my cum will make it past her teeth. I watch her fingers go inside her mouth and feel my cock hardening all over again. I pull my underwear and pants back up, buttoning them quickly.

She doesn't look me in the eye, and her face stays neutral as she reaches down and gets every bit of cum off her stomach and into her mouth. She opens her mouth wide open, fixing me with her pink tongue. "See, all gone. Now let me go."

"Fine. But first, your punishment."

Her eyebrows draw together and she laughs. "Wait. What? That wasn't my punishment?"

"No." I walk over to my bag and pull out my special gift. I've been wondering when to use this. Now seems like the perfect fucking time. I hide it behind my back and grab her arm with my other hand, tugging her off the table.

"Put your underwear on." She stares at me warily, tugging them back up her hips. I move my hand from behind my back, and pull the part of her underwear between her thighs down slightly with my pinky finger and insert my device inside her panties, positioning it right against her clit. It's nestled perfectly so the only way it will come out is if she pulls it out.

She shrieks. "What the fuck is that?"

I stride over to my backpack and pick the remote out. Pressing the red button once earns a small sound from her, and I press the black button to stop it. "You're going to wear the vibrator through your whole class. I'll be pressing it off and on and watching through the windows to make sure you don't take it out." I glance at the clock. "And it looks like class is starting…now. Don't think you want to be late."

"Ugh, I hate you," she mutters, pulling her pants up and grabbing her bag and leaving. Grabbing mine, I follow her back the way we came to her door. She walks inside and I glance in to see her sit at a lab table, similar to the one she was just laying on. Some girl next to her turns her nose up at her and scoots her body further away.

After five minutes go by, I press the button. Wil jumps slightly on the stool, straightening her back. I don't press the black button for two minutes. The moment I do, she relaxes on the stool, throwing her hair over her shoulder.

I let fifteen minutes go by the second time, pressing the red button three times to medium vibrations. I watch that hand fly to her mouth. Mm, I wonder if anyone can hear her moaning.

Reluctantly, I switch it off. Back and forth, I do it, occasionally being stopped by others passing by who stop to talk to me. When her class is nearing its end, I press the red button five times, putting it into high vibrations. Her fingers lock around her arms, tightening to the point that they turn red. Her head goes down to the paper on her desk and she visibly shudders on the stool.

After a few minutes, I shut it off for the last time. She's probably soaking wet right now. I palm the remote in my hand and think about how good she tasted on my tongue.

Fuck. I shouldn't be thinking about this. Heath is out there somewhere, dead or alive, and she's the only lead I have. I need to keep trying to get answers.

Suddenly, every person starts putting their work away in their bags. Class must be over. It felt like no time at all, standing here for two and a half hours.

I shift my weight from one foot to another before making the decision to leave. I was going to get the vibrator back, but that might cause something else entirely. As I walk down the hall and leave the building, I feel my dick finally start to calm down.

CHAPTER ELEVEN

Mera

All weekend, he avoided me. Not that I mind it. Our sorority did charity work downtown and so did his fraternity. Every time we crossed paths, he wouldn't even scowl at me or ask me if I remember anything from that night.

He was surprisingly helpful and I almost thought for a second that he was someone else completely as he talked to the homeless.

I still don't understand why he did what he did last Thursday. And, I threw that stupid vibrator away. I could feel his gaze on my back my whole bio class, yet when I left the class he was nowhere to be found, so of course I went to the bathroom right away and threw it out.

If he wants me to replace it, I'll just give him the money for a new one, not that he'd really need it.

"Got your outline done?" Peyton asks.

"Yeah, I stayed up until two getting it done." I rub the sleep out of my eyes and yawn, walking inside history class.

We sit in our respective chairs and I lean against the wall and look back at them.

"Tsk tsk, Mera. You procrastinate too much," Scar says, wagging her finger at me.

"It's a bad habit," I groan. "Plus I've been so stressed lately. That petition only needs 405 more signatures. There's no chance of it making 5k right?"

Peyton and Scar look at each other and back at me.

"No way," they say at the same time.

"Thanks for being optimistic." But I know if the same amount of people sign it this week and next week as they have been the past few weeks, I'll be at 5k by the end of the month. And then the board will have to make a decision.

But I'm not a danger to anyone and I don't deserve to be expelled.

I'm innocent. I have to be.

But those fucking notes aren't helping. I've been getting them daily since Halloween night. The day after I got *"Next time, no one will be around to save you."*

I think they know I'm close to bringing them to the police because of the one I got yesterday.

Show the police these and your roommate gets it.

So many people go in and out of the sorority, I'm nowhere close to figuring out who it is. Everything has just been... hopeless. The only thing I can do is keep trudging along.

Everything else may be shit but I have the best grades here than I've ever had.

"Class will now begin," Professor Harper says. "Please pass your outlines up front."

I bend down and pick it out of the folder in my bag and place it on my desk.

If I was smart, I'd get the 10 page paper out of the way this weekend. But that's probably not going to happen.

Turning back to Peyton and Scar's table, I take their two outlines and stack them on-top of mine and pass them to the guy sitting in front of me.

As long as I can get as good of a grade on this as my bibliography, there's a chance I might still score an A. With a minus attached, of course. I don't know anyone who's just getting a regular A on this.

The creaking of the door opening draws mine and everyone else's attention. Callan strides in, completely unbothered by the stares as he sits down in the empty chair next to me.

I pull my chair in closer to the table, facing forward and dig inside my bag for a pencil and notebook.

"Mr. Goldsworthy, do you have a good reason for arriving late?" Professor Harper booms.

The rest of the class is so quiet, the only thing you can hear is her brown sandals as she walks down the carpeted path to him.

"The printer was tweaking."

"So am I correct in assuming you don't have the outline worth 10% of this assignment?" she asks, stopping at our table.

She narrows her eyes at Callan, but Callan doesn't flinch. "That's correct."

"There are no second chances, Mr. Goldsworthy. You've

already forfeited your 10% for your sources. The highest possible grade you can get on this assignment is 80%. You understand that if you don't turn in the paper before Thanksgiving break, you will not pass this class?"

"Yes," he answers cooly.

She stares down at him for a minute longer, the tension in the room rising at the silence. Her mouth opens and closes a few times before she clears her throat loudly. "Let's not waste any more class time." She whirls around and walks back to the front of the room. "We're starting chapter 21 today."

"Old bat. Any other teacher would've let me turn it in tomorrow. Stayed up all fucking night for nothing," he mutters angrily, digging in his bag and throwing a notebook on the table.

So he didn't lie. Amazing.

I scribble the date at the corner of my paper.

"Do you have a pencil?"

I hear him, but why should I give him what he needs? After all the trouble he's caused me. All of the threats and forcing me to…

God. I need to keep my mind on U.S. History.

Professor Harper brings up a projection of the Bill of Rights and I rush to write them down before it's gone. She never leaves enough time to copy all of anything in my nice handwriting, so my notes are always scribbles.

A rough hand touches my arm and I jump.

Turning my head slightly to the left, I find Callan's eyes fixed on me. "A pencil."

"Are you talking to me?" I whisper, touching my chest. I glance around the room. "I'm sure there are plenty of other people who have pencils. Maybe ask Scar behind me."

"Just give me a pencil," he whispers angrily. "I need to

pass this class so I can stay on the basketball team."

"And I need to get an A in this class, so shush," I whisper back and continue scribbling madly.

He leans down to my ear. "Give me a pencil, or I'll touch you right now."

My cheeks heat up and I glare at him. "You wouldn't."

He grunts. "Fine, have it your way. Let's make the class smell like you, princess."

I feel a tug through my belt loop as I get pulled closer to him.

My heart beats faster as I realize if either of the two guys turns around they'll see, but even more embarrassing, Peyton and Scar will see his hand doing something.

"Wait, wait. I'll get the pencil."

I twist down to look inside my bag and spy another mechanical pencil and put it directly on his notebook. "There."

He smirks and leans to my ear. "That's great. But you're too late."

Grabbing the pencil with one hand he takes it far out of my grasp and with his right, puts his hand inside my panties. "Spread your legs, princess."

I shake my head quickly.

His cold eyes meet mine, growing darker by the second. His warm hand goes to one leg, pushing it as far right as possible, and the other as far left. My thighs are nowhere near as strong as that one hand of his.

His eyes lock with mine and my breath stills in my chest as I feel his hand go into my underwear and touch my clit.

I throw a hand over my mouth as his finger circles it. God, I hate how good this feels.

He dips his finger down lower and his eyes widen slightly. "You're already wet, princess?"

Fuck. I clench my jaw together and look away. "Look at me," he whispers.

I ignore him only to feel him pinch my clit. "Mm," escapes my mouth. Just loud enough to get Professor Harper's attention.

"Do you have a question Ms. Karden?"

"No, ma'am," I say as I feel a finger slip inside me.

Out of the corner of my eye, I see him staring toward the front with a neutral expression.

She nods and continues prattling on about the Bill of Rights.

"Look. At. Me."

I slide my eyes toward him to find him looking down at me with a heated stare. His finger slowly slides back and out. The sudden emptiness causes me to gasp softly. Luckily my hand over my mouth is enough to muffle it.

He brings his finger to his mouth, moving it inside and then taking it out. A heated shiver goes through me and I focus back on my paper. Why does he always do that? Acting as if I'm the best thing he's ever tasted.

Next to me, I hear the sound of pencil against paper. I should be focused on mine, but now I'm hyper aware of him. His slow breathing, the smell of his soap, his arm only inches away from mine.

No. I need to stop. History. I am in history class.

I can't and shouldn't get used to this.

I slide my chair back to its usual spot and continue writing down notes.

I get to Art a minute before class starts. There's never any use in coming early. I settle down in the seat next to his and look up to the board for the next project. It's already been a day explaining to Scar and Peyton exactly what Callan was doing. Though it was obvious by their faces that they didn't believe a single word out of my mouth.

'Why else would he suck his finger like that?' Scar kept asking.

Sooo fucking embarrassing.

I was so sure he'd ditch again, but he's here even before I am.

"Okay class, your next project is on the board. You know the drill," Professor Schmidt announces. "Please read the board first before asking any questions. Last week's project is due today. Give it to me now if you haven't already. I'll pass back the ones to the people who did theirs early."

A drawing of a neighborhood in two point perspective. Ugh. I hated one point so much. This is going to suck. My eyes glaze over as I stare at the board until I hear a throat clear. "Mera."

I blink quickly and find Professor Schmidt standing next to our table.

He glances down at the papers in his hands. "I'm not sure what's going on. You usually do such great work."

I wouldn't call any of my work great. Honestly, I struggle through it and what comes out in the end is passable to turn in. This time it was relatively easy to chisel on the blackboard surface a picture of someone of interest. Sure it sucked because there's no second chance with chiseling. Once the white shows up, it's there. I chiseled Kit Harrington, and I enjoyed the hell out of it but–

He places my project in front of me and what I see is *not* Kit Harrington. In fact, I don't even know what it is.

"This is supposed to be Kit Harrington," I tell him,

moving my fingers over the chiseled marks. There's barely anything left of his gorgeous face.

It's all a mess of scratches all over. There's almost no black left in the paper at all.

"Someone messed it up," I yell, standing up and looking around. Everyone turns to look to see what all the noise is. Some annoyed, some unaware, some blank. But there was a smaller class last Wednesday, more than usual because of Halloween. I simply dropped my project off and left giving someone the perfect opportunity to fuck it up.

Professor Schmidt clears his throat. "Do you have any evidence of this, Mera?"

"Of course I do. I even took a picture when I was done because I loved it so much." I pull my phone out of my pocket and scroll through my pictures to find it.

"Here!" I thrust the phone into his hand and he squints down.

Nodding, he hands my phone to me. "That looks nothing like what you turned in. I'd say that's definitely a 28/30."

He turns to the rest of the class. "Who did it? Who messed with Mera's drawing?"

No one says a word, some looking at each other and others rolling their eyes.

"Well? Which of you was it?" I yell. "Which one of you bitches did it?"

"Now Mera," Professor Schmidt says. "Simmer down. I'll get to the bottom of this." He walks to the front of the class. "Everyone will get an F on this project too if no one fesses up. So who did it? I won't report you to the Dean this time."

What the fuck? No! The person who did this absolutely should be reported.

"It was him," a girl's voice says. "I saw him grab her project and go at it with his chisel."

I follow the pointed hand up front and see a buff guy with a buzz cut. His shoulders are so broad he has to be involved with some kind of sport.

"Mr. Mackenzie, is that true?"

He scoffs. "Fine. Yeah I did it. Why does she get to get away with murder? My team is suffering because of her and we still don't have a replacement captain. This was supposed to be our year."

In a flash, the seat next to me is suddenly empty and the body that was there is now up front, right in front of that guy's face.

"You don't mess with someone's art. Each piece, no matter how bad, takes effort and work. Creativity and time. You don't steal that away from anyone no matter what they've done."

He laughs. "Your brother is rolling in his grave, wherever the fuck his body is. I can't believe you're really standing up for this bi–"

The guy's head goes flying back as he gets punched into the guy sitting next to him. The guy scoots back letting the guy fall to the ground. Mackenzie struggles to get up, flailing his arms.

"Mr. Goldsworthy!" Professor Schmidt yells running over.

I cover my mouth as Callan kicks the guy once twice, twice, three times by the time Professor Schmidt reaches him, pulling him away. I get a glimpse of Callan's wild eyes as he looks around the classroom. "None of you get to decide that she's guilty." He points his bloodied thumb to his chest. "*I'm* the fucking judge, jury, and executioner. Remember that the next time any of you think of pulling shit like this."

My jaw drops open as he meets my eyes for a second. The darkness inside them makes me gulp worriedly.

"M-Mr. Goldsworthy, I'm afraid I'm going to have to send you to your father."

"That's fine." He goes up front and snatches a blank paper, comes back to his seat for his bag and leaves.

A buzzing in my head starts as Professor Schmidt clears his throat. "Mr. Mackenzie, feel free to go to the nurse's office."

I stare down at my ruined project and raise my hand. "Can I please go, Professor?" I'll just get a blank paper next class and turn it in on Monday.

Sighing, he rubs the back of his head. "Sure, it's the least I can do. I'll count you as here for this class."

I grab my bag, slinging it over my arm and take off. I need to know why he did that. But I never catch up to him, so I wait outside the administration building.

Ten minutes later, he comes out with his signature frown. "Hey."

He glances at me and moves past me.

"Why did you do that?"

He stops in his tracks and turns to look at me. "I think I already explained that pretty well. Art should never be destroyed by anyone's hands but the creator's. That's all there is to it."

"Well…" I grit my teeth, struggling to say the words that I owe him. "Thank you for that. I wanted to punch the guy myself. If I hadn't taken the picture, who knows if I would've gotten credit or not."

"Don't thank me."

He walks away, going the opposite direction of the fraternity, to the parking lot.

Where is he going?

Oh well. It's none of my business. At least I have an excuse to eat dinner early today.

People are pouring inside the dining hall when I get to the doors.

Tonight seems like a good night for Chinese, and it's evident other people think so too judging by the long line in front of the Chinese restaurant.

"Mera! Merrrraaa!"

Brandie?

I turn around just in time to feel an arm go around my shoulder. "Hey, what are you doing here? Art class get out early? Though I can't be surprised with how lax you said he is."

"No, he let me leave. Some guy trashed my project so I asked to leave early for…emotional distress."

She gasps and covers her mouth. "That's just horrible. Did he send him to the Dean? He better have."

"Nope."

She rolls her eyes. "He really is lax then."

"Callan punched him in the face though."

She raises an eyebrow. "What? I thought he hated your guts."

"He does." Well, he did. Maybe still does? I don't fucking know. He plays too many games with my mind. And those looks he gives me when his fingers are inside me. I wonder if he had that same look on his face the first time he did it. "He's just passionate about art."

She seems to accept that as she nods. "You're going to eat with us right?"

"Who's us?" Please let it just be Jamie and their boyfriends.

"Jamie, Emerson, Brett, Gemma, Ashlynn, Luella, and…"

At this point I just know it's coming so I finish her sentence. "Collette."

I've been avoiding her every time I see her in the food hall so I don't replicate what happened that first day. I've been doing great at it, until now.

"I think I'll pass. See, I have PTSD from the first day–" I start with a laugh.

"Yeah, I saw. You spilled that orange juice on her. That has to be all under the bridge by now though, don't you think?"

"Ha!" I laugh so hard my stomach starts to hurt. "That's funny. Collette *hates* me. She still thinks I'm responsible, just like Callan."

I make my order and wait by the sound counter for five minutes for it to come out. When it finally does, Brandie smiles widely. "Come on, let's go. I'm not taking no for an answer."

She grabs my arm and hauls me to the table. It's so hard saying no to her because she's always so helpful. And she deals with my nightmares without complaining about them. Once I finish eating I can leave too.

Collette glares as I approach the table. "Did you have to bring the klutz with you?"

"Coll, don't be mean," Brandie says with a pout, taking the chair with a tray in front of it.

"Congrats, klutz, my dinner is ruined," she spits.

I sigh. "I told you this was a bad idea."

Jamie peeks her head around Brett and Brandie. "Well, *I'm* glad to see you, Mera."

"Mera's cool," Emerson agrees.

Brett nods and smiles in my direction. "Yep."

"I guess if half the table disagrees..." Collette murmurs, annoyed by their responses.

"Ah, actually more than half," Gemma pipes up. "Mera, we haven't eaten together since that one day with those guys."

"You mean the assholes who were harassing you?" Seems like it just happened yesterday, but it really has been so long.

"Someone harassed you?" Collette asks, turning toward Gemma.

Gemma pushes her glasses up her nose and turns to me. "Luckily, Mera was there because I had no idea what to do...again."

Collette rolls her eyes. "I told you, just stand up for yourself. Tell them off. You don't need *her* to do it for you."

Gemma looks away from Collette, crossing her arms over her chest.

"Hey," I say, leaning forward to look at Gemma. She glances up at me. "It's okay to have friends stand up for you. What are friends for if they can't stand up for you against the assholes?"

I'm slowly starting to figure out this whole friend thing, and the way Collette talks to Gemma makes me uncomfortable for her.

"She's right, Gemma. If I was there I would've stood up for you, er, at least I would've tried," Luella says in a soft voice.

Ashlynn pats Gemma's arm. "They better be glad I wasn't there. In fact, hey, do you remember who it was?"

"It was so long ago, I have no clue," she says with a shrug.

I shove a piece of orange chicken in my mouth.

Ashlynn glances at me. "What about you? Do you remember?"

Swallowing quickly, I shake my head. "Nope, but if I see them again, I'll know right away. Assholes."

"Who's an asshole?" a voice says, coming around.

I glance behind me to find Noel with Tyrell and Vincent

at his side.

Turning back in my seat, I look up at Gemma who shakes her head quickly.

"Why are you guys clamming up now? I want to hear the juicy gossip too," Noel pulls a seat from a nearby empty table and drags it to my right, while Tyrell and Vincent do the same.

"Just haters bothering our little nerd," Collette says, patting Gemma's hand. "She's so quiet she's easy to pick on."

"It wasn't because of that," Gemma snaps, yanking her hand away. "It was because I'm fat and ugly."

Everyone grows uncomfortably quiet and I pick at the food on my plate, moving it around, unable to look at anyone else.

Collette breaks the long silence. "Gemma, I thought we talked about this. No negative talk. You look great the way you are."

Gemma's staring down at the food on her plate.

"I agree. Like I told you before, you're beautiful Gemma."

"How dare someone talk about my diamond like that," Noel says in a joking tone.

"Your *what?*" Collette shrieks.

Gemma looks mortified as she glances away from him.

It seems like he's not giving up on her any time soon. Jeez, I feel bad. She looks like she doesn't want to be anywhere near him.

Brandie swoons. "That's sooo sweet. Brett, why don't you call me your diamond?"

"But, I like baby better."

"That's so basic," she mumbles.

"But really, who was it, Gemma?" Noel asks in a firm tone.

It shocks me enough to make me glance at him

immediately. All laughter is gone from his eyes as he tilts his head and observes Gemma. "I probably know them. So, tell me."

She looks to her left at him. "I don't know. And if I did, there'd be no reason for me to tell you."

"My man, shot down all over again," Vincent says with a chuckle, clapping Noel on the back.

Noel moves his shoulder, throwing his arm off. "Shut the hell up and speak for yourself." He gets out of the chair and storms off.

"Ouch," Emerson says, covering his mouth.

Ashlynn bursts out laughing.

Vincent glares at her clenching his fists. "Whatever. Let's go, Ty."

Tyrell nods as Vincent gets up, following after Noel.

"Hey," Tyrell says, stopping near me. My eyes widen since he never approaches me. His blue eyes are a lighter shade than Callan's, but that's not all. Tyrell's aren't cold, but they're empty. I find that more frightening. "How did Callan get suspended? He won't tell us, but I heard from someone else that it has something to do with you. Coach is going to be furious tomorrow when he doesn't show up for practice."

"He did?" Collette asks. "What did you do, klutz?"

"It wasn't my fault. Some guy trashed my art work and Callan got angry and beat the guy up."

Tyrell nods. "He does take art seriously. What a shame our captain won't be there though. Thanks for letting me know. Take care." His eyes glance to the end of the table. I don't have to look to know he's looking at Luella.

He turns around and leaves.

"What the fuck is going on between you and Callan?" Collette asks.

I lock eyes with her. "Nothing."

"Don't lie to me. He fucked you didn't he? Ugh, what's wrong with him? He could sleep with literally anyone else!"

"No. We did not." It sounds convincing to me. Too bad Callan practically insinuated that we did himself.

I shovel the remainder of my cold food in my mouth. I've had enough of this for the day. And it's been a long day.

After saying goodbye to everyone, sans Collette, I walk outside, colliding with someone immediately turning the corner to the doors. It's dark only in this area so it's easy to run into someone if you aren't paying attention.

"Oh sor–" the girl starts, wincing.

I blurt, "It's my bad. I was in a hurry."

She steps forward out of the shadows and into the light outside the dining hall.

Oh I know her. She's Kori, Jamie's roommate.

She walks several feet around me, like I have some kind of contagious disease and she doesn't want to catch it. "Whatever, just stay away from me."

Since I've already had enough of today, I turn around quickly and catch up to her right before she goes inside. "What's your problem with me?"

She pauses as a slow smile spreads across her face. "You kept terrible company and I want nothing to do with people like you. Satisfied?"

"Kept as in Heath?"

Her eyes sparkle cruelly. "You're probably better off now. Consider yourself lucky you got away."

"What the hell does that mean?" I ask, crossing my arms.

She shrugs. "Not my job to educate you. Do your own digging." With that, she walks through the door leaving me completely puzzled.

Just what did Heath do to her?

Maybe Callan knows.

CHAPTER TWELVE

Callan

Thanksgiving break. I'll finally have a fucking break next week after running around like a chicken with its head cut off.

President duties, fraternity duties, school, following leads, and not to mention being the captain of the basketball team.

Miraculously, I'm managing to pass all my classes. They aren't the perfect grades Dad expects like Heath's, but I think searching for my brother is worth more than my college experience. I only have one brother after all.

Juggling all this shit isn't easy.

When I walk into history Wednesday morning after missing the last three classes, I'm ready for another boring lecture from Professor Harper. As I make my way to my seat,

I can't help but notice the different colored folders on every student's table in attendance.

Why do they–

Oh fuck.

I collapse in my chair and run my hand over my face, stopping at my chin.

How could I fucking forget? That long ass paper is due today and I didn't even start it. I pushed it off, expecting I'd get to it some point later, but later came too fucking quickly.

I'm screwed. My dad is going to kill me.

I jam my fist into my forehead. Come on, think. You're Callan Goldsworthy. You can get out of this. Come up with an excuse, any excuse.

Fraternity meeting took up a lot of time. I was setting up for the Christmas charity event. But why would she give me a pass when she knows I haven't even shown up to class?

I rub the bridge of my nose.

My first F in college and it's only the first semester.

I glance to my right at Wil's empty seat. Maybe I won't be the only one failing.

"Class will begin in one minute. Everyone start passing your folders to the front."

The hardness of a plastic folder nudges against my back. I turn around quickly to find Red handing me a clear folder and Tall Boy handing me a green one.

I grab the both of them and pass them to the guy in front of me. I turn back around to them. "Where's Wil?" I bark.

Red tilts her head to the left. "You hear something Peyton?"

Tall Boy taps his chin a few times and shakes his head. "No. Not a sound."

"Oh, fuck you guys," I snap, and turn back around in my seat.

THE PRINCESS AND THE BULLY

Red snickers and Tall Boy whispers something.

"Class will now–"

Suddenly, the sound of the door opening makes Professor Harper pause.

A flash of bright blonde hair moves quickly inside and past me.

"Right on time, Ms. Karden. Please hand in your folder."

Wil smiles broadly. "Of course, Professor."

She bends down and picks a pink folder out, plopping it on her desk and passes it forward.

I guess I'm failing alone then. Of course she'd turn hers in.

I run a hand down the back of my hair as I watch the stack of folders get picked up by the professor starting on the left.

My jaw drops as she starts counting them. Fuck! Why is she counting? Why can't she just take them and put them on her fucking desk.

Grinding my teeth, I clench my fist under the table.

"You look panicked, Callan."

As my name leaves her lips, I turn to glance at her.

She raises an eyebrow. "You didn't do your paper, did you?"

I don't respond, crossing my arms and leaning back in my chair. Of course she wants to fucking rub it in. I think after class we'll play another game.

Professor Harper booms, "So far everyone's turned theirs in. Great job, class."

She moves over to the next row. I'll be the odd one fucking out and she'll call me out.

"Ask me nicely," she whispers.

My eyes widen as I turn my head in her direction. "What?"

She pulls her bag off the ground, sitting it on her lap between the table and her body. The moment she does, I spot a dark blue folder. She moves a few things away and touches the top of it.

No fucking way there's a paper in that folder.

"I finished mine last weekend, and I had some time and figured that you probably weren't going to do yours. You didn't even do the outline or turn in your sources. And don't worry, I made sure it sounds like someone else wrote it."

Fuck. If I accept this, my worries are over.

"Time is running out. Better hurry."

I look up to see Professor Harper in front of the row to the left of ours.

Is it worth my pride to ask the girl who might be partially or fully responsible for my brother's death for a favor?

No. I don't think it is.

I'll sink on my own. It's not like it hasn't fucking happened before.

But I'll lose my spot on the basketball team.

"No."

She sighs, setting her bag on the floor. "Fine."

Plop.

She sets the folder on the table right in front of me.

"You're really giving this to me, just like that?" I ask, touching the edges of it. "I didn't even do what you wanted, princess."

"Despite the fact that you're a major asshole and I hate you for everything you put me through, I do owe you. You punched that guy in the face for me remember? And you got suspended." Her eyes meet mine for a second before she turns back to the front. "Just know this is a one time thing."

I open my mouth to respond that I don't need her pity

when I hear Professor Harper call out, "Callan, is that your folder? Pass it up already."

Wil keeps looking straight ahead with a blank face.

What will it look like if I put it away in my bag or even hand it back to her?

No. I'm stuck with passing it up front. And...I do need to stay on the team. Sports have always helped keep my anger at bay.

The guy in front of me holds his hand out.

After placing it in his hand, Wil lowers her voice, "Now we're even."

I punched a guy in the face, and I didn't even do it for her. But she spent hours saving my ass. How can I call that even? No. It bothers the hell out of me but I owe *her* now.

After class, I check my phone notifications as I leave the building. Guys messing around in the group chat. Missed call from my dad? And a notification from BookSmarter?

I open the BookSmarter app to a message that flashes on screen saying 'Your petition has been submitted. Please wait for the result.'

Wait. *What?*

I click on it, finding it locked at 5k signatures achieved at the top.

Shit.

The board will be meeting about this soon then. I still haven't found the answers I need. She can't go anywhere.

"I hope you're happy."

Whirling around, I find Wil with teary eyes glaring at me. She swipes a finger at the corner of her eye.

"I don't deserve to be expelled. I didn't do anything. If anything, my life is being threatened!" she yells, her lips quivering as she covers her face.

Is she talking about what ever happened on the lake on Halloween?

People around us slow to a stop at her outburst. Nosy fucks.

"Let's talk somewhere private," I murmur, grabbing her by the arm and dragging her away.

Her eyes widen. "No!" she tries to tug her arm out of my grasp. "I don't want to talk to you or do *that—*"

"Shut up, Wil!" I scream, gripping her arm tighter. I stare into her tear-filled eyes. In a lower tone, I whisper. "We're just going to talk. Got it?"

Without waiting for a response I continue on, taking her to the basement, locking the door behind us.

This time, I flip the light on, letting her go and lead the way to the couch. She sits at the opposite end, as far away from me as possible.

"Let's get one thing straight," I start, "I did not start that petition."

She snorts. "Don't fucking lie Callan. Your name is at the top and it's connected to your BookSmarter account." She shakes her head, crossing her arms and leaning into the arm of the couch. "You must really think I'm stupid."

"I didn't fucking do it, okay?" I still haven't figured out how they hacked my fucking account. "Someone hacked my account and made it."

She looks at me with disbelieving eyes.

"Why would I make a petition that might possibly get you expelled when you're the one and only lead behind my brother's disappearance? Every tip I've gotten from people saying they've spotted him somewhere or his car have been dead ones. The memory of that night is somewhere in your head, and I need it."

She uncrosses her arms and clasps her hands together.

"You should've told me."

"How would I know that petition would actually make it to five thousand? Shit is hard to do. Besides, you don't tell me shit right away. You never even told me how you ended up with Silverstone."

A small smile forms on her lips. "Yeah. I know you hate the guy for whatever reason, but I like him."

A strange heat moves up my chest as I digest those words. "You what?"

"I mean, I almost feel like we're friends. Though he does sort of act like he's interested, I'm not into him like that but he's fun to talk to."

Hearing those words eases this annoying feeling of rage. "You don't want to be friends with him," I mutter, unclenching my fists at my sides.

"He saved my life. I was drowning. Someone...tried to kill me."

The rage returns at full force like a flash. "Who?" I bark, turning her chin to meet my eyes. "What did they look like?"

Her lips flatten as something like pain flashes in her eyes. "Like you. They were dressed like you, Callan. I thought *you* were drowning me."

I let go like I've been burned and turn away.

Of all the things I would ever do to her, I would never ever drown her. The feeling of the water seeping into every fiber of your being. The burn in your lungs as you suffer without oxygen. The light leaving you with only the darkness.

No.

I lock eyes with hers. "I wouldn't do that. I might have choked you that night, but that's as far as I took it. After I left you there I went back to AAA with my friends."

"They must have grabbed one of the masks you guys left

behind. But Kane saved me. The guy swam off and ran for it when he saw him."

For once, Silverstone was useful for something. But this begs the question. "Is there anything else you haven't told me?"

She opens her mouth and closes it a few times. There's something she isn't saying.

"I remembered something recently. The night before, you know, the night of the third round of the hazing, I found bruises all over Heath's abdomen."

What the fuck? Bruises?

"Maybe they were from football. They started practice as soon as school began."

"No," she insists. "These were a deep purple color and there was something else. A weird symbol was bruised into him. Almost like a fork, but it was super tiny. I thought maybe you might have beat him."

Me? Beat Heath? "I would've been just as bruised and you would've seen them on my body. Neither of us win when we fight each other." Could he have gotten into a fight with someone else?

She covers her mouth. "Maybe it was the person who made him disappear."

Could be. I need to ask around and see if someone else might've noticed it too. A small fork symbol. What could that even mean?

"Anyway, do you know where the meeting is going to be? I need to go so I can plead my case. I refuse to be expelled."

"They don't allow anyone else in the meeting besides board members, so no, you can't come." I think I have a plan and I can't let her interfere in it. I've learned a lot about how this college works. Not because I wanted to. This might be the one time that information is useful.

I stand up off the couch and move out of the way. "Let's go. I have a lot of shit to do."

Her lips flatten as she gets up, moving past me quickly.

I grab her arm before she's out of my reach. "Hey." She glances up at me with worried eyes. "You aren't going anywhere so don't worry about it. I still need my answers."

Her expression doesn't change, in fact there's something else in her eyes. Something I've seen reflected back in my own in the mirror many times. Hopelessness.

My stomach twists into knots and loosen my grip. Why am I filled with the need to reassure her that she isn't going anywhere?

I push it away, letting go of her arm, and eventually hearing the door close.

My plan will work.

I move my hair to the side and glance at myself in the mirror before strolling in. There's no one at the front or side desks to stop me. All of the lights are dimmed because there's no one here.

It's the first technical day of vacation. Sunday. Campus is pretty empty and all of the teachers, assistants, and administration are gone.

The only people in the building are in one of the conference rooms.

Striding down the hall at a leisurely pace, I glance through the glass doors of each one, looking for the group of stuck-up assholes. Stopping at the last one, conference room number five, I spot twelve heads. They're all here then. All except for one.

I cover my mouth to stop the smile from spreading across

my face. I can't afford to laugh. I need to keep a straight face.

Pulling open the glass door, I step inside and maintain an air of seriousness around me.

Murmurs fill the room as they talk amongst each other, glancing at me. The murmurs stop when I take the spot at the head of the table.

"With all due respect, Callan, that spot is for the dean," one of the ladies say.

"I understand that perfectly, but he isn't here." For the life of me, I can never remember the names of these people. They've come over our house so many times, but I can only really remember six of them.

"Callan, son, where's your father?" a voice I know very well asks.

Strong dark brows, heavyset, and dark blue eyes. Tyrell's father, the newest member of the board.

I shrug, "I don't know Mr. Sonnenfeld. I was told that I needed to come and stand in for him until he gets here. He doesn't want this meeting to take up any more of his time than it needs to. So, gentlemen, ladies, please vote on the expulsion of Ms. Karden."

They all look at each other, chattering loud.

"Callan, I don't think we should vote without talking about this," Mr. Hardington blurts.

Noel's father pushes his glasses up his face, looking ever the nerdy pharmacist.

"Mr. Hardington, when my dad does show up, I believe he'll love to see that we used our time here wisely. You all are aware of my brother's disappearance, I assume?" Looking around at all of them, most people nod.

"We're so sorry for your loss," Mrs. Hardington says, patting my hand.

Everyone else voices their agreement.

I force a few tears to my eyes. "Thank you. All of you. So you know exactly what she might've done to my brother. Everyone seems to know the circumstances so there's no need to not vote. She deserves to suffer for causing my family pain. Let's vote."

They nod, taking in my words, and grabbing the pencil and paper from the center of the table.

A sly smile forms on my lips as I watch them write their answer down and place it back in the center.

As soon as they're done, I motion for the stack to be passed down.

"Your father will be very pleased," Mr. Iverson says.

Luella's father with his giant blond beard looks ecstatically at the pile.

I don't have to read these to know they all voted yes for her expulsion. It'd shock the hell out of me if there was even a single no.

"He would be." I pick the first piece of paper up and unfold it. "Yes," I announce.

"Wait, Callan, what are you doing?" Mr. Hardington asks.

"Reading the votes of course," I say, pulling the next one open.

He stands up quickly, adamantly hitting his hands against the table. "But you can't do that!"

"I agree, Callan." Mrs. Hardington stands up next to her husband. "We only read them once the dean is ready to vote."

"But he is," I respond darkly. "These votes are final once they've been passed to the person sitting in this chair. My father isn't here, and I don't think he's coming. You see, his car had a little trouble."

Okay, I might have pulled a few wires out with Tyrell's help. So damn lucky to have a friend who knows so much about cars.

"And his phone is broken," I say in an over the top sad voice.

"I just talked to him a few hours ago," Mr. Iverson yells.

"Of course you did, Mr. Inverson. It's such a shame that electronics can stop working so fast. He'll order a new one soon, I promise you, but unfortunately that won't help him right now and his vote needs to be cast."

"You can't do that!" Mr. Sonnefeld shouts.

I chuckle and straighten my tie. "The rules clearly state that if the dean does not show up to cast his vote, a family member can stand in for him and vote in his stead. I'm a family member, am I not?"

"Why are you doing this, Callan?" Mr. Browning asks.

Ashlynn's father is the only one who doesn't look peeved.

"I'm simply fulfilling my duty so we can close this petition."

He seems to be satisfied with that answer as he nods. "Fine."

Everyone else whispers to themselves as I look through, opening every vote

All of them say yes as I suspected.

"Let the verdict be known that this is a no," I say smoothly.

Everyone erupts, pushing the room into chaos.

"That is not the way your father would have voted," Mr. Hardington says crossly.

"Maybe not," I reply, playing dumb. "But there's nothing you or anyone else can do now. The dean has the final say whether all the votes are yes or no. Once the decision has been made, it can not be overturned and the petition can not be repeated. Wilhelmera stays."

Some of them are slack jawed and some of them are yelling questions, but I don't have to answer anything. The only thing I have to do is throw all of these votes in the trash and write the outcome on this petition.

I pop the cap of the pen off with my mouth and scribble 'no' in the petition decision spot in the top right corner of the paper. Grabbing my phone from my jacket pocket, I snap a pic of the petition in case they decide to try not to file it.

"I hope you all understand, I only voted this way because once she's out of the country, there's only so much we can do. She's responsible somehow, I know it in my gut." As those words leave my mouth, I'm left with a bitter taste. Especially when they all clap. But why? "Nice to see all of you again. Have a good holiday." A weight is lifted off my shoulders as I walk out those glass doors and get back in my car.

I glance down at my father's phone in the cupholder and finally let myself laugh. I laugh until I almost cry thinking of my father's face when his car broke down on his way here. And when I took his phone and peeled off? Fucking priceless.

If everything could work out for me like this, I'd be set.

I scroll through my phone and find her name, hesitating with my finger hovering above it.

I can almost hear her firm tone if she were to answer and her stubbornly saying she doesn't want to talk to me. I can almost picture how she'll sigh with relief at hearing that she won't be expelled. A slow smile spreads across my face at the thought.

No.

My brother's face flashes in my head and anger slowly pushes to the surface again.

I need to stay focused. Stop thinking about her.

I'll let her read the verdict in the email.

CHAPTER THIRTEEN

Mera

I haven't had a good night's sleep since Tuesday night. It's Monday. They should've had the meeting by now. I should've heard something.

God, I hate being kept waiting.

Just give me the bad news already.

The only thing I got was an email telling me the decision on the petition would be emailed.

I haven't gotten any notes since Saturday, so whoever's been sending them is gone with their family on Thanksgiving break. I don't know how to feel about that.

Suddenly, I feel a vibration on my bed and find my phone ringing. It's Mother.

I take a deep breath and press accept.

"Mera, have you heard the decision yet?"

"No," I respond slowly. "Did they call you with it?"

She sighs heavily. "No. But I do know that it won't be the answer either of us were hoping to get. I spent all day Friday and Saturday talking to the board. Every single member was adamant that their vote would be no."

No.

"They could've changed their mind. They know I'm a princess."

"That doesn't matter, Mera. I couldn't bring myself to call Antoure. I think you should start packing your bag."

My breath stills in my chest.

"Please, Mother. Let me come home."

"No," she says firmly. "I told you not to screw this up. I told you if something happened you'd be on your own in the U.S., and you will. If their decision is to expel you, we'll block all your cards and you'll be on the street until you figure out something. You won't be coming home until four years are up, regardless if you're in school or not."

"But Mom. People know who I am. What if something happens to me?"

"You should've thought about this more. I told you not to drink. You even walked around the school in nothing but your underwear! You enjoy embarrassing us."

"That wasn't my fault!"

She completely ignores me and continues on, "I told you to focus on your classes. You didn't have to get involved with that boy. I realize that old friendships are hard to break but–"

"I just wanted to have fun for my first sorority party. You act like I wanted this to happen," I exclaim.

"You just don't make good decisions, Mera. Cate has never gotten in trouble during her time in college–"

"Stop!" I yell. "I don't want to hear about Cate!"

There's a moment of silence. "Fine. Call me when you get the verdict."

"As if you care," I scream and hang up.

After I hang up, I stare at the phone, waiting to see if her name pops up again. But it doesn't. She really doesn't care.

Father never sticks up for me so he must be just as disappointed.

That's all I ever do. Disappoint them.

The tightening feeling starts again. When I feel like I can't breathe. I tug at the collar of my t-shirt and lay back.

Everything is so quiet. I wish Brandie and Jamie were here. There's no one else in the sorority but me. Peyton and Scarlett have gone home for the holidays too.

I need to eat something to make myself feel better.

Running down the stairs, I go to the kitchen and pull out a few vanilla ice cream cones with chocolate encrusted from the freezer and eat them at lightning speed.

Ding ding.

What's that?

Ding ding.

It sounds again.

Is that a doorbell? Our doorbell?

I've been here for three months and I've never heard it before. The door is always open.

But who could that be? Did someone order something?

I rush to the door, opening it to find a mess of orange hair. Why the hell didn't I look through the side window first?

"Hi!" Ginger says brightly.

I glance behind her and raise an eyebrow. "Hi?"

"I just came to tell you that you're going to be expelled."

"How do you know?" I ask, feeling a panic rise from my chest.

"My dad is on the board. He told me every single member voted for you to be expelled."

My stomach drops. No. She can't be right.

"The funniest thing is, the dean didn't even vote. Callan was the final vote. Somehow he showed up in place of his father and told everyone in the meeting that you're the reason Heath is dead."

What?

"Wait, I thought…"

She pokes her bottom lip out. "Oh you thought, didn't you? You thought Callan paying you extra attention meant something. You thought he'd help you get out of this? I thought you were stupid before, but you're dumber than a box of rocks if you thought Callan doing all of that meant something." She starts cackling and the sound grates on my nerves as every second goes by.

"Go fuck yourself, Ginger."

"Oh don't get so upset, princess," she says in a baby voice. "Truth is, you don't have any friends at all. Every person I've seen you with signed that petition. Even our sorority officers. Gemma, Ashlynn, Luella, and of course Collette signed."

My stomach starts to twist angrily and I gasp as my chest tightens.

"Oh, you didn't know? Your roommate and her friend Jamie signed it too. But the most priceless thing is those first two bozos you were with. Peyton and Scarlett, right? They were the ones that put the petition at five thousand. Their votes were the last two!" She laughs loudly. Every laugh from her mouth sounds fainter and fainter.

The blood in my veins is rushing to my head so quickly and I can't deal. Gasping, I clutch my chest.

"Pathetic. You're absolutely pathetic. Anyway, I just

wanted to tell you the good news. Callan isn't the only one who played a great game with you. Enjoy the plane ride home, princess."

With blurry eyes, I see the orange in my vision leave. Stumbling backward quickly, I close the door and collapse against it.

I breathe quickly and deeply, clutching my head at the rising headache.

I should've known not to trust or believe in anyone. Blinking slowly, I let the tears fall down my face. Before I came here, I was fine not having friends. Now, I feel completely empty and used. I was fooled real well. I guess I can't sense betrayal as easily as I thought.

Slowly, I walk up the stairs back to my room. I grab my phone and call my friends, but neither of them answers. Some of them sending me straight to voicemail. I just need one of them to answer. Just one.

I wait a while for either of them to call me back, but none do. They must be busy with their families.

Maybe Ginger was bullshitting me about them signing it. I shouldn't just take her at her word. In lightning speed, I log onto Booksmarter and find the petition. There's a lock on it now of course, but every single name is listed.

Hours later, I've gone through every single name and my eyes are burning from looking at my screen for so long. Sure enough, they're all there. Peyton and Scarlett

I sit like that on my bed until the sunset seeps through my blinds.

I guess the only real person I could count on is dead. And he's not coming back.

My parents are disappointed. My sister hasn't called me once.

My friends secretly despise me. I was wrong in thinking

they'd overlook what I said when I was drunk on those videos. I was wrong to think I could get a new start.

Maybe I don't deserve a new start at all.

Maybe…I should give the person writing the notes what they want.

The moment I think about it, that thought is stuck in my brain.

In a flash, I strip off my clothes leaving me in my underwear. I turn my phone off and leave it on the nightstand.

The walk to the lake is a short one because I barely think about it.

It's perfect because I almost died here almost a month ago. This time there's no Kane to save me. He's with his family. Everyone is.

The campus is a ghost town. I don't see one soul on my way to the lake.

And when I get there, it's peaceful. Nothing but the sound of the animals hiding in the bushes. The occasional bird or two. The smell of the lake water fills my lungs with every deep breath.

This is a pretty place to go.

Strolling around the perimeter, I look for a big rock that's still possible for me to carry.

It takes a while, but I eventually find one and start back to the other side of the lake. If I go in on the side that's shallow, I might lose my nerve. I need to go off the deep end.

I step up to the dock and slowly make my way across the rotting wood to the end.

One jump and keep ahold of the rock. A few minutes of pain and this will all be over.

My parents won't have to feel disappointed. My friends

won't have to lie. My sister won't have to worry about her bratty sister.

Everyone will be better off.

It only takes a few steps.

Squeezing my eyes shut, I take a deep breath, clutch the rock to my chest in my arms tightly and take a running start until I drop into the water.

The temperature is overwhelmingly cold. Colder than it was that night. Then again, the temperature outside is colder than it was on Halloween. It's so close to winter.

Oh. I'll miss my favorite holiday, Christmas.

I'd be homeless though, so I guess that really doesn't matter.

This is the right decision.

It feels like my body is sinking faster, but I don't want to open my eyes to check. I don't want to see the vastness of the water in front of me. I don't want to see the leaves, branches, and other debris. But it doesn't take away from feeling all of it brushing against my skin.

All of a sudden, I realize I've run out of air.

This is it. I open my mouth and let the water rush in. The water is freezing cold in my chest yet my lungs are on fire. I can't hold the rock anymore.

I let it go, and feel the whoosh of the water as it sinks down past me.

Please let this be enough to end this.

All of a sudden, something grabs me around my waist, making me pop my eyes open. My hair falls in front of my face as I'm pulled backwards.

No.

Reaching down, I feel a strong, toned arm.

No, I don't want to be saved! I want to yell.

But it's too late. The water gets lighter until my head

breaks the surface. Coughing hard, I expel all of the water that built up in my lungs. Fuck, that hurts. The disorienting feeling of seeing the now dark forest around me instead of the silent water makes my head feel dizzy.

But who would even be around to save me?

The arm doesn't let go all the way until we're on the shallow end, dragging me to the rocky shore.

My body shakes as I cough and cough, little bits of water escaping every time.

After taking a few deep breaths, I finally turn around to face my unwanted savior.

"Callan? Why would you?"

He crouches down next to me, getting up in my face. "Why would *you*?" His brows are furrowed and there's a scary rage in his normally emotionless eyes. One that's threatening to burn me.

"That's none of your business! You had no right to do this."

"No right?" He grabs my chin. "I have every right. You don't get to die, Wil."

He lets go and runs his hand over the back of his sopping hair. "Fuck! You have no idea how much that took. I…" He breathes deeply, inhaling and exhaling quickly and pacing around.

I glance down to find he's still wearing his shoes. My eyes travel up to his clothes sticking to him. Especially his short sleeved shirt.

"Why would you try and do that? Tell me right fucking now."

My eyes start to fill with tears. "I was so close," I murmur.

His eyes darken. "You're never coming to this lake, ever again," he says in a threatening tone. "And you're not going to die any time soon. Whatever is going on, it can't be so bad that you'd just want to end it all. Where's the fight in you Wil? That stubbornness in you. I know it's there because you use it against me all the time!"

Every single word he says is a shot to my heart. I don't want to hear him talk any more.

I use my hands to push myself off the ground and start walking back to the sorority. I'll just have to do this another day when he isn't around.

"Are you listening to me?" he yells.

Hard arms circle my body and I feel myself being lifted off the ground.

"Let me go!" I shriek.

"No. Not until you listen to me." Defeated, I let myself lay across his shoulder with his hand on my ass.

He brings me straight to the sorority keeping one hand firmly locked around my wrist. He grabs one of my bags and starts tossing clothes in before moving to the bathroom and forcing me to point out my toothbrush. He tosses that in along with my hairbrush and makeup bag. "If you need anything else, speak now."

"My phone."

With a grunt, he grabs my phone and tosses it to me and finally grabs my bag in his hand. He forces me out the front door, locking it behind us.

He leads me out of Sorority Row to Fraternity Row and stops in front of AAA where his Lambo is parked.

He shoves me in the passenger side and tosses my bag on my lap. After he gets in, he starts the car. His signature scowl is once again on his face as we take off.

I stare out at the road ahead of us, watching as he gets on the highway, oh wait, freeway. I don't know where we're going, but California at night on the road is so different from

Kardenia. The lights are glittering and the rushing of the vehicles are hypnotizing.

Callan zips in and out of lanes, coming extremely close to clipping numerous cars. I clutch the door, hanging on for dear life until he finally exits the freeway.

He zips down a few streets with tall modern looking buildings until he stops in front of a gate. He hits the buzzer and a voice comes on. "Mr. Goldsworthy, good to see you."

Callan grunts in response and zooms in the moment the gate is fully opened.

In the blink of an eye we go up a hill and around, passing mansions as we go, until he pulls into the driveway of one of them.

It's like a mini castle.

He yanks me out and I haul my bag along with me. The whole house is glass and dark wood. The tile I step on is a beautiful marble, but I don't have much time to admire any of this because I'm being dragged up the stairs, of which there are no railings, and to the first door on the right.

The moment I walk in, I spot the huge bed agains the far wall.

"Leave your bag on the ground."

"Your house is pretty nice."

He sighs. "I didn't bring you here to show you my house. We need to talk about what happened."

"What's there to talk about? You ruined it."

"Of course I ruined it!" he explodes. "You're in that much pain that you felt the need to end it?"

Changing the subject, I eye my bag. I feel gross. I can't stay in this underwear. "Can I change?"

His mouth thins. "Fine. Hurry it up."

I grab my bag off the ground and move to the other side

of the room where it looks like the entrance to the bathroom is.

He moves quickly, blocking me from getting any further. "No, you'll take it off here."

My face heats up and he smirks. "It's nothing I haven't seen before."

Of course. Why would I think he would let me go off and change. He loves to watch me squirm.

I squeeze my eyes shut and pull off my underwear and bend down to find a shirt and another pair of underwear and shorts.

"You know, I brought you here to talk, but maybe we'll do something else too." I glance over my shoulder to find him perched at the end of his bed, eyes planted right on me, specifically, what's between my legs.

Heat starts pooling in my stomach so I rush like a madwoman to find any pair of panties and throw them on, and then any old shirt.

My face is on fire as I flop next to him.

There's a long pause. I don't want to be the one to break it so I stay quiet. I'm fine with not telling him anything. "Talk to me, Wil."

"I just realized that the world would be better off without me. My parents should've stopped after Cate."

"Fuck off with that. If they didn't care they wouldn't have shipped you here. And your sister cares I'm sure."

I wish he'd just stop talking. "No. In fact, I haven't talked to her since the night of the third round of hazing. I've left numerous messages and they've piled up to the point that I can't even leave any anymore."

He frowns. "Don't you find that strange?"

"She's in her last year of college and attending all of those fancy events with my parents. She's probably up to her ears in work. She can't even check on me for one minute."

"Fine. Let's just say they don't, but what about Tall Boy and Red?"

"What the..." a laugh escapes my mouth as I realize he means Scarlett and Peyton. Slowly it dies in my throat as I remember exactly why I know they don't really care about me.

"Did you look at the names on your petition?"

He groans. "I told you I didn't fucking make it. Why would I look at it?"

"Because their names are the last two on the list. They fucking signed it!" I cover my face with my hands. "I thought they were my friends."

He's quiet for a moment. "Well, you have that roommate of yours, Brandie right? And Jamie?"

"They signed it too."

In a low tone, he says, "Impossible."

"Check it yourself if you don't believe me. Enjoy those few hours it takes to go through all those names. Even Gemma, Ashlynn, and Luella signed it. Not that we're close but..."

He grunts. "Collette might have forced them to. They follow her lead, after all. But that doesn't mean they hate you. It doesn't mean you should kill yourself."

I take a deep breath and blurt, "I'm out okay. I've been expelled. Whatever you did or tried to do, whatever. It didn't work."

"The fuck are you talking about?" he says in a scary low tone, so low that I have to look away from him.

"No." He grabs my chin and forces me to look into his eyes. "Talk. Now." His eyes are blazing with anger again.

"I heard from a source—" I start.

"Not a fucking reliable one," he inserts.

"–That every board member voted yes on me being expelled." He lets go of my chin and my heart thunders in my chest.

"Okay, partially reliable, but it doesn't matter because the most important vote said no."

"What do you mean?" I say, feeling a surge of hope at his words.

"My plan worked perfectly, princess. I fucked with my dad's car and stole his phone. He wasn't able to get to the meeting. I stood in for him and voted no. His vote can overrule every other vote, and that's exactly what happened."

I cover my mouth as I muffle the gasp, but I can't stop the tears of relief from welling in my eyes.

"There's no one in the office this week so you won't get the decision until they're back. But you're not going anywhere."

"Oh my God," I murmur. I launch myself forward and grab Callan, hugging his arm. "Thank you, thank you!" Instantly, I feel the warmth emanating from his body. I hate how comforting it is.

Shit, I almost ended it all and I didn't even need to. So what if I have friends, I still have my spot at the university. I still have a chance to prove to my parents that I can be more than a party princess.

He clears his throat. "Now that you know that, are you still pissed that I saved your ass?"

"No. I'm…very grateful. Thank you, truly."

His eyes lock with mine as he grabs me by the throat, pulling me in. His eyes darken as our I stop only inches away from his lips. "Never do that again. Do you understand me?"

Nodding quickly, I glance away, but he squeezes so tightly, I know he wants me to keep looking at him. His grip loosens only slightly. "Say it. I need to hear it, Wil. You scared the shit out of me. I was at the far end of the lake when I saw you run off the dock."

"I won't," I say, in a raspy tone.

He lets go and something flashes in his eyes and then his lips are on mine, for the first time since the basement.

They're soft and threatening at the same time. Threatening to consume everything in me as his tongue dives past my lips. As our tongues move together, heat pools between my legs and I moan softly at the sudden need I feel.

Every time he touched me, this is what was missing. His lips on mine. I hate that I need this from him.

Suddenly, the warmth of his lips and tongue are gone. His eyes darken as he presses my forehead to his. "Stay here with me so I can keep an eye on you. Just until break is over."

"Aren't you going to have Thanksgiving with your family?"

"No," he says in a firm tone. "It won't feel right without Heath."

Like the cold water of the lake, bringing Heath up changes him. His gaze is cold as he backs up and takes off his still wet shirt and pants.

The rest of the night, we eat pizza in silence as he flips through the channels on his eighty inch TV mounted on the wall. After a while, it sounds so far away, I know I'm tired. His silk sheets are identical to the ones at home so I fall asleep the moment I cover myself with it.

Faintly, it must be in my dreams, I feel a pair of lips press against my forehead and a whisper of my name. "Wilhelmera."

CHAPTER FOURTEEN

Callan

I wake up to the sound of a deafening cough in my ear. Blinking slowly, I peer over to find a moving lump under the covers.

I rub my hand over my face and clear the sleepiness from my throat. "What're you doing princess?"

Her voice is muffled when she responds so I yank the covers off of her.

"No!" she screams, trying to grab the sheets and blanket to pull back over her. I keep a firm enough grip that she isn't able to do so.

"What's the big..." I start and notice her face. Puffy red eyes, snot leaking from her nose, and her normally pink lips are pale. "Are you sick?"

She sniffles. "Yes, and I look like a train wreck." Her

hands go up to her hair as she goes to fix the messy bun from last night.

"You just look absolutely fucking miserable, actually. But that's what happens when you decide to go swimming in cold lake water on a chilly overcast day. Learned your lesson yet, princess?"

She groans and sniffles. "Just shut up and point me in the direction of the medicine cabinet."

"Just stay put, okay? It'll be faster if I go get it." I lean over to my night stand and toss her the box of tissues. "Blow your nose. That sniffling is driving me nuts."

She glares and sniffles once, twice, three times on purpose with a grin.

I grab the box of tissues from her hands, take a tissue and shove it in her left nostril. "Blow."

She frowns and finally does, making her nose turn a deep shade of red.

"Thank you," I say, getting up and trudging to the bathroom. The medicine cabinet upstairs is to the right of the mirror. I grab the cold med box and cough syrup and bring them back.

On my way back to the bed, I go in the mini fridge and grab a bottle of water. I'm glad I keep this thing stocked.

I toss them on her lap, to which she snatches them up. Right after she gulps everything down, with a swig of water, she glances at me out of the corner of her eye. "You don't have to babysit me, you know, if you have stuff to do."

"I don't. It's Thanksgiving break." I lie back on my bed, parallel to her.

Her eyes move down from my face. "Are you going to put on a shirt?" She blinks quickly and her hands snap out and grab a tissue as she sneezes.

"Why should I? I'm in my own house. And it's nothing

you haven't seen. Now just rest and…here." I toss her the remote from my nightstand. "Watch whatever you want."

A look of surprise flashes on her face, but she grabs the remote regardless and goes straight for Netflix.

She emits a squeal of joy when she finds that popular vampire show about two brothers in love with the same girl. "I'm starting from the beginning because I'm assuming you haven't seen this."

"Do I look like I want to watch the love story between a girl and a vampire?"

She looks from me to the screen. "No, but you might surprise yourself."

And surprise myself I do, because hours later we're halfway through the season I'm glued to my fucking bed. "There's something about the bad brother that makes me think she belongs with him."

She laughs in a nasally voice. "What makes you think so?"

"Well, she's good right? And he's bad, so together they even themselves out. Plus he's just a hell of a lot more interesting. Don't lie and tell me you like the other brother better."

A sly smile spreads across her face. "Maybe I do. You'll have to wait and see."

Before she starts the next episode, I glance at the clock on the wall to see how many more we can fit in to find it's already almost time for dinner. Somehow we skipped lunch.

"Why don't we eat first before watching more?"

She nods. "Yeah, I just don't think I can eat anything heavy." Her hand goes to her throat and she moves her fingers slowly, massaging it. Her voice has gotten raspier as the day has gone on.

"We'll just order from the cafe down the street. Chicken noodle soup, okay?"

She nods, coughing hard into her elbow. "I can pay for my own food this time."

Not this again. Last night it took forever to order because she kept insisting she'd pay for her own. "Like I said last night, my dad has plenty of money. Stop worrying and rest."

I order a bowl of chicken noodle soup for her and a turkey sandwich and chips for myself.

She taps me on my arm, her cold finger making me jump as I set my phone down.

"What is it?"

She hikes the covers up her face. "I just want to say, I'm sorry for yesterday and getting mad at you for saving me. If you hadn't…I would have…"

"Just stop," I say firmly.

She tucks her bottom lip into her mouth and sighs. "It must have been difficult to save someone you hate so much." Her tone is so low, I can barely hear her.

But those words make my blood run cold.

Do I hate her? Would I have laughed and enjoyed her company all day if I did? When was the last time I absolutely despised her?

She smiles wanly. "Want to watch another episode while we wait?"

I don't respond, staring into her eyes. The intensity of my stare makes her falter a bit as she goes to reach for the remote between us. Before she can grab it, I pick it up and sit it on my nightstand.

"I don't hate you." The words leave my mouth so quickly, so effortlessly, I didn't even stop to think before saying them. And it shows on her face.

An 'O' forms on her lips and she shakes her head. "But Heath."

I press a finger to her lips. "Don't talk about him."

THE PRINCESS AND THE BULLY

Every single time I think about her, and then him, I get this murky feeling in my gut.

And I still don't know for sure if she has anything to do with his disappearance. Months ago I was positive, but that's slowly been weathered away. Sitting here right now, I'm more convinced that if she was around when something happened to him that she would have done everything to prevent it.

But that's not even the first thing that pops into my head anymore. The only thing I can think of is how betrayed my brother would feel by how badly I want to fuck his girlfriend. Maybe subconsciously I pushed it off for that exact reason.

Having her in my bed, sleeping next to me, is a whole new level of control I'm doing my damndest to maintain. Not to mention hearing her shower this morning and I couldn't even watch. I could only picture the rivulets of water cascading down her body.

I wish just fucking someone else would help. I had a girl right in my arms, about to plunge myself into her yesterday morning when I heard Wil's voice in my head instead of the girl's. When I looked down at the girl beneath me, I didn't see her, I saw Wil's lust filled eyes and her plump breasts, her flared hips. It wasn't the same.

I was on my way to her when I followed her to the lake and saw her jump in.

"I don't hate you either," she says, interrupting my thoughts.

Moving my hands down quickly, I hide my growing erection. "Glad we're on the same page." But even if we weren't, I'd fuck the hate away until the only thing left is her begging for my cock.

I grab the remote and start the next episode. Halfway

through, I get a notification about a visitor and okay it to the security guards. I go downstairs to grab the order and get crackers from the kitchen before going back up.

Her eyes brighten as I toss the crackers to her. "Thanks! How'd you know I can't eat soup without them?"

"You can't or you won't?"

She smiles. "I won't."

Spoiled. Right.

"And if I didn't have any?" I ask, shoving my sandwich in my mouth.

"I would have ordered some, with my *own* money."

Of course she could try. She doesn't know how much I like to blow my dad's money on everything. It's my favorite thing to do.

I don't tell her though. Instead, I finish my sandwich and watch her slurp down her broth after eating the chicken and veggie parts out.

When we're both done, we continue watching the show, and the further we get, the easier I can see how much she loves the bad brother. Even when he's intolerable to the main character, she smiles.

But we don't reach the end, not even when it's midnight.

She sniffles and blows her nose. "I'm sleepy. I think I need sleep."

"Go to sleep then. I won't stop you."

She nods, blinking sleepily. "I'll just use the bathroom first." Instead of that long shirt she was wearing last night, she's been wearing this clingy pink tank top since she got out of the shower with lacy underwear. My eyes stay glued to her ass as it jiggles while she stumbles to the bathroom.

My dick starts to come alive in my pants again and I quickly adjust myself, finishing just as the toilet flushes and she washes her hands. "I think I might have a fever. Mind if I find the thermometer?"

"Sure, go ahead," I call. "Just look in the third drawer."

I hope to hell it's there. I don't pay enough attention to my housekeeper when she tells me where she arranges things.

"I don't see it. Mind if I look around some more?" she barely gets out before she starts coughing.

I pause before answering. I've never let a girl go through my stuff before. Never slept in the same bed with one either. "Go ahead."

The sound of the drawers opening seems to echo throughout the room. She sniffles. "I can't find it." She comes back, looking pale and exhausted as she covers her mouth and makes a low sound in her throat as if she's holding something in.

"If you need to cough, just cough." I move off the bed and collect her in my arms, holding her to my chest as I lay on the bed. "You don't need a thermometer. I can already feel how hot your body is. I'll get you a cold water."

Nodding, she moves off of my lap and I curse myself for not putting that mini fridge closer to my bed. But I get her the water, turn off the lights and lay down next to her. She sips it so quietly, I would've thought she was using it as an ice pack if I wasn't facing her. But I guess she decides to, because she holds it to her chest.

"Night," she murmurs, turning her back to me. Last night she was so far away, almost to the edge of the bed. But tonight, she didn't scoot away. He stayed in place, her head planted in the middle of the pillow, no covers on her.

I know I should turn over and go to sleep, but I'm not tired. I'm wide awake. She's so close I can smell the shampoo in her hair from her shower this morning. I sniff the air, breathing deeply.

Wil might think she looks completely unattractive. The truth is she still looks just as gorgeous. Her smile might've lost a bit of its enthusiasm. Her hair might've looked wild. Her eyes swollen and her nose red from sniffling and blowing it so much. But my erection is still here, reminding me of the fact that my attraction to her isn't something that will disappear.

It's more than her body, and that thought scares the shit out of me.

I trail my fingers down the straps of her tank top as she snores away. Not softly either, but super fucking loud snoring just like last night. I thought it might've been a fluke but this is her normal volume.

When my fingers reach her hips, I stretch my hand out and grab it firmly.

"Mmm," she mumbles in her sleep. Scooting back and forth restlessly, I watch her stop with her ass barely an inch away from mine.

I'm sick. I know I am. She's sick and here I am wanting to fuck her so bad she won't be able to get out of bed in the morning. She's so close. And I've kept myself under control this whole time. *Just a little.* I need just a little to stave off this hunger. I move my hand off her hip to pull my sweatpants down, revealing my fully erect cock.

I grip her hip tightly and edge closer, moving my cock against her ass, still covered by her underwear. Gritting my teeth, I find the material of her underwear to be very fucking annoying against my cock.

I'll just be quick. She won't wake up.

I pull her underwear down, completely off her ass and thrust my cock upward between her cheeks. It's like heaven is cupping my cock, but fuck...her pussy is only an inch away. One shove in the right direction and I'll be inside her.

The thought makes me rub against her ass faster, earning a low groan from my throat.

A sweaty hand touches mine and I freeze when I realize I don't hear her snoring anymore.

There's only the barest hint of her breathing.

"Callan." Her voice comes out short and breathy. Shit, maybe she's feeling worse.

I could lie and tell her that I thought I was dreaming or come up with some shitty excuse, but I think the truth is better.

"You're too fucking tempting Wil."

That sweaty hand clutches mine tightly, squeezing. "Don't stop what you're doing. Keep going. Though, I'd prefer if you were between my thighs again."

Lust surges through me at her words, and I instantly oblige, thrusting myself between her thighs and rubbing against her clit.

She lets out a low moan. "Feels so good," she murmurs, moving her hips to keep pace with me.

Fuck. It does.

The wetness leaking between her thighs and the tight clasp of them coupled with her moans don't help me last long as I pull back, fisting my cock and finishing on her ass.

She's so quiet, I touch her arm. "Are you okay, Wil?"

But she's already fast asleep again.

I clean her up quickly with a hand towel from the bathroom and lie back down.

How am I going to survive sleeping in this bed with her for the next four nights without fucking her?

CHAPTER FIFTEEN

Mera

I never thought I'd say it but Callan isn't so bad. I thought by now he would've let me go back home, but he's accepted me into his space as if I've always been here. The whole time I was sick he took care of me. We finished the show this afternoon and I cried all over again. It turns out he loves shows like that one as much as I do since he isn't fighting with me about watching the spinoff show.

He still tries to control a lot of things though. I haven't paid for a meal since I've been here and he refused to let me help make Thanksgiving dinner. Maybe I could've saved the disaster of a meal that came out of it. Actually, scratch that, I haven't made a meal for myself in my life. It would've come out worse. But at least I would've had something to do instead of watching him make it all day. He also disagreed with me ignoring my parents' calls. He thought they'd fly out here after not hearing from me, but surprise surprise, social media says otherwise. They were pictured on their way to the southern castle since it's getting cold there. Their calls aren't the only ones I ignored though. But I don't want to face any of them yet. Not until I have to.

I never thought I'd feel better somewhere alone with Callan than in my own bed at the sorority. Everyone at school will probably show up tomorrow to get ready for their Monday morning classes. Callan will probably take me back tomorrow afternoon so tonight is the last night I'll share a bed with him.

It's the last night and he still hasn't done what he did that second night. Waking up to feeling his cock against my ass was a surprise I didn't know I wanted. My only regret is I was at my sickest that day and I couldn't even enjoy it.

God, I'm crazy. I should want him to respect me while I'm sleeping. All I want is to feel the high I get when he touches me.

"I got it, Coach. Practice at dawn on Monday." While he's talking on the phone sitting at the edge of the bed, I walk to the sink and brush my teeth.

I'm bent over, reaching for the bag of cups under the sink when I feel his presence and his intense gaze on me, but it doesn't last long. As I straighten my back, cup in hand, I watch him in the mirror as he grabs his toothbrush from the holder and brushes his teeth too.

My eyes are drawn to his whole naked torso in the mirror. His arm muscles flex as he moves the toothbrush around on his mouth. I'm so caught up with staring that he finishes and clears his throat, toothpaste stuck in the corners of his mouth. "Are you going to use that cup?"

"Definitely not," I say as I stick it under the water and fill it up. I swish it around in my mouth and spit it out.

He grabs the paper cup from my hand and fills it up with water. "Careful of my germs," I tease.

He spits out the water and chuckles. "I've already tasted all your germs, princess."

I get back in the bed first, facing away from his side of the bed.

A few minutes later, the lights go off and I feel the bed shift as he lays down on his side.

"Night," he says.

"Night," I murmur, grasping the sheet in my hand.

Straining my ears, I listen to the sound of his breathing. After a while, it starts to slow dow and he emits soft snores.

I guess this is it. There won't be anything tonight.

Biting my lip, I think back to how mind blowing it felt when he ate me out at school. Every flick of his tongue was erotic. And his fingers, God his fingers, rubbing against my clit.

Quietly, I move my hand under the covers and move them to my underwear. How did he do it? My face flushes as I realize I've never touched myself before.

I never wanted to until him.

Slipping my hand inside, I touch my clit for the first time, rubbing my finger over it. It feels good, just not as good. His fingers are so much larger and longer than mine. These fingers feel so foreign. I cover my mouth quickly before a moan can escape. A zing of pleasure reaches my toes and I twitch, continuously moving my fingers around my clit.

I stretch my fingers down lower, moving my lower body slightly to meet my hand as I put a finger inside. I'm already so wet. But I don't feel as full. It's not the same. I push the covers off completely annoyed when I notice I don't hear the snoring anymore. Freezing, I turn around to find Callan with his eyes wide open, staring at me. His mouth is flat and his eyes are fiery.

"I felt the sheets move, princess. And then do you know what happened?"

I hold my breath and watch as he closes the distance between us. "I smelled you." His hand goes around my thighs and he moves my underwear to the side and shoves his fingers right inside, making me gasp and arch my back against him.

"You're so fucking wet. What were you thinking of?" he whispers in my ear.

I don't respond, too focused on the feeling of his fingers inside me. Stopping abruptly, he yanks his fingers out and I'm left deprived of him once more. I let out an annoyed noise. There's no way I'll tell him I was thinking about him and it made me horny. "I just needed a little release."

"Oh? Is that so?" he pulls his fingers out of my underwear and I turn my head slightly to meet his eyes. There's a knowing smirk on his face. "You may continue what you were doing."

Fucking hell.

"I'm going back to sleep. Keep those loud moans of yours to a minimum."

He starts to turn over and I turn and push his shoulder. "Asshole!"

With a grunt, he stops, nodding slightly and then in a flash he's on top of me, pinning my body to the bed with his hands on my arms and his legs on either side of mine.

"I've been holding back all week. I'm not holding back anymore, Wil. Why should I keep holding myself back when you're so willing to touch yourself right next to me?"

He bends down close, mouth only inches from mine. "I'm not letting myself wait any longer." His lips come crashing down on mine, consuming me fiercely and completely. My breaths mesh with his as his tongue delves deep into my mouth.

If I thought the first time he kissed me was intense, it's nothing compared to this. I can't even process that statement. Does he mean what I think he means?

Every touch and lick makes my body shiver with pleasure and moan at the deliciousness of it all.

He pulls back and yanks my panties down quickly, followed by my shirt. He never wears a shirt to bed, so the only thing on him is his sweatpants. Those come off in a flash and suddenly, there's nothing left between us. It reminds me of the night during the third round of hazing.

His eyes are so hot on mine, I can't catch my breath. He bends down, lips going to my neck as he sucks on the skin there. His large hands move over my arms to my chest, testing the weight of each breast in his hands.

"And these," he squeezes my breasts in his palms causing a sharp moan to fly out, "I felt them push against my chest the night of the hazing, but you've never felt my hands around them before."

He lets go momentarily until his fingers find my nipples. "The soft dusky pink of these are my favorite color," he murmurs, scooting himself back and sucking one into his mouth.

I moan low in my throat at the shocking feeling of the hot wetness of his mouth. Heat gathers between my legs as his hand works my other nipple, twisting it sharply and causing a sting of pain that makes me gasp.

He switches to my other nipple, sucking and licking at it like his life depends on it. I tighten my thighs together as pleasure zings through my body. He hasn't even touched my clit.

His mouth comes off abruptly as he grabs my mouth in a deep kiss again. His tongue is completely tangled with mine, when I feel his hands go to my inner thighs and spread them wide open, exposing me to the air.

The cold air is a shock to the heat. A finger glides over my pussy, not going inside, but touching the wetness that's leaked out.

He pulls his head back, and our lips come apart with a pop. "Princess, you're so wet and so damn ready for me. I'm not waiting and I don't fucking care anymore."

"Care about–" I start and pause, feeling the head of his hard cock nestled against my entrance.

"There is no saying no," he says in a low warning tone. I only have one second to think about that as I feel all of him at once shoved deep inside my pussy.

I cry out immediately, tearing up at his invasion. Fuck, that hurts. His cock is so much thicker than even three of his fingers.

"Wil."

I glance up slowly to find him staring at me like he's seen a ghost. Eyes wide open. "Are you...are you a fucking virgin?"

Heat rushes to my face and I glance away. He grabs my chin quickly, yanking my face back to face his. "Not only did I feel that, but I also saw the pain on your face. Tell me right now. Tell me the truth."

His gaze searches mine and his hand leaves my chin and goes down to my throat. "Answer me!" he yells. The hand on my throat tightens.

"I am!" I exclaim.

His hand stays locked around my throat as he shakes his head. "That doesn't make sense. Are you trying to tell me that you never fucked my brother or anyone else for that matter?

All those parties and you never ended up in a bed somewhere?"

God. I'm sorry, Heath, but I have to tell him the truth.

"I never slept with anyone at home because every guy wanted to sleep with me just so he could say he slept with a princess. I wasn't going to let that happen. Just like I never kissed anybody before I came here. Heath was…"

His eyes darken. "Heath was your first kiss?" His hand leaves my throat as he leans his head back to look at the ceiling, the vein in his jaw ticking.

"And Heath and I were never really together like that. I didn't think of him that way and he didn't think of me that way. We never had sex. It was more of a I scratch your back you scratch mine."

Callan tilts his head down with a weirdly satisfied expression on his face.

"Is that what you were talking about when you said you didn't care anymore? You thought about me being Heath's girlfriend."

He nods. "But you know what?"

"What?" I ask, searching his eyes.

He grabs a thigh in each hand and thrusts himself forward. My back arches off the bed as I gasp at the pleasure it causes. "That means that you're mine. Don't let anyone else fuck you."

His eyes are so fiercely locked on me, all I can do is nod.

He pulls himself out smoothly and drives himself back in. "Fuck this is what I needed. Your tight pussy clenching around me so tightly."

Every dirty word only makes me open my legs wider for him. Something inside me starts to build, rising quicker than I've ever felt.

"Have to get deeper," he murmurs, rocking himself in and

out. He yanks my legs up, his cock resting at my entrance as he places a leg on each shoulder.

I breathlessly watch as he holds my legs, and thrusts back in with a groan. "Fuck that's it. Do you feel me, princess?"

"It feels so good," I say with a moan.

His thrusts are so deep and relentless, I can hardly think. I can only feel him. Think of him. He's consuming every part of my being. And it's so much.

With a cry I feel wave after wave of pleasure hit me.

"Princess, I need you to tell me. Tell me you're on the pill."

I'm still coming down, but I shake my head quickly. His eyes flash dangerously as he continues to pump inside me. Every thrust sends pleasure racing through me and I cry at how good it feels. He's doing it again. Pushing me to another orgasm at lightning speed.

"Look at me, Wil."

I stare at him with tear-filled eyes. A slow smile spreads across his face. "You're going to need to get on it."

He pounds into me fucking me hard into the bed and I come with another cry, screaming his name.

He thrusts in once more with a grunt, and I watch his eyes shine in the darkness as I feel him twitching inside me. "Did you just...?" I ask in a low tone.

Slowly, he lets my legs down, and he picks me up into his arms, planting me on his lap without letting his cock leave my body. "I'll never not come inside you, Wil."

Those words send pleasure shooting down my spine and he consumes my lips.

I pull back and bite my lip. "But what if–"

He silences me with another mind blowing kiss and pulls back. "Get on birth control if you don't want my child in your belly."

Gasping at his words, I'm left completely speechless. He

gently lays me back down and eases his cock out of me. Instantly, I feel empty, but I also feel incredibly sore and exhausted. I'm about to roll over when I feel his hand spread my thigh apart from the other one.

"You bled a little, princess. It's mixed in with your wetness and my cum. But I'm glad I was able to make your first time one of pleasure."

I nod sleepily and he seems to notice how tired I am because he tucks me under the sheet and lies down next to me.

The last thing I remember is his fingers teasing my entrance and feeling one breach my entrance while he says in a gravelly tone, "I'm just going to push it back in so it stays where it belongs."

I wake up to the smell of bacon and syrup, the aroma permeating the air.

Popping my eyes open, I find a tray of bacon and pancakes on the nightstand. I'd think last night was a dream if I didn't feel the aching in my lower half.

"Eat up," a gruff voice declares.

I glance up to find Callan leaning against the doorway shirtless in his sweatpants.

Wincing, I sit up. "Not yet." I feel his cold eyes watching me as I get out of the bed. Ignoring his stare, I walk slowly to the bathroom and use it.

When I wipe, I notice the spots of blood on the tissue and inside the toilet when I flush.

All of a sudden it hits me. I slept with Callan. Callan Goldsworthy took my virginity. He can brag all he wants about taking it to anyone. Everyone else will think I'm a whore for sleeping with both brothers when I fucking haven't.

And Callan...what are we? Fuck buddies?

Should I now expect us to have sex like that regularly now? Last night the horniness won over my reason. I didn't ask any questions. I just wanted his cock in my pussy. But now, I have to know.

I rush to the sink and push the soreness to the back of my mind as I grab a pair of underwear and a shirt and throw them on. Callan watches me from the edge of the bed with a raised eyebrow. I bring the tray to the sitting area and sit on the couch while I eat off the square plate.

"You don't usually eat over there. And what's the hurry? The food isn't going anywhere," he says with a chuckle as I chew quickly.

But I finish it quickly regardless and lick the syrup from around my mouth.

"I ate quickly because I want to know...what are we Callan?"

He sets the empty water bottle on the nightstand as his expression changes to a scowl. "What do you mean?"

"You said some wild things last night. I know sometimes people say things in the heat of the moment."

He crosses the room in a flash, eyes dark and planted right on me.

I frown up at him when he reaches me. "I sat over here so we could have a real conversation without our bodies getting in the way."

Nodding, he leans down and traps me against the couch between his arms. "I thought what I said last night was pretty clear. You're mine and no one else's. What else is there to know?"

Maybe I was expecting too much, because my heart sinks a little.

"Should I fuck you again to show you just how much you belong to me?"

"No," I respond smoothly and school my expression to hide my disappointment. Part of me was hoping he would apologize about everything he did to me. All of the fear and anxiety. Halloween night.

He presses a chaste kiss to my lips. The first of its kind. His cold eyes soften slightly. "What do you think about going back tonight? Are you anxious to go back?"

"Not really." In fact, I'm dreading it.

"Good. Then we have the whole day ahead of us. Let's go out to the backyard since it's not overcast today."

Excitement rushes over me at the thought of finally going outside again. I saw a few glimpses of the rose bushes from the kitchen but now I get to see everything up close.

"Wil." A hand touches my shoulder. "Wil."

"Hmm?" I rub at my eyes. Callan's calling me?

Lips press against mine. "Princess, you have to wake up."

Why am I so sleepy?

My eyes pop open to find it's still dark. "What's up?" I ask sleepily.

"Remember you were so tired after washing your clothes and packing that we decided not to go back? It sucks, but we've got to get back because I have practice."

Groaning, I put the pillow on top of my head. "You go back, I'll stay here."

He sighs and there's a pause. "I know you don't want to face them because they all signed that petition, but you'll have to sooner or later. Fuck them if they don't want to be your friend anymore. Now come on, show them that you're fine on your own."

His words are like a bucket of cold water. He's right. I came here on my own expecting to continue to not have friends. I was fine.

With renewed vigor, I get out of his warm bed and get ready to go.

I'm going to be okay.

I unlock the door and walk inside just as the sun starts to rise. My bag hits the door as I close it causing a loud sound. Heads peek out from the foyer and I wave with a wide smile. They roll their eyes with grouchy looks and I go up the stairs.

When I get to my room, opening the door slowly, I find Brandie and Jamie talking to each other in whispered tones.

Brandie gasps. "Oh my God, Mera! I've been so worried about you. I thought you said you weren't going back home for the holiday."

Jamie grabs me in a tight hug. "We thought something happened when you weren't here when we got back. We checked the status of the petition to make sure you weren't kicked out. Congrats by the way!" She lets go and she and Brandie high-five.

Funny she brings that up. I don't know how to act knowing they signed the petition, so I shrug. "I was off with a friend."

They look at each other. "Didn't you say all of your friends were off spending the holidays with their families?" Brandie asks.

Hearing her talk as if nothing's wrong finally makes me snap. "Why did you guys sign the petition?"

Jamie raises an eyebrow. "What are you talking about?"

"I read over each name that signed and both of yours were on it."

Brandie shakes her head. "Impossible." She pulls her phone out and stares at it for a long while as she moves her finger over it. "What the hell. It's in my list of signed petitions. This is unreal. Of course I didn't sign this. And neither would Jamie."

Jamie nods in agreement. "We're your friends, Mera. We'd never hurt you like that."

"Someone must have hacked me," Brandie snarls angrily. Her angry face is surprisingly scary. "I'm contacting the administration office today. There's obviously some security bug in the Silverstone's app."

Is it possible then that neither Scarlett nor Peyton signed? I need to talk to them right away.

I grab my school bag and check through it quickly and find everything I need for history still in it. Good.

Before heading out, I give them both short hugs. I feel so much better knowing the truth. If their answer had been different and they really did sign it on purpose, that would have been fine too because it would be the truth. "See you guys later."

I go directly to the dining hall and sit at an empty table. It's early enough that it isn't super crowded yet. As more people start to pile in, the tables fill up. All six other chairs around my table stay empty.

A yawn escapes my mouth as I rub at my eyes.

"Mera?"

My hands drop to the table when I see Peyton and Scar

fast walking to the table. They grab the two seats in front of me.

"What's going on? You called and didn't answer when I tried to call you back?" Scar says with a hurt tone in her voice.

Peyton grunts. "Same here. Not going to lie, I felt guilty because I thought something might have happened to you. I called Scar and we both came back early on Saturday to look for you."

I cover my mouth with my hand. Are these the kinds of reactions from people that would sign a petition to have me thrown out? But it doesn't stop me from asking. "So you didn't sign the petition to get me expelled?"

Scar looks at me as if I have a third head. "Girl. Everything okay up here?" She taps the side of her head with her index finger.

"I checked the petition and you and Peyton have the last two signatures."

Peyton frowns. "No fucking way." He pulls out his phone and after a few minutes he exclaims, "What the fuck!"

"Is she correct, Pey?"

"Yeah. What the fuck is going on? I'm changing my fucking password, dude. You should do the same."

Scarlett pulls out her phone and moves her fingers over it. When she's done, she reaches across the table and grabs my hand. "Mer, have more faith in us please? You and Peyton are both my best friends. I would *never* betray you." The truth shines in her eyes as she says it and I breathe a sigh of relief. Out of everyone, it hurt the most to know that her and Peyton were the ones that put me over. The first two people I met after Heath. They've become so important to me in such a short amount of time. I'm glad I don't have to be without them.

I watch three chairs at the other end of the table get pulled out and sat in by Gemma, Ashlynn, and Luella. Luella waves shyly while Ashlynn nods. They have full plates of breakfast food in front of them.

Gemma pulls her glasses off and cleans them with her shirt before pushing them back on her face. "Mera! Did you have a good break? I saw they didn't expel you. I'm sure everyone has seen by now. That was a shitty petition that Callan made, by the way."

"I did. I'm glad I'm not going anywhere. Hey, since we're on the subject, did Collette make you sign it?"

Gemma blinks quickly. "No. I refused to. So did Luella and Ashlynn. Right, guys?" she asks turning to them.

They nod and Luella speaks softly, "You're innocent until proven guilty."

"You might be a spoiled party girl, but you're no killer, Mera," Ashlynn says with a chuckle, shoving a piece of toast in her mouth. "You? Kill somebody? No. I know the type and it isn't you."

Now wait a fucking minute. Just how many of those signatures on that petition are actually real? I'll probably never know. It doesn't matter right now. Like a load has been lifted off my shoulders, I take a deep calming breath. All of the tension and stress I built up thinking about this is gone.

"Thanks you guys."

They all start eating and I look at the empty spot in front of me. God, I'm starving. What I wouldn't give for Callan's bacon and pancakes? Or even the sausage and hash browns he made Thanksgiving day.

A plate of ham, eggs, and waffles slides in front of me. My eyes widening, I turn around, but there's no one behind me. I hear the telltale sound of the chair next to me scraping against the floor as it's pulled out. I can't help the small smile that forms on my face when Callan's eyes meet mine. I've grown so accustomed to their coldness, that they don't make me balk now. They're a part of him.

"Thanks," I whisper.

"Callan, if I'd known you were bringing plates I would've put my order in too," Ashlynn comments, glancing at my plate.

And then, something happens that makes the atmosphere shift. An arm slowly goes around my shoulders and I freeze in place as everyone's eyes widen at the movement of that arm. "Sorry Ash, I only get breakfast for Wil and Wil only. Capice?"

Ash looks between us. From my flushed face to his and smirks. "So you guys did fuck, huh? Callan wasn't lying on Halloween."

Scar shrieks. "Girl! I thought you said it was nothing."

"It was!" I exclaim.

Callan leans down to my ear and whispers, "When have I ever been nothing, princess?"

The combination of his breath hitting my ear and his words make me want to crawl away from embarrassment. But a princess doesn't crawl, she smiles, and holds her head up high.

They all give me knowing looks as if they can easily guess the kind of thing that Callan whispered to me, except Gemma who just looks confused.

And I certainly don't protest when she changes the subject.

My phone sounds off in my pocket. My dad is calling?

I hit answer and hold the phone up to my ear. "Mera, how are you doing honey?"

"I'm...okay," I answer in a low tone.

I'm still angry they refused to let me come home for this

holiday. Though, I wouldn't have had this week with Callan if I had gone home.

"We're sorry we didn't fly you home for the holiday. How about we make it up to you by letting you come home for Christmas? You can even bring a few friends if you'd like."

That means I wouldn't miss the annual Christmas Eve ball.

"Yes!" I blurt.

And I get to go *home*.

My dad sighs with relief. "Good. We're looking forward to seeing you. We love you Mera."

"Love you guys too."

I hang up to find questioning faces.

"Something happen, Wil?" Callan asks, glancing at the phone in my hand.

I nod excitedly. "How would you guys like to spend Christmas in Kardenia?"

CHAPTER SIXTEEN

Callan

It's cold and rainy when we get dropped off in front of ZDB. If it wasn't for the rain we would've walked over here, but it's been pouring since yesterday afternoon. It's 2:15 AM and we're set to leave in Mera's plane at six.

"I can't believe you talked her into letting us come," Vincent says with a yawn.

"No. What I can't believe is that he got an invitation first!" Noel yells irritably, glaring over his shoulder at Silverstone.

He smirks. "Isn't it obvious? Mera and I are friends. She barely knows you guys. Besides, why would I ever turn down going to a place as beautiful as Kardenia?" He glances in my direction and I glare at his arrogant smile. "Besides, if my *friend* offers, it'd be rude to turn her down."

"Just shut up," I mutter. It's too early in the morning for this shit. Tyrell, Emerson, and Brett stay quiet as we all spread out underneath the overhang on the concrete porch to get out of the rain. We're actually on time, unlike the limo and the girls.

The black Escalade limo pulls up before the girls come out, so we pile in. Everyone else goes through the Gull Wing door while I enter through the regular one in the back. I start to close the door behind me when something stops it in place. I glance back to find Silverstone's hand at the top of the door. "The captain's chair is reserved."

He shrugs. "Fine with me."

He moves past me and I close the door quickly. He sits in the very backseat, behind the other captain's chair.

"Morning gentleman," the older limo driver says through the limo divider.

I let everyone else respond, relaxing back into the seat.

Last night's game was a hard win. We went into double overtime but managed to squeak it out. We needed this win so I pushed myself hard. I'm fucking exhausted.

I rest my eyes, opening them quickly when I hear the sound of the Gull Wing door opening. Brandie and Jamie slide in first, sitting in the empty spots on one side next to Brett and Emerson, respectively on the shorter side. Gemma, Luella, and Ashlynn slide in on the longer side and stay close to the door, putting a good amount of room between them and Noel, Tyrell, and Vincent. In a flash, the irritable look on Noel's face is gone. He closes that distance by sliding closer to Gemma, but before he can stop next to her, she puts her suitcase on the seat with an annoyed look.

"Morning, Gem."

She doesn't respond, completely ignoring him, as Red and Tall Boy slide in next to Ashlynn. I roll down the window quickly to see Mera about to go in through the Gull Wing door. "Back here," I call out, and roll the window up.

The door opens a few seconds later and she smiles, not looking anywhere near as tired as I thought she'd look. She gets in, going around my suitcase, and sits in the other captain's chair. She's about to throw her suitcase behind her when I mutter, "There's someone in the back."

Her eyes widen and she turns. "Kane! Why didn't you say anything? It's so dark back here."

In the darkness you can see his pearly white teeth when he smiles widely at her. "I much prefer sitting in the back."

Mera opens her mouth to respond, when I turn and ask, "Think we can get a move on? If we're any later we might miss our flight."

Her mouth thins and she sighs. "Actually, we're just waiting on one more person. And not by choice. I only found out an hour ago that she was coming along."

The door next to me opens and I'm face to face with my sister. "Morning, dear brother."

"Coll?" I blurt.

I thought she was going to spend Christmas alone with our parents like Thanksgiving.

"So you were just going to run off without me with *her?*" She leans in, turning her head to the right to look at everybody else. "*Everyone* was just going to run off without me."

"Um, excuse me, Miss Ballerina," Red inserts. "This is Mera's home we're going to. *We* have no say."

She scoffs. "That's a load of shit. She invited them," motioning to Noel, Vincent, and Tyrell.

Noel gasps in an exaggerated way. "Uh, Mera's our best friend. Your fault if you didn't fucking notice Coll."

She glares. "Well, luckily, Ashlynn isn't exactly quiet when she talks on the phone and I heard her whole conversation with her parents."

Ashlynn crosses her arms. "You're not exactly quiet yourself."

"So you better have room for me on that plane," Coll says adamantly.

I roll my eyes and glance at Wil. "Is there room?"

She nods, but she doesn't look happy about it. Coll smiles. "See. No harm done."

Coll steps in between the suitcases and moves in between the captain's chairs to the back.

"Oh my God," she squeals. "Why didn't you say something you creeper?"

Silverstone responds to her in a low tone I can't quite make out, but whatever. I slam the door shut. "Someone tell the driver he can leave."

Eventually, we make it on the plane ten minutes before six.

It's pretty large. Larger than the one that my father uses for his business trips.

Wil and I stay in the back right corner.

"I'm so glad to be going home," she murmurs, leaning against my shoulder. She looks like she's ready to drift off at any second and I feel the exact same way.

I'm glad for a different reason. Spending Thanksgiving away from my family was a lot less stressful. Now two holidays back to back I won't have to deal with my dad's attitude and watch my mom automatically agree with every word he says.

And I won't have to look at Heath's empty chair. Heath...

Clenching my jaw, I lean into the headrest and turn my head away from Wil's peaceful face.

When we get back, I have to keep searching for answers.

Her sprawling castle up the hills are a sight to behold. The closer we get, the more her face lights up. Brighter than I've seen it before, and it's a good sight to see. Her parents sent several SUVs to get us from the airport.

Once we enter the gates, Wil is out, running full speed toward the castle steps. Wil says the central Kardenia castle is the largest and she wasn't lying. Five times the size of my family's mansion, the castle is humongous, perched atop of a large hill surrounded by trees and a huge lake in the distance. The moon is partially hidden behind the dark overcast sky, but every ornate design of the castle reeks of magnificence and care. I can see why Wil loves it so much, but a strange wave of deja vu washes over me looking at the many towers and windows. I've never even seen pictures so it makes no sense.

The rest of us get out of the cars, grabbing our luggage with us. I grab Wil's hot pink suitcase for her.

Despite it being the middle of the night, most of us are wide awake after sleeping on and off during the plane ride.

"Hey Mera," Noel calls. "Can I live here instead? You can stay in California."

"Absolutely not!" she yells.

It takes a few minutes for us to get up the many steps as the cold wind hits us. Should've worn some fucking gloves. But when we finally get up there, Wil is underneath an alcove facing away from us and the grand doors are wide open with three people on each side of the doors in maid and butler costumes.

"Welcome to Kardenia," they all exclaim at once, way too cheerily for people who are used to this timezone.

Wil turns her head back and motions us forward. "Come on, I'll show you guys to your rooms."

It's a long trek, down hall after hall and past room after

room. We finally reach the East Wing on the second floor. She gives us each our own rooms, right next to each other. I flip the light switch to find the one she graces me with is pretty damn nice and clean. Everyone else closes their doors, wanting to rest until breakfast time. I leave mine wide open.

It doesn't have that dusty smell to it. The walls are a light shade of gray and the bed is made with at least six pillows stacked on top.

"I'll let you rest then," she says, glancing inside and then to me.

I drop everything on the nice marble tile and cross over to her. "I don't need to rest." I grab her in my arms and inhale her scent off of her hair. Even after a long plane ride, she still smells like heaven. "Unless you rest with me."

She pushes a soft hand against my chest. "My parents will kill me if they discover me in bed with you."

"There's so many rooms, Wil. How will they know to check this one?" I murmur.

She starts to falter and I take that chance to pick her up in one arm, she emits a shocked gasp as she wraps her arms around my shoulder. I flip the light switch off and shut the door quickly and carry her into the darkness. By the wide smile on her face I know I made the right decision.

I drop her in the middle of the bed and move toward the left side. "Who needs so many fucking pillows?" I shove them off the bed and she crawls to the right, shoving hers off and laying her head on the remaining one. She lays on her side looking at me.

I reach forward to grab her hip but she slides away from me upon seeing my hand move.

"Don't."

Her word draws my anger forth and I lay my hand back on my side. "Why?" I bark. "We've hardly seen each other this past month. With the charity work and basketball, and fucking finals."

Her mouth turns downward. "Stop. I don't want any part of this vacation ruined. Let's just rest for now, okay?"

Because I want her to have a good time while she's home, I keep my trap shut, clenching the hand underneath myself into a fist as she closes her eyes. She moves her hands under her face, pressing them together and snuggling into the luxurious bed beneath us.

I only know she's truly asleep when she starts to snore.

What the hell does she want from me?

While she's asleep, I carefully move back, easing off the bed and watching for any change in her face.

When I'm off, I go to the window and pull back the curtains. The moonlight barely shines in, but it's enough for me to see her face from the chair in the corner. I go in my bag, pushing the clothes aside and grabbing my drawing tablet and a pencil. When I finally get in the chair, I set to work, drawing every inch of her face as she sleeps with her hands underneath it. The moment I'm finished, something flashes in my mind.

A girl with wild bright pink hair looking out from a treehouse.

A treehouse?

I peel back my drawing of Wil and start fresh on a new page.

Suddenly, I can see it so clearly. The ladder going up, the treehouse wrapping around the trunk of the tree several feet up. The bird's nest perched at the top on the roof of the treehouse.

A rainy day…and…

A sharp pain inside my skull hits me out of nowhere and I grimace, holding my head.

Maybe that's my cue to stop.

I close my drawing pad quickly and set it on the small side table next to the chair.

Quietly, I go back to her and stare at her face until I feel myself drift off too.

The knock on the door jolts me out of a deep sleep. I sit up quickly, rubbing at my eyes. The sun is shining in through the window and hitting the wall near the door.

"Is Princess Mera in there?" a voice calls out.

"Oh fuck," I mutter, and shake the still-sleeping Wil.

She's on her stomach now with her hands underneath the pillow under her head.

"Wil," I say quietly, shaking her side.

She groans and pops one eye open. "What?"

The knock sounds again and a look of horror hits her face. She mouths 'shit' and jumps out of the bed and hides in the corner parallel to the door. I can't help but chuckle at her scared expression. She glares angrily at me as I open the door.

The young maid at the door smiles and glances around me, speaking loudly. "His and her majesty would like their daughter and her friends for breakfast in the dining area. No one can currently find Princess Mera, but if you see her, please let her know that they still expect her to be prompt."

"Got it," I respond, in a gravelly voice.

With a nod, she leaves and I close the door quickly.

Wil moves herself off the floor, hands over her face and groans. "Martha totally knew I was in here."

"And?" I ask with a laugh. "We weren't actually doing anything."

She flattens her hair on her head. "It means she's going to go and tattle to my parents. And then they're going to question you. Not to mention my sister."

She acts like it's the end of the world, but it was bound to happen sooner or later. By the way she's acting, she never expected it to. And that pisses me off.

"I'm going to change," I mutter gruffly, and dig in my bag.

As if she notices my change in mood, she doesn't say another word, perching herself at the end of the bed.

When we're done, we both walk out and knock on our friends' doors, and get no answer.

"They must all be at the table already."

A short while later, we walk into the central part of the castle where the dining room is. The chatter coming from inside can be heard all the way to the stairs. Several maids and butlers are stationed at the entrance who immediately curtsy and bow at Wil.

Wil goes to walk through the arched doorway, squaring her shoulders. I follow right behind. There's two empty seats. On one side, all of the guys sit, and the girls on the other. Situated at the ends are a regal looking man and woman who immediately eye Wil and I.

All chatter immediately slows to a stop and Wil exclaims, "Mom, Dad!" Her father extends his arms and she runs right into them. Wil hugs her Mom, too, just not with the same energy. Though I can guess why after overhearing her phone call with her mother outside the police station.

What the fuck do I say? Hello your majestys, I'd love to get permission from you to keep fucking your daughter, and by the way can she stay in California forever?

"Saved a seat for you buddy," Noel calls out and waves.

Trust Noel to always chime in at the right moment.

Wil takes the remaining seat in the middle of the girls and I take the other one, between Noel and Tall Boy.

The Queen rings a bell, and immediately trays come out with food, coffee, and orange juice. It takes a while for them to serve all of us, but once we've all gotten our food and drink, the Queen sighs happily.

"It's so nice to see you home, Wilhelmera."

A wave of annoyance passes over Wil's face.

She glances between her mom and dad. "Where's Cate though? I thought she'd be joining us for breakfast."

An uncomfortable look appears on her dad's face. He doesn't look like he wants to answer her question. Her mom looks at her plate for a while and then sighs.

"Well?" Wil yells. "What are those looks about? Where's Cate? I haven't heard from her in months."

Her mom crosses her fingers together. "Unfortunately, Cate won't be joining us for Christmas this year."

"Why?" Wil asks, eyebrows furrowing as she looks between her parents. "We've never spent Christmas apart."

"Your sister met someone," her dad finally responds. "She wanted to spend the holidays with him instead."

"And she knows that I'm here?" Wil asks, hurt evident on her face.

I don't feel like I should be listening in on this conversation.

They nod and she scoffs. "No. That doesn't sound like Cate at all. Who is this boyfriend of hers?"

"We don't know," they both say at once.

"Bullshit!" Wil yells.

"Young lady!" her mother screams back.

Wil's mouth flattens. "The only boyfriend Cate has ever had was Duke Floyen's son and they broke up after high school. Even when she claimed to care for him they never did anything together besides go to public events." Anger flares in her eyes. "I haven't been able to call her, she hasn't posted on social media. I haven't even seen her in the news."

Her father sighs. "This last year at University is taking a toll on her. I believe she wanted to get away from it all with this new guy."

"With bodyguards then? Keeping watch in the shadows?"

"No," her father responds.

And now even my bullshit monitor is going off. What the fuck is going on with this?

Her parents share a look. There's something they aren't saying.

Wil's stubbornness isn't letting it go. "How did they meet?"

"She saved his life and they started seeing each other right after that. I hope we get to meet the young man soon," her mom says, reaching for her fork.

Wil's eyes narrow. "Call her then. Call her right now."

But her mom does no such thing, instead slicing the pancakes on her plate.

"Mother?"

Her mother looks up in my direction. "Callan, isn't it? It's so good to see you again. It's hard to believe it's been thirteen years."

Wil looks furious at being ignored. I want her to get the answers she's looking for, but I also can't ignore the Queen.

Wait. I go over those words in my head and turn to look at her. "Your majesty, did you say again?"

I can feel my friends staring at me. Fuck off guys, this is not the time.

She blinks quickly. "Why yes, we've met once before years ago. Do you not remember?"

Across the table, I meet Wil's puzzled eyes.

"Honey, don't you remember he fell?" the King asks, taking a bite of toast.

Wil's eyes widen and her mouth turns into an O. "Oh my God."

"Mera, dear. You didn't tell him? You two were the best of friends that day. You didn't want him to leave."

"You're Rain Boy," she says, covering her mouth after those words slip out.

"Rain Boy?" I ask.

Her dad nods. "Yes, that's right. She kept asking for you when you left and she could never remember your name. That name stuck even after we corrected her. I'm sure you know how stubborn she can be. She kept remembering how hard it rained that day and came up with that. Rain Boy. You also had a cute name for our little girl, too."

And then it hits me all at once, a flash of a girl with bright pink hair. The same flash of pink I've been seeing every time I look at Wil. "Pinkie."

She jumps in her seat, a look of shock in her eyes as she looks at me as if she's seeing me for the first time.

"Pinkie! That's it!" her father yells. "You couldn't pronounce her whole name and it was the first time we let her dye her hair pink."

That drawing and those flashes. I remember now. "I'm sorry, Your Majesty. I lost my memories of that day. It's only starting to come back to me now. I fell from the treehouse trying to get the bird's nest off the top of it. It was hailing and Wil cried because she was afraid the birds would get hurt. I climbed up on the railing and got the bird's nest off. When I tried to get down, I slipped and fell off. Hit my head on a rock."

"Our meeting ended when Mera came running, tears running down her cheeks. They rushed you to the hospital and only told us you were okay. It's a shame you two didn't remember until now. Though that doesn't matter does it?" her dad gives us a knowing expression as he chews his eggs.

"I tried to tell you before you left, Mera. You weren't going to be completely alone at school. The Dean's son—" her mother starts and stops, looking at me anxiously.

"The Dean's son..." Mera murmurs.

"You just happened to meet my brother, first," I mutter. My parents knew, yet how could they not have sent me instead of Heath?

Would anything have been different if I had been sent to show her around instead? No. I probably would have ditched her the moment I took her to her dorm and gave her her schedule.

"Cate and Heath, weren't they friends too?" Wil asks.

Her parents shake their heads.

"Catherine and Heath didn't get along from the moment they met. While you and Callan ran off to play, they refused to."

Heath, who was friends with everyone? That doesn't sound like him.

"I bet you feel pretty stupid now, man," Vincent says with a laugh.

"Well, wait a minute, where was I?" Collette asks.

"Who knows? And who cares?" Wil says, turning to look at her toward the end of the table.

"Wilhelmera," her mother chides.

"Sorry Mother, what I meant to say was," she turns to look at Collette, "five year old you was doing something *so much better* than us. We're so sad you couldn't come. It would've been so much more fun had you been there."

Collette glares, staring at her like she's roasting her alive in her head.

Those two will never fucking get along. But I don't care about that right now.

I remember something from that day. Something that her parents don't know.

The innocent kiss between two kids who had crushes on each other. Heath was never her first kiss. I was.

She notices me staring and her cheeks turn pink. I know she remembers and more than ever, it's clear.

Wil has always been mine.

And I intend on showing her just how true that is on this trip.

CHAPTER SEVENTEEN

Mera

Ever since that breakfast ended, Callan's done nothing but stare at me. Like he wants to eat me up. It's been hours since then. After hearing about the famous treehouse, everyone made me take them there.

It was weird being there again after not going there for so long. Of course we didn't go up, but being there with Callan again was weird and I think he felt it too. He kept looking at the rock he hit his head against, still partially stained brown with a spot of his blood.

Since the ball is tomorrow and I'm the only one with something to wear, we have to go shopping for everyone else. The moment I knew I was coming home, I had Mother order a custom made gown and today we're picking it up.

Kara's Dress Shop can't be beat with their styles and

quality so I know they'll have plenty of gorgeous dresses on the rack for the girls.

Callan wanted to ride with me to the marketplace, but I jumped into the car with Scarlett and Peyton at the last minute.

"I can't believe I'm going to a fancy ball for Christmas Eve," Scar says with a huge smile.

"Not only that, this place is the most beautiful place I've ever seen. No wonder you didn't want to leave. Look! No traffic!" Peyton yells as we move right along down the highway.

"When we graduate, I hope you guys will come and visit me."

Scar exclaims, "Why the hell would I turn down an invitation to come back? I'll visit so much you'll get sick of me."

"Same here," Peyton agrees.

We exit the highway and head for Main Street, where all of the nice restaurants and shops are. I already know what to expect, but I don't think they will. "Okay guys, when we get out, look straight and walk forward. Do not stop. Follow me into the dress shop no matter what they say. The paps know I'm back and they want comments."

"I got this," Scar says with a nod.

Peyton grunts in agreement.

As we turn onto Main, I immediately notice the paps standing around with their cameras in hand. They're clustered on both sides of the street. One of them points directly at our car and the flashes start.

The car stops right outside the dress shop and hordes of paps come rushing to get to me before I'm in the shop.

But I'm already at the doors with Scar and Peyton on my heels.

"Mera, Mera, how does it feel to be home?"

"Are these your friends?"

"Do you have a comment about the disappearance of Heath Goldsworthy?"

They always seem to have one question that grates on my nerves more than any other.

I smoothly turn back, giving them a broad smile and wave. They shout and cheer and I yank open the doors, holding it open for Scar and Peyton.

A short woman with black hair and gray streaks comes out from the back. "Mera, dear! It's so good to see you." She moves around the counter, rushing over and immediately grabs my cheeks. "I was so excited to get that order. Finally, I got to make a dress for my favorite customer once again."

I give her a tight hug. "You're so sweet Ms. Kara."

Suddenly, I hear the sound of the door opening again. Since the shop is closed to everyone else today for my appointment, that has to be everyone else.

She looks behind me. "It's so nice to see your friends." In a louder voice, she says, "Hi, I'm Kara. My assistants and I will be dressing you all for the ball tomorrow."

A devious smile comes over her face and she leans in to my ear, whispering, "Which one of these handsome men is your escort? Or are you going alone again?"

I can already feel his presence at my back with his gaze on me.

She straightens and her eyes widen. "I think my question has already been answered. I can't wait to get his tux for him." She whirls around and claps her hands quickly. Her assistants come running and she gathers them into a circle.

"You're coming with me on the way back, princess." My cheeks heat up and I turn around. "Actually I think I'll ride with Peyton and Scarlett again."

He opens his mouth to respond when Kara pulls him away, much to his displeasure and gathers him with the other guys.

Her other assistants approach the girls, so I leave them all to talk and decide while I focus on finding a new pair of shoes to match the dress.

Four hours later, the cars come to pick us up with our attire for the ball. I narrowly slip into the car with Peyton and Scarlett.

The paps were waiting right outside for us and got a ton more pictures.

"To The Crown, please," I tell the driver.

"Yes, princess."

It'll be a late lunch and if we're going anywhere, I'd love to take them to my favorite, and of course, the most expensive restaurant downtown, The Crown.

Scar sighs happily. "I've never had a dress this gorgeous before and it fits me like a glove."

It's a beautiful, deep red to match her red hair and it suits her figure perfectly.

"Thanks again for paying Mera, I promise I'll pay you back," Peyton remarks sheepishly.

I never mind paying for friends. It's only when it's demanded of me that I mind. Peyton and Scar are nothing like that. "I invited you guys so it's the least I can do. I'm just happy you were able to come."

Twenty minutes later, we're stopped right outside the doors. Tall dark doors with tinted glass and gold around the edges. The restaurant towers high above, having five floors to it.

THE PRINCESS AND THE BULLY

The top of the building has gold rods that jut out, almost making it look like a crown.

A few people walking by stop and stare as I stop outside the doors, waiting for everyone to gather. They whisper to themselves, making it super obvious that they want to be nosy and see what we're doing.

Kane whistles. "Fancy. Mera, you're really treating us today."

Peyton clears his throat. "Um, are you sure they have enough room for all of us, Mera?"

An excitement builds in me. "Let's go inside and find out, shall we?"

I pull the door open, and walk up to the hostess table only a few feet past the barren seating area.

The hostess is busy on her tablet when I stop in front of it. Without looking up, she says, "If you don't have a reservation, you'll have to leave."

"No reservation," I respond.

She glances up with an annoyed look that quickly changes to one of glee. "Princess! You're back."

"It's good to see you Emily, can we go up?"

She glances at my friends behind me and smiles widely. "Of course, go on up. I'll have Pierre grab sixteen menus and arrange the table."

"Great, thanks," I say, moving around her table and going for the elevator. I press the up button and it immediately comes.

As I step in, and turn around, I tell everyone, "Fifth floor." It'll take a few trips since this elevator is tiny.

Callan, Collette, and Kane join me inside. When it dings, we step out to the top floor full of empty tables. "Welcome to my family's own floor."

"Showoff," Collette murmurs.

I shrug. "Well, I mean, my parents do own it so...yeah! Fun to switch things around, you know, since I'm going to a college that *your* parents own."

The door to the stairs opens and a panting Pierre rushes over. He bows quickly and slams the menus on the table in the middle of the room. "So good to see you again, princess."

Pierre is always the one to serve my family because he has a great attention for detail. He's never once messed up an order, even with the giant parties we've had on this floor. Dragging two tables to each end of the one in the middle, makes one big long one.

"Don't worry about the chairs, Pierre, we'll grab those ourselves."

He grins and wipes the sweat from his brow. "Thank you."

I sit in one of the chairs already at the table and Callan sits next to me. Kane and Collette sit across from us.

"I didn't know you wanted to sit with me so much, Collette."

She glares. "I didn't feel like getting my own chair."

Of course she didn't.

A few minutes later, everyone is seated and Pierre's waiting at the end of the table with his notepad open and ready.

I already know what I want, but everyone else is looking over the extensive menus.

Suddenly, under the table, I feel Callan's hand on my thigh, squeezing it, once, twice, three times. Heat starts to pool beneath my stomach and I bite my lip. I can feel his intense gaze studying my every reaction. I'm about to whisper for him to stop when I feel my phone vibrating in my pocket.

Emily?

I answer the phone and she says, "I'm so sorry to bother you, princess. Your other friends are here. Should I send them up?"

Other friends?

That could only mean three people.

I clench my jaw together and think about what to do, when Callan squeezes my thigh again. "What's wrong?"

I put my hand over the phone. "Some leeches are here to feed."

Kane leans in. "Who's here?" he booms.

Collette raises a questioning eyebrow.

All other conversation stops as everyone turns to stare at me.

"My old friends," I say slowly.

Scar stands up from her chair near the left end of the table. "You mean those three bitches you told me about who haggled you for your money?"

Peyton stands up with her. "You told us they forced you to take them to The Crown all the time."

"They must have seen I was back and known that I'd come here."

"Princess?" Emily asks on the other end of the phone.

Scar flops back in her chair. "Send them up. Send them up!" she yells.

"I agree," Gemma adds.

I hesitate, flip flopping back and forth between telling them to come up and telling Emily to make them leave so I don't have to see them again.

Brandie giggles from the right end of the table. "Come on Mera, do it. I'd like to teach those scummy fakes a lesson."

I don't know what she means by that, but how can I say no when it sounds so fun?

"Let them up," I say and hang up.

"Does everyone know what they want for drinks at least?" I ask, touching the gold trim on the menu.

I hear enough 'yes's' that I nod at Pierre, who takes them all down. As the door to the stairs close behind him, the elevator dings and in walk my three so-called friends.

Four months and they still look the same. Greed shines in their eyes as they look around the table at my friends and I.

"Mera!" Amanda shrieks and comes around the table to hug me from behind.

Evelyn follows suit. I turn my body slightly in the chair. The only one who doesn't touch me is Josh, and that's because of the stare down between him and Callan.

Callan's hand is practically glued to my leg, and as Josh's eyes flit down, I know he sees it too.

Josh's smile falters for a second as he turns to me. "I missed you, Mera. Think you could ask *someone* to move over so I can sit next to you?"

By someone he can only mean Jamie or Callan and I don't think he means Jamie.

"The only guy she's going to sit next to is me."

Josh frowns. "And what about what Mera wants?" He looks pointedly at me, but I don't say a word.

I'll never forget how pushy Josh always was. Not only for my money, but for my attention. For that reason, he's the most annoying out of the trio.

"I'm fine where I am, Josh, actually. Why don't you go and pull up a chair with Amanda and Evelyn?"

His mouth flattens. He truly thought I would say something different. I hold in a laugh.

"So you're gone for four months and suddenly you decide to ditch your friends for some rich snobs?"

Noel shouts, "Hey buddy, we're cool rich snobs, thank you very much!"

I hold back a laugh.

"We've been your friends since freshman year of high school. We partied with you day and night, whenever you wanted to. We skipped out on lots of things to be there for you."

He looks so serious. It's almost like he really believes this shit. That he's actually a good friend.

"So you three paid for your own drinks and paid for your own food while you guys went out too then right?" Scar asks, perching her head on the top of her hand with her elbow on the table.

Amanda gasps. "Hey, wait–"

"Or what about making up excuses so you could get money out of her?" Scar continues.

Evelyn stands up and gazes down the table at me. "Mer, are you really going to let them do this to *us*?"

Josh scoffs. "Obviously she's being used by everybody here. They all secretly hate her, I know it. That's how it was in high school. *We* were the ones who told you who to look out for and I'm telling you right now, every single person at this table hates you. Do you know how pathetic you are Mera for just going along with this?"

I mean, they were mostly wrong, everyone at this table is my friend except for one person.

Collette coughs. "Uh, excuse me, but the only person who gets to call Mera pathetic is *me*. So how about you parasites go and find someone else to attach yourselves to?"

Her words leave me stunned and by the look on everyone else's face at the table, they are too.

Callan stands up, towering over Josh, "Yeah. How about you listen to my sister and go?"

Josh clenches his fists at his side, looking from Callan to me.

Amanda sighs. "Come on, let's go. I can see we aren't wanted anymore."

Evelyn looks teary as she eyes me. As if tears would do anything to turn this around for them.

Josh turns and stomps over to the elevator, with Amanda and Evelyn right behind him. And when they're gone, a rush of relief washes over me.

I'm done with them. I never have to see them again.

"I don't know how you managed to be friends with them for so long. Just from this small amount of time I can tell how annoying they were," Gemma muses.

Jamie touches my hand. "We'll never take advantage of you like that. And I think we're all honored that you invited us."

At that moment, the elevator dings and Pierre comes in, moving tray after tray from the elevator of drinks.

After placing each drink in front of the person who ordered, he takes down our meals and is gone again.

"Let's toast to friendship," Brandie says, holding her glass of wine up. "And to Mera."

"To Mera," everyone except Callan declares, glasses clinking together.

"To Wil," he murmurs in my ear and takes a sip of his tequila.

All of us girls are chattering excitedly as the ball is about to begin. They're all in my room because they wanted me to do their makeup, well, except Collette. But finally, they're all done and I'm all done. I did mine fast so I wouldn't sweat it off.

All eight of our gowns are different colors with different cuts and each one of us looks gorgeous from head to toe.

We all look like a bunch of princesses, honestly.

I gaze at myself in the mirror to check for anything out of place. I try and smooth down a stray strand of hair in the front. Most of it is in curls down my back. The other part is a piece taken from the front left and a piece from the front right put together and held by a jeweled clip.

With careful hands, I move them over the skirt of my princess ball gown. A beautiful rose gold color with diamonds of every size covering the sweetheart cut corset.

"I guess we should get down there," I say, twirling around for one last check.

"Who plans on dancing?" Scar asks.

Brandie pipes up, "Me! I'm sure Brett is going to look so dreamy."

Jamie smiles, "Me too, probably? Hopefully Emerson wants to."

Collette turns her nose up. "I'll be just fine sitting by the bar."

"Guys don't ask me to dance," Gemma quietly remarks.

"Why don't we dance together then?" Ashlynn suggests looking at Scar, Gemma, Luella, and me. "To the fast songs at least. Those slow ones can fuck off. No offense, Mera."

"Sounds good," Luella says, clapping her hands.

Nodding, I finish my outfit up with a tiny princess tiara and slip on a pair of heels with a chunky transparent heel. Out of all of the ones at the shop, these looked the most comfortable while at the same time looking the least probable to not make me do something clumsy like falling over my own feet.

When we walk out, all of the guys are waiting.

My eyes go straight to Callan, his cold eyes turning hot

the minute he looks me up and down. His hair is gelled and pulled to the side and his tux is immaculate. He looks so hot, my breath catches in my throat. And then, I spot the cutest thing in his pocket. A gold flower with rose gold diamonds encrusted inside. When did he get that?

He grabs my arm and leads me down the hallway, fast, away from everyone else. "You shouldn't have worn that dress."

I glance up at him. "Why?"

He inhales deeply. "Because it's taking everything in me not to pull you in any room we pass by and rip it off of you."

A choked breath escapes me as he leads me to the grand stairway by the ballroom. "But just wait," he murmurs.

Just wait for what?

I'm left wondering as the ball starts. What does he want to do?

I try to keep my head in the game as my parents show me off to all of the attendees, talking to them, dancing with my father. I'm finally free so I find Callan in the corner, talking with Tyrell, Vincent, and Noel.

I grab his hand and drag him away, toward the stairs, but instead of going with me, he instead tugs me to the dance floor where a slow song is playing.

I'm still uncertain about things between us. He never apologized for anything he did to me. For filling me with fear and constantly worrying for my life. For choking me to the point where I almost passed out.

The hate between us is gone, but what's left then?

I don't know when I'll figure it out.

There's only one thing I know for sure, and that's that I want him again. Should I give in? I was able to stop myself yesterday morning when we arrived, but now, with how devastatingly handsome he looks, and how hard he's been pushing I can't deny how much I want him.

"What're you thinking about so hard, princess?" he whispers in my ear.

"Nothing," I answer, probably way too quickly.

He presses me into his hips and I feel something rock hard between us. "You know what I'm thinking about though, don't you?"

I shake my head quickly and he leans down, His hot breath hits my ear and I can't even put my mind to the dance movements anymore. I'm following his lead now automatically.

"I'm thinking about how much I need to be inside you."

A low gasp escapes my mouth and my cheeks heat up, glancing around slightly paranoid at the people around us to make sure they didn't hear.

"You want it too, I know you do," he whispers gruffly.

I don't get to respond, because he grabs my hand off his shoulder and leads me away, quickly up the grand staircase.

My heels click softly against the tile as we stop at a bench along the side of the wall.

Down below, I can still hear the song we were dancing to slowly coming to an end and people softly talking to each other.

He pulls me into a rough kiss, capturing my lips and nipping at them with his teeth.

Waves of electricity flow through me, and I gasp softly as his lips move to the side of my neck, sucking hard and then biting down.

I emit a soft whine and his hand covers my mouth quickly. "I love hearing every sound you make, just try and keep it down."

He sits on the bench and pulls me down on his lap.

Underneath me, I feel his hand moving as he undoes the button and the movement of his zipper coming down.

Right now? Right here?

He's really...

My thighs tighten together as moisture starts to pool.

He pulls the skirt of my gown up and yanks my underwear to the side. A long finger slips in, and I bite my lip hard to keep myself quiet.

"You're so wet for me, Wil. You can't wait either, can you?" I close my eyes as I feel the head of his cock brush against my entrance.

The sensation coupled with the anticipation of knowing that he's so close to being inside me causes me to move my hips back and forth, rubbing myself on top of him.

He groans low in his throat. I wish I could see his face this time.

His hands move to my hip outside of my dress and he pulls me down onto his cock in one go.

I cover my mouth, muffling the moan in my throat. A zing of pleasure goes to my toes. There's no pain at all this time.

"You're tighter this time, princess. Is it because anyone can walk by and see us like this?"

He pulls my hips up and thrusts his cock up into me. The pleasure hits me harder than before. Maybe because it was my first time, or maybe because we're in public, or maybe it's this position.

I push myself harder, meeting him as he pounds into me, and he emits a strangled groan that has me moving faster, until the pleasure becomes so much, I lean back against him and he covers my mouth as I cry out, coming on his dick.

Wave after wave of pleasure washes over me, but he's still fucking me hard, making everything feel so heightened. My toes twitch in my heels and my body shakes and another wave hits me and I come all over again.

"You look so pretty when you come, Wil," he whispers.

As he's still slowly rocking into me, I hear voices faintly, and sit up. They're coming from the staircase.

Two minutes later, two people round the top of the staircase and my eyes widen in horror.

Callan is still inside me.

And it's my mother and father.

"Hey guys" I exclaim in a hitched tone.

She smiles. "There you are darling." Turning to my father, she inclines her head, "See I told you she snuck off with him. Oh to be young and in love."

My body quakes at that last word and I feel Callan twitch inside me.

Biting my lip, I twiddle my fingers together.

"Don't worry, we aren't mad at you sweetheart, we snuck off plenty of times together too."

Snuck off, yeah. Those are the words for what we're doing.

"One of those friends of yours was looking for you. He didn't seem too happy that he couldn't find you."

"One of my new friends or old friends?" I ask, even though I know the answer.

"That old one who used to come around all the time."

Josh.

Underneath me, I feel Callan's hips move back just slightly and move forward, moving his cock deeper inside.

"Eeep. Ooookay! Well thanks for letting me know," I say looking between them and motioning with my eyes for them to leave.

My father gets the hint before my mother does.

He grabs her shoulder and ushers her back to the staircase. "Let's let these lovebirds enjoy themselves."

The minute their voices can't be heard anymore, Callan leans up forward. "That was a close one. Do you know how tightly you were clenching around my cock? I almost came, Wil."

I gasp as I feel him twitching inside me again. He moves my hips up and pulls me back down onto his cock.

"Your pussy belongs to me, Wil," he groans as I feel him jerk his hips up, filling me with his hot cum. "Don't deny me anymore."

A hand goes around my throat as he pulls me back and thrusts his tongue inside my mouth, just as roughly as his cock entered my pussy. He pulls back and touches my forehead to his. "Better go clean up." His eyes are hazy with lust. "My cum is going to start leaking out the moment you get off my cock."

My eyes widen at the realization. The closest bathroom is on the other side of the hall.

"Clench those thighs together, princess."

God, and I haven't even had the time to get on birth control.

Luckily, my period came so I'm clear from last time.

With a sharp gasp, I move off of his cock and immediately take off down the hall as fast as I can while keeping my thighs pressed together. I look like a duck waddling awkwardly. Luckily no one is around to see. When I get to the other side, I walk into the unisex bathroom.

Most of the stalls are empty, but since I'm in such a rush, I take the stall closest to the door. I clean up quickly, feeling my body heat up when I see his cum made it partly down my legs.

He came so fucking much.

When I'm done, I flush the toilet, and pull the door open, running right into someone.

"Wh-what? Josh?"

His eyes are angry and red, as if he's been crying.

"Do you know how hard I worked?" he asks quietly.

"What are you talking about?"

"I worked so hard to be the guy you wanted. You leave for four months and you come back with some asshole. And just like that, I'm out. Four years, Mera."

"Josh, you weren't–"

"*Four fucking years*," he thunders. "So what is it? Is his dick big? Is that it?"

He backs me into the stall for a second, but I push forward, trying to move around him.

He blocks me with his body. "No. You aren't getting away from me this time. I bet my dick is just as big as his if not bigger." Reaching forward, he grabs me by my wrist, so tight I wince.

In a flash, I hear the slide of his pants going down. He pulls me to the wall by the sink and I kick my leg out trying to get him in the crotch, but he blocks me.

He yanks my skirt up so I'm flush against his crotch and I can feel his erection.

"I will never want you Josh. What part of that don't you understand? Maybe Amanda or Evelyn are more your speed."

He curls his lip as I try to wrench my wrist out of his grip, but he only punishes me for it by slapping me across the face.

My cheek stings as he wrenches my underwear to the side.

No. *No.*

He pushes a finger into my entrance. "Look how wet you are." He laughs eerily. "You can't deny it."

I spit in his face. "I'm not wet for *you*. I'm wet for Callan and only Callan."

His face twists into anger and he yells, putting a hand at my throat and choking me just as hard as Callan did Halloween night.

I let out a choked scream. Screaming one name only and begging that he'll hear me. "Callan!"

In what seems like slow motion, I feel his hips move forward as I start seeing flashes of light in my vision. The bathroom door opens with a bang and just when I feel his disgusting penis against my entrance, he goes flying away and I can breathe again.

I inhale sharply, clutching my throat and straighten my dress.

I hear the sound of gurgling and look down to find Callan's back with Josh on the floor. Josh's hands and scrambling around madly, scraping at the sides of the bathroom stall.

Callan is drowning him in the toilet. "You touch what's mine, and you die," he says in a low tone. "I thought you got the message yesterday, that Wil was mine, but I guess I didn't make it clear enough. Every inch of her belongs to me. Only I get the pleasure of touching her, kissing her, feeling her clenched around my dick. You're a sorry sack of shit."

I approach Callan, softly touching his back. "Callan, just leave him. Please, I need to get out of here."

Callan glances back at me, his eyes dark. As Josh's hands flop to the ground, Callan suddenly pulls away, pulling him back and letting him fall to the ground next to the toilet.

Josh gasps, coughing hard.

Callan throws a glare in his direction and clutches my hand. He leads me out and down the hall.

It's a long way back to my room, but when we finally get

there, I collapse onto my bed. Callan's hands move to my feet as he slides my heels off.

I hear clothing moving around in the darkness and then I see him get on my bed in just his white shirt and black pants. He gathers me in his arms and rubs his hand along my arm.

"Thank you," I whisper, even though I don't need to. No one's anywhere near here.

He grunts. "Wilhelmera, never be afraid. If you ever find yourself afraid, call for me. Or fuck, even call my phone. I will come for you as fast as I can."

My eyes feel teary and I rub at them quickly.

In a soft voice, he explains, "I'm glad I ended up following you to the bathroom five minutes after you left. I hope you know if I ever see that bastard again, he's dying for real next time."

Nodding, I inhale, smelling Callan's clean scent and let myself become consumed by it and the beating of his heart. And we just stay like that in the darkness of my room. Laying quietly together with no one barging in to bother us.

CHAPTER EIGHTEEN

Callan

I'm in a deep sleep when I hear my phone going off.

Fuck it's too early for this shit.

Didn't I just get back to AAA after an early morning practice?

I feel around on my bed and grab my phone, hitting accept quickly when I see the name on the screen.

"Princess," I groan. "I'm trying to sleep before class this afternoon."

"I know, I know, I'm sorry. It's just, I got back to my room and all of my clothes have been destroyed."

"What the fuck?" I rub my eyes and sigh. "Why would someone do that?"

She doesn't respond, staying quiet. "Wil?"

Her voice comes out shaky, "I just…I called my parents and they're sending clothes over, but I won't be getting them for a few weeks. I hate international shipping. Do you think, well..." she hesitates.

"Just spit it out. Stop beating around the bush," I snap.

She sighs. "Can you take me shopping for a few things after your class? Maybe I'll get two outfits and cycle through them? It'll be super fucking embarrassing, but oh well."

"Are you kidding?" I sit up, stretching my arms above my head. "We'll get at least a month's worth of clothes to replace the ones you lost. I'll ditch today. Meet me outside in a few."

"Thank you!" she squeals.

"See you soon, princess." I hang up and glance at the phone to find it's already past noon, though it would have to be if she's calling me now.

I throw a shirt on and get in my Lambo and go.

When she gets in, she shows me a picture on her phone of all of her clothes strewn across her room. Some spray painted. Some torn. All completely wrecked.

"No one saw anything?" I ask, looking over my shoulder and taking off.

"No. No one ever sees anything," she mumbles, mindlessly watching the road.

"What?" There she goes again, being vague.

"It's nothing. Just thanks for taking me."

Our relationship changed after the Christmas Eve ball. We went straight to my house instead of her staying at the sorority alone for New Year's.

The past month and a half we haven't been able to keep our hands off each other. But there's always something she seems to be holding back. Something she won't say. We've argued about it so many fucking times.

It has to be because she doesn't trust me enough yet.

When we get to the mall, everything is decked out in pink and red and there are hearts all over the place.

A couple pass by us, holding hands and speaking softly to each other. I'm close enough to hear them say 'Happy Valentine's Day' to each other.

Valentine's Day.

What a stupid holiday.

She smiles, looking around. "Before we go shopping, I want to go to Godiva. Is that okay?"

"Sure."

It's on the second level of the mall, but when we get there it's packed. Thirty minutes later, we're at the counter and she picks out some milk chocolate and some milk chocolate with caramel in the center.

"I'll pay for it," she says, handing her card to the cashier.

Frowning, I shake my head at the cashier. "Take my card. Now." I hand it off and she takes it looking from Wil to I.

"I wish my husband was that enthusiastic about paying for my stuff. You two are such a cute couple. Happy Valentine's Day!" The cashier hands me the card back.

Wil smiles, but it doesn't reach her eyes. Why? "Thank you."

She's quiet as we take the escalator back downstairs to the clothing stores.

I grunt and grab her hand. "Wil. If you wanted us to do something special today, we could have."

She squeezes my hand. "No. It's okay. I know we're not... well we're not there yet." I'm about to respond when she steps off as the escalator reaches the bottom. She brings me to the first store on the right. "Let's just shop for now and talk about it later, okay?"

I nod, but I'd rather just tell her, I want to spoil her every day of the year. Give her whatever she wants when she wants it. She doesn't have to wait for this day to get chocolate and flowers.

Shit she's turning me into a sap. Me, Callan Goldsworthy, a sap.

Who claimed he would never be tied down by any one girl.

But Wil isn't just any girl.

We're in the food court eating Chinese food when I hear the tell-tale click of phone cameras.

She sighs. "They're taking pictures again."

"Let's just finish and go," I tell her, glaring around as a warning to anyone who thinks about following us back to my car.

The whole world knows about us now and the whole world is judging her so fucking hard for dating Heath and now me. No one but me knows their relationship is fake.

She doesn't want to explain to the police why she didn't tell them before.

We get up, throw our trash away and set the trays on top of the trash can.

I grab all of her bags in one hand and wrap my other arm around her shoulder.

"Thanks for today. I really did have a good time. Are you going to be at the party tonight?"

I've missed out on the last few, trying to keep focused on my classes. Since it's Valentine's Day, I'll go to this one.

"Sure."

As we're about to leave, I pass by a store that makes me stop and stare. A watch shop.

"Callan?" Wil asks. "Why'd we stop?"

"I just remembered."

I'll never see that watch again.

The watch that Heath was supposed to give me the night he disappeared. Wherever that watch is, it's lost with him.

"It's nothing."

She frowns at me and she looks like she wants to ask, but she lets it go. But as we get back in the car, I can't help thinking back to that night, like I have so many times in the past six months.

"I can't believe I have to room with Silverstone," Vincent yells angrily. "Of all the fucking guys."

"That's just the way it goes, man. Heath didn't do it on purpose, chill."

"Ty, want to switch with me?" Vincent asks, elbowing Tyrell in the arm.

Ty blinks twice. "No. Don't ask again."

Vincent scratches his head. "Okay. Can't say I wasn't fucking expecting that. What about you Noel?"

Noel snorts. "Absolutely fucking not. He's the type that wouldn't leave the room for the night if I had a lady over. He'd just sit there and fucking watch. Tyrell isn't like that, right buddy?" Noel claps him on the back and Ty doesn't look enthused.

"I'm going to sleep before the party. No one wake me up for any reason, whatsoever." I head up the stairs, close my door and flop on my bed. Luckily it's a single. My brother knows I don't get along with just anyone.

I set an alarm on my phone for eight. As I'm about to lock it, I check social media and see a bunch of posts with my grandfather's picture on them. Why are these still showing up on my timeline? His funeral was over two weeks ago.

My mom's father. Unlike my father's father, he didn't believe I was a failure. He always told me I had potential to do great things. He told it to my siblings and I equally, not just one of us.

A kind man, and he's in the ground from one stroke.

While my other grandfather is in wonderful condition and he's fucking older.

He can keep whatever that asshole gives him when he dies, but I deserve to have something from my mother's father. While he was a rich man, he left everything to my mother. Not that she's in need of anything because my father gives her whatever she wants. But her father was a sucker for my mom.

He left his prized watch to the three of us. Naturally, my father gave it straight to Heath.

But I want it.

He's been putting off giving it to me for long enough. Should've fucking given it to me this week. Instead he's been running around with her.

Last night was priceless. With any luck, she'll be crying to her parents and be on the next plane out of here.

I fall asleep to the flash of pink.

When I wake up, I text him about the watch one last time, telling him he needs to be here by three AM no matter what. He responds with a thumbs up and a text saying he'll be here and he has something to talk about with me too.

Good.

On the other side of the door, music enters the air and it steadily grows louder. Guess the party is starting.

I knock on Tyrell and Noel's door and get no response. Then I knock on Vincent's hoping to God I don't have to see Silverstone's face.

Neither of them answer.

Where the fuck are they?

Well, I know where Vincent went. He's forever following Ashlynn around like a puppy. He went to ZDB.

Noel will follow the women. He could be anywhere. It'd be most convenient for him to go with Vincent to ZDB.

Which means, Tyrell went with them.

Well, I refuse to go.

Not tonight.

Tonight I want to actually enjoy myself.

I get down the stairs and go into the kitchen, grabbing a beer from the tap and drain my cup. It's good, just not what I'm craving. I grab a fresh bottle of tequila from the counter and take a swig. Fuck yes. That's it. That burn sliding down my throat is nice.

"Callan," a voice says.

God, I'd know that fucking voice anywhere. I wanted to have fun tonight. Not party with her attached to me like a remora.

I turn around to find Ginger. She has heavy black eyeliner around her eyes, so thick she looks like a fucking raccoon. Her orange hair falls around her shoulders and she has a black headband on.

"I'm ready," she purrs.

I back away quickly and take another swig. "Ready for what?"

Most girls follow my brother around the moment they see him. But Ginger? Ginger is different. My brother doesn't exist in her eyes. She's been trying to get me to sleep with her since high school.

The only reason she hasn't is because she hasn't been able to follow my one rule.

I made it up on the spot as a way to stop her from getting in my pants, but by the excited look in her eyes, she's finally done it. In my brother's image, a girl can only sleep with me if she drinks a bottle of Jose Cuervo, while his is a bottle of Absolut.

"Give me the Jose Cuervo."

Fuck.

Think and think fast.

I turn around and grab the new bottle and hold it in front of her. She grabs it with her hands and pops it open. I can't count the number of times she's attempted this. She has to just be overconfident.

I eat my words when she finishes the bottle in fifteen minutes.

She slams the bottle on the counter and leans into me with a pink face and hazy eyes.

"It's time," she slurs, "you, me, your bed. Now." She jumps at me and I grudgingly hold her in my arms.

I bring her up the stairs to my room and she flops on the bed. "I made it!" she yells excitedly, putting her arms in the air.

"Now fuck me Callan. Fuck me right fucking now." She's too anxious to get my dick inside her.

"Ginger," I mutter, rubbing a hand over my face and leaning against the door. What the fuck do I do? I don't want my dick anywhere near her.

"I did it fair and square. You owe it to me now. You owe..." She blinks slowly and her eyes slide closed.

"Ginger?" I stride over to her and lean my head down to her chest to make sure she's still alive.

Her heart is still beating.

I move back and watch her face and the slow rise and fall of her chest.

Lucky. Thank fuck I got lucky tonight.

I stay in the room for a long time, on my phone and when a respectable time passes, I leave the room and go downstairs.

The rest of the night, I spend listening to music and drinking until I'm buzzed.

Heath never shows up. When I call his phone, it goes straight to voicemail. Who knows how long it's has been turned off?

Hours later, after everyone's either left or passed out on the floor, I'm in my room listening to a sleeping Ginger when I get the text from Collette with the picture.

Heath Goldsworthy is dead.

What the fuck?

She calls me a second later, uncontrollably sobbing and telling me the last time anyone saw him, he was with Wil in her room, and they were fucking.

It's too much of a coincidence that one week into her existence in my brother's life, this happens. She has to be partly if not fully responsible.

Princess or not, she's going to pay. She won't get away with this.

"Callan, are you going to get out of the car?"

Blinking quickly, I gaze past her and notice we're sitting in front of ZDB. By the looks of it, the party's already started by the loud music and the people loitering outside.

I turn the car off. "Yeah. Let's go."

If I'm being honest with myself, it's been almost six months. I'll never see Heath or that watch again.

CHAPTER NINETEEN

Mera

I walk inside ZDB and go straight for the alcohol. Every party I've been to since that first one, and there've been several I decided to attend, I haven't had a drink. I've been too nervous to, afraid that somehow something terrible will happen again and I won't be able to remember.

But tonight, I need it.

I had a great day with him at the mall. I didn't expect us to spend Valentine's Day together. I try not to expect anything of him so I don't get disappointed. It's hard when he shuts down on me out of nowhere. The minute he got in the car he was back to being ice cold and distant. He's only acted that way a handful of times since we got back from Kardenia, each time I want to tell him he can talk to me, but how can I expect him to open up when I still haven't told him about the notes?

There's so many of them now, the bottom drawer of my nightstand is full to the brim. I've gotten used to the threats on my life. Their new thing is to threaten Callan's.

Every day I'm tempted to throw them all in a bag and show him.

But they've made it very clear, if I tell Callan he'll die just like Heath did.

This is their way to make me suffer.

So tonight, I drink.

I grab the bottle of Absolut from the counter, pour a shot and throw it back.

"Hand me the Jose Cuervo, Wil," I hear Callan say behind me.

His eyes are cold as they look from the bottle of Absolut to me.

I pick up the brand new bottle of Jose Cuervo, and just as he opens his hand to take it, an orange blur snatches it away.

Gritting my teeth, I watch Ginger shake the bottle. "Callan, this time I won't fall asleep."

Rage fills his eyes and he thrusts his hand forward to snatch it away from her. She moves her hand back, moving it behind her back and shakes her finger at him. "No, no, no, Callan. You know the rules. I finish this, we go find a room."

"Ginger, I'm not doing that anymore. That game is over with," he says in a dangerously low tone. "Hand me the fucking bottle."

She turns around and tilts her head back, keeping the bottle straight and letting the liquid slide down her throat.

She stops after a few seconds, coughing hard.

She's halfway there. Fucking hell.

I glance at the counter and notice two more bottles of Jose Cuervo.

A sense of deja vu washes over me as I grab the bottle in my hand.

"Wil," Callan says with a sigh. "You don't need to do that. I'm not going anywhere with her."

Her eyes widen as she watches me unscrew the cap. "Just let me do it. I can do it." And I'll have to do it fast.

I put the bottle to my lips and gulp it down, feeling the burn as it goes down my throat. My face feels hot as I close my eyes and keep drinking.

Vaguely, I hear her trying to gulp it down.

I stop to take a breath, gasping for air, and looking at the bottle. A fourth to go. I haven't drank anything this fast in a long time.

I only had a few glasses of alcohol at the Christmas Eve ball.

I refuse to be outdone.

I gulp the rest of it down, and slam the bottle on the counter at the same time she does.

She screeches, "No! I did it first. I finished my bottle first." She slams her hand on the table and screams, "He's going with me!"

Wiping my mouth on my arm, I stare her down. "Is that so?" I move to the counter, a little slower than before, as things start to feel further away. The volume in the room is a lot higher.

I grab the last bottle of Jose Cuervo and gulp more down.

"Wil!" Callan yells, reaching for the bottle. I change hands and push him away.

My head feels so heavy. I gasp as I pull it away and set the bottle on the counter. Half of it is gone. "His dick is mine."

"Bitch!" she yells loud enough for anyone to hear over the blaring music. And hear, a lot of people do as they turn around to look.

I slump back against the counter. "No. You're the bitch. He's mine," I slur.

"I'm not doing this game anymore with you Ginger. In fact, I don't want to see your face again."

Ginger hiccups and tears leak from her eyes. "No." She hiccups again. "No, you can't do that. Everything I do is for you, Callan. It's always for you."

Callan's arm goes around my back as he lifts me up to his side. We walk into the living room. He looks around and booms, "Cut the music. Someone cut the fucking music now."

All of a sudden, the music is gone, and I glance around to find everyone staring at us.

"No one better fucking approach me again with a bottle of Jose Cuervo expecting me to take them to bed. It's not going to happen."

"Yeah!" I yell, throwing a random hand up and moving my hand, pointing at everyone. "Try it and I'll kick your ass. And then I'll ban you from my country."

Somewhere off in the crowd, I hear Noel clap his hands. "Woo, yeah. Mera!"

"Play the music," Callan barks, turning around and urging me up the stairs.

The music returns as he pushes me inside my room and closes the door.

I stumble back until my legs meet my bed, and lay down on it with my legs hanging off the edge.

"Don't do that again."

I tilt my head down to look at him to find him crossing his arms and staring at me coldly.

I did it so that the orange haired bimbo would leave, yet he's acting like I did something bad.

"Why?"

"I had it handled. I didn't need you to do that, Wil."

He glares and I'm so sick of it, I look back at the ceiling. "Whatever. I could, so I did."

"I'm going to drink more." I hear the sound of the door being pulled open and the click of a lock.

He's locking the door?

It slams closed, shaking the room, and I stare at the ceiling, watching it, when something clicks.

The locking of the door.

The slamming.

It replays in my head, over and over, until I suddenly remember.

Holy shit. I sit up way too fast and stare at the wooden door. I know what happened that night.

"Tonight's going to be fun, roomie," Brandie says, putting a Maroon 5 poster on the wall.

The wall her bed is against and the walls on her half of the room are decked out with posters, I almost feel like I'm back in my own room at home.

I didn't bring any with me.

"It is." Heath had some errands to run, but he should be here soon.

"You and Heath look so adorable together. What did he think about what his brother did last night? Is his brother into you or something?"

I move the strands of hair sticking to my face. "He wasn't happy." Shit, that doesn't sound convincing enough does it?

"He was super angry and furious. I haven't seen him so mad before. He said he was going to punch him right in the face the moment he saw him."

She smiles. "Wow. What a guy, willing to fight his brother for you. I hope Callan doesn't try and get in the way of your happiness. He's always seemed bitter, even in high school."

"Oh you went to high school with him?"

She nods. "Yeah, I think quite a few of us in this sorority did. The older girls with Heath of course."

Outside the door, the music starts, signaling our cue to go out and join the party.

I can't drink a ton, but that doesn't mean I can't drink some.

"Oh! And if you and Heath, uh you know, decide to do the deed, and you want to use this room, just text and let me know okay?"

My cheeks heat up at the thought of Heath and I in bed together. That thought feels so wrong. "I'll definitely let you know," I say slowly.

She smiles. "Now come on, let's enjoy the party."

She opens the door and I follow her out.

Some EDM song is playing as we walk to the stairs. There's a ton of people dancing and drinking together. I don't see Scar or Peyton yet. They should be here soon. Brandie waves and mouths 'see you later' when she gets wrapped up in the arms of a tall blond guy.

Maybe, I'll head for the drinks first.

When I walk into the kitchen area, I spot a familiar face in the corner of the room, sipping from a red cup and scrolling through her phone. Gemma!

"Hey!"

She glances up. "Hi, Mera." She glances back down at her phone.

I grab a cup of beer and walk over to her. She straightens with a look of surprise in her eyes. "What's up?"

I shrug. "I'm just waiting around for Heath. He should be here any minute."

"Hey, thanks for what you said last night," she says, tucking a hair behind her ear.

"No biggie. I meant it."

Her eyes widen as she looks past me, and I turn around to find the same guy who took her back here last night coming toward us.

He walks slowly, in an exaggerated way that lets me know he thinks highly of himself. Too highly. With a bottle of Absolut in his hand.

"Princess." That's the only greeting I get as he zeroes in on Gemma. "Nice to see you again, Gem."

She ignores him, still facing me. "I have to go, Mera."

She walks between him and I, walking to the living room.

"Where are you going, nerd?" he turns and follows her as she walks back into the living room. I follow behind him, and almost run into him when he stops.

He's got Gemma's wrist and refusing to let go.

"Just hear me out. Let's go out once. Anywhere you want, my treat."

Gemma squares her shoulders and fixes him with a look of pure annoyance. "Not interested."

"Just give me a chance, I'm a pretty cool guy," he insists. "I'm not asking us to fuck on the first date if that's what you're afraid of."

She clenches her jaw, closing her eyes for a second and pushing her glasses to her face before opening them. "No. How many times do I need to say it for you to understand?" It's yelled so loud, the entire party around us stops to stare.

I can't see Noel's face, but Gemma's face pales a little as she stares at him and tries to wrench his hand off her wrist.

"We're going to talk somewhere private," he says, in a tone so much like Callan, it makes me jump in on her behalf.

"Let go of her. She said no."

He turns to me with a murderous expression and I back up a little.

"Hey, I thought this was a party."

I glance around them to see Heath looking around the room

puzzled. When he sees me, he smiles and the dimples on his cheeks show. "There you are."

I move around Noel and Gemma and walk over to Heath, who puts an arm around my shoulder. "He won't let her go," I whisper.

He squeezes my shoulder before walking over to Gemma and Noel, stepping between them. "Why don't you let her go, man? She's just one girl. There are plenty of other girls interested."

Apparently his grip loosens, because Gemma wrenches her arm away. She scowls and rubs her wrist. "I'm not interested in going out with anyone. If I was, I'd go out with..." she trails off, "someone like Heath. Too bad he's taken."

Heath smiles, and I know him well enough now to know he's uncomfortable with her statement. "You're sweet, Gemma."

The rage on Noel's face suddenly lessens, and he's back to smiling. "My bad, Gem." The tension in the room lessens and everyone starts paying attention to the music again.

He looks from me to Heath. "Sorry." He turns around quickly for a moment, shuffling around and holds out his half drank bottle of Absolut. "Here, have the rest, I wiped the top off. No germs."

Heath doesn't look like he wants to take it, so I step up to Gemma's side and accept it, handing it to Heath. I just want things to stay calm so they don't escalate. "Thanks Noel."

Heath takes several swigs and Noel smiles. "Have a nice night." He leaves after glancing at Gemma once more.

She turns to Heath and then me. "Thank you both. I'm uncomfortable with men. Mera knows that."

Heath hands the bottle to me. Only about a fourth of it is left, so I finish it off.

It feels so good to drink again. I need more. "Let's go to the kitchen. See you later, Gemma."

She gives us a wave, and when we get to the kitchen, people are all over the place, more so than before. Tons of people are gathered around the beer tap, guzzling it down.

"Heath! There you are!" a voice yells over the music.

It sounds only vaguely familiar, but when she bounds over, I know exactly where I remember her from. The very first fucking day. The freshman dorm. What's her name?

"Hey, Jenny," Heath responds.

She smiles widely, completely ignoring the fact that I'm standing right next to him.

"Let's play that game of yours. I prepared all summer for this." She grabs a big bottle of Absolut and unscrews the cap.

Heath shakes his head. "No. I'm not doing that anymore. I'm off the market, Jenny."

"No," she voices, "you aren't."

"Standing right here, bitch," I say, waving my hand in front of her face.

She laughs. "Then let's see you do it. Drink that bottle." Her eyes move to the other full bottle of Absolut on the counter.

A smile spreads across my face and I hold in a laugh. She thinks she can beat me? With Absolut?

"Mera, you don't have to do that. I'm not going to fuck anyone but you," he says, loud enough for her to hear.

She shakes her head, "No. See you didn't announce it before the party like you usually do if you're in a relationship. This is valid." She puts the bottle to her mouth and tips the bottle high enough for the vodka to go down.

"It's going to be fine, Heath." This is my job right now, as your girlfriend, to fight off the other bitches trying to steal you away.

I tip the bottle back and as soon as I feel that burn, I feel like I'm back in George's bar in Kardenia.

"Your parents didn't want you to drink a lot," he whispers.

But I don't let that stop me. I never have.

Even if it's a bad idea, I have to do this.

It takes about ten minutes for me to get it all of it down, but I do. And before her at that. My face might feel hot and the room might be spinning a little, but I did it.

And Jenny is pissed.

A fourth of her bottle is left and she slams it on the counter. "It's fine," she snaps. "Because pretty soon, Heath will dump you. He'll find someone better. He always does. Isn't that right, Heath?" She says looking pointedly at him. "You fuck until it gets serious and then it's over." Her gaze shifts back to me. "So be careful, princess. Don't let him too close. He might look sweet on the outside but he's a monster underneath."

"And yet you still want him?" I ask, confused by her obvious lust for him.

"Sometimes it's the monsters that draw you in. And once you're in, you're held captive. Forever." She grins. "So I'll wait my turn. Remember Heath, I'll be whatever you want me to be."

"Let's just go up to your room." He moves a hand over his face.

We go up, passing people in the hallway making out.

When we finally get inside, I sit at the edge of my bed and he sits with me.

"You know, she's right," he murmurs.

"What? About you being a monster?"

He nods. "I did something horrible just last year." His face is so conflicted, and sad, I feel like I have to ask.

"What happened? You can talk to me, you know. I am your 'girlfriend' after all."

A slow smile spreads on his face. "It's better you don't know. Let me keep that good guy image up in front of you."

"Everyone makes mistakes Heath." I know that better than anyone with all my drunken escapades and the messing up of ceremonies at home. I'm not that great at being a princess. "All you can do is do the best you can. You're only human."

He stays silent as he lays back on my bed and I lie next to him.

"It's good to see you again, Mer. This time, I'm allowed to be your friend."

"What do you mean?" I ask, turning my head to him quickly.

He chuckles. "We met once before when I went to one of your castles. I was about nine and you were this spunky five or six year old with bright pink hair."

I laugh at that. I had to beg Mother to let me and the day she did, I remember being so excited I showed it to everybody who worked at the castle at that time. "What? How come you didn't tell me before?"

"I wanted to see if you'd remember on your own. You haven't so I thought I'd bring it up. You invited both Callan and I to play with you. He didn't look too happy and my father didn't. He wanted me to stick around and play with your sister."

I giggle. "Cate never wanted to play, though. Not even with me. She'd rather read or write. Learn about our country's history. I had to beg her to play."

"She didn't like me very much, I could tell. Every time I went to say something she'd react like she didn't want to hear it. We ended up not saying anything to each other at all. Then...I think...Callan had an accident." Abruptly, Heath's head lulls back.

"An accident?" I ask and gasp when I remember. "He's Rain Boy. Oh my God. He's Rain...Boy." I peer at Heath and find him passed out on my bed.

What the fuck?

And why do I also feel myself getting so drowsy–

Everything goes black.

Dimly, I hear the sound of someone muttering and pop an eye open to see Heath sitting at my bed, clutching his head. "I have to get back to AAA."

"Heath?" I rasp.

He turns his head to look at me. "Mera? Are you okay?"

"I think I drank too much," I slur, "I feel funny. What time is it?"

Rubbing a hand over his face, he checks his phone, "Just after two. I have to go." He leans over me and presses a chaste kiss to my cheek. "I'll see you tomorrow, okay?"

"Mm, see you," I murmur, leaning up to see him open the door, lock it quickly, and close it behind him.

My eyes feel so heavy, I just want to go to sleep. I need to turn the light off.

I pull myself to the top of the bed, reaching over to my nightstand for the light. My arm is stretched as far as it can go, can't it? So why can't I reach the light?

I flail my hand forward and that momentum carries me forward as I reach the light switch and yank it. The lights go off and I sigh happily at the darkness when I go to roll over and over extend myself, colliding with my headboard, and passing right out.

The next sound I hear is the sound of someone pounding on the door urgently.

I call Callan's phone immediately to tell him the good news. He comes back with a cup of beer and listens as I tell him exactly what happened.

When I finish, I expect something. A 'thank you,' or at least a 'finally' since it took me so long. But he doesn't do any of those things.

His eyes are colder than ever, and when I'm done, he turns around and leaves, telling me he'll see me later.

This is the one thing that's been torturing me for months.

I do feel bad that I don't know more. There's nothing I can do about that though. The only useful thing that was locked away in my memories is that Heath left here just after two. Between two and eight AM, someone killed him and he and his car disappeared, never to be seen again.

I lie back on my pillow and move my hand underneath it to push it further into my face when I feel a piece of paper.

Not this shit again.

I pull it out to find a picture with a note wrapped around it.

The picture makes my stomach drop.

It's me. What I think is me?

That platinum blonde hair has to be mine. It stops right in the middle of my back like mine. And that's my pink hoodie that hasn't been seen since that night. That's not the most horrifying part. The most horrifying part is the date. That's the night he went missing and…I'm standing in front of Heath's car with the door open and what looks like Heath inside?

Tossing the picture away, I stare down at the note.

I told you, guilty. Want that hoodie of yours back? I've been holding on to it, just for you. You'll have to wash it first before using it again since it's covered in his blood.

No way. There's no way. I remember it all. That can't be me. I didn't do anything to Heath.

CHAPTER TWENTY

Callan

I haven't been feeling anything since Wil told me what she remembered two weeks ago. I've been going about everything on autopilot. School. The fraternity. Basketball.

Coach forced me to run laps because of how reckless I was with the ball.

And Wil... Wil and I have been on autopilot too. We spend time together, yet apart. Too content to sit in silence together. We haven't fucked since the day before Valentine's Day.

It's not her fault that all of this happened.

I do feel guilty for assuming she did something to him at first.

Something has been on her mind since the night she told me. Every time we're together, when she thinks I'm not looking, I see her looking over her shoulder. Is she afraid of the person who broke into her room and destroyed her clothes?

A lot of people here still aren't fans of hers. Something like this was bound to happen. But she acts like it's more than that.

She's coming over today to study for our political science midterm tomorrow.

I open the door to a knock, and Wil shoots me a small smile. "Let's do good on this one."

Nodding, I step aside to let her pass and close the door to the loud shouts emanating from down the hall.

She settles onto the floor, leaning up against the front of my bed, and I sit beside her.

She pulls out her flashcards, her preferred method of studying and quizzes me first. Once I've gone through them several times, only getting a few wrong each time, I go through them and quiz her.

After the second round, she clutches her head. "I kind of have a headache."

"Let's take a break."

I choose that time to get off the floor and grab two water bottles from my mini fridge.

Mine is the only room in the fraternity with one.

I toss one to her and she gulps the water down.

"Hey, Callan," she speaks in a soft tone. "Something has been going on for a while."

Her careful tone makes me stare hard at her. "What's been going on?"

Suddenly, my phone goes off, vibrating in my pocket. Dad.

If this isn't an update on Heath I don't want this call. I'll find an excuse and get off quickly.

"Hold on," I tell Wil and answer.

"How're you doing son?" Dad asks in a monotone voice.

"Fine," I reply back in the same tone.

"Good to hear. Listen, I just wanted to let you know, after talking with the police about what you said Mera remembered, we've all decided that it's in our best interest to stop searching for Heath."

Like a sucker punch to the gut, I feel fucking sick. "You can't do that, Dad. He needs to be found."

Dad sighs. "And someday, I'm sure we'll find it. The bones, maybe. But we don't know anything, all leads have been false."

"There might be more leads!" I shout. "Why are we giving up so soon?"

"It's been six months. I'm afraid it's time for us to let him go. I've put plenty of money and time into trying to find him. A lead isn't just going to appear out of nowhere, six months later. We have to just accept it. He's gone and let him rest."

"No." This is why I fucking hate him. What kind of father gives up after six months? If something had happened to me, he would've given up after six months? And Mom is just letting him? "You can't do this."

"I am, and I did. It's over beginning tomorrow."

"Fuck you!" I yell into the phone and hang up.

Wil looks at me with wide eyes. "I'm sorry. I can't believe he's given up so easily."

I hold my head, trying to contain the headache forming. "You need to go."

"We aren't done studying yet, I still need to go over it a few more times."

"Do it in your own room," I mutter and open the door for her.

She frowns. "Just because you got bad news, doesn't mean

you get to treat me like shit again, Callan. I'm not your enemy."

"Just get out." I can feel my anger rising with every second. It's leaking out in small doses, and getting to her. I need her out before it consumes me completely. "I'll talk to you later."

"Talk to me about this. Don't just shut down," she says, getting off the floor and touching my shoulder.

"I don't want to talk!" I shout. "Now get the hell out. I have things to do." Like talk to my sister and see if she'll help me turn things around. It's a long shot. But I need to do whatever it takes to keep this investigation open.

"If I walk out, I'm not coming back in, Callan. Ever." Her mouth folds into sadness and her eyes get teary.

But right now, I'm too mad to care. "Leave."

Because when I want her back, I'll drag her back in, kicking and screaming if I have to.

She inhales deeply, goes back to grab her bag off the floor, shoving her flashcards in and runs out.

I close the door and immediately dial Coll's phone. She answers after a few rings. "What?"

"Did Dad call you yet?"

She sighs. "Is this about Heath? Yes, he told me last weekend that he was thinking about shutting the investigation down. I don't want him to shut it down either, but there's nothing we can do except keep trying on our own to find something else out."

"There has to be more. There's something out there we're missing."

"Talk to your friends again. Maybe there's some minute detail that they glossed over the first time you asked them?"

It's a good suggestion. In fact, I'll ask everyone again. "Ask your friends again too, then. They were there that night."

"I've asked so many times," she says with a frustrated sigh, "but sure."

I go to rush away, opening the door, when I realize how nice that scent is. Wil's scent. I'll make it up to her. Right now, this is more important.

When I get to Tyrell and Noel's room, Vincent is there too, listening to music on Tyrell's bed while Tyrell is on the floor and Noel is on his.

"What's up buddy?" Noel asks, looking up from his phone.

"My dad is shutting the investigation down."

"Oh shit," Vincent mutters.

"Sorry, man. Why don't you pop a squat and try and chill for a while?" Noel asks.

I shake my head. "No. I came to ask you guys, one last time. What do you remember from that night?"

Noel's smile leaves his face. "I remember acting like an ass and Heath stopping me. Heath went into the kitchen with Mera, came back out and went upstairs with her. I left ZDB around midnight after sulking over my first rejection."

Vincent clears his throat. "I was there until two, but I was watching Ashlynn all night." He grimaces. "And what about Heath?"

He blinks quickly. "I never saw him come out of Mera's room."

I look down to Tyrell on the floor.

His mouth flattens. "I stayed out in the backyard all night long...watching Luella with some other guy. I-I was fucking miserable. I wanted to beat his face in."

"And Heath?" I ask.

He tilts his head back. "He went up with Mera and I didn't see him again."

So nothing new. Fucking hell.

"Thanks." I leave, slamming the door behind me, ready to go back to my room when I run right into Silverstone.

He inclines his head toward the room he shares with Vincent.

When he closes the door behind me, he walks to his bed and sits at the end. "So I heard they're closing the investigation."

"How do you know that?" I ask slowly, watching his face as he smiles widely.

"I know a lot of things. And what I know for sure is that I'm the only one who can help you. So ask me what I know, Callan, ask me nicely."

Anger rises from my chest and I pull him up by his black t-shirt. "Tell me what the hell you know, Silverstone."

"That's not nicely. But I'll let it slide, just this once." He shoves my hands away. "I saw Heath come down the stairs that night. He didn't look well. Maybe he drank too much booze, who knows. I know I did. I watched him run into three people and the last one helped him to his car. That car left the parking lot and I never saw him or it again."

Clenching my fists at my side, it takes every fiber in my being to not punch this asshole right in his fucking face until it's completely bruised. "You couldn't tell me any of this sooner?" I snap. "And who were the three people? No one came forward and said any of that shit. How do I know that's the truth?"

"I didn't say so sooner because I fucking hate you, Goldsworthy." He smirks. "And who those three people are aren't important. I have no reason to lie."

"Except to fuck with me," I blurt.

"Believe me or don't, that's fine with me." He shrugs with a smug look on his face.

I leave without another word, heading back to my room.

When I get inside, I go to call my dad, stopping as my finger hovers over his name in my contact list.

No. He's already given up on finding Heath. This is only for Collette and I to know, and no one else.

But something still doesn't make sense. How the fuck could Silverstone know so quickly that the investigation was shut down? Does he have an in with the police? Does one of them *call him* with updates?

And if so, why keep tabs on Heath? Heath who he despises just as much as he despises me. Even more concerning, did he really tell me everything this time? He better hope to God he did.

Kane Silverstone has hated me since the moment he met me.

"Callan. This is Kane. You guys both like to play with cars, don't you? Go outside and play while Kane's father and I talk business."

I nod and grab a green car for Kane and a blue one for me.

"Thanks." *Why doesn't he look happy? The green car is the better one since somehow I messed up the blue wheel.*

We go outside of the building and I line up my car. "Hey, let's see who is faster." *He'll be happy when he wins.*

He stares blankly at me for a few minutes and finally nods. Does he feel sick or something?

Kane sets the green car down, crouching down next to me.

"Ready?" *I ask. Before I can say go, he pushes the car forward. His car goes all the way to the grass and flops over.*

"Hey!" *I yell, standing up and pointing.* "That's not fair. You have to wait until I say go."

He laughs. "I won. Now go get it so we can go again." *His eyes are different than everyone else at school. Why is he looking at me like that?*

I walk down to the grass and go get it anyway, handing it to him. He sets it down and I crouch next to him. "This time, let's wait until I say go." He's going to win anyway since the wheel of mine is messed up.

"Ready?" He nods. "Go!" I yell.

I push the car and watch it go a short ways, eventually spinning out while his gets to the end of the grass again.

He laughs and shouts, "Haha, you're still a loser! Want to go again?"

But I don't. And I don't want to be called a loser. That's mean. Heath said when people say stuff like that they're bullies.

"I'm not a loser," I mutter. "I knew your car would win. My wheel is messed up." I walk over to the blue car and pick it up. "Here, you can try it and it'll do the same for you."

He snatches it from my grasp and pushes it forward. The same exact thing happens and he glares at me. "What kind of idiot keeps a messed up car? My dad will buy me a new one if mine breaks."

"My dad would too!" I yell. "I just like this one because my brother gave it to me."

He glares. "Your brother makes stupid choices then."

I hate him. Kane. No one talks about my brother like that. "You don't talk about my brother like that."

"I can say what I want. I'm Kane Silverstone."

I clench my fist. I want to hit him. I feel so angry. Dad says hitting is for older people though. I'm only six. Dad might get in trouble with Kane's dad.

What should I do?

Maybe if we do something else he'll act nicer. "Why don't we go to the lake for a swim? They'll take a while in there."

A smile that I can only think of as creepy spreads across his face. "Yeah, that sounds like a good idea. Let's go."

I put my blue car on the ground next to the green one and start walking, leading the way to the lake.

Dad says most students are off campus for the rest of the week so no one should be there.

I wish I had a better idea. Mom will be mad when she sees my wet clothes again and maybe even madder because she told me not to do this until the sun is out all the time again. If there was other fun stuff to do here I would do it.

Kane stays behind me. I look back at him a few times to see what he's doing. He isn't doing anything though, just smiling in a weird way.

It's a long way to the lake and it can sometimes be confusing with how many trees are around. It's a lot easier now since the leaves have fallen off.

When we finally get there, I stop at the edge and point to the dock. "Why don't we jump off there?"

He nods. "Sure. We'll race to see who's faster." Something in his expression makes me feel scared. Maybe it's the fact that he's still smiling?

I start walking and try to ignore the feeling in my chest. When I get there, I take my shoes off and he does the same.

"I'm a pretty good swimmer. Are you?" he asks, looking at the lake.

It's not the pool at my house, but it's still pretty fun. "I'm pretty good too."

He jumps in place. "I'm ready then. We'll run when you say go."

"Ready?" I pause and watch him stick his leg out and his arms straight back. "Go!"

I take off, running straight down the old dock. Where's Kane though? I don't see him. As I hit the water, I go down, and move my arms to go back up when I hear a splash.

A splash that's way too close.

And then I feel it, hands, two hands pressing on my head.

Did Kane land on me?

I try and swim away, but his hands stay on my head. What's he doing? I need air.

I tap his hands expecting him to realize his mistake and let go. He only presses me down harder.

Wait. This isn't funny. This isn't fun. I open my mouth as my air runs out and water comes rushing in. It isn't a fun feeling.

I try to kick my legs to send myself above the surface. It doesn't work. He has me held down. I can't breathe. My chest hurts so bad.

Dad said I need air to swim which is why I shouldn't swim too deep in the lake. Without it I'd die.

I don't want to die.

"Kane! Kane!" I yell in the water shaking my head. "Don't let me die, please."

My mind goes to Heath. My brother would save me. Please let him hear me somehow. "Heath! Heath! I don't want to die."

And then, everything goes black.

Until I hear a voice calling me. A hand on my chest. Something wet on my lips.

But I can't breathe. It hurts.

"Callan! Oh my God!" That's my mom's voice.

I blink and cough out the water from my mouth. A lot of it comes out, and I feel sick.

I suck in as much air as I can, and look around. I'm right next to the lake.

The lake. I turn to stare at it, still trying to breathe.

All of a sudden, that lake doesn't look like much fun anymore. The dark water in the center looks angry. Like it'll pull you in and never let you go.

I don't want it to pull me in.

"Callan, promise me you won't swim without us, ever again," Mom says tearfully.

I'm still staring at the water when she shakes me. "Callan?

Callan? Can you understand me?" I don't say anything as I still remember how it felt to not be able to breathe.

"Oh my God, something's wrong with his brain."

"Hey, Call." That's my brother's voice. I turn my head and see him.

"Heath," I whisper, and stumble to get up and hug him. "I thought I was going to die, Heath."

"You didn't die. I got there just in time. Sam's dad dropped me off and I saw your cars outside, but you weren't there. I went in and found out you were missing and ran straight here. I'm glad I got there just in time before you drowned. Didn't I tell you swimming can be hard? It's okay to take a break."

Blinking quickly, I shake my head. "I didn't have trouble swimming."

Mom touches my shoulder. "What do you mean?"

I glance at the person that hasn't said a word this whole time. And what I see is terrifying. His eyes are wide and his face is red. He looks like he's about to burst. He shakes his head once and does the zip it thing.

He doesn't want me to tell on him.

No. The truth is the most important thing. That's what Mom says.

"Kane tried to drown me," I say, burrowing into Heath's side.

Mom laughs. "Callan, don't make a joke. That's not funny. We can't accuse innocent people just because they were there during an incident. Kane didn't know you were drowning. That doesn't mean he drowned you."

Why doesn't she believe me?

"Callan, is that what happened?" Heath asks.

I shake my head and tell them everything. When I'm done, she scoffs. She says I made the whole thing up because I don't like Kane.

It's true, I don't. But I wouldn't lie. I promised her I wouldn't lie about anything.

She walks with us back, patting Kane on the back, whispering to him so I don't hear. But I do. She doesn't want Kane to talk to his father about this and that she'll make it up to him for having to deal with me.

I cry silently rubbing the snot that comes out of my nose. Heath pats me on the back and whispers, "Hey, I believe you. I think Mom is just trying to keep Dad happy like she always does. And for some reason that means keeping Kane happy."

It sounds right to me, but it doesn't make me feel better. I hate her. And I hate Dad. I hope Heath never leaves me.

"Don't be alone with Kane again, okay? Have your two friends with you, Noel and Vincent."

I nod. Noel and Vincent would be on my side. They're my best friends. They'll hate Kane too.

When we get back, Dad is angry at me for leaving. Kane's dad asks what happened and Mom tells them both. Dad is even angrier because he thinks I lied. Kane's dad isn't angry though. He looks kind of sad at me. Why? Does he know I didn't lie?

When Kane goes to leave, I realize he's been staring at me the whole time. Watching me with a weird look. When he's really gone, I feel a lot better.

Dad tells Heath and I to wait outside and not move so he and Mom can talk.

When we get out, Heath hands me the green car. "Let's race again." He grabs the blue car.

"But Heath, you know you'll lose."

He smiles. "It's okay if I lose to my little brother. Now let's do this."

I'll never fucking forget that day. Drowning in the lake with Silverstone's hands on my head. I know he remembers it too, the fucker. To this day, he's never once apologized. And for that reason, I will always despise him.

For years, I wondered why. Even up until now. What about me did he hate so much that day? What made him decide to try to kill me? We barely even talked to each other. Because if my brother hadn't come, I would have died. My mom runs too slow in heels in the dirt. I know that now.

After that day, I vowed to never step foot in that lake again. The thought was too frightening. The lake water was in my dreams every night for a long time. Every night I fucking drowned, over and over and over again.

But I did. I ran for the water without looking back to save her. And I'd do it again. When I got into that water, I wasn't thinking about myself. I was thinking about having to live with the fact that she died the same way I almost did. But I got to her in time.

Someday, I'll have to open up and tell her why I hate seeing Silverstone near her. Whenever she brushes me off saying he's not so bad, I want to explain why he is. He's better at hiding how fucked up he is. But I can't yet. It'll be giving her more insight into why I'm so fucked up. I never even told Noel and Vincent after it happened. I just tried to forget.

Trusting hasn't come easily since then. I need to work on trusting her so she'll trust me. Once I've calmed down and thought over every fucking detail again, and talked to everyone in AAA, I'll force her to talk to me. I refuse to let this be the end of us.

CHAPTER TWENTY-ONE

Mera

He froze me out like it was nothing. He's been next to me for four classes of Political Science acting like I don't exist. I wish it didn't bother me every class, but each time I see him start to look my way, I hold myself back from turning and talking to him first.

Scar thinks we were doomed from the start, reminding me all over again how she warned me about the Goldsworthys. Not what I wanted to hear.

Brandie and Jamie both think he'll come around.

It doesn't stop my heart from shattering into a million pieces.

Does he tell every girl they're his and act hot and cold?

It doesn't matter anyway. I'm done trying and hoping for something different. He walks right over me and never apologizes. Only ever whispering hot things in my ear to melt my resolve away.

That's never happening again.

I need to keep my head focused on my studies. Political Science with Professor Harper again today. If it's even possible she's stricter with this than she was with U.S. History. I think she has more of a love for politics than she originally let on.

As I leave Sorority Row and head toward class, I spot a few pieces of paper on the ground. Ugh, litterers. But one piece rolls over as a breeze moves by.

The shaking of the trees around me are nothing compared to the shaking my body does when I see the front of that paper.

I bend down, picking it up to closely inspect the picture. It's the same fucking one from under my pillow on Valentine's Day. I pick up the other two and find the exact same thing.

Whoever it is printed these.

All of a sudden, I realize everyone around me has a similar white paper in their hands as they stare at me with looks of hatred and distrust.

But this isn't me. It can't be me.

How many people have seen this? Where did it come from?

Oh my God, how am I going to go to class with everyone seeing this?

Everyone. Oh fuck, Callan. I have to tell him before he sees it.

He always gets to class after I do. I don't know if he went to the dining hall or if he's coming straight to class from AAA.

Shit, what do I do?

I turn around quickly and collide with a broad chest. Callan's intimidating presence is like no other, so when I glance up, I know I'll look into his eyes. Those cold eyes that will suck me in and freeze me solid. I slowly move my gaze up, locking eyes with him and becoming slack-jawed at the pure darkness in them.

"Come with me, now," he says quietly.

"If we're not going to class, I'm not going with you."

His jaw tics and he grabs my arm, pulling me toward the building. Everyone stares as we walk by at a furious pace.

We pass Scar and Peyton who are arguing with Collette in front of the classroom, all of them holding the paper. When they see us pass, Collette shouts and tries to run after us, but Callan turns around and yells, "Do not follow us."

My heart pounds quickly as he pulls me up the stairs to the roof. The last time I was here flashes in my mind. Callan shedding me of my clothes, leaving me in nothing but my underwear and throwing them off the roof.

I tried so hard to get away that day.

And now, here we are again on the roof. He wrenches my bag off, tossing it to the side and I back up. He didn't even bring one.

His face is stony as he stares me down. "Wil. What is this?" He waves the paper around.

"It's not me!" I yell. "I promise it isn't."

"It looks an awful lot like you. I looked at it carefully, hoping that somehow it'd been photoshopped. But there's no hint of it being photoshopped. It's real."

His eyes are so dark I can't breathe. The rage coming off of him is dangerous. With every step toward me, I instinctively back away, moving closer and closer to the edge.

I think quickly, trying to say something, anything that

would stop his advance. "I-It might be real, but it isn't me! I didn't think it would–"

His eyes widen and he turns his head slightly to the side. "You didn't think? So you've seen this picture before?"

Shit. I feel the roof's edge hit my legs and I stop.

Shutting my eyes quickly, I take a deep shuddering breath. I have to come clean about those notes and my hoodie.

"What are you hiding, Wil?" he says in a low tone. "This is where you tell me everything." I nod and he booms, "All of it!"

"The person who destroyed all of my clothes, they've been tormenting me since Heath disappeared."

"Tormenting you how?" He crosses his arms.

"They send me notes, leaving them under my pillow. It was slow at first, only once a week, sometimes twice a week, then before I knew it, it was a daily thing."

He steps closer, but I have nowhere to go. "And what did those notes say?"

"That…that…" Fuck what's he going to say.

"Don't get quiet now. What did they say, princess?"

I close my eyes and blurt, "That it's my fault Heath is dead."

He stays quiet for so long, I have to open my eyes. I expect to see the rage and hatred, the ice. None of it is there. The only thing there is hurt. "And is it?" He runs a hand over his face, stopping at his chin, eventually gesturing to me. "Is it your fault that my brother is dead?"

"*No.* No, it isn't."

In a flash, he grabs me by the neck, squeezing hard. I start to see stars and it's painful. It takes me back to Halloween night. Tears form in my eyes as I gasp. "Please, Callan. Just listen to me." *There were more notes.*

"I'm done listening," he says gruffly. For a few seconds, I wonder if he's going to throw me off. Does he really care about me so little? Did these last few months mean nothing to him?

But he pulls me away from the edge. He pushes me to the ground harshly, letting go of my neck.

I gasp for air, but lose it again as he kneels on the ground and takes off my shirt. "Wait, Callan."

His hands move behind me to my bra, and I hear and feel the tug as he unclips it, throwing it off to the side. He meticulously moves down, peeling my jeans off, and leaving me only in my panties.

And then, in broad fucking daylight, he rips my lace panties off ruthlessly leaving me naked to the world. But not for long as he puts his other knee on the ground, one on either side of me.

"Callan, please. You got what you wanted. My clothes are off and I'll have to parade around naked. But please, let's talk."

His eyes are so cruel as he laughs. "Do you know what you did, Wil? How much this fucking picture hurts? The time for talking is over. I don't want to hear another word out of that lying mouth of yours."

He picks the pieces of my shredded panties up and stuffs them into my mouth. I try to ignore the subtle taste to them after wearing them for ten hours.

One hard hand goes to my side and he flips me on to my stomach and forces me on all fours. I hear the sound of a zipper going down and my heart sinks. I sputter, trying to eject the pieces of my panties from my mouth.

His hands go to my hips, catching them in a bruising grip. I quake at the feeling and gasp when I feel the head of his cock against my pussy. I spit the last of my underwear out and cough.

"You're going to feel every bit as hurt as I do, right now," he says calmly.

But doesn't he know how hurt I've felt over him never apologizing for making me afraid and fearful? Not one apology. I don't want this.

And then he thrusts inside, all the way to the hilt.

I can't help but cry out at the feeling of friction. It hurts. Tears well up in the corner of my eyes.

Down below us, I hear a few people ask, "Did you hear something?"

"Hear that, princess, you better keep quiet." He pulls back and thrusts back in. I press my lips together as tears flow down my face.

It hurts, but knowing that his cock is inside me starts to do something to me. My body starts to burn. Even on a cold day like this.

He grunts. "You're getting wet. I guess you don't mind a little pain." He reaches under me and grabs my breast, twisting my nipple and pulling it.

I let out a low moan and clamp my hand over my mouth. Why does every touch, every thrust, feel so good yet so horrible at the same time?

I move my hand off my mouth. "I-I did it for you. They killed Heath."

He slows his thrusts. I have his attention.

"They said if I told you about the notes, th-they'd–," he moves so deeply in me, I feel him push against my cervix and shiver.

"They'd what, Wil? They'd what?" he mutters, pulling out and snapping his hips forward.

"Kill you. They'd kill you. They already killed Heath, I

didn't want..." And abruptly, his pace quickens again, pounding into me relentlessly.

"The minute you got the first one, you should've shown it to me!" he yells.

"You hated me!" I scream back. "You thought I had something to do with his death. You didn't believe my memory loss for a long time." He pauses, balls deep inside me, finally giving me the chance to think more clearly.

"You never fucking apologized, Callan. Not once. You threatened to fuck me here before, remember that? And even before that, in the third round of hazing? What about in the basement, both times? Or how about when you choked me until I almost passed the fuck out?"

My arms shake as I pant, taking one shaky breath after another. "Why would I show *you* notes from someone threatening to kill me?"

"The person from the lake dressed like me," he murmurs.

"You pushed me away like I was nothing when I just wanted to help. I was on your side. So now you know, I was already hurt before you did this." A sob escapes my mouth as my eyes burn. "So go ahead, keep fucking me. You'll never be inside me again. I fell in love with you, despite it all. But no more."

He pulses inside me and I bite my lip. There it is, out there in the open. What I've been thinking since he saved me from Josh in the bathroom. Somehow, I fell in love with Callan Goldsworthy. I thought maybe we were headed toward him feeling the same, but someone who loves me would never do this.

He pulls me back off my hands until my back is flush against his chest. His lips go to my neck, sucking hard and biting down until I know I've bled. His hips move underneath me, moving back and forth as he fucks me hard.

I'm lost in an endless cycle of pleasure as he makes me orgasm so many times I lose count. It feels like forever that our bodies are joined, but his release does eventually come, and I get that same rush I always feel when his hot cum releases inside me.

Thank God I got on birth control the day after he kicked me out.

His grip on me lessens enough that I shove his hands away and scramble on my legs toward my clothes.

"Wil."

I ignore him, putting my shirt over my head. When I stand up, I immediately feel his cum leak out. As I pull my jeans up, I can feel it seep into the cloth.

He grabs my chin, forcing me to look into his eyes. They're back to their default setting of coldness. "I need to see those notes if you still have them."

"What if I don't want to?"

"Wil," he says in a low threatening tone.

"Fine." I was half-expecting it already. "But once I give them to you, I don't want to see you again."

I slap his hand off my chin with all the force I can manage. I'm so exhausted and sore. Even bending down to grab my bag is hard. Somehow, I'm able to and take the lead back to ZDB. By the look of the sun, it has to be closer to noon now.

Everyone across campus stares and when I open the door to ZDB, the girls inside stop and stare.

"Shouldn't she be at the police station right now?" one of them asks.

I roll my eyes and stomp up the stairs to my room. The door closes behind me and I feel Callan's intense gaze as he watches me open the bottom drawer of the nightstand.

And there they are. Every single note.

He reaches around me and starts grabbing them randomly, reading them and throwing them on the floor. I settle on my bed, letting my body relax and recover.

It takes a long time, reading over hundreds of notes and eventually seeing a smaller version of the photo that was printed everywhere. When he's finished he slams the drawer shut. "You should've told me, Wil."

"Well, now you know. And now there's nothing else to be said. You can grab them and take them with you if you want, either way, you're leaving."

He glares. "You want me to leave knowing the amount of times they've threatened your life? And are they talking about that pink hoodie you wore your first week here?"

I don't feel the need to answer any more of his questions, so I ignore him completely. "Leave."

"Fine!" he yells, going back to the drawer. "Let me make sure I get all the notes." He slides open my top drawer.

"Wait there's nothing–" I sit up in horror at the hint of what I see sitting in the drawer.

That can't be.

In a strangled voice, Callan says, "Wil."

All of a sudden, there's a banging on the door. "Police! Open up. We received an anonymous tip that there's evidence in this room."

Fuck, my parents are going to kill me.

Callan stares down at the notes and the hoodie. "Wil. If they see this hoodie, they'll think you did it."

And at the same time, there could be DNA of the person who really did this on that hoodie. I still believe that wasn't me in the picture.

"Open the door," I tell him.

"If this door isn't opened in the next five seconds, we're breaking it down!" they yell out.

What the fuck? They can't do that!

He closes the drawer and opens the door. "Officers, she didn't do it," he snaps.

One officer goes for the closet first, the other one watches us. He starts rifling through my side and then Brandie's. They'll start to go through her stuff soon if I don't point them in the right direction. Heath's green eyes flash in my head. Heath with his smiling face and dimples showing. Always there to help me. His body is somewhere rotting.

These notes won't help identify the killer, but that hoodie will. Callan is standing right in front of my nightstand with an unreadable expression.

"It's in the nightstand."

The cop by the door goes into the nightstand and whistles. "That tip might've solved this case."

The officer by the closet laughs. "Well isn't it our lucky day. You hear that, boy?" he asks, talking to Callan. "You're finally getting the answers you hassled us for. Guess she really was guilty like you insisted that morning. Who would've thought, a princess being a killer?"

"We're going to need you to come in for questioning."

"You don't have to, Wil." Callan glares at the officers. "They legally can't make you. You're a foreign dignitary and you have diplomatic immunity that prevents them from forcing you to go with them."

"You're right, but if I go I'll be able to explain my side, and that picture. Heath deserves it."

Callan nods slowly. "Call me when they're done and I'll come get you."

I breathe a sigh of relief and don't look back as they usher me down the hall. I ignore the stares, the loud whispers, the jeering, all of it. As they push me into the squad car, I finally feel relieved because I'm not holding anything back anymore. And maybe now that they have that hoodie, something will change and they'll be able to find the sick person who did this.

Everyone thinks I'm guilty. How could they not? But I know the truth. I didn't do it.

I've been here for almost twelve hours at the police station and I've officially reached my limit of explaining things. We went over everything again, starting from the beginning, the day I came to campus.

First to the two officers that showed up at the sorority today, then the two I originally talked to, and then the captain.

They took the notes at Callan's urging and they all believe they were fabricated to make me look innocent. Unfuckingbelievable. Of course they asked me to write and see if my handwriting matched, which it doesn't. But they said I could've easily hired someone to do it for me.

What I keep coming back to is, why would I put that picture out there if I actually did do it? They don't have an answer for that.

They're slowly putting the case together to prove I had an accomplice, a man. The accomplice took the picture as a trophy for me. And I hired the accomplice to also be responsible for taking care of Heath's body.

Since they can't charge me, they want to charge him. But there is no accomplice!

Finally, they leave me alone, long enough for me to call my parents.

Neither of them answer the phone the first time. The

second time I call, Father answers the phone. "Mera? We're just waking up. How's everything?"

"I'm at the police station."

"What? Why?" he asks. On the other end I can hear my mother saying something in the background, and he responds, "She's at the police station."

I hear a gasp and sigh. Please don't let her take the phone away from him.

"They found my hoodie with Heath's blood on it. Someone tipped them off anonymously. And there's a photo of me in the hoodie the night he disappeared, in front of Heath's car, and it looks like Heath's in it."

"Mera, how do you know the blood on your hoodie is his? Maybe it's–" he starts.

The person who did this? Unlikely they'd give me a hoodie with their DNA on it that would lead me right to them. "Give me the phone," I hear Mother say, slightly muffled.

There's the sound of silence, and then crystal clear, she says, "Why is that boy's blood on your hoodie?"

"It was taken that night. They must have used it when they did whatever they did to him."

She sighs. "Maybe it'd be best if you came home. This sounds like a lot for you to deal with, and I think this way we could keep a better eye on you. This might've been a mistake on our part."

Leave? When I've finally found friends? Not to mention I've worked so fucking hard to keep my grades up. College isn't easy. Now it'll have been for nothing. I guess I shouldn't tell them about the notes. They'd really make me leave then.

"No. I don't want to leave."

"One more thing and you are, Wilhelmera. Someone is playing a dangerous game and you need not stay involved."

She hangs up, and I put my phone away. Right away, a cop comes in the room. Clearly he was listening in.

"I'd like to go back to my sorority now."

He doesn't look too happy, but he opens the door and walks me to the front.

It's just past midnight when I step outside in the night air. I pull my phone out to call Callan, but pause and remember what he did to me earlier. If I call him, I'm basically crawling back and saying it's okay.

I can't do that anymore.

I call Scar. She doesn't pick up the phone. Peyton answers on the third ring in a sleepy voice, "Mera? Oh shit, Mera! What's going on? We saw the picture and we were worried about you. There were rumors that you'd been arrested, but that can't be, right? They can't arrest you."

"No, they didn't arrest me. I came voluntarily to try and help with the case. Scar didn't answer her phone, do you think you could ask if she'd come pick me up?"

"Um, Scar isn't here. When I went to sleep she was, but she must have gone out for something."

"That's weird. She has class early tomorrow morning, right?" Unless it was canceled.

"Yep. But she does it often. Right, you wouldn't know since you only roomed with us for a week." He clears his throat and a little of the gruffness disappears. "I'll wake up randomly during the night and she won't be here. I asked her about it once and she told me it's her mother. Always asking her to run errands for her. One time I waited up and she didn't come back for hours. Always comes back smelling kind of funky, don't tell her that."

So she could be gone for who knows how long. I guess I need to find another ride. Only, there's no one else. Brandie's anal about her sleep and I think Jamie's the same way.

Gemma doesn't have a car. Luella and Ashlynn do, but I don't know how they'll feel after Collette's talked to them about what was found in my nightstand. "Well, it sounds like I might be shit out of luck. Talk to you later, Pey."

I hang up, and walk down the parking lot to the sidewalks and start walking. It's still cold. It's not quite spring yet. With each car that goes by, I feel more pathetic. What did this trip to the police station even do? They treated me, once again, like I was a criminal. Like there was no other explanation except that I'm guilty.

By the time I reach campus, I'm freezing, and by the time I walk into ZDB, I'm exhausted and tired. The police station didn't seem like it was *that* far away.

No one's downstairs when I get inside, thankfully. When I get in my room, Brandie is fast asleep. There's an empty spot where my nightstand is. That'll be a nice reminder in the morning of what a shit day this was.

Maybe, I should go home.

Despite my tiredness, I get myself in the tub and wash the dried cum from my legs. I lean back and fall asleep.

In my dreams, I see Cate, and she looks completely disappointed in me. "Who told you to give up so easily? Keep fighting to prove your innocence."

But all I want to do is hug her. I miss her.

When I wake up from my dream, the tub water is cold with a slightly dirty tinge to it. I wipe the tears from my eyes, and get myself out of the tub.

Hearing her voice in my dream made me realize how long it's been since I've heard it. The only thing that would prove my innocence is if I had an alibi, and I don't.

CHAPTER TWENTY-TWO

Callan

After Wil's gone, I'm walking toward the end of Sorority Row when I spot my sister, stomping angrily down the sidewalk.

She shakes the paper with the picture on it in the air. "Have you seen this?" she yells.

People on both sides of the street turn to look at us.

When she finally gets to me, she asks, "Why do you look like that? Where's that anger, Callan? Shouldn't you be fucking furious? Any other time you'd be flying off the handle."

I snatch the paper from her hand and rip it to pieces, letting them fall to the ground. "This isn't her."

Coll yells, "What the fuck. I needed that!" She glares up at me, narrowing her eyes. "What happened to searching for answers about Heath? That picture proves we were fooled.

How can you deny the truth that's right in front of you? That's her fucking hoodie. Didn't you see the 'Princess M' all glittery on the back, shining in the photo?"

She's right, but it's time I start doing something. Trusting the woman that's captured my heart and soul. She's been dealing with those notes on her own for so long. It's no wonder she tried to kill herself during Thanksgiving break. People may think I'm a fool for believing her words. It does look like her in the picture, but something I should have about is things aren't always what they seem.

This person didn't just take Heath away. They're trying to take her away too. "If you can't trust her, then you need to trust me." I stare down into Coll's frustrated eyes and sigh. I wish I could tell her about the notes. It's not my place to. "Coll, you know I wouldn't say this if there was even a shadow of a doubt that it's her. I wouldn't lie to you. I'm going to keep looking for answers."

She glances away. "Fine. Just keep me updated, okay? You must really be in love with her. Who'd have thought, my twin brother, in love with that klutz? Just what is it about her that you love so much?"

Love. There it is again.

She said it on the roof and it's been echoing in my head ever since. It has to be what I feel. There's no other word to describe the need I feel to keep her by my side forever. The yearning I feel to see her smile and laugh. The rage I feel when someone wrongs her. I would've killed Josh that night if she hadn't stopped me. She shines like the brightest light, brighter than the sun, breaking the shadows that cover me.

"I do. I love her."

She nods. "Then you should know, I overheard Dad talking and someone is trying to get her deported back to Kardenia.

My stomach drops, picturing her getting onto her plane and never coming back. "What the fuck? Who?"

She shrugs. "I don't know. All I heard were the words princess and deported."

Fire explodes behind my eyelids. No. He's not going to get away with that. I'd burn this whole school to the fucking ground before I let him get her deported.

I move past her and I distantly hear her say, "Don't forget, keep me updated. I don't think Dad is on campus today, by the way."

Fucking hell. I need to get to my Lanbo.

As I turn into Fraternity Row, a red blur stops right in front of me, making me run right into her.

"I've been calling your name the last few minutes and you ignored me."

I stare down at her miffed expression. "This isn't the time, Red." I need to find my dad wherever the hell he is.

"Scarlett. My name is Scarlett. I'm your girlfriend's best friend, remember?"

Girlfriend. I've never used that word before when it comes to Wil. I've never used that term with anyone else either.

"I know who you are," I bark. "What do you want?"

She crosses her arms. "I just want to make sure you know, that's not Mera in that picture."

"I'm aware of that," I respond with a grunt. "But how are you so sure of that?"

Anger flashes in her eyes. "Because I trust my best friend."

"Right. So what did you need?"

"You've slept in the same bed as Mera."

I rub the bridge of my nose and feel my anger surge. "Yes. What of it?"

"So you know that she snores. Sometimes, she snores

pretty loud. How come not one person in her sorority could tell the police that they heard her snoring the night he disappeared? It's not like her room is at the end of the hall either."

The wheels start turning in my head. She's right. Even if one person heard, that would give Wil an alibi. But no one ever came forth to say they heard her sleeping.

"They're all hateful bitches in that sorority. Someone had to have heard her, they had to. I just wanted to put that on your mind. I'm going there right now to kick some asses until someone tells the fucking truth." She smiles widely with a look of determination in her eyes. "See you later."

She walks past me and a wave of admiration flows through me. I'm glad Wil has friends who believe in her as much as I do.

I walk down the street and get to the parking lot, sliding into my car quickly, and turning it on.

First, I find where he is. When I unlock my phone, I notice the massive amount of messages from Vin, Ty, and Noel. And even more inside our shared group chat. I don't have time to answer those now.

I call my mom, and hope she isn't off having drinks again with her friends. When she does that, she never answers the phone.

The phone rings for a while, and just when I know it's going to go to voicemail, she picks up. "Callan? Is everything okay? Listen, I know you saw that photo–"

"Where's Dad?" I snap, interrupting her.

"Callan, there's no need to bother him right now. He's busy today, dealing with business somewhere. He'll be home late today."

Son of a bitch. "Busy trying to get her deported, huh?" I yell.

"Wh-what are you talking about?" Mom asks, an air of confusion in her tone.

"Of course. You never know shit about what he's doing." I hang up the phone and slam my fist against the wheel. Anger and fear start a war inside me. Leaning my head on my arm against the wheel, I breathe deeply and think.

He must be trying to talk to his judge buddies to find a way to get her deported. Going to my parents' house now won't do a fucking thing.

There's a click as the passenger door opens. Turning my head to the right, I watch the last person I want to see right now sit in my passenger seat.

I lean back and run my hand over my hair. "Get the fuck out of my car, Ginger."

She frowns and crosses her arms over her chest. "You're so mean to me."

"I mean it," I murmur in a low tone. "I don't have the patience to deal with you today."

She pokes her bottom lip out. "I just wanted to make sure you were okay after seeing what that snake did to Heath. You saw the picture right?"

"Wil isn't a snake. Of course I saw the fucking picture."

She scoffs. "And you're okay with it?"

"It isn't her, okay? Now get the fuck away from me."

She shakes her head. "That's her hair. It's as long as it was when she got here. That's her hoodie. You have to believe that, Callan. Don't let her brainwash you. You're so much smarter than that." Her hand reaches forward to touch my shoulder and I push it away.

"Don't touch me," I snap. "Now get out of my fucking car. If I have to tell you one more time, I'm dragging you out."

Her lips flatten. "She deserves all of this, Callan. Why can't you see that?"

I stare right into her eyes and slowly say, "That is the woman I love. It's way past fucking time you realize it'll never be you. No matter how much you beg, no matter how much you flaunt yourself in front of me, I'll never love you."

Her lips quiver and she yells, "We'll see about that!" And to my utter relief, she throws the door open and gets out. Ginger stomps away, and I watch her walk away in my mirrors.

I shut my car off and inhale deeply. While I wait for it to be night, I need to be alone. There's too many fucking people around to bother me. I get out of my car and lock it.

Where can I go to be alone? If I go to AAA, everyone will have questions for me. Questions I don't feel like answering right now. I know Ty, Vin, and Noel are wondering about me. I'll send off a short text in the group chat so they don't worry. Without reading any of the messages, I type a reply quickly that I'm fine and I'll talk to them later. I shove the phone back in my pocket, feeling vibrations hit my leg. That's them responding.

I know I owe them more of an explanation, but the only person I want to talk to on the phone is at the police station.

Mindlessly, I keep walking, ignoring the stares and the people who try to stop and talk to me. Somehow I end up somewhere I don't enjoy being. In the woods surrounding the lake.

I walk around the perimeter, watching the ground to make sure I don't stumble over any tree roots.

When I've made it around fully once, I start walking again, kicking at the dirt. The stupid fucking dirt.

I should be with Wil right now. Talking to the fucking police.

Flopping down onto the ground, I let myself slump against a tree in the woods on the east side of the lake.

A bird squawks above my head and I see it fly down across from me and stop in front of a tree a feet away. It starts pecking away at the ground.

Wil would find that bird cute. When it stops, its head pops up and the sun overhead hits the ground. Something shiny catches my eye. What is that?

I move off the ground and walk closer. The bird squawks and hops away a few feet before taking off into the air when I get there.

I bend down, moving the dirt and leaves off the object and my heart drops. What is this doing here?

This has to be it. I've seen it thousands of times. Bringing it up slowly, I hold it up to the sunlight. My grandfather's watch.

The gold circular clock face, the silver band with the gold strip down the middle. I turn it over to find the engraving. *'To my husband, I love you forever.'*

A birthday present from my grandma who died a few years ago. My grandpa was heartbroken and the light in his eyes was never the same after she died. There was only a glimmer of it whenever he looked down at this watch.

How did it end up here?

I dig in the ground where I found it, searching for something, anything to point me toward Heath. But I don't find even a scrap of paper. So then, how did it get here?

Fuck, Heath. What the hell happened to you? Who helped you in the car? Who's in the picture and who took it?

I glance up at the sky and stare as the clouds in the distance start rolling in to cover the sun. I hope to hell they aren't an omen of something to come.

CHAPTER TWENTY-THREE

Mera

I can't believe I allowed myself to skip class the rest of the week. But each time I wanted to get out of bed and get ready, I couldn't. So I emailed every one of my professors hoping they'd point me in the direction of what I missed in the books and tell me what the homework was.

Every professor responded professionally. Even Professor Harper. For some reason she enjoys my work and let me know that class wouldn't be the same without me. But the more I've thought about my parents' words, the more they ring true.

Maybe I should go home.

After I find a way to tell my friends that is. I silenced all notifications on my phone so I wouldn't get bombarded. Brandie and Jamie are the only ones that have seen me since

I got back here to the sorority. I've kept the door locked otherwise. Gemma, Ashlynn, and Luella have all come to talk to me together and separately. Peyton and Scarlett have both tried to talk to me, even through the door. I'm lucky that none of them believe it's me in that picture. It doesn't stop me from feeling miserable.

Since I've been anchored to my pillow 24/7, I haven't gotten a single note. But I know this isn't the end. They'll keep slowly torturing me somehow.

But above all, I can't stop thinking about Callan. I didn't call him that night to pick me up and I haven't heard from him since. Maybe he's tried to call or text, but I can't find the desire to check those yet.

Deep inside though, I know, if he really wanted to see me, he'd be at my door threatening to kick it in if I didn't open it.

Maybe he really is done with me. Why did I tell him I was done with him? I'll never be able to quit him. He's burrowed in so deep, I can't think of how my life would be without him.

The booming of the thunder outside makes me jump for the millionth time today. It's been storming outside all day long without letting up.

I flip my phone up and down in my hands, wondering if it's worth it to even try to call *her*. My sister.

The phone goes straight to voicemail as it always does. And her voicemail is still full.

"Why?" I ask out loud.

Why couldn't I have a normal college life like every other person? Maybe this is life's shit way of saying I don't belong here. I should listen.

The next name I press in my contact's list is my mother's.

She answers the phone with a sleepy, "Hey, Mera." Shit, I forgot it's super early in the morning in Kardenia.

"Mother, I want to come home."

She sighs. "You ignore our calls all week and suddenly decide that you want to come home?"

"I'm sorry. Everything just overwhelmed me. Just please, let me come home."

There's a pause and she says, "Of course. Okay, in the morning we'll talk about everything. Can you give me at least four more hours of sleep before you call again?"

"Sorry," I say quickly and hang up, hoping that she'll get back to sleep and wake up in a decent mood. I lock my phone, lying back in bed with it on my chest, when I hear the sound of sharp rapping on the door.

Frowning, I stare at the door. Everyone left for the playoff game thirty minutes ago if they wanted to get good seats in time.

If Callan and his team win tonight, they only need one more win to move on to the second round.

So who could be knocking on my door?

I turn the lock, unlocking it and pull it open to find the last person I thought I'd see. Her angled eyes don't look at me with hatred this time.

"Hi, Kori? If you're looking for Brandie–"

"No. I'm looking for you. Can I come inside?" she glances behind me and I suddenly feel self conscious about the mess on my side of the room. Now she's going to hate me and think I'm a complete pig. Or a spoiled princess who doesn't like to clean up after herself.

"Sure," I reply, moving aside for her.

She sits gently on the edge of Brandie's bed and stares at me.

Her gaze is slightly unnerving so I glance around. "Is there something I can help you with?"

She tilts her head down for a second and sighs. "I have to

apologize for something. I should have told you sooner. I let my hatred for him get in the way of being a decent human being."

I sit at the edge of my bed, watching her as she moves a strand of her hair away from her face.

"Callan came and talked to everyone the night you were at the police station. He asked all of us if anyone heard you snoring the night Heath disappeared. At first I was going to deny it again."

Deny it again? So she did hear me snore! Someone heard me. I do have an alibi.

"I heard you snoring on the way to my room that night. He paid special attention to the girls who room around you on this floor. He reminded me that you're innocent in all of this. Even for becoming friends with Heath Goldsworthy. I just wanted to let you know before I go to the police and tell them so they can stop bothering you with their questioning."

My heart swells at the thought of Callan coming through for me again. "I can't thank you enough."

A small smile forms on her face and she nods. "Well, my girlfriend is saving me a spot at the game so I better get going."

She stands up to leave, when a thought pops into my head. This is the moment to ask since I never got the opportunity to ask around on my own.

"Why do you hate Heath so much?"

Kori turns back, only inches away from opening the door and sits back down.

"Last year, Nadine and I came out of the closet. For years, she had guys falling over her, asking her out on dates, asking her father's permission to date her, but she refused all advances. We secretly dated all throughout high school with no problems. The minute we were out, guys were furious. So furious that..." she trails off and gets a far away look in her eyes.

She glances down at her hands. "One night, we were roofied at a party. It was late, there weren't as many people around. It had to have only been seconds that we set our drinks down for. My body was stiff. I couldn't move. I was only able to watch as a group of guys picked us up and put us in their cars. Drove us to the forest surrounding the lake, where no one could hear."

My heart sinks as I already know what's coming. I cover my mouth at the horror they must have felt.

She wipes the edge of her eyes and inhales deeply. "They made me watch as they did it. Each one of those bastards. My poor Nadine. But then, by some miracle. Someone came. Heath happened upon us somehow. There weren't any other cars nearby so he must have been wandering around."

Oh fuck, Heath. Please don't tell me...

"He took one look. They told him to mind his own business, and he kept walking. Wouldn't you hate him too if the same had happened to you?"

I nod, feeling sick to my stomach. How could Heath walk away like that? Is this the mistake he vaguely told me about?

"I'm so sorry," I murmur, folding my hands together.

She finally looks at me again with teary eyes. "Nadine hasn't been the same since. I don't know if she'll ever come back to college for class, but she never misses a basketball game. She says it makes her feel alive again. Her professors have been letting her do all her work online at the request of Mr. Silverstone."

With a frown, I ask, "Mr. Silverstone? As in Kane's dad Mr. Silverstone?"

She raises an eyebrow and slowly says, "Yes. Nadine Silverstone."

My jaw drops to the floor. "You and Kane are close I've heard and he's never once talked about her?"

"In passing, just not her name," I respond, trying to process things in my head.

If someone didn't stop someone from raping my sister, I'd be pissed off. Did Kane kill Heath?

She stands up for the second time tonight. "I'll talk to you more sometime soon, Mera. You aren't as bad as I thought you were."

I smile automatically as she leaves. My mind is far, far away though. What if Kane did it?

Those hints he gave me about him seeing something. Have I been talking to Heath's killer all along? Does Callan know what Heath did? How could I have ignored Callan who told me himself that Kane was bad news?

I lie down on my bed and stare at the ceiling. That basketball game needs to hurry up and end. Not that I want it to go badly, but keeping this to myself is weighing on me.

I don't know how long I lay like that when I hear the door knob turn. That's right, I forgot to lock it after her.

"Kori? Did you forget something?" I turn my head to look and sit up quick when I see orange hair underneath a hood. Only one person I know has hair like this.

"What the hell do you want?" I snap. Ginger does nothing but antagonize me. And try to steal Callan away.

She moves the hood off of her head, taking a few steps forward, and stopping right by my bed. Way too close for my liking.

"Why couldn't you be satisfied with Heath?" she asks quietly.

"Does it really matter? Callan didn't want you even before

he was interested in me. You two went to high school together, remember?"

She shakes her head several times. "No," she says in a low tone. "I was so close to being with him. So fucking close. By the time we graduated from high school he was warming up to me. Despite the fact that his brother whispered in his ear from time to time and told him not to stick his dick in crazy. Me? Crazy? But his brother isn't around to whisper anymore." A sinister smile spreads across her face.

I reach forward ever so slightly toward my phone. "What do you want, Ginger?"

"I want to get rid of Callan's distraction," she states cheerily.

Fuck this. I turn to my phone, pushing my body forward as I reach and successfully grab it in a flash. I'm just about to hit the recent calls and call the first person listed when she starts cackling and I register the shadow too late as something crashes into me and everything goes black.

I come awake to feeling a finger in my mouth. Why is there a finger there? I tilt my head up to look and immediately come face to face with Ginger's crazy eyes. Something slides down my throat and I gasp.

"What the fuck did you do?" I scream. Going to touch my throat, when I realize something doesn't feel right. My arms hurt like hell.

Why are we in the bathroom? Why am I in the tub?

And then, I stare down and scream because the water isn't clear, it's red. This weird feeling, I know it now. The slow leakage of all of the blood in my body.

I find the source of my pain to be two long openings, one on each arm. My blood is pouring out into the water and I'm completely naked.

Shivering, I glance at her. She's holding a razor blade in

one gloved hand and a pocketknife in the other. "I was tempted to cut you more, one on each leg too, but then I realized if I did that, I wouldn't get to talk to you some more before you die."

Die.

There's that word. That word that I wanted to come true during Thanksgiving break. But now? I don't want this.

"You move to get out of that tub, and I'll stab you in your eyeball," she says, holding her pocket knife up to eye level.

What should I do?

"Did you kill Heath and masquerade as me?" I ask quietly.

She laughs. "You're talking about that picture right? That's priceless. Someone out there really hates you and Heath. Maybe even more than I do. No, I didn't. I had nothing to do with that. If I wanted to kill him I would've done it years ago after the very first time Heath stood between the love of my life and I."

"Psycho," I bite out.

She grins. "It's just a happy coincidence that he's dead. And now, when you die, Callan will need me. He'll look for comfort and my arms will be wide open."

How fucking delusional can you be?

Ginger needs to…

I blink slowly as my head starts to feel heavy.

"Oh the pill is starting to work. Pretty soon you won't be able to move and you'll only be able to sit and watch yourself die." She laughs loudly. "Brilliant plan right?"

Fuck. I should've gone to the basketball game.

Suddenly, I hear a sound that makes my heart beat faster.

The creaking of the door opening. Please let it be one of my friends. Anyone. She reaches forward to cover my mouth but I bite her fingers and she shrieks.

"The bathroom," I scream, "I'm in the bathroom."

Seconds later, the bathroom door flies open and I gasp when I see Callan's face. His eyes are confused at first. They don't stay confused for long. "Callan," I whisper, feeling tears well up in my eyes.

He's dressed in his game uniform. It's completely soaked along with his hair. The rain is still streaming down his face from his hair.

His eyes are absolutely murderous as he yanks Ginger by her shirt and throws her against the wall. I glance up at them to find him lifting her by throat off the ground. "I told you to stay away from her." He pulls her head back and jams it back into the wall. "But you don't. And you do this? To my princess?"

"Don't kill her, Callan," I whisper, feeling really drowsy.

"Why the fuck shouldn't I?" he yells, glancing from her to me. "Look at you, princess. If I hadn't gotten here." He slams a fist on the other side of her head and yells, "Fuck! I'm wasting time."

The hand around her throat tightens and she gasps, "But I love you, Callan. I did this for us."

"I don't love you," he says in a low tone. He holds her there for a while, and the moment her head lulls forward, he lets go. Her body sinks to the floor and he moves toward me with a dark expression.

Both hands dunk into the crimson-tinged water, going around my legs and my back. He pulls me up and holds me close to his chest in his arms.

"Sorry about your uniform," I mumble, blinking slowly.

The rush of cold air as I get out of the tub feels too sensitive to the cuts in my arms.

He sets me on the bed. "It's halftime and the only thing I

could think about was seeing you. I ran here to see you for a moment, hoping it'd get me back in the game. I'm glad I came." He presses a kiss to my forehead. "Let me call for help. Keep those pretty eyes on me, princess."

Moving to the side of my bed, he searches my only remaining night stand. "Where's your phone?"

"Ginger had it," I manage to slur out.

He rushes to the bathroom and I stare up at the ceiling, trying and fighting to stay awake.

A few minutes later, he comes back stomping around and looking everywhere. "Fuck! Your phone isn't with her. She doesn't have her phone on her either. I left my phone with my shit inside the locker room."

The despair in my chest crests and I feel my heart sink. Walking over to the vanity chair, he pulls it away from the vanity and pushes it underneath the bathroom door knob.

"Listen to me," he says, "I'm going to get help. Someone has to be around here somewhere. I'll be back once I've called for help."

"You're leaving?" I ask weakly.

He bends down, touching my cheek, "I'll be back as soon as I can." Without another word, he runs out. I try to think of something, anything, to help me stay awake. My arms feel like they're throbbing, but it's dulled by this drowsiness I can't overcome.

The minutes seem to drag on alone. But then I hear something faintly. Footsteps. Callan's back!

Wait, the footsteps echoing sound more frequent than just one person walking down the hall. He brought someone to help?

I watch the doorway, looking into the darkness of the hallway and breathing easier now that help is coming.

But it isn't Callan's face I see. It's Brandie and Jamie who come in, followed by their boyfriends, and I breathe a sigh of relief. I don't know how or why they're here, or even how Callan missed them but they look shocked when they notice the condition I'm in.

"What happened?" Brandie says rushing over.

Jamie gasps. "We left the game early because they started losing without Callan. Who did this to you?"

"Ginger. Just call for help, please." Everything is starting to get hazier.

Brandie pulls her phone out and I hear the sounds of the buttons dialing. The phone goes to her ear as she looks at Jamie. I stare at her confused when she doesn't say anything into the phone. She pulls the phone off of her ear and shrugs. "Sorry, but it looks like no one's coming to help you, Mera."

I stare hard at them. At all of them. From Brandie's smiling face to Jamie's blank expression to Brett and Emerson's smirks.

No way.

The air inside the room starts to suffocate me all at once and I gasp wanting to touch my throat, but it's completely impossible to. I can't move a muscle.

"I trusted you," I rasp.

"Oh that bubbly personality of mine worked, see I told you guys it would!" she says with a happy clap turning to them. "All I had to do was beg Collette to let me room with you. She was more than happy about that."

"Don't act so happy. I told you sticking Ginger on her was a good idea and that worked out well too."

"Poor Ginger," Brandie says with a sigh. "Poor, dumb, Ginger. Callan came and interrupted her job, didn't he? Is she dead in the bathroom? Well, good thing he did since now you get to learn what happened to Heath before you die."

All the moisture in my throat dries as tears start to pour down my face. "No."

The evil coming off of them in waves is smothering me. "Callan. Where's Callan?" I ask.

They shrug and Brandie comments, "None of us saw him. Must have run off campus for help since we didn't see him on the way here from the gym. It'll be a while before he gets back. By that time, you'll be dead."

I breathe a little better knowing that he's out there and he's okay. It doesn't stop the sick feeling in my gut from being betrayed and crushed by people I thought were my friends.

"Did you like those little notes of mine?" Brandie asks with a wink. "I can't take all the credit though. Jamie did come up with quite a few. I wrote them super fast in case you decided to check them against my own writing. Oh and did you love the petition? That was Jamie's idea. We found out Kane's account is an admin one and happened to figure out the answer to his security question. From there it was easy to get into the other accounts."

Jamie stares at my arms, "Brandie, we're saying all of this while her towels are still wrapped around her arms."

"Oh, right," Brandie says, pulling the towels off of my arms. I have no control over them so they fall right onto the bed, soiling the blanket again.

I glance behind them at Brett and Emerson for the first time to find them staring at me with a weird gleam in their eyes. If I wasn't paralyzed, I'd shiver under their watchful gazes.

"What happened to Heath?" I finally ask. The question that's been tormenting me every day for months.

She smiles. "That doesn't really matter in the grand scheme of things. Heath's body will never be found. That's his *ultimate* punishment. We had fun though when I donned that copycat wig and stole your precious hoodie."

"Not him dying," I slur. "You robbed him of his fucking life."

"And he deserved it," she says with a shrug, looking back at the three of them.

"Brett and Emerson here aren't our boyfriends by the way. We put on a pretty good act, huh? See, Heath ruined their lives last year. Brett and Emerson were just trying to have some fun in the woods late at night at a party."

My blood runs cold as that starts to sound way too familiar.

"This girl had been teasing them, you see. So they and their buddies decided to teach her a lesson. Well her and her *friend*."

"You two raped Nadine."

"Heath got us kicked off the team the next day, right when a NFL scout was going to be at our game. Coach only let us come back when Heath disappeared," Brett adds.

"You're sick. You all are," I spit. "And what did Heath do to you two?"

Jamie scowls. "He dumped me last winter when he found out I was only seventeen and he got a new girlfriend right away, forgetting about me completely. But I was happy when he left her too."

Brandie smiles. "We met at orientation and hit it off but he dumped me a month later. I tried contacting him the rest of the summer and he ignored all my fucking calls. Not cool, Mera. Not cool. Jamie and I happened to meet on a We Love Heath forum."

God, things like that actually exist?

"But you see, even if Heath found a new girlfriend, we knew she'd get dumped just like we did. That was all that kept us from making his life hell. We knew he'd never be satisfied or happy." Brandie pauses and edges forward to my side. "Until something happened. You showed up and all of a sudden you're the bright new shiny thing. The instant it was confirmed you two were a couple, the both of us could tell something was different."

Every word sends another blade into my heart. I am responsible for his death.

"Never once did he announce that we were together anywhere, yet with you he paraded it in front of the world."

It was fake, I want to cry out. It was never even fucking real.

"So, yes. Heath deserved to die. He didn't deserve to be happy if it wasn't with us," Brandie says, pulling a knife out of her purse. "Turns out he chose wrong though, didn't he? You moved on so quick with his brother. How *sick* is that? He would've been better off with Jamie or me. But anyway, now you know. Before you die, tell me one thing."

My heart pounds in my chest frantically as the knife hovers above my stomach.

"What?" I manage to ask.

"Did Heath fuck you?" she asks, peering at me with wide eyes.

I'm assuming the correct answer is no. If I'm going to die, why should I give them the satisfaction of hearing the truth even if it's what they want to hear? No matter what I say, they're going to kill me.

"Yes."

Brandie looks visibly disturbed and Jamie's jaw drops open, showing more emotion than she's shown all night. "So we were right. She was special," Jamie mumbles, turning to Brandie.

There's no way. Could Heath have been...a virgin? What about all of the girls that completed his challenge?

Whatever, might as well roll with it. I muster up every bit of energy I can. "I guess it would also suck to hear that he asked me to marry him that night. Guess he fell in love with this pussy."

Brandie screams bloody murder and just as the knife starts to come down, I watch it go flying from her hand, landing on the bed next to me.

I try with all my might to move my hand, but nothing happens.

My head swims as I turn my head to see the cause and find Callan wrestling Emerson to the ground.

My eyes bulge out as I watch him jab a knife into Emerson's side several times. Emerson falls over, collapsing and clutching his side.

I hear loud shouts from the bathroom. Oh God, Ginger's awake again.

"Hang on a little longer, Wil," he says calmly, thrusting the knife at Brett who dodges it.

Jamie and Brandie are on the floor with Emerson trying to help him stop the bleeding when he motions with his head to the knife on the bed next to me.

"Call–" I gulp. "Callan." But my words are so low now. He didn't hear me. Brandie snatches the knife up and moves toward Callan. He seems to notice her coming as he shifts to look at the both of them at once.

But not Jamie.

Jamie, who kicks him in the leg, causing him to buckle and Brandie finds her opening, shoving that knife right into his shoulder.

His cry makes my heart jump out of my chest. He hangs his head lowly, clutching his shoulder. "Fuck."

And then, like a flash, his knife that he was holding with his injured arm is in the air as he jumps right at Brett. He doesn't move back in time as the knife slices right across his neck. Blood pools out of it quickly and a look of horror comes over his face as he coughs blood and falls to the floor. There's loud gasping noises as he tries to breathe and then there's silence.

Brandie yells angrily and dives for Callan. All I can do is watch as she goes low, stabbing him right in his stomach. Callan's face twists into pain and I sob as his blood spills to the floor. But she goes still and shudders. When she falls backwards, I'm barely able to see Callan's knife stuck in the middle of her chest. Jamie runs past Callan, out the door, neither of us being in any shape to chase her.

Callan hobbles over to me, slumping at the edge of the bed. He clutches my hand, touching his bloody one to mine. We're both completely saturated with it. The walls of my room are blood splattered. It's everywhere. "They should be here any minute," he murmurs. "You're going to be okay."

The banging on the bathroom door won't stop.

"We," I say.

His face is pale as he winces. "I'm sorry you were betrayed. And I'm sorry you had to see me do that to people you thought of as friends only an hour ago."

"S'okay." I don't want him to talk at all, but he continues.

"And I'm also sorry for all of the shit I put you through. I was wrong for everything. I'm sorry for what I did on the roof. And I'm sorry for not checking on you this week. My dad…was trying to deport you. Tried to find him all week."

Don't say all of this now. It's too much to say. Too much to process I can only manage to say, "Stop."

He nods. "You didn't deserve any of this. I heard everything they said. Don't think you killed Heath. They did." His eyes soften. "I love you, Mera. I guess you won the game."

He falls back with a sickening thud against the floor as his hand slips from mine.

"Callan." I chant his name. "Callan."

As everything starts to slip away I murmur my final words, "That name sounds foreign coming out of your mouth. It's Wil. Your Wil. You can't just say you love me and pass out like that. You have to hear me say it back."

In the distance, I hear the ambulance wailing, but they're too late.

Way too late.

And I allow myself to be pulled into the darkness.

The beeping of the machine is the first thing I hear. It's so loud.

I peek an eye open and find the whiteness of a medical room. I'm in a hospital?

And then, all at once, I remember everything.

Oh God, Callan. Is he alive?

Please, please, be alive.

I stare around the room and spot no light around the window. Is it still night?

I move a leg off the bed, wincing as I have to use my arms to grab the IV drip. After I'm off the bed, my feet hit the cold floor and I walk slowly, keeping hold of the IV drip as I open the door.

A nurse on her way to another room spots me leaving mine. "Hey, you aren't supposed to leave your bed," she gripes. "Wait right there and I'll get you back to your bed." She disappears into the room she was heading into.

No! I don't want to lay down a moment longer. I move down the hall, looking in each room to find they're empty. All of these rooms are larger sized private ones. They're much more expensive. It's sad that there are some empty ones when people could use these. When I get to the end, I peek through the window and spy a familiar head of dark hair in a bun. Collette.

I open the door and her and two other people, an older looking Callan with strips of gray through his hair and a striking woman with red lipstick and bloodshot eyes.

"Princess of Kardenia, I don't think you should be in this room," she utters, wiping at her eyes with a tissue.

While she looks completely wrecked, Mr. Goldsworthy is stone faced. "I think it's best that you go and rest. You've both had an ordeal."

"What she needs to do is stay away from our son," Mrs. Goldsworthy insists.

I stare down at the bed, finally laying eyes on Callan. The machine says he's alive, but his body is wrapped up and his face is still as pale as it was the last time I saw him. At least he's alive.

"Mom," Collette blurts. "Let her come in. Don't you see her arm shaking?"

I glance down to the arm holding the IV pole and sure enough, it's shaking like a leaf.

She moves off of the chair she was sitting in and offers it to me, to my complete surprise.

"Callan is lucky to be alive. If that knife had gone deeper into his stomach he'd have been dead. The wound in his shoulder was worse. You've both been asleep for an entire day. It's Saturday night."

Thank God. When he wakes up, I have a lot to say.

"Those four in the room," Collette murmurs, "what happened to them?"

"They killed Heath and wanted to kill me. Callan came just in time."

Collette's eyes widen as she covers her mouth. "Oh my God." It comes out muffled and I hear a gasp next to me and watch their mother grab Mr. Goldsworthy and cry into his shoulder.

"Where's his body?" she asks, a lone tear sneaking out from the corner of her eye.

"I don't know. They never told me." I wish they had.

"We'll get it out of the orange haired one," Mrs. Goldsworthy remarks.

I turn to face her. "Sorry, but Ginger wouldn't know. Only the other four would."

"The other three in the room are dead," Collette says in a low tone.

"Jamie isn't. The fourth member of their little group. She ran out of the room before Callan could get to her."

Mr. and Mrs. Goldsworthy look at each other and stand up. "Thank you for letting us know," Mr. Goldsworthy says, touching my shoulder.

The moment his cold hand touches my shoulder, I get a sick feeling in my gut. He smiles. "Thank you for all of your help."

And thank you for trying to get me deported, I almost say.

"While they're gone, I'm calling everyone in," she says in a hurried tone as she pulls out her phone.

Minutes later, a group of eight walk in.

Immediately, Luella, Ashlynn, and Gemma surround me.

"We're so glad you're okay. We wanted to see you, but

they said since you were asleep they could only let family in," Luella says with relief on her face.

Gemma sighs. "I've been trying to figure out what could've happened. Ginger was no help at all. She just kept crying about Callan. The only thing I could come up with is they killed Heath and wanted to kill you too. Am I correct?"

I nod slowly, and there's a shocked silence.

Callan's three friends have a weird look on their faces. Scar isn't facing me. Peyton shakes his head, "How could we have known? They hid their true faces behind those masks so well."

"They said it was my fault," I mumble looking at my hands.

"No, Mera. That's not how it works. They took it upon themselves to kill him," Gemma explains.

"They saw me as a threat. They thought Heath had finally found the girl meant for him. But they were wrong!" I exclaim.

"Heath only cared about me as a friend. We…had a fake relationship. That's the part that kills me. They believed our act so strongly. I should've never agreed to it."

Collette frowns. "So you guys tricked me and everyone else."

"It wasn't my idea. But it still hurts that because of that scheme, Heath is dead. I hope they find Jamie and figure out where his body is."

"Jamie was in on it too?" Ashlynn gapes.

"I was right again," Gemma says. "I told you. If Emerson was there, Jamie must have been too."

"And what about Nadine?" Collette asks.

"Innocent," I say. And Kane is too. I feel guilty for thinking he might have killed Heath.

We all sit in silence after that. Soaking it all in. I manage to find a clock and notice it's almost 9 PM.

At some point, I fall asleep to the sound of the machine beeping. And when I wake up there's no one around except for Callan and I.

I slide closer to his bed and touch his hand, being careful of the IV.

"You saved me," I say softly. "My knight in shining armor. I love you Callan. Rest as long as you need to." I let his hand go and lean over onto his leg, resting my head on it ever so gently.

CHAPTER TWENTY-FOUR

Callan

There's something warm on my leg. It's a little heavy. I blink my eyes open and look down to find a messy platinum blonde bun. That beautiful head of hair can only belong to one person.

I shut my eyes, seeing Wil on that bed completely naked and soaked with water and blood. I thought we were both going to die in that room. I was scared shitless I didn't save her in time. If only one of us was going to make it out, I wanted it to be her.

From the end of Sorority Row, I saw the four of them go into ZDB. I was going to run and stop them until I saw the knife. I stole a phone from some girl I found walking and called 911 and immediately ran into ZDB.

I grabbed a knife from the kitchen and went upstairs. I got to hear almost all of what they said. With every word about Heath, it felt like that knife was twisting in my gut. I've never felt a blind rage like that before. But I also felt guilty for listening to them talk while Wil lay fucking paralyzed on the bed unable to defend herself. She was depending on me and only on me.

But now, it's over with. I'll never let her suffer like that again as long as I'm still breathing. She's going to be okay.

Not a spec of blood can be seen on her hospital gown or her hair.

Why is she lying here?

I look past her at the silver pole. She's hooked up to an IV and monitor just like I am.

"Wil," I rasp.

She jumps up quickly, straightening and staring at me with wide eyes. "You're awake." She reaches forward to hug me, pulling back at the last minute when she eyes my shoulder.

"I probably shouldn't hug you. Are you in pain? Should I call the nurses? The doctor?"

"No. They have me hooked up to some good fucking stuff." I gesture to all the tubes and wires in my arm. I don't feel any pain at all. The only thing bothering me right now is knowing that the people responsible for my brother's disappearance were so close right from the start. I never knew or even suspected.

After all of that fucking detective work.

"I should go look for your sister and parents," she says with an exhausted smile. "They'll want to know that you're awake."

"What day is it?" I look toward the window and find it's at least night time.

"It's Saturday night. Everyone was just here not too long

ago. Maybe they still are." I grab her wrist before she can leave.

I don't want her to leave my side yet.

Scooting over a little, I make room in the bed for her. "Come lay next to me, princess. Everyone else can wait a little longer."

I can still feel the pull of sleep. I don't know if it's the meds or my body trying to help me recover.

Slowly, she lays her body down next to mine, making sure not to touch me. Her face is only inches away from mine as she lays her head on the same pillow.

She wets her lips for a moment and sighs, speaking softly. "Right before Ginger showed up, Kori, Jamie's roommate, came to talk to me."

Kori. I only know one person named Kori. "Kori as in Nadine's Kori? She's Jamie's roommate?" I should say was. If Jamie isn't dead by her own fucking hand by now, she'll be in jail, not back at college. I wouldn't be surprised if she took the easy way out.

"She told me about what Brett, Emerson, and those other guys did to Nadine. Did you know about that?"

I shake my head. I was still a senior in high school. The only way I would've heard about it is from Heath. "Heath never told me. That was my first time hearing about it." I did wonder why Nadine wasn't here. I assumed she took a leave of absence.

"For a while, I thought Kane might've killed Heath because Heath didn't interfere. I'm glad I was wrong." Her eyes are regretful as they stare into mine.

If she was willing to think that about Silverstone on her own, maybe it's time…

Time I tell her why I fucking hate him.

There's no one else on this Earth alive now who knows. It's just me.

Her eyes are open, trusting, loving. To deserve all of that, I need to give her all of myself in return. "He might not have killed Heath, but he's still a monster."

She opens her mouth to protest, when I say in a low tone, "He tried to drown me when we were kids. Out in the lake."

She freezes, mouth hanging open. Confusion, anger, sadness, they all flash on her face before she cups my cheek in her hand.

"What happened?"

So I tell her, finally opening up. It's hard going over the details, experiencing the drowning all over again as if it just happened yesterday. But by the time I'm done, I know it was fucking worth it.

Now she knows what I see every time I look at him and understands me that much more.

It's Friday night when I finally get wheeled out of the hospital. Wil got discharged a few days ago and has been sleeping in my room ever since.

She walks next to the wheelchair until it stops at the edge of the sidewalk next to Coll's G-Wagon. The nurse opens the passenger side door and I hoist myself out of the wheelchair and use the side step to get in while Wil hops in the backseat. I've only felt the smallest amount of soreness in my shoulder since yesterday. But I still feel the ghost of the knives digging into my flesh. It's annoying and I hope it eventually goes away.

Ty, Noel, and Vin visited when they could. Coll has been

hanging around more, actually getting along to my surprise with Mera.

My parents have been scarce. No fucking explanation why. My mom saw me the night I woke up, but every time since, it's only been my fucking dad. They keep dodging my calls and don't answer texts. I hope it has something to do with Jamie, but I don't know anything.

Mera's parents both talked to me on the phone, thanking me for saving Mera's life. They sounded so grateful and thankful, it made me realize how different they are from my own parents.

Tonight will be the first time I've seen them since Tuesday. Both Mera and I were invited over. And while I don't want to go, they're insisting because they have something to tell us over dinner. Coll was invited too so it must be something important.

The ride to my parents' mansion is quiet. When Coll pulls up, the gate is wide open.

"Do you need help getting out?" Wil asks from behind me.

"I'm good."

She opens the door for me anyway, holding it open while I slide myself out, avoiding the side step.

Both of my parents are waiting at each end of the table. There's no food set out this time, which is fucking strange.

There's two seats on one side and one on the other so Coll sits alone on the other side.

I stare at my father's face, waiting for him to speak, but his eyes are on my mom, and my mom, doesn't look like herself one bit.

Never in my life have I seen her look this haggard. This worn down. Her mascara has run down her face. She's always looked put together even when we were kids. Something isn't right.

"Go on, Antoure. Tell them," she spits.

My eyes are still on Dad as he looks between Coll and I.

"Kids. I need you to understand…" he starts and pauses to glance at my mom who's staring daggers at him.

"Let's start with the good news," he says finally. "Jamie was caught on her way to Mexico. She confessed that she and her friends murdered Heath."

I only feel relieved for a second. While I love hearing that, the bad news is like an anvil hanging over my head.

Underneath the table, I feel Wil's hand over my fist. She forces me to open my hand, intertwining her fingers with mine. My other hand still remains in a fist.

"How?" I ask. Since finding the blood on Wil's hoodie, I've wondered if they stabbed him to death.

It'd make sense if they did since that was what they were going to do to Wil.

"How is it not important, Callan."

"What do you mean?" I ask, looking between them. "Did Jamie still not confess to where his body is?"

Coll leans back in her chair. "Yeah, I mean at this point, she'd want to divulge all the details for an easier sentence. So where is Heath's body?"

"You're wasting your time. You both are," Mom says in a low, disturbed tone. She sniffs and tears pour out of her eyes. "We'll never get Heath's body because your father is a selfish bastard."

"What the fuck?" I scream.

Mera gasps next to murmuring, "Why?"

Collette stands up out of her chair, and yells down the table, "We need to put Heath to rest."

Dad folds his hand together. "It's in the best interest of this family that his body is not recovered."

What the fuck is that supposed to mean? I'm a thread away from dragging my dad out of his fancy chair and punching him bloody until he tells me what's going on.

"He's had me locked up in this house since Sunday. But my contact at the police told me everything. Jamie was alone in the room with your father for a minute. She was on the verge of telling the police where his body was only minutes before their chat. Now? She won't say. They've given up trying to find out." Mom wipes her eyes.

"What the fuck, Dad?" Coll yells.

"I'm telling you all, we can put him to rest without his body," Dad says calmly.

"But that's not the worst of it all. He didn't realize it'd been recorded. What he said to Jamie. My contact watched that minute of footage and the only thing on that tape was him telling her not to talk about where his body is and her agreeing." She turns to look at him. "That could only mean he's known all this time where his body was."

In a flash, I'm out of my seat and pulling my dad up out of his chair. Fuck the soreness in my shoulder. I get right in this fucking face and yell, "Where the fuck is my brother's body? Where is it?"

I always knew my father, Antoure Goldsworthy, was a monster. But not this kind of monster. All this time I was scrambling to find Heath, looking for signs, clues, trying to find out if there was any chance of him still being alive. He was laughing at me. He knew. He fucking knew I'd never find talk to Heath again.

"Let go of me, right now, son," he says, staring at me with eyes too much like my own. But I don't. I drag him to the wall behind him and throw him against it.

Immediately, he wrenches my arm away, twisting it to the shoulder and causing me to cry out. The pain shocks me so I'm wide open when he backhands me. But not for long, because I finally get my shot in. I punch him right in the face and blood explodes from his lip.

Distantly, I can hear Wil call my name, but I can't hear it. My blood is pounding too hard. My heart is beating out of my chest. I want answers and I want them right fucking now.

But with every punch I get in, he gets in one. They hurt like a bitch with the ring on his hand, but I accept that pain.

"Stop!" I hear my mother yell, very close to me.

A soft hand touches my shoulder, and then right in my ear, I hear Wil whisper, "Callan. Stop. We need him to be able to answer us."

My dad is slumped against the wall. His face red and turning purple with a black eye. My nose hurts like hell. I think it might be broken. I swipe at the blood dripping down and stare at him. "You're going to tell us where his body is." I turn around to Wil who's right next to me and my mom a few feet away. Coll is sobbing at the table.

"Callan," Wil says in a stunned tone.

"What?" I snap. But I can't help it. The anger is still here, raging inside my body. She touches my cheek. "Pitchfork."

What the hell is she talking about? This isn't the time for this. I'm about to pull her hand away from my face when she pulls it away, covering her mouth. She glances around me, staring at my father.

"It was you," she says.

"Him what, Wil?" I blurt, staring at my father who narrows his eyes at us.

She turns her head and locks eyes with me, speaking softly, "The pitchfork, Callan." She points to the ring on my father's finger. "That marked your face. And it marked

Heath's chest. The night before he died, remember how I told you he had those marks on him?"

What? But his ring, it's not a pitchfork. In my head, I picture his ring. An A and G inside of a circle. But the A and G are intertwined in a way that if put together, faintly if you see it from the side, it might...

"So I hit him, what does that matter?" he spits.

For as long as I've been alive, and old enough to understand, I've known that Heath was my dad's pride and joy. Always comparing us and forever making me feel like second best. Like I was never good enough.

For the first time, I don't understand. "What did Heath and you argue about that day, Dad? What was so horrible that you had to punch him like that?"

A disgusting smile forms across his face and right as he opens his mouth to respond, I hear the pounding of shoes.

Our butler bursts into the room. "Sir, I'm sorry to interrupt but there's an uninvited guest that is only minutes away from entering. We tried to stop him but he's holding a gun. The other servants and I are going to hide." He runs off with fear in his eyes, yelling for the maids and other butlers.

What the fuck?

"What kind of business dealings are you doing, Dad?" I yell and turn away to ask my mother when I notice the strangest fucking thing.

My mom's face doesn't look worried one bit. In fact, if I had to say, she looks relieved. She might be happy to die, but I'm not. And I'm not going through this with Wil again. She will be protected this time along with my sister.

I grab Wil's hand and fast walk to my sister and push them under the table. Wil's eyes are shiny as she tugs on my hand. "Please, get under the table with us."

I shake my head. "No. I'm sorry." I need to know what my dad has going on.

"Callan, don't be stubborn, there's plenty of room," my sister snaps. "You don't know what kind of psycho is going to walk through that door."

"Just call 911," I respond, putting the tablecloth down and hiding them completely.

Moments later, the sound of one of the front doors banging open echoes throughout the whole house. I straighten quickly, ready to face whoever comes through that door. The footsteps are light. This person is running.

I don't expect to know the face that runs through the doorway. Part of me pictured it being some foreigner looking for money that my dad owes them. Somebody else. Not him.

He stops as he enters the room, glancing across the long table at me, moving his eyes around the room until they lock on my father with my mother in the corner near him.

"Antoure," he says in a low, dangerous tone, ignoring me completely.

"Legis," my father says, smiling with blood stained teeth.

"Your son did a number on you, already I see." In his left hand at his side, he's holding a pistol.

From behind him, I hear the sound of feet hitting the tile once again. Did he bring someone with him?

And there in the hall, my greatest enemy appears. He steps forward, staring right at me. Does he have a gun too?

"What the fuck is this Kane?" I ask, having to use his name so his father doesn't think I'm talking to him.

He grits his teeth. "I told him *not* to come."

Ignoring the both of us, Mr. Silverstone steps forward. "Marguerite told me that you won't be putting Heath's body to rest."

My father stares at him and bursts out laughing. He laughs so hard, he holds his stomach, with one hand back, holding him up against the wall.

"So you're here to convince me with that gun?"

"Where's his body?" Mr. Silverstone asks quietly. "I won't ask again."

I glance from Mr. Silverstone to my dad. Back and forth, back and forth. The wheels start turning in my head.

My dad looks him straight in the eye. "I will not tell you or anyone else."

"Oh my God," I hear Wil say under the table. I hear a quiet, "What?" from Collette.

And it all clicks in my head, sliding into place. I stagger back at the realization and stare at Kane Silverstone.

Kane Silverstone has hated me since the moment he met me. He's known since then. He's known this whole time.

"What?" he barks out, but by the way he dodges my eyes, I know that he knows I've figured it out.

"You'll tell me," Mr. Silverstone says, pressing the gun against my dad's chest, "and you'll tell me right now, unless you want to die."

My dad laughs. "You won't shoot me. You don't have the balls to, Legis."

Mr. Silverstone backs up and rubs his hand down his face. "That's my *son*, Antoure. He needs to be put to rest. His mother and I want his body put to rest."

"What the *fuck*?" Collette shrieks underneath the table, causing everyone to look over for one second.

How long has my dad known? Did Heath know?

Mr. Silverstone shakes his head. "You think you're invincible, Goldsworthy. But you should know that a father's love for their child eclipses everything else, even for a coward like me."

Far away, I hear the sounds of police sirens and an ambulance. But they're too late.

All I can do is watch as my dad suffers at his own making. No one moves to stop Mr. Silverstone as he steps back and in slow motion, raises the gun and fires. I turn away as I hear my dad's body hit the wall.

"What did you do, Dad?" I hear Kane shout.

Under the table, I hear Collette sobbing. Wil moves the tablecloth away as she jumps out from under it and grabs me, pulling me into her arms.

Stunned, I lay my head on top of her hers, anchoring myself to her like my very own safe harbor. I stay locked in place as the chaos around us unfolds.

It's only later, after I'm home, at my own house do I hear everything from my mother on the phone.

Wil and I listen together with Collette as she tells us that he's known since a car accident happened when I was younger. It was only my dad and Heath in the car and Heath was hurt badly.

He needed a blood transfusion and my dad offered. They found out that way that there's no way Heath was my dad's son.

My mother had an affair with Mr. Silverstone. It turns out she's always loved Mr. Silverstone, but her parents wanted her to marry the more "worthy" person, my dad.

Ever since he found out, she's worked extra hard to keep my father happy, but she's been miserable for years.

The next thing she tells me shocks me to my core. Since he found out, my father has secretly despised Heath. Forcing him to push himself and make himself better so I'll get frustrated and motivated enough to beat him, becoming better.

My father never hated me. He only wanted to push me, and make me into a mirror image of himself.

She thinks he'd been beating Heath for years, taking his paternity out on his body.

But did he know for sure? No one knows.

If he did, how could he never tell me any of this? How could he suffer so fucking bad silently?

And how could his life be snuffed out like that?

My brother didn't have the perfect life I thought he did.

After the phone call, Collette finds a guest room to hole herself up in. She's furious at our father and inconsolable because the whereabouts of Heath's body are still unknown.

My dad is in a coma, and because he's the only one who knows where Heath's body is, we won't be able to ask again until he wakes up. The bullet went right through his chest, narrowly missing his heart. He still had internal bleeding that had to be corrected during surgery.

Wil and I are walking upstairs to my room when I get a call from Noel. Shit. I forgot to tell them. This is probably all over the news by now.

I click answer as we walk through the doorway. "What's up Noel?"

"Dude! What's going on? It says your dad got shot and he's fighting for his life in the hospital."

"He's not exactly fighting for his life. Yeah, he did get shot though."

"What the hell happened?" he explodes.

"It's a long story. If you come over tomorrow–" I start when he grunts and says, "Hold on."

There's a few muffled voices in the background that gradually get louder. Vin and Ty must be with him.

The voice on the other end changes, and it's Ty. "Hey, do you guys need anything? F-food maybe?"

I clutch my stomach and realize that we both never did get to eat. I place my hand over the phone and ask, "Are you hungry, princess?"

She holds a thumbs up in the air.

Eventually one of us would have realized and we would've ordered something.

But if they're fucking offering, I can't turn that down. So much has happened, I just want to lay in bed with my princess and try to relax.

"Yeah, In n Out sounds good. I'll reimburse you when you get here."

I already know Wil's order to which she cracks a smile that I know it, and they know me well enough to know mine, so I hang up and wait for them to get here.

When they show up with the food, Gemma, Ashlynn, and Luella pop up, tagging along with them, bringing food for Collette too. And what ensues is a night full of retelling and talking.

All nine of us in my huge living room. Not all of it is about my dad or Silverstone.

Some of it is about nothing at all. Noel cracking jokes. Vin encouraging him. Ty sitting quietly.

And some of it is about spring break which is only about a week away.

Over those few hours, though I try to escape from thinking about him, I do. I think about Heath and it sinks in that I'll never fucking see my brother again.

CHAPTER TWENTY-FIVE

Callan

It's a cool March morning, but the sun is out. Two days after my dad went into his coma, my mom decided that we should move forward and have a funeral for Heath. I argued against it, but my mother believes my dad, even when he wakes up, will never tell us where his body is.

And because of how fucked up my dad is, I'll never know why he's holding on to this secret so hard.

So today, here we are, burying an empty coffin today.

It's the first day of spring. The birds are chirping. Everything is growing back. Around this time last year, Heath and I decided to go to the Bahamas for spring break.

Not this year.

As his coffin sinks into the ground, I feel the tears well up in my eyes. Wil clutches my arm, wrapping her arm around mine and leaning into my shoulder.

I turn away first, striding past my mom and Mr. Silverstone, Kane, Collette, and the rest of our friends and family.

Dane and his father, my uncle showed up, as well as Sophie and her father, my oldest uncle.

I appreciate that they came despite the fact that Heath isn't actually related to any of them. But I don't feel like talking to them or anyone else. I want to be left alone with Wil.

Both of us still have school work to finish online before spring break starts. So we work our asses off the next two days, finishing our work at the end of the day on Friday. She groans, leaning back against the couch. "Finally we're done."

"Yeah, finally." I shut my fucking laptop and relax back into my bed.

I hear the sound of her moving off the couch, and eventually feel the bed move as she gets on top of the covers with me. She lays her head on my good arm, and I play with the pieces of hair around her face.

Through all of this, I never got to tell her again.

"I'm sorry, Wil."

She tilts her head up to look at me and we lock eyes.

"Thank you for not leaving me. For not giving up on me and us."

Her eyes get shiny and she scoots up so our lips are only inches away from each other. Our breaths mingle and I inch myself down, pressing my lips against hers. A fire starts blazing inside me as her tongue and mine collide at once, touching, writing, moving together like a dance.

She moans into my mouth.

I move to flip her over and she says, "Don't do too much work."

"I'm healed, princess." I lean over, flipping her so she's underneath me and press my crotch against hers so she'll feel how badly I want her.

"I'll never take you on the roof again, in complete anger and rage, princess. I promise you." I press my forehead against hers and she sighs happily.

"Thank you." She's quiet for a moment as her face heats up. She softly says, "It's okay if you're rough, though. I know that roughness is all you and I want you to be yourself in every way."

She's one of the very few people that's only expected that of me. Never to be Heath. Only me.

We both shed our clothes and I grind my hips down against her, moving my cock against her folds.

I can feel her wetness coating me. She gasps low in her throat. "Are you sure you're okay to do this?"

"More than sure," I say as I start to push inside her. When I'm fully in to the hilt, I stare into her eyes and move my hands down to her hips. "I love you, Wil."

A tear slips from her eye as I pull back and thrust back in. She moans and I lay on top, pressing my body flush to hers as I move my hips back, rocking forward. Her gentle arms wrap around my shoulders as she moans into my ears.

It feels so fucking good. I know this is where I belong. Right here, in her arms forever, balls deep inside her. Wilhelmera Karden is the other half of my soul and I'll never let her go.

Mera

Callan fucks me so hard, I can't see past the pleasure he bestows upon me. I've already orgasmed three times, and he's still going, pushing inside me like he can't get enough of me. I can't get enough of *him*.

Finally, I feel him slow down. He grunts, "I can't put it off any longer." With a groan, he closes his eyes and pushes all the way inside me, and I feel him twitch. The small warmth I feel makes me glow with happiness.

He's still hard inside me, as his fingers move down and slide toward my clit. "Callan," I gasp. He pulls out, flipping me over onto my stomach, grabs my hair and yanks me back, impaling me with his still hard cock.

I cry out at the suddenness of it and he holds my hair as he fucks me from behind, causing a whole new orgasm to wash over me. "You orgasm again princess? I felt you tighten around my cock. Let's go for number five tonight."

Every thrust sends electric waves to my toes. I don't know if I can last another round. But if we're going to, I want to feel him come inside me one more time. I meet every thrust, pushing my hips back to meet his.

"Think we should stay locked in my house all of spring break? I'll tell the guys to fuck off and I'm busy feeding my princess's pussy."

My cheeks heat up at the thought of Callan and I fucking like bunnies for a whole week with no interruptions. I'd feel sore, but it'd feel oh so good.

"What about my friends?" I moan out.

"Tell them you're too busy getting railed to care about anything else. We'll let them listen as you cry out and beg me to fuck you harder, then they'll definitely understand." He pulls me back by my hair so my back is flush against his chest. "How does that sound?"

His hands go to my breasts as he twists both nipples at once, thrusting into me. "We can't...do that," I respond panting.

The last time we were in this position, we were on the rooftop. "Fine. We'll go ahead with our plans, but no matter where we are, I plan on fucking you just like this," he whispers in my ear, pulling my hips down to meet his cock. That fifth wave washes over me, so quickly and so powerfully, I can't do anything but shudder and cry out his name.

With a low groan in his throat, he pumps his hips and I feel him spurt inside me for the second time. "Fuck, Wil." He kisses my neck, in a few places and his lips on my skin make me feel so sensitive, I quake. "Don't do that. I might fuck you again."

Suddenly, I hear the sound of my phone ringing. It feels wrong to feel him slide out of me, but he does, and I move over to my night stand and grab my phone. It's my dad. It's too early in the morning for him to be calling unless something happened.

"Dad?" I ask, answering the phone.

On the other end, he's quiet for a moment. "Can you come home, honey?"

At the serious tone in his voice, my heart drops. "What's wrong? Is everything okay?"

"We'll talk when you get here. The plane should be there in about three hours." He hangs up the phone right after, and my head spins.

My stomach twists and Callan moves up behind me, "What's wrong princess?"

"I have to go home. The plane is on the way."

"I'll come with you."

Shakily, I move off the bed and head to the bathroom. I hold my head in my hands and sigh. I fucking hate when people do this shit. Now I have to stay worried the whole plane ride and poor Callan has to deal with me.

After I get out of the bathroom and wash my hands, I get right in the shower. I hear the sound of the shower door opening and glance behind me. Callan holds up his hands. "No funny business. We get to waste less water and I get to stare at your body while you wash, that's it."

Even with the anxiety I feel, he makes heat rise to my cheeks as we wash our bodies together. He keeps to his word, and when I get out, I'm surprised to find our bags by the door, ready.

"I work fast," he says with a smirk.

We get a car to pick us up and take us to the airport, and not too long after, we're in the plane on the way to Kardenia. I fall asleep, off and on, thankful when sleep overtakes me so I don't have to worry about what I'm walking into.

By the time the plane lands, I've thought of every scenario. Our country is bankrupt. They've decided to disown me. Our cousins are taking over as monarchs. They're not letting me go back to college after spring break. Any of those are preferable over the one that really hurts my heart.

That my sister's mystery boyfriend did something to her. You hear about it so often. She might be a princess, but she's still vulnerable to that kind of thing.

Maybe my sister will be the first to greet me and put that worry to rest.

By the time we touch down, it's 9 PM at home. We get in a waiting car that takes us to the castle. I hold Callan's hand, seeking comfort and preparing myself.

We enter through the gates and go up the long driveway. When we stop in front of the steps, I spot Angelina who immediately runs down to grab my bags. "Welcome back, princess."

I smile to be friendly and then a thought occurs to me. "Hey Angelina, do you know why I'm back?"

Servants often hear a lot of things. Even things you don't want them to hear. The castle is huge and things can echo easily.

Her eyes widen and she shakes her head. "No."

She definitely knows something.

Callan grabs his own bags, walking up the steps behind Angelina and I. As we walk in the grand doors she points forward, "Your parents are having a late dinner for you two. They're waiting in the dining room."

She glances at Callan. "You can set your bags here, I'll have someone bring them to a guest room for you." She moves her gaze toward me. "And of course these will go in your room, princess." She curtsies and runs off.

I bite my lip, staring into the hallway that leads to the dining room.

"I'm right here, princess," Callan murmurs to me, clutching my hand and squeezing it.

I breathe slowly, and start the walk to the dining room. As I'm almost there, I hear the clinking of glasses and silverware along with the smell of good food.

My stomach grumbles in response. I was too hungry to eat before the airport and too hungry to eat on the flight so I'm starving. But my stomach is going to have to wait.

I turn into the room first, under the bright lights of the chandeliers hanging from the ceiling. My mother and father are at each end of the table.

Neither of them look sick. Thank God for that. I can rule

that out. But they don't exactly look well rested. Both of them have dark bags underneath their eyes and they look gaunter than they did when I came home for Christmas. I glance at the table, noting that there are only two chairs besides the ones they're sitting in and they're across from each other.

I take the one furthest from the door while Callan bows to both of them and sits in the other.

"Why don't you make your plate, dear?" Father asks, gesturing to the food.

"Yes, there's a good spread," Mother adds.

"No," I say quietly. "I need to know exactly why you asked me to come back home before I take one bite, and believe me, I'm starving."

The allure of the smell of the fresh food makes me snappier and less patient than I'm trying to be.

Mother and Father stare at each other across the table, exchanging a few looks.

"Someone fucking say something!" I blurt.

"Language, Mera!" Mother exclaims.

"I'm sorry, but after sitting on a twelve hour flight, no, after getting a call fifteen hours ago telling me I need to come home and knowing that there's something wrong without even having a hint of what it is, has made my imagination go wild. So just, *tell me*."

"It's hard to say," Mother says in a small voice.

Father sighs. "Mera…"

I glance at Callan across the table and his brows are furrowed as he worriedly stares at me.

"Your sister is missing," they both say at once.

No.

Somewhere deep inside, I knew this had to do with her. I just didn't want it to be true.

"When was the last time you spoke to Cate?"

They look at each other. "Please, don't misunderstand. We love your sister, but she's also a princess of a country. If other people were to hear that she's missing..." Mom starts.

"We don't need to look weak, like we can't keep watch over our girls. Any person might try to travel the world trying to find her and use her to extort us for money," Father says.

My blood pounds in my brain and a massive headache is starting to form as I gasp, "When?"

They look sorrowfully at me.

"When?" I scream.

"The last day of August," Mother says, tearfully.

Seven whole months. My sister has been missing for seven whole months.

"So you lied on Christmas, about her spending it with some guy?"

"It was the only thing we could come up with," Mother says, wiping her nose in a tissue.

Callan clears his throat, speaking for the first time as he asks, "Did you say, August 31?"

Something about that day sounds super familiar, and that's when it hits me. "That was the last day I spoke to her. I spoke to her that night."

"We saw her that morning when she left for the university. She never came back that night," Father says slowly.

"After a week we knew something was wrong. She's gone off and done her own thing a few times, but she's always contacted us. We were still hoping she was just busy at school with her schoolwork. Then, we discovered something," Mother adds.

"What? Discovered what?" I yell, desperate to get

something, anything that'll let me know they're close to finding her.

"She took the plane. The last call she made was to you, and it was off the cell tower near SGU. It was around 2:15 AM on September 2."

"No way. I don't remember getting a missed call," I say, dread filling me.

I glance down at my phone but the farthest it goes back is Christmas. Fuck, why did I delete everything?

"Can you think of any reason why your sister would go to your college?" Father asks, folding his hands together.

My heart drops as I remember our last conversation. I told her I was being bullied. Did she actually come to comfort me? Or maybe to teach Callan a lesson?

"I told her I was suffering and I think...she wanted to help me feel better. She didn't tell me she was coming. I wouldn't have gotten drunk that night if I knew." I put my head in my hands. "It's my fault. If she still hasn't been found, something bad had to have happened to her."

"None of her cards have been touched, no social media. We talked to her friends and her professors. No one has heard from her. They're all staying quiet for now, but we can't keep this quiet forever," Father says regretfully.

"We wanted you to come so we could tell you," Mother says slowly. "If your sister isn't found by the time you graduate, we're going to need you to step up."

I sit up straight, hands falling to the table. "Step up? As in, the crown? Becoming queen?"

She nods slowly. "You'll be the crown princess and you'll have to start studying to take it over and—"

"No," I murmur. "No," I repeat more firmly. "That's not me. That's Cate. She was trained since she was young for that spot. I don't know anything about that, Mother. I'm just the party girl."

She smiles sadly. "There'll be no one else but you, honey. Let's hope something turns around, hm?"

I shove my chair away from the table and run out of the room, up the grand staircase, down the halls, until I reach my room, and slam the door.

"Cate," I cry. My heart hurts so fucking bad.

I throw myself on the bed and sob into my pillow. A few minutes later, I feel a warm hand against my back. "They'll find her, Wil. She might've gotten tired of her life here and needed a break."

"No." I lift my head out of the pillow to look at Callan. "She would never shirk her responsibilities like that. That's me."

He rubs my back in circular motions.

"Plus," I say quietly. "We both know that when someone goes missing at Goldsworthy University, it isn't good. You had the same faith about Heath, remember?"

His hand freezes in place and falls away.

"But Heath wasn't a fucking prince. He was just a regular guy."

I scoot over to allow him to lie with me. He moves a stray piece of hair out of my face.

"No matter what the future holds for you, Wil. I'm here and I'm not going anywhere. I promise you." He pulls me into his arms, letting me cry into his chest.

"We'll find her," he murmurs against my hair.

I know he wants me to believe it, but that sinking feeling in my stomach tells me otherwise. The first big party night of the year was wild. People on campus partied until late into the night. Anything could've happened.

But I know somehow, I'll get through it. Even if she's never found. We'll both get through all of this. Together.

"I love you, Wilhelmera Karden of Kardenia" I hear him whisper as I start to drift off.

I whisper back, "I love you too, Callan Goldsworthy" and let myself drift away.

EPILOGUE

Mera

Two Years and 9 Months Later

It's warm and there's something hard against my ass. "Mm, Callan, we leave early in the morning."

He moves an arm around my body. "I told you I wanted to make love to you tonight, Miss Advisor." He calls me it every chance he gets since Collette gave me the final open position.

Things between her and I are a far cry from how they used to be.

His hand slips down beneath my panties until he reaches my clit and starts rubbing.

"Callan, we're leaving in six hours for the airport. We need to get some rest."

He bites my earlobe. "Let's rest on the plane instead, princess."

"No, listen. It's been stressful. I want to be able to talk to everyone before we get there. I'm so nervous about all of this."

He pulls his hand out and kisses my neck. "I know. Everything is going to be fine."

They're finally going to announce my sister is missing to the public. There are only six months left until graduation and after that, I'll be ushered back home and officially made crown princess.

It leaves a bitter taste in my mouth, knowing that I'm taking the place of someone who deserved it far more than I did.

I miss my sister everyday. It's hard to believe she's been gone for so long. There's been no trace, no sign of her anywhere. It's like she never came on campus.

I'm not alone in my grief though. Callan thinks about Heath all the time. I still remember like it was yesterday, meeting him next to the administration building's parking lot.

"Hey, can you do something for me? I think I left my phone in the bathroom. Can you go and get it for me?"

I turn back to him. "Sure?" I move out from underneath his warmth and the covers and walk to the bathroom. His phone, sure enough, is sitting on the counter.

"Why would you leave it here?" I ask, looking at it curiously.

I turn around and walk back into the bedroom and stop in shock when I see Callan on one knee and a huge rock in a black box angled out toward me.

"Wilhelmera Karden, Pinkie, you drive me absolutely nuts sometimes–"

I cover my mouth as I start to tear up.

"But I could never imagine myself living this life without you. Will you stay by my side forever with this ring on your finger?"

I'm so happy I could burst. "Are you okay with being king of a country?" I ask with a laugh.

He smirks. "I think I'd be a great king, with the help of a wonderful queen. One who I would bow to any day."

I walk toward him and put my hand out, biting my lip. "Then, yes."

He slides the ring up my finger, standing up and grabbing me in his arms. He lifts me up in the air and lets me down slowly, our lips coming together in a deep toe-curling kiss.

He whirls me around, lifting me off and the ground, and we fall over on the bed. "How about now? How about a little engagement sex?" he whispers, against my ear, his hot breath driving me wild.

"Engagement sex it is." His eyes heat up as he puts my legs around his hips. Heat pools in the bottom of my stomach as I feel his cock bulging against my panties.

How did I ever hate Callan Goldsworthy?

It's a cold morning when we get to the plane with all of our friends around us. I get so cold, I stuff my hands into my pocket. I feel something scratchy brush against my hand. Ouch.

What's this? I pull out my right hand, to find a folded, crumpled up piece of paper.

I don't remember putting this here.

I unfold it, and my jaw drops as the blood rushes to my head. I'd know that penmanship anywhere. No one else I know uses cursive like that. No fucking way.

I love you, baby sister. Live the life you were meant to live. Keep this note to yourself.

How long has this been in my jacket? I washed this jacket last week. I gaze around the airport with tear-filled eyes.

"Princess?" I hear from next to me.

I turn around and gaze at Callan.

She told me not to tell anyone. Callan isn't just anyone. I pull him away from our friends and shove the paper into his hand.

He glances at the paper and then up to me. "And you're sure this is real?"

"It is," I insist. He hands the paper back to me and I stare down at it.

Somewhere, out there. My sister is alive. I wish I could see her and tell her how much I miss her, but I'm satisfied with this tiny note.

For now.

Gemma

Present

I wonder why Callan and Mera had to run off to Kardenia so quickly. I hope that everything's okay.

They said they'd be back Monday morning when we leave for Cancun.

I didn't want to come to this party. I would've rather stayed in my room all night long. But Luella and Ashlynn are always dragging to them.

Tonight we're at AAA or the lion's den as I call it. I hang by the door like I always do, away from the epicenter of the party.

The music is pounding and everyone's laughing and excited for the coming week. I wish I could get excited. If there's anything I know for sure, it's that my vacation will be spoiled by *him* again.

Kardenia was great, but everywhere I looked. Boom. There he was.

No matter how much I tried to chase him away, it hasn't worked yet.

He doesn't remember and I don't want him to remember.

Sighing, I look down at the empty red cup in my hand. Might as well get another drink.

I step inside the kitchen and fill it up with the generic beer.

As I go to turn around, I bump right into a hard chest.

I glance up to find glittering brown eyes staring down at me.

Ugh, and here he is.

I push my glasses up my face.

"Move."

But he stays still, an immovable wall. He snatches the cup

right out of my hand and drinks all of the beer. He smacks his lips. "Thanks. I was parched, Gem."

Angrily, I turn around and fill my cup up again.

When I'm done, I feel him pressed right against my back. "Stop standing so close, Noel."

"Are you going to go out with me?" he whispers.

"No!" I yell. "Never. Why don't you get it through your head? It'll never *ever* happen."

There's silence behind me. I feel the loss of his warmth against my back so I turn around. His brown eyes aren't glittering anymore. They're completely dark.

As dark as they were the very first night he asked me out and I embarrassed him in front of everyone. He leans his head down and instinctively I move my head away.

"There will come a day that you will want and need me. And I look forward to that day, Gem."

As if. It'll never happen. I won't *allow* that to happen.

He backs away, hands in his pockets.

I will never get along with Noel Hardington.

This series will continue with The Nerd and the Bully and it's on pre-order at tiffanyransier.com/the-nerd-and-the-bully

Want to talk all things Goldsworthy University? Join the spoiler room: https://www.facebook.com/groups/goldsworthyuniversityspoilerroom

AUTHOR'S NOTE

Thank you for getting to the end of The Princess and the Bully! I truly hope you enjoyed it. Callan and Mera have a special place in my heart. If you did, please leave a review, I'd really appreciate it. Gemma's story is next and it's a heart-wrenching one. I hope you'll continue along this journey with me.

Tiffany

ALSO BY TIFFANY RANSIER

The State Family

Alaska

Nebraska

ABOUT TIFFANY

Tiffany Ransier is a USA Today Bestselling multi-genre author. She loves writing twisty, heart-stopping novels. She has a love for diving in to different worlds and making theories about books and shows.

She lives in SoCal with her boyfriend James Ransier, another author. They are the parents of an adorable Siberian Husky/Shiba Inu mix named Peg.

When she's not writing or reading, she's swimming in her pool and obsessing over anime.

- facebook.com/TiffanyRansier
- twitter.com/authtiffransier
- instagram.com/authortiffanyransier
- goodreads.com/TiffanyRansier
- bookbub.com/authors/tiffany-ransier
- amazon.com/author/tiffanyransier

Made in the USA
Monee, IL
08 February 2022